Advance Praise for Drawn in Ash

You could read *Drawn in Ash* purely as entertainment and it would be an enjoyable, compelling ride. But slow down just enough and you'll see how Otte has drawn from our current cultural moment, using both a futuristic setting and ancient biblical symbolism, to show how all of human history is caught up in the issues facing Everys, Narius, and the world in which they live. It's about America. It's about ancient Babylon. It's about race relations, reparations, colonialism, and community. It's about war and peace, religion and politics, diplomacy and radicalism. Otte balances all of these themes perfectly, weaving them into a cohesive narrative tapestry—a truc work of art that undergirds the action and mythology of the story. John Otte has created a fully-realized world that mirrors our own, allowing us to explore all of these difficult topics in a fresh way that's free from the familiarity and bias of reality. That's what the very best fiction does. It allows to explore reality in ways we can't explore within reality. We think, we learn, we grow in this fictional world, then we return to our reality with a new perspective. *Drawn in Ash* is absolutely captivating—the best sci-fi I've read in a long time. — Josh Olds, book reviewer for LifeIsStory.com

John W. Otte has done an astounding job of building an authentic world filled with a variety of fascinating cultures, intriguing magic, and political intrigue. Within this science fantasy backdrop, Otte writes a captivating story filled with thoughtful and emotionally powerful characters and a slow burn romance that kept me glued to the page—it's the sort of book you can't put down. I loved Everys and

Narius and so many others and found the story gripping. *Drawn in Ash* is a must-read for both fans of sci-fi and dystopian fantasy. — Jill Williamson, award-winning author of the *Blood of Kings* trilogy and the *Kinsman Chronicles*

Clever, imaginative, vivid. With his reimagining of an ancient story, John Otte helps us see our modern world in a fresh way. *Drawn in Ash* builds a complex world full of difficult choices and heroic characters and an un-put-downable plot with themes that will linger long after you finish the story. When life surprises us, there is One who can reveal our purpose. — Sharon Hinck, Christy award winning author of the *Dancing Realms* series

When I pick up a book by John Otte I know what to expect: exciting action, charming and lovable characters, and thought-provoking themes. *Drawn in Ash* is an imaginative and exciting fantasy novel full of unique magic, intriguing politics, and high stakes. — Matt Mikalatos, author of *The Crescent Stone*

Drawn in Ash

John W. Otte

Geeky Grace Books

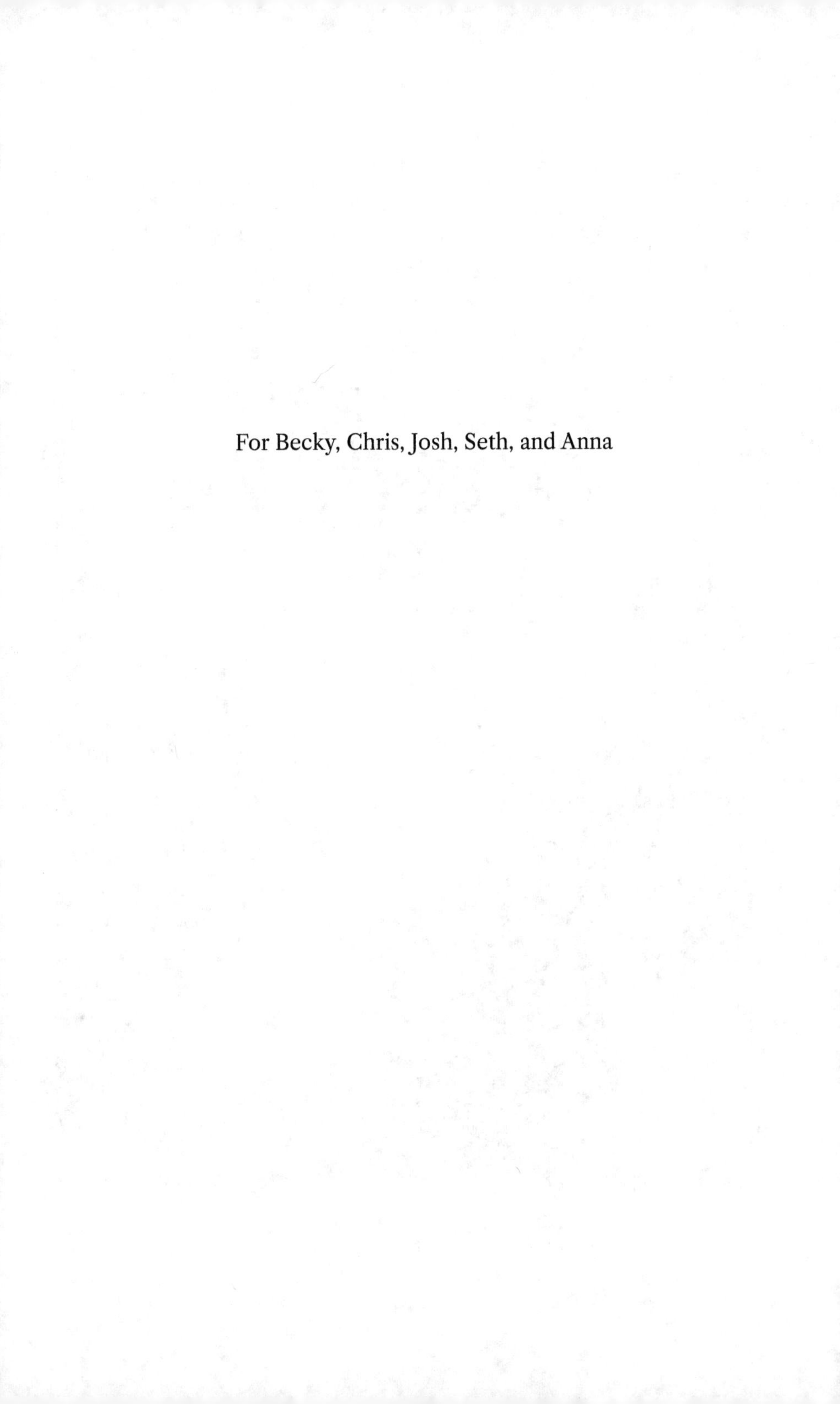

For Becky, Chris, Josh, Seth, and Anna

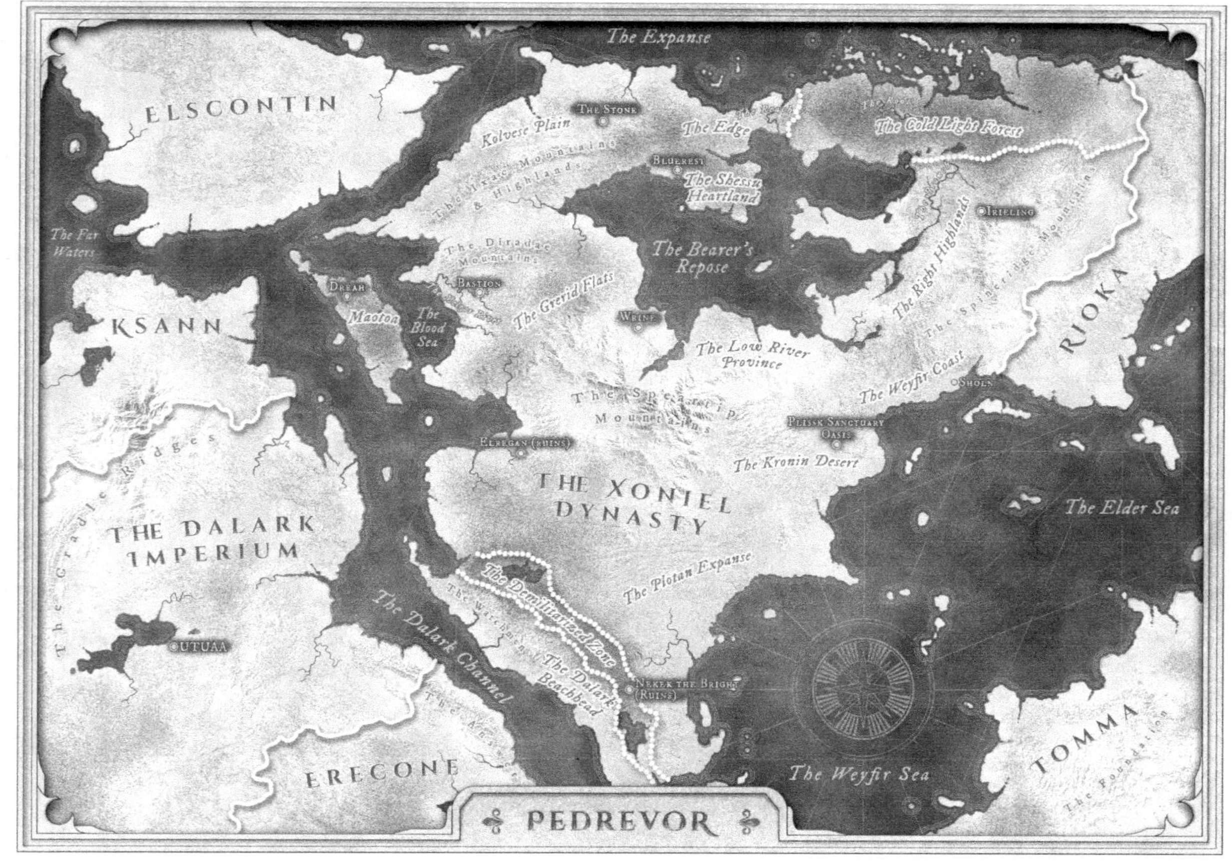

PEDREVOR
ELSCONTIN
KSANN
THE DALARK IMPERIUM
ERECONE
THE XONIEL DYNASTY
RIOKA
TOMMA
The Expanse
The Stone
Kolvese Plain
The Edge
The Cold Light Forest
The Diraxac Mountains & Highlands
Bluerest
The Shessu Heartland
The Far Waters
The Diradac Mountains
The Bearer's Repose
Irieling
Dreah
Bastion
The Grerid Flats
Maofon
The Blood Sea
Weine
The Right Highlands
The Low River Province
The Spiderridge Mountains
The Spearleip Mountains
The Weyfir Coast
Sholn
Plissk Sanctuary
Oasis
Elregan (Ruins)
The Kronin Desert
The Elder Sea
The Cradle Ridges
The Piotan Expanse
Utuaa
The Demilitarized Zone
The Watchhand
The Dalark Channel
The Dalark Beachhead
Nexek the Bright (Ruins)
The Weyfir Sea
The Foundation

Narius looked over Bastion, the city a vast field of lights. Breathtaking, a reminder of the many souls who lived under his rule.

It was the last thing he wanted to see.

Someone cleared his throat.

Narius closed his eyes. "Is she gone?"

As Paine stepped up next to him, Narius studied his chief adviser. Even after all the drama, Paine was the paragon of stability. His dark skin positively glowed in the night air.

"Is she gone?" Narius injected some steel into his voice.

"She just left, Your Strength." Paine coughed discreetly. "About the duke's recommendation..."

"No." Narius turned to face the vizier. "No one is to harm the—" What should he call her? "—the former queen, understood? That would only make the situation more dangerous."

"Allowing her to spread lies is better?"

"We won't do that either." He resisted the urge to glance at the darkened room. He knew he wouldn't spot the out-of-place shadow. "Isn't that right?"

Sure enough, Tormod, his spymaster, emerged.

"I've already begun the disinformation campaign." Tormod offered Paine an oily grin. "I've suggested half a dozen different theories to the press as to why the queen left: mental illness, sordid affairs, potential treason. Her voice will be drowned by the noise."

Paine sniffed. Narius understood his disappointment. Paine and Viara had never gotten along. That was probably why the vizier favored a quiet assassination. But it wasn't honorable. Even Tormod's plan seemed too heartless.

"Then it's done," Narius whispered.

"Not quite, Your Strength." Paine turned back to him. "Unfortunately, Istragon has already begun agitating."

Not surprising. Istragon, the supreme prelate, was supposed to be the spiritual leader for the Dynasty. Instead, he usually spent his time finding things to disapprove of. "Let me guess. He finds the current situation 'unacceptable.'"

"He fears the Dynasty will not fare well with you in your present... condition."

Narius snorted. Leave it to the prelate to make it sound like he had contracted a disease. He turned back to Bastion. Istragon was a simpleton, but Istragon's fears would be shared by many within the Dynasty.

Of course, there was one potential solution, the best in Narius's mind by far. "Any reaction from the Dalark Imperium?"

Paine wouldn't meet his gaze. That spoke volumes, but Narius wanted to hear it.

"Paine?" he prompted.

The vizier sighed. "I have already made discreet inquiries with Ambassador Alezzar regarding your desires."

"And?"

Paine shook his head. "Emperor Devroshan still won't allow it."

Of course the old fool wouldn't. Such an obvious solution to so many problems, and the senile fossil didn't have enough sense to see it.

Narius looked up. If only the Perfected Warrior, the Water Bearer, or any of the other gods were real. If only there were someone who could give him what he actually wanted.

But he couldn't wallow. "Very well. Contact the prelate and tell him that the situation will be dealt with."

Paine hesitated, a frown tickling his brow. "If I may be so bold... how?"

Narius waved the question away. "I leave that up to you. Find someone. Anyone. I want this taken care of by the end of the week. Is that clear?"

Paine nodded. "As you say."

Narius glared at the city. Being the ruler of so many people meant he had to make sacrifices. He had done so before. What was one more?

Hopefully, though, they would find someone pleasant to be his queen. At this point, the universe owed him.

2

Inkstains, she was late *again!*

Everys rushed out of her apartment. She only paused long enough to make sure her emergency pen was tucked in her pocket, then she flew down the stairs. She poked her head into her shop as she passed. It didn't look like anyone was lining up at the front door.

Hot air poured down her throat the moment she stepped outside. The humidity was bad enough, but with the added stench of garbage from the restaurant next door, Everys gagged. She hurried out onto the streets of Fair Havens.

She skirted around a crowd gathered by the local crier. The image of a well-dressed Grerid man filled the screens on the column as he shared the latest news. "—still no word on whether King Narius has picked a new bride. Rumor has it the palace has interviewed dozens of eligible women, but none have caught his fancy."

Everys snorted. *This* was news? The criers rarely shared anything important, and never anything relevant to Fair Havens. Why not report on the crushing poverty most residents in Fair Havens experienced? Or the lack of education? Or how the Dynasty's bloated military budget could relieve so much suffering in Fair Havens and other neighborhoods like it? But no, obviously the most important news was about the king's love life or lack thereof.

As she slipped around the crier, she bumped into someone. She turned to apologize, but stopped short. A man with blue-tinged skin and dusky hair glared at her. A Weyfir. Not a surprise. A lot of the races lived in Fair Havens.

"Watch where you're going, scribbler." He spat the last word like it tasted bad.

She bristled at the insult. She should have been used to such hostility and hatred, but it always stung. Everys rolled her eyes at his back, debating whether or not she should hurl a fake apology at him. But no, she was late enough as it was. So, she turned and headed down the street.

As she rounded a corner, she came up on a wall of people clogging the intersection. Everys, at least a head taller than most of the people in the crowd, popped onto her toes to see what caused the jam. Bastion constables and military police formed a ring around one of the buildings, most of them trying to disperse the crowd. That many constables in Fair Havens was odd enough. But the military too?

Then she saw why. The building was covered with a new coat of graffiti. "RETURN THE HEARTH" and "FREEDOM FOR THE COLD LIGHT" had been painted in bright green letters, along with hastily drawn pictures of the Bastion skyline burning while two large trees loomed behind it. Everys shuddered. The last thing Fair Havens needed was Cold Light terrorists. She shook her head. So much broken, so few people willing to work on solutions.

Spotting an opening in the crowd, she slipped through to the empty street beyond. She pulled her digital scriber from her pocket and checked the time. Still running late, but maybe if she hustled, she could slip in right at the end.

Something crashed in the alley to her right. Her head snapped around, and she touched the pen in her pocket, if only to reassure herself. At first, she couldn't spot anything, but then she saw five wiggats slinking down the alley. She grimaced. The vermin weren't native to Bastion. Instead, someone had accidentally imported a wiggat horde from the Ixactl highlands. Since they didn't have a natural predator, the wiggat population exploded, especially in neighborhoods like Fair Havens. Most of the residents had learned to give the creatures a wide berth, and Everys knew she should just keep moving.

But then she heard the sound of someone faintly crying for help.

Everys hesitated. It was none of her business. And she was late. But another plea and the distinct hiss of wiggats sent her jogging into the alley.

She skidded to a halt when she found the vermin. Sure enough, the winged felines had encircled an old Grerid woman. She looked near death, wearing thread-bare clothing, her dark skin pocked and creased like it was made of water-damaged leather. She weakly swatted at the wiggats and the vermin easily dodged.

Then they noticed Everys. Five of them faced her, snarling and spitting. Everys took a step back. Something rattled above her. She glanced up. Six wiggats glared at her from their perches on the surrounding buildings. So much for retreating. She'd have to use more drastic measures.

Everys yanked the pen from her pocket and snapped it in half. The ink's acrid smell filled the alley, but it was quickly, thankfully, swallowed by the stench of garbage. She daubed some ink onto her finger and hastily smeared it onto the pavement. The rune she had in mind wasn't complex: a half-circle peppered with dots along the inside, with smaller squiggles radiating from the flat side and ending in diamonds. She glanced up at the wiggats. The horde advanced on her, ignoring their original prey. Good. They were in for a rude surprise.

Everys added the trapezoid which bisected the half-circle. There. Done, though the trapezoid's angles were too loose, the radiating squiggles too sloppy. It'd work, but she could have done better. Everys pressed her hand on one of the lines and willed the spell to activate.

Fire burst from the rune's center, and tendrils slapped each wiggat, missing the woman. Everys breathed a sigh of relief. Combat runes weren't her specialty.

The wiggats, screaming their indignation, clambered up the walls to escape. Everys nodded. As tempting as killing the vermin had been, unnecessary death was a sure way to get rebuked. She braced herself anyway, just in case the Singularity objected. When nothing happened, she darted forward to the old woman.

She was in rougher shape than Everys had thought, clearly suffering from a chronic illness. Her lungs rattled, and Everys didn't even have to touch her forehead to feel the heat.

Everys drained the rest of the ink, and then threw the pen's broken pieces into the trash. Once again, she worked quickly, sketching out a lesser healing rune. While she knew a more powerful variant, she couldn't use it. Old vows, old familial promises echoed in her mind. The lesser might not be as effective, but she had no choice. She knew this one better than the fire attack, so her finger moved practically on its own. This rune was more organic, like a fern unfurling on the woman's cheek. Sworls and curls intertwined and branched out. Everys frowned. She could only do so much without accurate information. She sketched in pain relief, strength, and healing then added a command to break the fever and clear her lungs.

But once the healing rune was done, she drew a different rune on the woman's other cheek. She had spent too much time on this already, and every extra second risked exposure. Within a minute, she had finished. She pressed her hands against both sides of the woman's face and, taking a deep breath, activated the spells.

A wave of light rippled across the old woman's body and soaked into her chest. She gasped, her back arching and her eyes opening wide, then she took a deep breath, one free of rattling. She met Everys's gaze, her expression filled with confusion.

But then she sniffed the air. Her eyes widened as she looked down at Everys's inkstained fingers. The woman's confusion gave way to terror.

"Get away from me!" the woman rasped. "I know... I know what you are!"

Then the second spell took hold. The old woman went limp in Everys's arms.

Everys released her held breath and gently settled the woman against the nearest wall. That was about as good as she could have—

Needles blossomed inside Everys's chest, and she fell onto her rear, clutching at her sides as the rebuke took hold. She screwed her eyes shut as the burning sensation clawed up her throat and blazed in her cheeks, the same place where she had drawn the runes on the old woman.

Everys gritted her teeth. This made no sense! Smacking around wiggats was fine, but healing an old woman wasn't? Or was it because of the amnesia rune? Did the Singularity want her to get caught?

Just as quickly as it came, the pain vanished. Everys took a ragged breath and checked on the old woman. The spells had consumed the ink, leaving no trace of what had happened. The old woman would stay unconscious for another minute or two as the toratropic magic erased her memories of Everys. Best leave before she regained consciousness and asked awkward questions. Everys found a rag and wiped off her hands before she hurried out of the alley, hoping against hope that she wouldn't be too late.

"You are late."

Everys glared at the acolyte. She wasn't *that* late. Based on the low droning coming from the armory, the morning rituals were still being performed. But she knew better than to antagonize him. If she attended the morning rituals regularly, it earned her tax breaks at the shop. If she attended daily, she could even earn her citizenship. She snorted at the idea. Tax breaks were good enough.

She slipped into the armory and hustled down the long hallway to the sanctum. She walked between statues depicting the Dynasty's lesser deities. On her right, the brooding Gravedigger. On her left, the twins Chance and Chaos. Flanking the sanctum's entrance were the kneeling Sun and Moons. And squatting over the door was the snickering Trickster. Everys didn't spare them more than a glance. Like most people living in the Dynasty's holdings, she knew they weren't real. They were mostly just good for making colorful curses.

As she stepped into the sanctum, she realized that the prelate and his acolytes weren't at the rostrum but stood at the weapon rack. She hadn't just been late. She'd almost missed the entire service. She skirted along the edge of the worshipers to find a place to watch. That wasn't easy; there were at least three hundred people packed into a space that should only have held half that many. Like so many things in Fair Havens, expanding the armory was on a perpetual to-do list that would never get done.

She finally found a spot near one of the support pillars. At the front of the room was the Warrior's statue, a ten-foot-tall carving of an imposing human male with distinct Hinaen features. The statue's eyes looked upward, his expression stern. His right hand was stretched out, his hand cupped to hold something. The prelate and acolytes carried a stone sword from the weapon rack and knelt before the statue. The prelate then rose and slid the sword's hilt into the statue's outstretched hand. Once the weapon was in place, the prelate turned to the assembled people.

"Today marks the beginning of Sword, a most auspicious month. During this time, we remember how the Warrior struck down those gods who stood between him and his beloved Water Bearer. His successors, imitating his strength, have struck down many enemies. The foul mage-kings of the Siporans, the Plissk and Dunestrider barbarians, and most recently, the Cold Light. Rejoice that the Dynasty is held in such strong hands."

Everys fought the urge to laugh. "Strong hands" indeed. She had heard the rumors about how Queen Viara had walked out on King Narius two months earlier. While she didn't know the queen's reasons, Everys couldn't blame her. The Dynasty's kings were all monsters. Violent, vengeful, power-hungry, just like the Perfected Warrior they emulated.

Water dripped on her head, and she sighed, resisting the urge to glance at the ceiling. Water sprinkled from vents in the ceiling, symbolizing the Water Bearer's blessing and marking the end of the ceremony. The people funneled through the exit where the water poured out of two spouts, each one held by a carving of the goddess. The prelate and his acolytes stood at the entrance, holding identity scanners. As each worshiper left, they pressed a thumb against the device, recording their attendance. Just her luck, Everys had to approach the acolyte who had seen her late arrival. He sneered as she passed.

"Be careful, scribbler," he whispered. "One day, we're going to finish the job."

Everys didn't meet his gaze, but she knew what she would have found if she did. Open hostility. Hatred. A desire to see her dead. While the Drywell Laws had been repealed forty years earlier and discrimination against her people was supposed to be a thing of the past, most of the Dynasty's citizens conveniently forgot that. As far as they were concerned, every Siporan was a potential mage-king, ready to use their dark arts to slaughter innocent people as they did in ancient times. The very notion was ridiculous.

Except Everys had used those "dark arts" before the service. Drywell Laws or not, if anyone found out, she'd be dead.

3

"Everys! Come see what I've got! You know you're going to like it."

Everys eyed the market stall. Gallik could surprise her with parts or even used electronics he got from who-knew-where, but most of the time, he called her over to ogle her. If Gallik actually did have a deal, it would be worth it. Just last month, he had sold her a crate of data scribers well below cost. She had sold them for a tidy profit. If he had something like that again, it might be worth stopping. But she didn't have time.

She shook her head. "Sorry, Gallik. I'll have to pass."

He grumbled, but she kept going. Calling this slow motion riot a "market" was charitable. At least a hundred open air stalls were crammed together, with merchants hawking their wares through shouts, innuendos, and barely contained aggression. Shoppers jostled each other through too narrow aisles. Everys grunted. The nobility never came down to markets like this. No, they stuck to cleaner, safer markets in better neighborhoods. She should have avoided the market, but with the military blockading the streets still, this was the fastest route back to her shop. She had at least thirty repair orders waiting. She had no idea how she'd get all of that done if she had to deal with customers too. Maybe she'd be lucky and she'd have help.

"Everys!"

Apparently she wouldn't. She knew that voice: the soothing baritone with a sharp undercurrent of greed.

She groaned. "Weren't we supposed to meet at the shop, Legarr?"

"Couldn't wait. I had to talk to you right away."

That made her even more uneasy. She turned to face him. He was short, but he made up for it with what he called "charm." He wore clothing that was almost fashionable, close enough he could pass in higher society. His brown hair had been cut short, similar enough to a military style he could be mistaken for a soldier. That's how her brother got through life: a little bit of charm, a little bit of swagger, and enough bluffing to make up the difference.

Everys crossed her arms and didn't say anything. Why tempt Chaos?

"So I found out about a new opportunity that's kind of a limited time deal. And I'm a little short on funds. Tilash keeps insisting we pay rent."

"Crazy idea." Everys had never met Legarr's wife. For all she knew, this "Tilash" was convenient fiction for Legarr's schemes. "Maybe if you came in and worked a shift at the shop like you promised you would before Mama and Papa left..."

He waved away the idea like he was shooing an annoying insect. "No time! Too many deals, and one's ready right now. All I need is an advance of 2,500 blades..."

"2,500 blades?" That was a lot of money, definitely more than she could spare. And she knew if she gave Legarr the money, she'd never see it again.

But then she also knew what Papa would say. *Family takes care of our own, especially since no one else will.* Except ever since Papa, Mama, and Galan, Everys and Legarr's older sister, left Bastion, that meant Legarr was Everys's only family. And vice versa.

She sighed. "All right, let's go to the shop and—"

"You leech, leave her alone!"

Everys jumped at the shriek. An older woman barreled into Legarr, whacking him with a long walking stick. The woman wore threadbare rags, their bright colors faded. Even though she was blindfolded, she smacked Legarr repeatedly until he fled. The woman turned to her and smiled.

"So you're blind this week?" Everys asked. "I thought you were supposed to be deaf."

"Now is that any way to talk to your auntie, dear?" the old woman asked.

"I'm sorry, 'Auntie' Kyna." She forced the words past her clenched teeth.

Kyna smiled. Everys swallowed a groan. Saved from one con by another. Kyna usually wandered through Fair Havens, pretending to have some sort of ailment. She would be "blind" or "deaf" or "mute" or "crippled." While most people knew to ignore her, a few still tossed her spare coins, which the old fraud eagerly scooped up. Everything about her was a lie, including the fact that she wasn't related to Everys at all. She insisted every Siporan called her "Auntie."

"We missed you at the conclave," Kyna said. "Your prayers, woven with ours, would have been a blessing."

Everys felt a stab of guilt. Technically, she should never set foot in an armory. After all, the Dynasty was responsible for overthrowing the Ascendancy four hundred years earlier. She shifted her weight, looking down at the ground. "I had to go. You know that. If I don't—"

Kyna waved away her words. "Yes, yes. The Dynasty will demand a little more in taxes or make your life mildly more inconvenient and unpleasant. What a horrible burden!"

Everys's cheeks burned. "It's not that simple."

Kyna tugged the blindfold off and held it out to her. "Perhaps you need this more than me."

Why was she standing there and taking this? She had to get back to the shop and open for the day. Everys spun on her heel and marched off.

"There are some things you can't run from, Everys!" Kyna called after her. "The Singularity has a way of catching up to you."

Everys snorted. The Singularity. If the God of her people was so powerful, why had He allowed the Dynasty to destroy the Siporan Ascendancy? Why had He allowed foreign tyrants to tear down Nekek the Bright and desecrate the Scriptotum? Why had He allowed the Siporans to rot for four hundred years? The Singularity catch up with her? All He ever did was rebuke her when she didn't use the runes the way He said she should. But that was as far as His interest went.

Instead of her absent deity, a foul mood chased Everys through the streets. The buildings loomed around her, feeling more like prison bars than homes or shops. She was trapped, sealed away. At least once she made it back to her shop, she'd be able to—

Someone down the street screamed. Everys's head snapped around. A wave of people stampeded down the street, trying to get away from...away from...

The crowd parted. A man wearing a long coat stood on the corner. He gestured wildly, shouting something she couldn't make out over the panicked crowd. Then he tore open his coat, revealing a vest covered in cylinders and wires and—

The world dissolved in a flash of light, thunder chasing behind it. An invisible hand slammed into Everys, knocking her off her feet. She tumbled across the street and landed in a heap against a parked transport. The world spun and juked around her, then dissolved into darkness and noise.

4

V oices buzzed around Everys. Her head throbbed in an unheard rhythm that sent jolts down her spine. She groaned, and the voices went still.

"Is she waking up?" A voice that sounded like boulders grinding together cut through the silence.

Everys risked opening her eyes. She stared at a khaki ceiling. Where was she? A tent? She tried to lever herself up, but two humans in medical garb appeared at her side.

"Easy," one of them whispered. "You're one of the lucky ones. Just got a little shaken up is all."

"But you still want to be careful," the other said. "We don't know if—"

"Can she be transported?" The person—a woman?—with the gruff voice laced her words with authority.

Everys looked down at the end of the bed and her head started to spin. An Ixactl woman sat across from her. Even though the Ixactl was seated, Everys guessed she had to be close to eight feet tall. She had flinty gray skin and black eyes beneath a sloping and knobby brow. Unlike other Ixactl, though, this woman's horns were shorn into ragged stumps. A red line had been tattooed across her eyes, wrapping around her head to her ears. Her black hair had been trimmed short, almost to the point of baldness.

But it wasn't the Ixactl's presence that stunned Everys. It was what she wore. Not a constabulary uniform. Not even a military uniform. No, she wore a dark blue overcoat with a large red shield stitched onto her shoulders. Why was a member of the royal guard here?

"I asked you a question. Can she be moved?" The Ixactl stared at Everys.

One of the medics blew a long breath out through his nose. "She could. I wouldn't risk it, though."

"Understood." The Ixactl rose. "Please come with me."

Though what she said was polite enough, Everys still felt the threat. She glanced at the doctors, but they had retreated. Obviously, she couldn't play sick, not after what the medics said. She could refuse. The guard hadn't said she was under arrest. But a Siporan, resisting someone in authority? Bad idea. She forced herself to stand, holding her hands at her side so the guard wouldn't see the way they trembled. The Ixactl woman led her to the exit.

They stepped out of the tent, and Everys almost tripped over her own feet. Four more royal guards stood at attention. Once the Ixactl passed them, they fell into step, creating a moving barrier between Everys and the rest of the world. Thankfully, she was taller than most of them, so she was able to get a peek at her surroundings. They were still in Fair Havens. Military personnel and constables swarmed the streets, clearing debris or interviewing the local citizens. But as the guards passed, people stared, both at them and at her. She shrank back, trying to disappear, but her height made that difficult.

"What's going on?" she asked the Ixactl. Clearly she was the commanding officer.

Either the Ixactl didn't hear, or she didn't want to answer. She led the group to a waiting military transport, a large vehicle on six thick wheels that had been painted a mottled green and gray. The Ixactl wrenched open a back door and offered a hand to her. Everys took it, although reluctantly, and the Ixactl boosted her into the back. She found a bench along the opposite wall and sat down. The guards piled in, two of them sitting on either side of her, the other two in seats that flanked the door. The Ixactl shut the door, and a few moments later, the entire vehicle lurched forward.

Cold sluiced through her. Where were they taking her? Did they think she was responsible for the bombing? Maybe. People blamed Siporans for just about everything. Or what if they knew about Mama and Papa and Galan? Could they have learned about why they had left Bastion? But if either of those were the case, wouldn't they have put her in manacles? The guards weren't exactly treating her like a prisoner.

"Can one of you tell me what's going on?" she asked in a quiet voice.

No answer. Everys glanced at her... companions? Escorts? Captors? They all stared forward, not even acknowledging her existence. Fear twisted within her, but finally, she wrapped her arms around herself and leaned against the armored wall, closing her eyes. Hopefully whatever they were going to do with her would be over quickly.

The transport halted with a jolt that woke Everys. She snorted, nearly jumping out of her seat. How had she fallen asleep? Her head ached and her mouth was dry. She desperately needed to stretch.

The door creaked open and the Ixactl said, "We're here. Come."

The other guards didn't move. The order must have been meant for her. She sighed and slid through the door into the bright sunshine. She winced and held up a hand to shield her eyes. When her vision adjusted, she gasped.

Standing before her was a large building made out of tan stones. Towers dotted with crystalline windows speared into the sky. She turned a slow circle and realized that the entire complex was enclosed by a wall that was at least thirty feet high.

Why had they brought her to the royal palace?

The Ixactl steered Everys toward the palace. A door popped open and an older Grerid woman stepped out. Everys hadn't met many Grerids. Most of them were fortunate enough to live in middle-class neighborhoods. This woman was plump with darker skin, olive-shaped eyes, and tightly curled brown hair streaked with white. She pierced them both with a scowl.

"What took you so long?" she demanded.

Everys flinched.

"My apologies, Matron Halis, but there was an incident in Fair Havens that complicated matters," the Ixactl said.

Wait, they were coming to find her before the bomb even went off? What had she done? Why was she here?

Matron Halis shook a finger at the guard. "We'll have words about this later, Redtale." Then she fixed her attention on Everys. "Well, come along. Let's get you ready."

Ready for what? Why did everyone seem to think she knew what was going on? But before she could ask, Halis dragged her through the door.

Halis led her through the halls, keeping up a running commentary as they went. "I apologize for the confusion, ma'am. I was against sending Redtale to get you. She still thinks too much like a soldier. And you know what they say about the Ixactl. Nothing but rocks between their horns. Are you okay? You look like you've gone through a warzone yourself. But no matter. The girls are waiting for us, and they'll have you ready before you know it. There's no way that we'll be late, not for something this important."

Girls? Ready? Late? The questions built up. She tried to pull Halis to a stop, but the Grerid woman was surprisingly strong and kept dragging her through the halls. They finally arrived at their destination, and Halis practically shoved her through the door.

Everys stumbled into a room larger than her apartment, filled with lavish decorations and plush furniture. Half a dozen girls waited for her, all younger than Everys by at least a few years. One even looked to be sixteen. They rushed forward, chattering in a variety of dialects and languages. Everys tried to catalog them. More humans, a Weyfir, and even a reptilian Plissk girl, who had large eyes with slitted pupils and scaly, green-tinged skin. And they were in a bedroom of some sort, one larger than her apartment. They escorted her deeper into the room toward another door.

"Get her bathed!" Halis ordered.

The girls led Everys into a bathroom and immediately started pulling at her clothing, trying to undress her. That snapped her out of her shock. She fought to keep them from stripping her, but there were too many hands. Before she knew it, they had practically thrown her into a shower.

"We'll be waiting right outside when you're done, ma'am," one of the girls said.

And then she was alone, standing in a small, tiled room with a large nozzle set in the ceiling. Everys turned a slow circle, her eyes wide, her body shaking. She took several gulping breaths.

"Ma'am, please hurry. We don't have a lot of time." The girl's voice was muffled, but Everys could hear a hiss to her words, the thready tone sounding like a Plissk voice.

"Time for what?" Everys demanded. "What is going on?"

"We have to prepare you for the ceremony!" The Plissk girl's tone suggested Everys should have known what she was talking about.

"What ceremony?" Everys asked.

Her question was met with silence. But she could feel the tension boiling off the girls through the door. She sighed. Fine. She could probably use a shower anyway.

The warm water was wonderful. Unlike her apartment, it didn't cut out. She wanted to luxuriate, but within a few minutes, the girls started making impatient sounds. So she finished up, using the soap she found in a nook in the shower's wall. The soap and shampoo smelled wonderful, a mix of flowery sweetness with a hint of citrus.

The moment she emerged from the shower, the girls pounced, drying her with large towels. Everys tried to ask more questions, but they were too focused. They wrestled her into a simple blue gown, half of them working on making sure it fit properly while the other half forced a comb through her hair.

Then Halis strode into the room. The girls stepped away from Everys, and Halis examined her from every angle. Everys wrapped her arms around her waist, wanting to disappear. Halis's expression didn't change as she finished her inspection.

Finally, the matron sighed. "I suppose this will have to do. The scratches and bruises are minimal, but if we had been given more time to—"

"What is going on?" The question exploded from Everys. "What am I doing here?"

That stopped Halis in her steps. She sputtered. "Y-you... you don't *know?*"

"Know what?"

Halis spun on her heels. "Redtale! Redtale!"

The guard stepped into the room. "She ready?"

"Yes, but that's not why I called you in here." Halis stabbed a finger at Everys. "Did you tell her why you brought her here?"

Redtale shook her head. "Wasn't ordered to. I assumed she knows."

"She most certainly does not!"

"What is it I'm supposed to know?" Everys asked.

The guard shrugged. "Not much we can do about it. Whether she understands or not, she's part of this. Time to go."

Halis spluttered, turned back to Everys. A frightened look flitted across her face, then she rushed forward, her hands fluttering over the dress, tugging at it, adjusting it, making sure it was just right.

As Halis worked, she whispered, "I'm so sorry, ma'am. I don't know why you weren't told, but you're here now. It'll be okay. Just be yourself and you'll be fine."

She offered Everys one last, half-hearted smile, then stepped out of the way. Redtale beckoned for her to follow. Everys didn't want to. She wanted to run, jump out a window, try to escape, or find a place to hide. But she couldn't. And Halis had said she was going to be okay. Taking a deep breath, she followed Redtale.

The guard led her through halls, walking a bit faster than Everys thought was necessary. They passed by what appeared to priceless works of art, paintings, and sculptures tucked into small alcoves, the sort of thing she would have expected to see in a museum. Redtale didn't even glance at them or slow down so Everys could. They came to two large, ornately carved wooden doors. A pair of guards snapped to attention, then hauled the doors open.

Everys stepped through, then halted. She stood in the entrance to a large, round room, surrounded by thick pillars that held up a soaring dome. A grand staircase led to a balcony, with half a dozen smaller balconies encircling the room. The royal ballroom! From the pictures she had seen, she would have expected ornate tables and chairs, the nobility in their finest sharing quiet conversation or maybe dancing to gently played music. But the room was largely empty, a nearly cavernous space.

A row of eight young women wearing similar dresses to Everys's stood on the opposite side of the room. Redtale motioned for her to take her place at the end of the line. As she crossed the room, she examined the other women. A shock ran through her when she realized she knew one of them. Well, not personally. But just about everyone in Bastion had seen pictures of Clarinda Gaines, the owner and Chief Executive Officer for TelleGlin. Her company's headquarters was in Bastion. She was tall for a Weyfir—even taller than Everys, which was saying something—with long teal hair that almost matched the tint of her skin. Her purple eyes sparkled as her gaze swept over Everys, as if she were sizing her up for battle. Everys shrank back, sure the woman wasn't impressed. Everys's olive skin was pockmarked with scars from a childhood illness. Her brown hair wasn't nearly as lustrous as the other women's, and she knew her brown eyes were hardly remarkable. She was no statuesque beauty, no stunning vision of sexual desire. And Gaines clearly thought so, given the way she smirked and turned away from her.

Everys forced herself to examine the other women. All of them appeared to be about her age, mid- to late-twenties, although she knew that Gaines was somewhere in her forties. All of them except Gaines were human, an even mix of Grerid, Hinaen, and Kolvese. No other Siporans, but that wasn't much of a surprise.

Redtale cleared her throat, so Everys hustled to her place. She risked a peek down the line. All of the other girls save for Gaines appeared nervous. Should she be? What were they doing here?

The doors to the ballroom opened again and someone walked across the room. A wave of pins and needles swept over Everys. It was Prince Quartus, the king's younger brother! He appeared just as he did in the news reports, handsome with ruddy skin and shining golden hair. His coppery eyes shone with mischievous light. Everys's knees jellied in spite of herself. Although she would never admit it, she had always harbored a crush on Quartus. Her parents would have never approved. After all, it was King Heronus, Quartus's ancestor, who had destroyed Nekek the Bright and the Siporan Ascendancy, forcing Everys's people into exile. But that didn't change the fact that Quartus was cute.

"Hello, ladies," Quartus said. "So glad you could be here today."

His gaze slid over them one by one. Everys frowned. Did he pause on her? The girls tittered nervously, although Gaines speared Quartus with a glare. Redtale cleared her throat.

Quartus sighed and gave a slight, dismissive wave. "I know, Redtale. I shouldn't interrupt. I just had to satisfy my curiosity. Chance's favor on you, ladies."

As Quartus left through a side door, the main doors banged open again. Everys jumped at the noise, then turned her attention to the newcomers. A squad of royal guards trotted through, fanning out along the wall.

And once again, Everys felt ready to collapse as King Narius himself strode into the ballroom.

5

S he was in the presence of the king. *She was in the presence of the inkstained king!*

Her heartbeat thundered in her ears. Sure, she had seen images of the king, but to encounter him in person? The official imagery made him appear more statue than alive, but she realized that there really was an otherworldly quality to his appearance. His hair was a shimmering copper, cut short. His jawline was sharp. And his eyes were golden yet cold. He exuded a quiet strength that seeped into the ballroom and drew everyone's attention to him.

The other women stood straighter and smiled brightly. Everys didn't. Her jaw popped open in surprise, her attention focused on King Narius. He was right there, the living embodiment of the Dynasty's will, the visionary of the Dynasty's future, the unleasher of the Dynasty's military wrath.

The direct descendant of the monster who destroyed her people's homeland.

That thought snapped her out of her reverie. How could she gape at him? He wasn't nearly as handsome as Quartus, even if he did carry himself with a stiff seriousness that made his face look like it had been chiseled from stone. Smudges and splatters, what was she *doing?* So what if she was suddenly in the presence of royalty? Nothing made him better than anyone else. So why was she still staring at him with her jaw dangling open like a broken store sign?

Everys forced herself to examine the people in his wake. She realized she recognized many of them from the news. There, that was Auriel Zammit, the Governor-General of Bastion. And behind her was... yes, that was Zolkin, First Speaker from the Hall of All Voices. And following him was Supreme Prelate Istragon. While she didn't recognize many of the others, she had to assume that they were all members of Narius's council, especially since the last person through the door was Vizier Paine, looking almost as regal as Narius himself in his robes of state. The advisers, fifteen of them by Everys's quick count, fanned out in a line parallel to the one in which Everys stood, all of them studying the women clinically.

"Really, Clarinda?" One of the advisers, a rotund man with a white horseshoe of hair, chuckled. "I thought you wanted a title."

"Why not aim higher?" Clarinda's tone was icy.

Everys risked a glance out of the corner of her eye. The CEO glared openly at the man who had questioned her—whom Everys recognized as Masruq, the Minister of Finance—before painting on a pleasant smile as Narius stepped up to her. The two spoke quietly, but it wasn't hard to spot the predatory gleam in Clarinda's expression or the way Narius kept a safe distance between them.

So what was she supposed to do? Maybe one of the councilors would give her a clue. But they watched Narius as he and Gaines chatted. Everys's gaze eventually landed on Vizier Paine. Out of all the gathered people, he was the most striking, standing just a little shorter than her. He had dark skin with a completely shaved head. His robes of office complemented his Kolvese complexion. He looked stately, regal, a pillar of calm.

But then Paine's gaze flicked in Everys's direction. The scowl he leveled on her knocked her back a step. He despised her. But then the expression vanished, and he turned his attention back to Narius.

The king had moved down the line, chatting quietly with the girl next to Everys. She strained to overhear their conversation, but their voices were too low for her to pick up on more than a few words. It sounded like they were discussing a winter home at Bluerest, but whether it was his or hers, she couldn't tell.

So what was she supposed to say when he got to her? The other girls appeared to at least know the king. And since they all appeared to be from the nobility except for Gaines, they traveled in the same social circle. What could she talk about with him? The price of food in Fair Havens? The crippling poverty? The way the constables behaved like they were in an occupied city rather than the Dynasty's capital?

And then he stepped in front of her, his golden eyes flicking up and down her body. But his expression remained neutral, almost grim, as if he were inspecting a soldier. Everys's thoughts froze. She was mere inches from the most powerful person on Pedrevor. Her mouth went dry as her mind tumbled in free fall, trying to stitch together two coherent thoughts—

With a snort, he turned and marched back to his advisers.

She blinked. That was it? Was this over? None of the other girls had moved. Instead, they looked even more anxious. Everys turned her attention to the men huddled around Narius. A heated discussion broke out, with some of the advisers waving in the direction of the women. Everys risked another glance down the line. Clarinda Gaines stood taller, her smile bright and confident. The other girls ran the gamut of nervousness. One looked ready to collapse.

She turned her attention back to Narius and his advisers. Most of them had fallen silent except for Supreme Prelate Istragon. The older man spoke in a harsh whisper she couldn't quite make out, but from his posture and expression, she could tell he verbally hammered Narius, punctuating his points with a jab of his finger. Everys wasn't sure what was more shocking: the prelate's obvious disrespect or Narius's restraint. If Narius was bothered by Istragon's attitude, he wasn't letting on. Everys's estimation of him went up, just by a little. She knew how much she would struggle to keep her composure with an old geezer lecturing her like that.

But apparently Paine wasn't going to stand for Istragon's attitude. The vizier interposed himself between Narius and Istragon, also whispering, making emphatic points with sharp hand chops. Istragon didn't back down, instead leaning in and almost thumping Paine in the chest. The other advisers clustered around Paine and Istragon, occasionally interjecting their own thoughts.

Everys ground her teeth. What, exactly, were they discussing so emphatically? Every now and then, Paine or Istragon would gesture in the women's general direction, but they didn't seem to be paying too much attention to them.

No, wait, one of the advisers was staring at her. Not the other women. *Her.* He was a lumpy little man, squat and his facial features bland. He had nothing overtly memorable about him, and she may not have noticed him at all if he hadn't been staring so intently at her. When their gazes met, his eyes lit up and a broad smile split his face. Who was he? Everys didn't recognize him. He shuffled up to Narius's side and pulled on the king's arm like an eager child. Narius frowned at him, but as the other man kept tugging, Narius leaned down to listen to what he had to say. The man whispered in the king's ear, and a strange procession of emotions flitted across Narius's face: irritation, confusion, curiosity, and then amusement. The two men turned and looked right at Everys with such a piercing intensity she considered hiding behind one of the other women.

Then Narius said something that stopped Paine and Istragon's argument. The vizier and prelate gaped at him, and then, much to Everys's surprise, Paine and Istragon started arguing with Narius together. But it was clear that whatever they were saying, it wasn't changing Narius's mind. The king crossed his arms and stared at them, stony faced until finally, Paine fell silent. After making a few more emphatic points, Istragon did as well.

Then the entire crowd of advisers turned and headed back to the line of women. Paine stepped in front of them.

"Thank you for coming. We will make sure you all get home safely."

Gaines looked frustrated, but the other women looked relieved. They tried to hide it behind masks of disappointment, but she could tell. They all headed for one of the exits. Everys tried to follow, but Paine cleared his throat.

"Everys, please stay here."

She froze. The advisers studied her with critical expressions, as if sizing up some sort of specimen. Istragon looked positively sick.

As soon as the other women left, Narius stepped up next to her. "Let us proceed."

Proceed with what? She shied away from him, but he shot a look at her that froze her in place. He roughly grabbed her right hand, the sudden movement holding her in place.

"This is most irregular," Istragon said.

"It's what you've been insisting on this whole time," Narius said. "Now do it!"

Istragon sighed and stepped closer. He offered Narius a disappointed look, then speared her with a venomous glare.

Everys looked between them, trying to piece together what might be happening. The king, standing next to her, with the Supreme Prelate before them. A cold wave sliced through her. What was going on?

Istragon held up his hands. "As he is the Warrior, she is the Water Bearer. As he strives for honor, she strives for wisdom."

Wait, she knew those words! She had heard them in the armory. They couldn't be serious!

"No!" She jerked away from Narius.

But he grabbed her hand in a vise-like grip and fixed her with angry, steely eyes. "Just get this over with."

Istragon dropped a hand on top of Narius's, the same one that held hers. "May you both be the ideal the other pursues." Then he turned sharply on his heel to the gathered advisers. "It is done. They are bound in marriage. May the Warrior's own favor rest on King Narius and Queen Everys, both today and for all the years to come."

6

Queen Everys? Had she really just become the Queen of the Xoniel Dynasty? No, this had to be a mistake. An elaborate prank. Or a nightmare. Because there was no way that any of this was real. It couldn't be.

But she wasn't waking up. And no one acted like it was a joke. Instead, the advisers applauded politely. Everys searched their expressions, hoping to catch a glimpse of something—anything—that would explain what was going on. Maybe the squat man who had spoken to Narius? But she couldn't find him. When had he slipped out?

Narius released her hand. "Get her settled, Paine. Then come down to the Amber Office so we can plan how to share this new development." He sounded like he was discussing something insignificant.

"Now wait just a minute!" Everys started after him.

Before she could catch up, though, Redtale and three other guards stepped into her path.

"Sorry, Blessed." Redtale wore a pained expression. "Go slow. Your husband's got a lot on his mind."

Everys laughed, a slightly crazed bark that could easily have turned into sobbing if she hadn't caught herself in time. She wouldn't give this audience the satisfaction of seeing her cry.

One by one, the gathered advisers offered their congratulations. She numbly stood there, the bland platitudes not really registering. The only person who didn't speak to her was Istragon, who sneered at her before storming out of the room. Soon only Vizier Paine remained.

"Queen Everys, if you would follow me, please?" From his tone, he didn't care what she did, but he headed for the exit.

Everys hustled after Paine. "Wait! What just happened? How can I be queen?"

Paine paused. "You are aware of the departure of Queen Viara?"

She held back a snarl. Of course she was. Everyone in the Dynasty's holdings knew.

"And you're also aware that, by sacred law, the Dynasty's king must be married for his reign to be legitimate?"

Oh. She didn't know that part.

Paine's lips twisted into a smirk. "I thought not. After searching for an appropriate candidate for months now, he has chosen you. Congratulations."

She didn't feel all that lucky. But Paine continued walking, and she hurried to keep up. "So does that mean I'm in charge of... something?"

"No, you are merely here to lend his reign the proper legal legitimacy. My suggestion is that you stay out of his way."

"Gladly," Everys muttered.

One of Paine's eyebrows quirked. "Take heart, Queen Everys. This life is hardly unpleasant. You will be provided with quarters, a staff, a stipend to cover your living expenses. There will be public functions you will be expected to attend and host. For example, a Queen's Court is scheduled for a few weeks from now. It would be a good entry for you into the nobility."

Wait, she was going to do what? Spend time with people who had no idea what she had been through, the people whose wealth and power had made the lives of so many in Fair Havens miserable? Oh, that would end well. But if Paine noticed her disdain for the idea, he didn't let on. Instead, he kept walking.

"So Narius finally found a new queen?"

Everys and Paine whirled around to find Prince Quartus leaning against a nearby pillar.

He stepped closer to her. "Welcome to the family."

Everys's cheeks burned at the open attention from the prince. Maybe if Narius looked at her the way Quartus was right now, she would have felt better about this whole arrangement.

"I'm afraid I didn't catch your name earlier," Quartus said.

"I-I'm Everys." Should she bow? She had no idea what the correct protocol was.

"Everys." The way he whispered her name caused a shiver to dance up her spine. "Well, let me give you some preliminary advice: be cautious who you trust in the palace. There are always half a dozen schemes brewing that can trip up the unwary."

"So does that advice extend to you as well?" Everys asked.

His smile turned impish. "Of course. Me most of all."

Another thrill shot through her.

Paine cleared his throat. "If we can continue, Queen Everys?"

"Oh, yes, don't let me interrupt you," Quartus said. "So much to learn, so much to see. But when you're settled in, do look me up, my queen. I'll give you a personal tour of the palace to show you what really matters."

And with that Quartus slipped away, whistling a jaunty tune. Paine cleared his throat again, snapping Everys out of her reverie. After a few more twists and turns, they arrived at a large set of doors, flanked by a pair of guards. They snapped to attention when they saw her, then quickly hauled the doors open. Paine motioned for her to enter.

She stood in a lavish living room the size of her apartment back in Fair Havens. There were three different seating areas, one around a low table, another facing a fireplace, and one clustered around a state-of-the-art vidscreen. Lavish rugs covered the marble floor. Beautiful but soulless paintings hung on the walls. Intricately carved stone arches led into other rooms. This couldn't all be for her!

Then her gaze landed on the line of young women who stood at attention in the middle of the room. She recognized most of them— they had been the ones who had helped her get dressed earlier. But the young woman on the end wasn't familiar. She was Hinaen and wore a smart business suit, her dark hair swept up into a tight bun.

Paine gestured to that woman. "This is Challix. She will be your assistant. If you need anything, you are to go through her. She will help you navigate your new responsibilities and duties. In addition..." Paine's voice trailed off. "Where is Matron Halis?"

The Plissk girl—Trule?—squeaked. "Your pardon, Grand Vizier. Matron Halis had to leave on a family emergency."

Paine scowled. "Very well. Until her return, you will oversee the queen's personal attendants. Understood?"

Trule blanched, but she nodded quickly. "Of course."

"Challix, I leave the queen in your care." With that, Paine left.

Challix stepped forward, her heels clacking against the stone floor. She examined Everys through narrowed eyes. "I will admit, you are not what I expected. But life can be filled with surprises, yes?"

Everys couldn't tell if Challix was being rude or not. She decided to assume she was and start disliking her now to save time.

"As the vizier said, I am your assistant," Challix said. "If there is an issue, you may come to me first so that I may address it. I will maintain your personal calendar, handle any and all official correspondence, and serve as liaison to the various functionaries of the Dynasty."

Challix clapped her hands, and the doors boomed open. Redtale and a number of guards tromped inside. They quickly snapped to attention in a neat row.

"You have already met Redtale, correct?" Challix asked.

"That's one way to phrase it," Everys replied.

Challix regarded her with a curious look. Redtale, for her part, kept her features impassive.

"Redtale is head of the Queen's Guard," Challix explained. "She will serve as your primary bodyguard when you leave the palace. She will also coordinate the schedule of the other guards to make sure that you are adequately protected at all times. Redtale?"

Redtale motioned toward one of the guards, a handsome young Dunestrider man. Much to Everys's surprise, he had a sword strapped to his side. Did he think he'd need to use it? In one fluid motion, he pulled the blade free, then knelt in front of her, setting the sword on the floor in front of him.

"My queen, I am Kevtho, fourth-child of my tent, Strider of the Ridge. I pledge my life and limbs to you and your honor. The sword is yours. If any should challenge, it is my blood that shall shield you. By the shifting sands, by the implacable heat, I swear this to you now."

Everys stared at him. What did any of that mean? She looked up at Redtale, then at Challix, hoping that they would pick up on her confusion.

Thankfully, Redtale seemed to understand. She mouthed, *Pick up the sword and give it to him.*

She gingerly picked up the blade. The sword was real, with enough weight that she almost dropped it. She fumbled it before holding it out to Kevtho, who took it, rose, and sheathed it before stepping back into line with the other guards.

"Uh... thanks?" she said.

Challix sighed. "Kevtho is your Swordbound, Queen Everys. Should someone challenge you to a duel—"

"If they *what?*"

"—Kevtho would fight in your place."

Everys's gaze hopped between Challix, Redtale, and Kevtho. This had to be a joke, right? But no one was laughing.

"People will challenge me to duels?" she asked.

"It is within the realm of possibility," Challix said. "As queen, you are a legitimate target for duels of honor and retaliation."

"It doesn't happen that often," Redtale said.

"Does Narius have a... what is he called again?"

"Swordbound," Redtale said. "And yes, he does."

"But his only carries the sword," Challix added. "King Narius would fight his own duels. Allow me to show you the rest of your quarters."

Challix didn't wait for Everys to respond. Instead, she started through the living area toward one of the arches.

"Admittedly, we did not have time to prepare your quarters properly. Should you wish to redecorate, we will be able to accommodate just about any request within reason. While you do have a stipend, it is not limitless, as Minister Masruq is fond of reminding me."

"How much?" Everys asked.

"Queen Viara left 1.7 million blades."

Everys's stomach dropped, and she suddenly couldn't breathe. *1.7 million blades?* She could buy her building with that kind of money! And that was just what the previous queen had left?

"Now if you'd come with me?"

They continued on the tour. Challix showed her a private study almost as large as the living room, then a kitchenette and dining nook, followed by a bathroom that could have fit a family of five back in Fair Havens. So could the bedroom, which was dominated by a bed so large Everys worried she'd get lost in it.

Finally, Challix led them back to the main living room area and headed to the door. "I will take my leave of you now, Blessed. I will let you get to know your personal staff and settle in. Never fear, we'll make sure you're well cared for."

And with that, Challix left the quarters. As the doors shut again, Everys wrapped her arms around herself. Why did it feel like she was really a prisoner?

7

At least her prison was comfortable. That thought didn't provide a lot of comfort. And her captors seemed a whole lot more scared of her than she was of them. Trule and the other girls hovered several feet away, tense and ready to fulfill her any demand. When she realized she was hungry, they ran to the palace kitchens. When she commented she was chilly, they started a fire. Maybe they would put on a show for her if she said she was bored. The only real excitement was when one of the guards came into the room and whispered something to Trule. The girl's scales paled and she followed the guard out of the room.

When she came back, she looked positively sick. "I'm so sorry, Blessed, but... but..."

Everys rose from the couch. "What is it? You can tell me." Hopefully her voice was soothing enough.

Trule hiccupped. "I have been ordered to bring you to the king's chamber."

"Why?" Everys asked.

Trule spluttered. "It... it is your wedding night."

It took a moment for what she said to sink in. Everys's stomach dropped into her feet. No. Not happening! He had barely acknowledged her presence earlier. And now he expected her to... to...

"And..." Trule's voice trailed off.

There was *more?*

"You need to wear this." Trule held out a small scrap of fabric.

That was supposed to be clothing? The material appeared nothing but blue lace, and there wasn't enough to cover all that much.

With dawning horror, she realized that was the point.

She took a step back and tripped over the hem of her dress. "No, no, no. I-I can't!"

Two of the girls caught her before she could tumble. Or were they making sure she couldn't escape?

Well, they didn't have to worry about that. Because she wasn't going to leave this room. Forget it.

Wait. No, she couldn't think like that. She couldn't hide. If she did, Narius would probably send guards to fetch her. So she would go to his quarters. But not to have sex. Not tonight and, as far as she was concerned, not ever. No, tonight would be a talk between adults. Maybe she could find a way out of this. After all, he hadn't looked thrilled. Surely he could be persuaded to see reason.

She nodded. "Fine. Let's go."

She turned to leave, but the girls blocked her way. She frowned at them, but they wouldn't budge.

"Please, Blessed," Trule said. "He was most insistent."

She glared at the lingerie. It was too bad she couldn't draw a quick rune on it and set the stupid thing on fire.

"Fine." She snatched it out of Trule's hands. Then she held up a warning finger. "But if I'm going to wear it, I'm going to dress myself!"

Everys pulled the robe around her shoulders. The cool air nipped at her bare skin, and there was far too much of it. Thankfully, no one would see her. As it turned out, there was a private passage between the queen and king's quarters. But even as she snuck through the dimly lit tunnel, she felt too exposed. Like dozens of eyes tracked her every move. Dissected her. Judged her.

After making their way up two flights of narrow stairs, they came to a doorway set in the featureless wall. Trule turned to her. "This is as far as I may go, Blessed. I will wait until you're... finished."

Wait, she would... what? Everys shook her head. "That's not necessary."

Trule gave her a desperate look. "But I have to. It's my responsibility."

Oh, no. The girl was going to start crying again. Fine. It wasn't like she was going to overhear anything anyway. Everys held up her hands in surrender. "All right. But I won't be long."

Trule's eyes widened, and her scales paled. Everys almost laughed at her horrified expression, but she caught herself. She gave the door an experimental push. It slid open silently, revealing a darkened room beyond. Taking a deep breath, Everys ducked into Narius's chambers.

She emerged into a spacious living room. A hearth filled one wall, made out of rough-hewn stones. A large portrait of the Perfected Warrior hung over the fireplace, the mythical hero striking a dramatic pose, clutching his broken sword in one hand, his battered shield in the other. The artwork was exquisite, easily the most impressive masterpiece she'd seen since arriving at the palace. Clusters of couches and chairs were scattered around the room, one group circling a vid entertainment console, the other low tables.

Everys crept deeper into the room, jumping when the door clicked shut quietly behind her. Apparently the secret entrance was next to a fully-stocked bar. She turned a slow circle, drinking in the room as a whole. A great space for hosting a party. But she got the sense this room was rarely used. The bar was too perfectly put together, the bottles too orderly, the glasses covered with a thin layer of dust.

"Hello?" She winced at how loud her voice was. She didn't mean to shout.

But where was Narius? Maybe in one of the other rooms? She picked one of the archways.

It led to an office. Not the Amber Office—the king's official study, which she had seen in images on the criers. No, this had to be his personal study. Not surprisingly, there weren't any physical books on the shelves. There may have been at one time, but with the rise of scribers, it made such archaic things unnecessary. And thanks to the Drywell Laws, most upstanding members of the Dynasty had avoided owning anything that contained ink as a way of further punishing the Siporans.

Instead of books, the king had a number of trinkets and knickknacks although there weren't nearly enough to fill the shelves. It gave the room an odd, empty feeling. Everys took a closer look at a few of them. Here, a piece of metal that looked like the remains of armor. There, a ceremonial mask from some province within the Dynasty. All of them carefully arranged on their own individual shelves. Again, she had the distinct feeling Narius didn't pay much attention to his momentos. A shame, really. Some of them, like the mask, caught her attention. As much as she hated to admit it, she wondered what the story was behind it. Who gave it to the king? Why did Narius feel it worthy of being displayed?

She moved on. A draft nibbled at her legs, and she pulled the sheer robe a little tighter. Where was the breeze coming from?

As she walked down the hall, she found the source. A large balcony overlooked Bastion, and from this angle, it was a beautiful sight. Towers poked into the sky, shining like they were encrusted with the stars themselves. And there, a dark ribbon winding through the heart of the city. The Melgor River, working its way from the Speartip Mountains to the Blood Sea. It was tempting to go out on the balcony and drink in the view, but the evening air chased her away from the balcony into another room.

Everys found herself standing in the king's bedchamber, and the sight brought her up short. It wasn't the expensive furniture, although she could tell it all cost a small fortune. She had expected that. No, what she hadn't expected was the mess!

Clothing was strewn across a couch in one corner, as if Narius had just dumped the lot of it there while trying to decide what to wear. And over on a credenza were close to a dozen scribers stacked precariously. And were those...? They were! Dirty dishes from at least four different meals on a tray in a corner. She frowned. Did the servants not know about this room? Or were they under orders to leave it alone?

She did her best to dance around anything on the floor. Part of that was out of respect for Narius, but most of it was basic survival. The last thing she'd want was a twisted ankle. As she walked, she catalogued everything she saw in the room. On the wall by the credenza, ten different pictures of Narius at various ages, posing with groups of Dynasty soldiers, wearing the same uniforms as them. She crept over for a closer look. These didn't strike her as being part of an official visit, but it looked like Narius had belonged to the various units. And from the way the other soldiers smiled and stood close to him, it looked like they genuinely liked Narius.

She glanced at the stack of scribers. Should she peek? Well, she had come this far, and besides, if there was something truly sensitive on them, they'd be encrypted, right? She picked up the topmost device, careful not to knock over the rest, then thumbed the power switch. The tiny screen lit up, a logo swirling across the surface before the screen displayed a wall of text. It didn't look like a report or anything official. Instead, it was a novel? The king was reading a novel? Or he had been, at one point. Everys scanned the words. Looked like a military story: heroic soldiers fighting against the despicable enemies of the Dynasty. She rolled her eyes. Figured.

She was tempted to peek at the mound of clothes, if only to get a sense of Narius's personal style, but she thought better of it. Besides, she couldn't tell if the clothing was clean or dirty, and she didn't want to risk it being the latter.

Instead, she moved toward the bed. Like the one in her room, it was expansive. It probably could have held three or four people with room to spare. There was a small mountain of pillows at the head, and the deep green comforter was wrinkled and twisted, revealing white sheets underneath. Looking at the way the blankets were pulled aside, she guessed Narius slept on the left, so she headed toward that side.

Another scriber sat on the nightstand, along with a half-empty glass of water. A lamp perched on three sharp legs. And... wait, what was that? Tucked behind the lamp was a digital frame, its screen blank. Everys chewed on her thumb, then decided she had seen so much already. Why stop now?

The screen lit up, displaying the face of a beautiful young woman.

Everys frowned at the image. This wasn't Viara. She had seen plenty of pictures of the former queen. No, this woman looked about Everys's age, maybe in her early twenties, smiling with prominent dimples. Her green eyes sparkled from flawless porcelain skin, her face framed by long auburn hair. Everys frowned. She was no expert, but this woman appeared to be Dalark. Why would the Xoniel king have a picture of someone from the Dynasty's fiercest rivals?

She found the controls on the side and advanced the images. More pictures of the woman, but younger. Standing in a field of wildflowers. Looked like an image from a sappy romance vid. And then the same woman sitting on the beach, coyly looking over her shoulder. And then...

And then Narius and the girl together. They had to be in their midteens. They sat next to each other on a short wall, their heads tipped together. It wasn't entirely intimate, but Everys thought she saw longing in the girl's expression, in the way she looked at Narius instead of the camera. So who was she?

"What are you doing in here?"

The harsh words startled Everys. The digital frame slipped out of her hands, and she whirled. Narius stood in the bedroom doorway. As she turned, the robe's slick material slipped from her shoulders and the robe pooled at her feet.

She stared at the king. While she had noticed that she was taller than him, she hadn't noticed how well built he was. He wasn't overly muscular, like Quartus, but his body suggested he was used to hard work and exercise. His clothing accentuated his arms, the flatness of his stomach. She caught herself staring and looked up to his face.

His golden eyes burned with fury.

Then she looked down and realized how this must have looked. She was on display, standing next to his bed. Smudges, this wasn't how she wanted things to go.

In one quick movement, she scooped up the robe and tried to put it back on. In her flustered state, she wound up tangled in it rather than wearing it. And the struggle was probably revealing more of herself than she intended.

"I-I'm sorry, but I thought you wanted me..." She winced at the phrasing. "I mean, that you wanted to see me. Here, I mean. No, not here here, but—"

He stormed into the room. She shied away from him. Oh, inkstains, this couldn't be happening. She braced herself, determined to keep herself from being pushed onto the bed.

But he didn't touch her. Instead, he jabbed a finger toward the door. When she didn't move right away, he snarled.

She got the message. She scurried toward the door, keeping as much distance between him and her as possible. He followed her out of the room, storming down the hall and into the living area. He pointed at the hidden door.

"Get out. Now!"

He didn't even wait to see if she would follow his orders. Instead, he headed back to his bedroom.

Tears warred with relief. She should be happy. But she couldn't ignore the way her body shook at the mere memory of his fury. She choked back a sob and spun to the door, shoving it open.

As promised, Trule waited on the other side of the door. The girl seemed surprised to see her, but that melted away to concern. "Blessed? Are you all right?"

"Just get me back to my room. Now."

As they made their way through the tunnel, Trule didn't ask any questions. Not that Everys would have answered, but apparently the serving girl knew to leave well enough alone. She even shooed the other girls away, then excused herself, leaving Everys alone in the bedroom.

The tears broke free. The chaos of the bombing, the fear of Redtale and her troops, the confusion she felt in the ballroom, the horror after the wedding ceremony, and now the anger in Narius's expression, it all boiled over as sobs wracked her body. All she wanted was to curl up in bed.

And then she realized that she didn't have any of her clothes. They were all in her apartment in Fair Havens! The only thing she had to wear was this ridiculous costume.

With no other options, she tore back the covers, burrowed underneath them, and sobbed herself to sleep.

She had been here. In his room!

It didn't seem real. When was the last time that Viara had been here before she'd left? Not for months and months. But his new wife, she had been here. Why?

The image of what she had been wearing assaulted his mind. She intended to seduce him, obviously. But why had she acted so upset when he'd caught her?

Narius shook his head. She had probably warmed up to the idea of being queen and wanted to get her hooks into him right away. Viara had done the same thing. His ex-wife had always loved her position more than him. This Everys was probably cut from the same cloth.

Admittedly, being with her was certainly enticing. She wasn't ugly. In any other context, he might have even considered her pretty in her own way. But she wasn't... she wasn't...

She wasn't *her*.

That's what made this intrusion even more painful. It wasn't just that he caught her in his room. He'd found her holding the pictures of Innana, scrolling through them with that condescending frown on her face. Judging Innana. Judging him.

He picked up the frame and looked through the pictures, angry that tears welled in his eyes.

"Why couldn't it have been you?" he whispered.

Someone cleared his throat.

Narius didn't even have to look up. "What is it, Paine?"

"I have some preliminary reports from the bombing in Fair Havens, Your Strength. Five deaths, dozens of injuries, a fair amount of property damage."

"The culprits?"

"The bomber himself is dead, but given reports, it was likely another attack by Cold Light terrorists."

Narius blew out a long breath. Of course it was. As if it wasn't bad enough the Cold Light weren't meeting their agricultural quotas, now they were attacking the Dynasty's holdings. He could already hear the arguments in his next council meeting. Duke Brencis would demand swift retribution. Elamak would side with the duke. Masruq would counsel restraint for the sake of the economy, and the argument would go on and on until Narius made a decision.

He sighed. "Leave the report on my desk. I'll read it in a little bit."

"Of course."

Narius looked back at the picture frame. "She was here, Paine."

"Who?"

"Everys. Just now."

He met Paine's gaze, and the vizier quirked a brow.

"Oh? I hope I didn't interrupt anything."

Narius snorted. "No."

Paine once again turned to leave.

"Paine?"

The vizier paused in the doorway. "Your Strength?"

"Have the doors to the passage between the queen's chamber and mine sealed. First thing in the morning."

The vizier hesitated, but he nodded. "It will be done."

Narius sat down on the edge of his bed, surveying his sanctuary. At least he wouldn't have to worry about it being invaded again.

8

As long as Everys stayed beneath the covers, she could pretend like nothing strange had happened. No bomb. No rushed marriage. No humiliating night in Narius's room. No, yesterday she spent her day in the shop. She made a few sales. Then she slept in her own room, and now, she was just being lazy. Today would be no different.

Except it was different. Try as she might, she couldn't ignore the too comfortable mattress, the too fine sheets. Everys poked her head out of the covers, looking up at a ceiling that soared above the bed, a beautiful fresco of flowering plants and flowing water. Fine. She might as well face her new normal, however strange it might be.

She rolled out of the bed, where she encountered another difference. Normally, her bedroom floor sent cold shocks through her feet. But even though she walked on marble, the floor was surprisingly warm. She set out for the bathroom, curious to see what ridiculous luxuries awaited her there.

"Good morning, Blessed."

Everys shrieked. Trule sat in an oversized wooden chair in one corner of the room. The girl squeaked in response, flinching as if she expected to be attacked.

"What are you doing?" Everys demanded.

"W-waiting for you to rise, Blessed."

Waiting for her to...? "How long have you been sitting there?"

Trule shrugged. "Since right before First Watch."

Everys gaped at her, then shot a look at a chrono by the bed. "You've been watching me sleep for the past four hours?"

Trule shrank in on herself. "Many pardons, Blessed, but we weren't sure what your morning routine would be. Queen Viara liked to sleep in, but Queen Felisa was an early riser. We didn't want you to awaken without us ready to attend you, so I volunteered to wait until you rose."

The girl was babbling, clearly terrified. Everys held up a hand. Trule stuttered to a stop, punctuating her final phrase with a squeak.

"Thank you, Trule. I appreciate your concern. But I don't need 'attending' in the morning. I can handle this by myself."

Everys turned to walk into the bathroom, but Trule bolted out of the chair and caught up with her, her eyes wide.

"But that's why we're here, Blessed, to assist you. Have we done something to displease you?" Tears welled in her eyes. "Have *I* done something to displease you?"

Everys sighed. "No, not at all. It's just... I'm not nobility. I've never had a staff to help me. I'm pretty self-sufficient."

Trule still looked on the verge of crying. Oh, inkstains! None of this was Trule's fault. She was only trying to help. So Everys motioned for her to follow. Trule hiccupped, a long tongue licking away her tears. Hopefully she wouldn't try to scrub Everys's back while she bathed.

Thankfully, Trule stayed out of the way. She looked ready to make suggestions several times, but she kept those to herself. When Everys emerged from the bathroom, the rest of her staff was waiting, each holding a different outfit. Everys hesitated, eyeing the clothes. They all looked expensive. They clearly hadn't been made for her. Did they really think she would wear one of them?

Trule must have read her hesitation. "We have laundered your clothing from yesterday, Blessed, but that outfit was deemed... inappropriate by Assistant Challix. We haven't had time to put together a proper wardrobe, but we were able to find some possibilities for the short term."

Everys's stomach flipped. Some of the outfits were riots of color that threatened to give her a headache. Others appeared shockingly skimpy. None of them appeared to be functional. What could she even do in one of those outfits?

A pit opened in her stomach. That was the point. She would always be a decoration and nothing more.

"What am I supposed to do with myself?" she whispered.

Trule glanced at her. "Blessed?"

Everys turned to the servant, latching on to a thread of hope. Trule would know. Granted, she was young, but she had more experience in the palace than Everys did.

"What did the previous queens do with their time? Like Viara. Or Felisa?"

Trule winced when Everys said both names. "I-I can't really speak about Queen Felisa, Blessed. She died before I came here. But the older servants say she took particular pleasure in organizing the royal household." When Everys gave her a confused look, she explained. "She made decisions about purchasing food, furniture, overseeing the palace staff. She also maintained King Girai's social calendar while hosting numerous Queen's Courts."

Everys blanched at the thought.

"As for Queen Viara, she preferred organizing parties for her friends. She also prided herself as a patron of the arts."

Everys resisted the urge to laugh. That was a very charitable way to describe what Viara did. The media was always awash in stories about Viara flitting from party to party, spending time with famous entertainers and vapid members of the nobility.

But were those her only options? Household dictator or vacuous socialite? Everys wanted to quiz Trule more, but the younger woman was already trembling. Maybe Everys would have to talk to Challix.

She sighed. Might as well get dressed. One by one, the girls held up possible outfits, all of which seemed more suited for a formal setting than for everyday living. After thirty agonizing minutes, Everys settled on a relatively tame dress, all flowing veils and bright colors. It would never have been her first choice for anything, but in a field of impractical contenders, it was her best option.

But once that was decided, that prompted a new fight. The girls expected half of them to slather on her makeup while the other half tried to wrestle her hair into some fashionable style. Everys argued with every suggestion they made. But when it was clear they wouldn't back down, Everys relented.

By the time they were finished, a stranger stared back at her from the mirror. They had applied bright blue to her eyelids and teased her lashes, creating a black border around her eyes. Her hair had been swept into a knot that flowed into an elaborate braid. And once they had her in the dress, Everys was stunned. She didn't look like a tinkerer from Fair Havens. This was no illegal toratropic mage. No, somehow, the girls had performed a miracle and turned her into something resembling a queen.

Everys burst out laughing. The girls startled, each of them flinching. Was this all it took to make someone look like a noble? A few strips of colorful cloth and cleverly applied cosmetics?

The door to her bedroom popped open and Challix breezed in. Her assistant wore a bright smile, one that faltered when she saw Everys. "My lady, you look quite... regal."

The hesitant compliment caused Everys to laugh even harder, which only made Challix look even more confused, but she pulled out a scriber. "Well, we have quite the busy day ahead of us. I've scheduled meetings with tailors to take the necessary measurements for a new wardrobe. That will take the better part of the morning."

"Why?" Everys asked.

"You will have to look through designs and fabric swaths to determine what clothing we should order and what styles are suitable for your unique personality."

Everys sifted through what Challix said. She knew an insult lurked in there somewhere, but Challix's bright attitude kept it too well hidden.

"And then, this afternoon, I have lined up architects and interior decorators to help us redesign your living quarters."

Everys looked around the room. Sure, the queen's quarters were overly lavish, but nothing stood out to her as needing to be changed. "Why?"

"When Queen Viara took up residence, she had the fresco added to the ceiling. And she brought in all of this furniture to meet her very exacting specifications. And she also renovated the sitting area. That required major construction that took—"

"You're expecting me to replace the ceiling and all the furniture?"

"If you feel it necessary. We have the money to make sure that these rooms are perfect for you."

"And that's all I'm going to do today? Pick out clothes and redecorate my room?"

"Not entirely," Challix said. "In a matter of weeks, you'll hold a Queen's Court. While Queen Viara started preparations, we'll have to tweak them to suit you better. Truth be told, we barely have enough time."

"What if I'm okay with the rooms the way they are?" Everys asked. "And why can't I just go get my clothes from Fair Havens?"

Challix looked positively horrified. "No offense, Blessed, but I'm quite confident that nothing you own will be appropriate. You need a new wardrobe at the very least."

Everys wanted to keep arguing, but from Challix's expression, that wouldn't be wise. "Fine."

Challix nodded, clearly relieved. "Very good. Now, if you'll excuse me, I have some correspondence to attend to."

With that, she breezed out of the room.

Everys glared after her, then looked around the room. Why did they expect her to change everything? She honestly didn't care. This really wasn't her room and, as far as she was concerned, never would be.

But then an idea occurred to her, one that caused a smile to tug at her lips. She could do something to make the room hers. Something that would cause the straightlaced members of the Dynasty to have a conniption. If she was going to do it, though, she needed privacy.

"Trule? Could you and the girls please step out of my quarters for a moment?" She hoped she had injected enough steel into her voice to make it clear this wasn't a request.

Although she appeared confused, Trule didn't argue, shooing the girls from the quarters entirely. The moment they left, Everys breathed a heavy sigh of relief, relishing the quiet. But she knew this wouldn't last long. If she was going to carry out her plan, she had to move quickly.

She darted to the door to her quarters and lined herself up on the frame. She took a deep, calming breath, and pressed her left hand against the door. With her right, she traced an elaborate rune.

Technically, according to the traditions of her people, she was supposed to paint these runes on her doorposts every morning as a sign of the Singularity's protection and sovereignty. But ever since Downcasting, when the Xoniel Dynasty overthrew the Siporan Ascendancy, the scriveners had decided that simply tracing the runes with one's finger was good enough. No ink, no outward sign, a concession for the perilous times, they called it.

Everys smiled as she set to work on the second rune and savored the rebelliousness of the act. The Dynasty had tried to destroy her people and their abilities, and now she was tracing runes on the queen's doorpost.

The first rune invited the Singularity to dwell in this space. The second bound her to His power and grace. The third served as a ward against evil intentions, and—

Something tugged at her heart.

She froze, her finger hovering over the doorframe. She recognized the sensation. If she had drawn a tracking rune to find someone using toratropic magic, she would have felt a tug in her chest in the right direction. But that shouldn't have happened, not with these runes and definitely not without ink. But the sensation was unmistakable. Somewhere within the palace, someone was using toratropic magic. There couldn't be any Siporans in the palace. So where was it coming from?

She opened the door and poked her head into the hall. Redtale, Kevtho, and the girls clustered around the door, almost blocking the path of someone walking by. It took Everys a moment to recognize Duke Brencis, the head of the Dynasty's military. He glared at her, but then his features softened ever so slightly.

"Is there a problem, Blessed?" His voice was a growl.

She took a moment to study him. He was Hinaen, which wasn't a big surprise. He had probably been extremely fit in his younger years, but his uniform pulled around his middle. His most striking features, though, were his eyes, a shining copper. The duke must have had a bit of royal blood in his family tree.

"Uh... no. I just thought I... I thought I heard something and..."

"Sorry if I disturbed you." And with that, the duke continued on his way.

Trule gave her a questioning look, but Everys shook her head and slipped back inside. Her finger trembled as she traced the last two runes.

Someone knocked on the door. "Blessed?"

Redtale's voice! She had to hurry. As soon as she finished the last one, she quickly pulled the door open.

Redtale and Kevtho stepped inside. The head of her guard looked over the room, her face pinched in a frown. "Everything all right in here?"

As Redtale asked the question, Trule peeked into the room. Everys sighed and motioned for her and the other girls to come back in. They scurried past the guards and disappeared into the rooms beyond to do who knew what.

"Just wanted some privacy is all," Everys said.

"Sounds like we're going to have an easy day of it, huh? Tailors and decorators? Light duty." Redtale shared an amused look with Kevtho.

That soured Everys's mood even further. Such a fantastic use of her time, making such frivolous decisions, when she could be doing something far more important.

But then the thought occurred to her: Why stop with just one act of rebellion? Why not add another?

"What else is happening in the palace today, Redtale?" she asked.

Redtale pulled a scriber from her pocket. "Well, King Narius has his usual full schedule: briefings with the various ministers, audiences with some of the ethnarchs, strategy sessions, and such. Prince Quartus—" Everys couldn't miss the venom lurking in her tone. "—well, he's supposed to be at the Hall of All Voices."

That caught Everys's attention. "What's he doing there?"

"Part of his duties," Redtale said. "A royal or noble is supposed to observe the workings of the Hall when they're in session. It's the prince's shift."

"A royal?" Everys repeated. "Does that mean I could go?"

Redtale froze, her features pinching into a scowl. "That sort of thing's never been done."

"There's a difference between 'never' and 'can't.'"

Redtale shifted her weight, the conflict clear on her face. That was answer enough for Everys.

"Let's go. I wish to join the prince in his observations."

"But what about the tailors and the decorators and all that?" Redtale asked.

Everys waved away her objection. "They can wait. I want to see our government in action."

Or, more accurately, avoid a boring series of meetings. No matter how she described it, she felt it was a much better choice.

9

Technically, the Hall of All Voices wasn't attached to the palace, which apparently caused some trouble. Redtale was obviously frustrated as she called for a transport. It was all ridiculous, though. Everys could see the Hall from her bedroom. She could have walked there in five minutes. But apparently that wasn't dignified or appropriate or safe, so they had to wait three times as long while her guards made the appropriate preparations. Then they hustled her through the palace and to a waiting transport.

Thankfully, this vehicle was comfortable, with wide, thick windows. Not that there was much of a view, just tall stone walls on either side of the road, one belonging to the palace and the other to some other government building. But then they turned a corner and there was the Hall of All Voices. A thrill ran through Everys in spite of herself. The Hall was beautiful. Whereas the palace looked like an ancient fortress, the Hall was glass and steel, shimmering in the sunlight. Spires rose into the air, each one twisted like a seashell. The Hall was a work of art. And yet, as breathtaking as the Hall was, it carried a not-so-subtle message. The palace was larger, more dominant, perched higher on the hill. It was clear which institution existed in the other's shadow.

The transport slid past the building's main entrance, then descended a ramp to a covered entrance. The guards exited the vehicle first, looking around the area before Redtale signaled for Everys to join them. Then they hustled into the building, through hallways and stairs, past offices and doors. Occasionally, someone would emerge from an office, only to step aside as Everys and her entourage hurried past.

Redtale led her to an elevator and waved her wrist across a black panel. The car shuddered and rose quickly. As soon as they were underway, Redtale turned to her.

"Since the Hall is in session, Blessed, we should go over the ground rules. When we get there, you have to remain silent. Observer, not participant. Understood?"

Everys laughed. "Do guards usually talk to the queen this way?"

Redtale didn't smile. "Not normally, no. But my job is to protect you. There's only so much I can do when the harm isn't physical. There are expectations for how a royal will behave in the Hall. Breaking protocol is one thing. Causing a disruption will be much worse."

Everys's smile faltered at Redtale's grim expression. Maybe this wasn't the best idea, not if she was going to stir up trouble. But then the elevator door opened with a sigh. After walking down a long hallway, they came to a single door that Redtale pulled open, revealing a small balcony with three plush chairs facing a larger room. Redtale signaled for her to keep quiet, and they slipped onto the balcony. As Everys did, she froze, transfixed by what she saw.

The balcony overlooked the Hall of All Voices, a cavernous room constructed out of marble and dark woods. It resembled a theater, with rows of benches facing a dais at one end of the room. Dozens of representatives were seated throughout the Hall, but very few paid attention to the podiums on the dais. There, an Ixactl glowered at the assembly, almost looking like a disapproving parent standing amidst her children's toys.

"...but that is the point, isn't it?" Her voice was a gravelly rumble. "While the Dynasty has indeed opened the door for many of us, we receive crumbs while the Xoniel keep the best on their table."

Everys settled into one of the balcony's chairs, drinking in the woman's words. She understood those feelings all too well. She didn't have to look at the gathered representatives to know there wasn't a single Siporan among them. That used to be mandated by the Drywell Laws, but even with those repealed, no Siporan had ever been elected to the Hall. The other races had adopted the Dynasty's prejudices. So long as they had their little scraps of prosperity, they didn't care whose backs they stood on.

"So what does the representative suggest?" Zolkin, the speaker of the Hall, asked from his seat. "Independence from the Dynasty?"

Laughter rippled through the room. The Ixactl representative's posture stiffened, but she waited until the noise died down.

"As if any of us could stand on our own. The Dynasty has seen to that, making us far too dependent on the king's benevolence. And yet, we all know the Dynasty's power is waning."

Everys's breath caught. How could she say that so openly? Her gaze twitched toward Redtale. Would the guards arrest her? But Redtale looked bored, not angry.

"We sacrifice our young to the voracious appetites of the Dynasty's military. We pour our hard-earned money into their coffers. We submit to their laws. But why? Because their armies once defeated ours? Because the same family has sat on the throne for generations? Because that one family freed us from Siporan tyranny four hundred years ago?"

Everys pulled back into her chair. Had the representative seen her?

Instead, the Ixactl representative sighed heavily and shook her head. "We have all seen the rot taking hold. Once, the royal family was worthy of respect. Of honor. Of fear. But now? Is it any wonder the Dynasty has never fully subjugated the Cold Light? Is it a surprise unrest simmers in every major city and province?"

To Everys, this sounded just short of treason. Shouldn't the representatives be scandalized? But most of them paid more attention to their scribers than what was being said on the dais.

"How can she say that?" she whispered to Redtale.

Redtale glanced in her direction and snorted. "The representatives have broad-ranging immunity when it comes to their speech in the Hall. They've said much worse."

Everys blinked. They had? Why hadn't she ever heard about that?

But Redtale didn't elaborate. Instead, she leaned against the wall and jerked her chin toward the dais. "Besides, Mossglade doesn't mean half of what she says. She's posturing for the clans."

"How can you be so sure?" Everys asked.

Redtale's lips pursed into a thin line. Her left hand idly stroked the stump of her horns, then her frown deepened. "Don't forget, you gotta keep quiet right now, Blessed."

Everys ground her teeth, but she did as Redtale said.

After an hour, Everys wondered why she thought coming down here was such a good idea. Nothing exciting happened. One after another, the representatives came up to the podium and ranted about the Dynasty's policies. They each urged their colleagues to take a stand.

Yet no matter how passionate each speaker was, no one seemed to care. So what was the point of any of this?

She caught Redtale's attention again. "Is this all that happens?"

Redtale shrugged. "People get into arguments every now and then. Those can be exciting. But for the most part, yeah, this is pretty typical."

Everys gaped at her. "But this is supposed to be a way for the citizens of the Dynasty to shape their future. To participate in the government."

"And it is," Redtale said. "What they're saying right now is being written down and the transcripts will be sent to the Ethnarch Parliament. They'll review the record. And if they find something important, they can pass along the recommendation to the King."

"But what they're doing here doesn't really matter. If the ethnarchs or Narius decide not to listen, none of what's being said here matters."

"I suppose that's one way of looking at it." From her tone, Redtale made it sound like what she was saying should have been obvious.

But it wasn't. Not to Everys. While she didn't pay close attention to the Dynasty's politics, she had heard enough of the propaganda. The Hall of All Voices was the way for the common people to be heard by their government. And the Ethnarch Parliament too!

"But it's all a lie, isn't it?" Everys insisted.

Redtale's jaw clenched, and her gaze darted toward the edge of the balcony.

"We might as well just shut down the Hall completely and send all of these representatives home because—"

"Who interrupts the proceedings of this chamber?"

The bellowed question smacked Everys like a physical blow. When had she stood up? When had she advanced on Redtale? She stood still, hoping no one would notice.

"Who is in the royal box? Prince Quartus, we have warned you against bringing... companions into these proceedings."

Everys stifled a groan as she realized who was yelling at her. It was Speaker Zolkin. She considered trying to sneak out again, but that didn't seem wise. Instead, she squared her shoulders and stepped to the edge of the balcony.

The angry expression on Zolkin's face dissolved into one of recognition, followed by absolute dismay. He stammered at his podium before turning to the assembled representatives. "Ladies and gentlemen, it is my distinct pleasure to, uh, introduce to you all Everen, King Narius's new wife."

Surprise rippled through the room. Everys cleared her throat, ready to correct Zolkin about her name, but then a hand tightened on her arm.

"We should go," Redtale whispered. "Wave, then try to leave without causing a scene."

Everys offered a limp wave, which was met by a smattering of half-hearted applause. Then she turned to go, only to run right into her chair. She almost fell over, but Redtale quickly pulled her back up to standing and hustled her out of the room.

She kept her head down as her guards hurried her back to the waiting transport. As soon as they were under way, Everys took a deep, shaky breath. "Well, that could have gone better."

Redtale fixed her with a withering stare.

Everys shrank in on herself. "Was it really that bad?"

"A queen breaking precedent, disrupting the Hall, and suggesting it be dissolved?" Redtale grunted. "I can't imagine how anyone would see that as a bad thing."

Everys swallowed a groan. Great. Just perfect.

10

The doors to the queen's quarters banged open. Everys winced. She'd expected a reaction but not this quickly.

"What were you thinking?" Paine stormed into the room. "So on your first full day in the palace, you decided to force your way into the Hall of All Voices and loudly denounce it as being ineffective?"

Everys's cheeks reddened. She wanted to argue, but that was unfortunately accurate.

Paine's face twisted into a snarl, but then he closed his eyes and took a deep breath. A calm mask descended on his features, one that made Everys distinctly uncomfortable. She glanced toward Redtale and her other guards, but they had all taken a step back and clearly wouldn't intervene.

"The story of what you did is already spreading through the Dynasty's holdings," Paine said. "We can no longer introduce you properly since you have created a political scandal that could upset the delicate balance of your husband's government."

Challix rushed into the room, clearly out of breath. Her gaze skipped from Everys to Paine, and then her cheeks flushed red. "My apologies that I was not here, Vizier, I—"

"And where were you?" Paine whirled on her. "What task was so important you left our new queen unsupervised?"

Challix's gaze dove to the floor. "M-my pardon, Vizier, I was working on a schedule of appointments for the queen. Tailors, interior decorators, and—"

"Indeed. Leaving the queen to her own devices?" Paine crossed his arms. "Perhaps we promoted you too quickly. Shall we send you back into the public relations ministry so you can write fluff about our domestic initiatives?"

Everys bristled at his condescension. "Hey! It wasn't her fault."

"But it was." Paine stalked past Challix and up to Redtale. "And not hers alone. I expected better of you, guard."

Redtale snorted. "I don't answer to you, Vizier."

"That excuse won't defuse this. There will be consequences." He turned back to Everys. "Do try not to cause additional scandals before your husband and I can untangle this one."

In a flurry of robes, Paine started for the door.

"Is Narius mad?" The question slipped out of Everys's mouth. She didn't even know if she cared. But given what happened the night before and now this, she wondered if he had been pushed too far. Why else wouldn't he be here?

Paine paused at the door but didn't turn to face her. "He is currently meeting with Speaker Zolkin and a number of representatives who were offended by your conduct. I doubt he's had time to be angry. That isn't Narius's way. But I would be careful not to tread where you do not belong. Are we clear?"

Everys's cheeks blazed. From Paine's tone, he clearly wasn't just talking about the Hall. Had Narius told him about what happened in his bedroom?

With that, Paine left the room, but he didn't take the anger with him. Everys felt it simmering as Challix glared at the floor. Everys took a tentative step forward, but Challix speared her with a glare.

"If you wanted to visit the Hall, you could have told me," Challix whispered. "We could have done it right."

"It wasn't so much that I wanted to go to the Hall as I... well, didn't want to be here."

"Picking out new clothes and furniture is that bad?"

"I guess? Honestly, everything Viara left is so much better than anything I've ever owned. I've learned to make do with what I have. It seems like a waste of time and money."

Challix looked ready to argue, but then her jaw clicked shut. She scrutinized Everys's face.

"I suppose that's true, isn't it?" There was no malice in her voice. "But we do need to get you a new wardrobe. Reusing the furniture is one thing. The nobility will notice if you wear Queen Viara's clothes."

Everys made a sour face, one that elicited a chuckle from Challix. "But then, if that is not something you would enjoy, I suppose we can find a way around that. What would you like to do with your time instead?"

The question caught Everys by surprise. She hadn't really expected anyone to ask what she wanted. So far, everyone expected her to be a decoration.

"Something... significant? Something that could actually make a difference."

"What do you mean?"

She waved a hand at her surroundings. "Tell me what you see."

Challix turned a slow circle. "Your quarters?"

Everys shook her head. "You may see a room. I see enough space to house two or three families. I see enough money spent on decorations to feed those families for years. I see—"

Challix held up a hand. "This isn't an election speech, Blessed. Are you suggesting that we just give the money to the poor?"

"Why not? You said I had an annual budget of what again? A million blades?"

"No, you have 1.7 million blades left. Your annual budget is closer to three million blades."

Everys's knees wobbled. But she quickly steeled herself. "So who says I can't spend that on something charitable?"

"Well, Minister Masruq, for one. He has control over the budget and how it's allocated. And the funds you're talking about are specifically earmarked for your personal living expenses."

"So can't we un-earmark them?"

"Not really, no. There are expectations, Blessed. Those funds are intended for the maintenance of your personal living quarters, for your wardrobe, and for giving gifts to worthy courtiers. Using them for any other purpose would be frowned upon!"

So let people frown! Who cared what the nobility thought? Maybe they would agree with Challix's so-called logic. But just a few days ago, Everys had been living in a small apartment above her shop. And now she was being told that she had enough money to purchase the building and...

A smile tugged at her lips as an idea began to form.

"You know what?" she said. "Forget I said anything. You're right. I'll use the money to improve my quarters and purchase gifts."

Challix visibly relaxed, smiling as well.

"And I know I've put you through a lot in the last day or two. Why don't you take a break? I'll see to the improvements myself."

Now she looked confused. "But I'm supposed to assist you and—"

Everys waved away her words. "Nonsense. I've done my own decorating for years, and I've always purchased my own clothing. I know what I like. I'll make sure it's all appropriate, don't worry. I'm sure Trule and the other girls will be more than enough to help me."

It took a few more minutes of arguing, but eventually, Everys hustled Challix out the door. When she turned back to the room, Redtale regarded her with a lopsided smile.

"Gonna be doing some decorating, huh?"

"Eventually. But first, where do I find Minister Masruq?"

11

The palace was more of a maze than Everys expected. The halls in the residential wing twisted and intersected in ways she couldn't fathom. It only got marginally better when they crossed into the administrative wing. There the halls were straight and crossed at orderly right angles. But there were so many doors, so many branching paths, she wondered if she would ever find her way around on her own.

Maybe that was the point. Maybe it was a way to make sure that the royals could never escape.

She followed Redtale and Kevtho as they led her to Masruq's office. At least, she'd have to take their word for it. There was nothing that distinguished this door from the others.

Everys stepped into a room filled with desks separated by short wooden walls. People bustled through the narrow walkways, carrying scribers and talking with each other. Others sat at their desks, concentrating on their tasks. But when Everys stepped into the room, silence. Within seconds, everyone had turned to face her. She froze, suddenly feeling self-conscious.

A young woman stepped forward, wearing a clearly fake smile. "Queen Everys, it's so wonderful for you to stop by. Is there something I can help you with?"

Everys smiled in return, although she hoped she looked more genuine. "I hoped to speak with Minister Masruq. Is he available?"

The girl's expression turned brittle. "Unfortunately, Blessed, the minister is quite busy today. He left explicit instructions not to be disturbed. And protocols do have to be observed. Perhaps I can find some time in two weeks?"

It wasn't really a question. And the oblique jab about protocol? Probably an attempt to shame her for what happened at the Hall of All

Voices. Everys recognized the effort to get rid of her. This happened every time she went to the banks in Fair Havens for a loan. But this time was different. Back home, she had been a desperate business owner. Now, she was queen.

"No, it wouldn't," Everys said. "His schedule may be packed, but thank Chance, mine isn't. I can sit here and wait for him."

The girl blanched. "Blessed, I'm sorry, but the minister is—"

"Yes, you made that very clear. But I only have a question or two that won't take more than five minutes. I'm sure he'll be able to sneak me in."

With that, Everys found a vacant chair. Her guards fell into place on either side of her and stared forward, although Everys thought Redtale was trying to stifle a smile.

The young woman gaped at her, then scurried away into the maze of desks. Everys watched her go, then let out a breath. But she didn't relax. The office workers kept glancing at her, clearly disturbed. Hopefully their discomfort would eventually lead them to actually do something.

Sure enough, a few minutes later, the young woman came back, wearing the same fake smile. "Blessed? I've just made Minister Masruq aware of your desire to meet with him, and as Chance decreed it, he has a few minutes right now. If you'd follow me?"

Everys rose. Her guards fell into step with her, and the four of them walked along the room's edge to a door made of ornately carved wood.

The door popped open, and an angry voice drifted out. "—not able to wait much longer, Masruq. The longer we delay, the more dire the situation at the border becomes. If he keeps diverting our funds to that secret project, we'll..."

The speaker emerged. Duke Brencis. Her guards snapped into a crisp salute, which he returned.

"Duke," Everys said. "So good to see you again."

He mumbled something and brushed past her. He didn't come in contact with her, but Everys still felt like she had to take a step back to avoid him.

Masruq's office was spacious, larger than her apartment back in Fair Havens. The far wall was one large window, overlooking the palace grounds and Bastion beyond. Rows of shelves lined the wall to her left, and there was a bar on her right. Hanging behind the bar was a large painting of a storm at sea, jagged lightning leaping between menacing clouds. As she examined the painting, a strange sense of nausea crested through her, almost as if she were standing on the ship in that maelstrom. But the sensation quickly faded. Across the room from her was a wooden desk with a computer terminal and not much else. The impression Everys got from the room was that of order and restraint.

Masruq stood next to his desk. He was a short man, rotund, with a horseshoe of white hair. His cheeks and nose were ruddy, his eyes so dark they almost appeared black. He appeared Hinaen, but maybe with a bit of Kolvese in his ancestry as well.

A warm smile burst on his face when he saw her. "Blessed, so good to see you! I apologize for my assistant. Klarre can be overprotective about my time. You are naturally my top priority."

The minister was a better liar than his assistant. He escorted Everys over to one of the chairs that faced the desk, then bustled over to the bar.

"Can I offer you a drink? I must confess, I'm not sure what your tastes are. I do have a particularly pleasing vintage of Dalark red."

Everys's eyebrows shot up. "Isn't that illegal?"

Masruq chuckled. "Oh, quite. The mutual embargo and all that. But even the most loyal citizens find ways to get what they want or need in spite of the Dynasty's prying eyes."

There was truth to his statement. Although she didn't frequent them herself, Everys knew of three different black markets in Fair Havens where someone could find goods smuggled in from Dalark. Some of her neighbors considered it a point of pride to buy those items, a small defiance of the Dynasty's overarching presence. It made sense that the nobility would have similar methods too.

"But my wine is more of a gray area. The bottle was given to me by Diplomat Alezzar the last time we knocked heads over the embargoes." Masruq pulled a bottle out of a credenza. "Don't tell Brencis. He'd probably confiscate it as a security breach."

A smile tugged at her lips. Masruq reminded her of a kindly grandfather. He may have been part of the Dynasty's apparatus, but she was more than willing to break the law with him.

"That would be fine, thank you."

Masruq nodded and set about pouring the drink. "I must admit, I'm a bit perplexed as to why you're here. Neither your predecessor nor the king's mother ever took an interest in the Dynasty's economy." He looked up from the glass. "Not that I blame them. If it wasn't my job, I probably wouldn't pay much attention either."

He came around the bar and offered a glass to her. She took an experimental sip. Sweetness burst on her tongue, chased by a mellow flavor she couldn't quite place. Definitely the best wine she had ever tasted, but then, her experience with such things was limited.

"I'm sorry to disturb you, but I was told recently I have access to a discretionary budget I can use to decorate my quarters and purchase clothes." She waved a hand at what she was wearing. "As you can see, I need to update a little."

"If it's any consolation, you look lovely," Masruq said. "And it is true, you do have those funds available to use as you see fit. But normally Challix or Matron Halis would be the one to talk to about that."

Everys nodded. "And I was told that as well. But Halis was called away, and Challix seemed rather upset after my blunder in the Hall of All Voices. And, quite frankly, I'm not comfortable with someone shopping for me. I was hoping to take a more direct role."

Masruq smiled. "I understand. My wife is the same way. I keep telling her the servants can handle most of the day-to-day affairs of our house, but she likes the more personal touch."

He sat down behind his desk and rummaged through one of the drawers. He pulled out a scriber and checked the screen. "According to my records, you presently have 1.72 million blades available to you. And this will have everything you need to access the funds." He chuckled and handed over the device. "Don't spend it all in one place."

She returned the smile. "I wouldn't dream of it."

He rose from his desk. "Unless there's anything else I can do to help you?"

Everys nodded, but her gaze hitched on the painting again. The waters in the center swirled and sloshed. At least, they appeared to for just half a moment, and then the effect faded. She blinked several times and blew out a shaky breath before nodding toward the artwork. "That's a most unusual painting. Very unlike anything else hanging in the palace."

He glanced toward it. "Yes, it is. *The Storm before the Calm* by an old Weyfir master. It reminds me that, even in a world of chaos, it is possible to chisel out a small amount of control if one is willing."

Everys allowed him to escort her to the door, which closed behind her with a resounding click. Klarre waited for her on the other side, all smiles and apologies as she escorted Everys back to the front door.

"Where to now, Blessed?" Kevtho asked.

Everys held up the scriber and smiled. Masruq was an adept liar, but so was she. She would spend a lot of this in one place. "Time to go shopping."

Within a week, Everys had made all the arrangements. It hadn't been difficult; no one cared what she did as long as she stayed out of the way. Keeping Challix in the dark proved trickier, but Everys realized if she made small decisions about wardrobes and decorations, that kept her assistant busy and happy. Working with the girls, Everys acquired computer terminals and had them installed in her private office. That allowed her to dig up the right data, make the right contacts, arrange for the deliveries, and everything else.

The only sticking point had been Redtale. The guard commander strenuously objected when Everys explained her plan, but when she shared her larger vision, she thought she saw the faintest glimmer of a smile in the guard's eyes. In the end, Redtale reluctantly agreed and did what she needed to quietly.

By the end of the week, Everys was pretty sure that everything was set and ready to go. She smiled. Everyone expected her to be a decoration, a powerless prop to be trotted out when Narius needed her. But she was going to make sure no one saw her that way ever again.

"You know, if I'm going to keep riding in this thing, I should be able to personalize it," Everys said.

"What'd you have in mind, Blessed?" Redtale asked from her perch in the front seat.

She shrugged. "Maybe replace the camo with flowers? Or paint it a nice shade of blue?"

Redtale laughed. "That's not up to regs, Blessed."

Everys smiled and tried to settle in, which proved almost impossible. At the very least, she'd have a more comfortable seat installed. And she wasn't as scared as the last time she had ridden in a military transport. This time, she was headed in the right direction. Back to Fair Havens. Back to home, even if it was only temporary.

"Any word from the advance team? How's it looking?" she asked.

"Last check was ten minutes ago. Area secure and the press is arriving." Redtale regarded her. "Have to say, you took me by surprise, Blessed. That's hard to do."

"How so?"

Redtale pursed her lips, then turned to face her fully. "Before we brought you to the palace, we did a thorough sweep of your background. Even did some careful interviews with neighbors and acquaintances."

They what? Ice sluiced through Everys. "Wh-what did you find out about me?"

"kar Bin Tusant Everys. Age: twenty-three. Raised in Bastion, specifically the Fair Havens neighborhood. Proprietor of the Broken Sword Shop. Financially stable with no evidence of illegal dealings. Spotty attendance at armory, just enough to stay on the good side of the tax laws. Parents and older sister left Bastion five years ago—"

Everys tensed. Inkstains, did they *know*? Had they figured out the truth?

"—without proper travel documentation. One younger brother, kiv Ren Tusant Legarr, involved in numerous petty criminal enterprises. Shall I keep going?"

Everys forced herself to blow out a shaky breath. If they knew where Mama and Papa and Galan had gone, what they were really up to, would Redtale have said? No, if they knew, there was no way they would have allowed her anywhere near the palace, right?

"You seem the sort not to seek attention. Not the sort to make a big show like... well, like this." Redtale waved a hand toward the front of the transport.

Smudges and stains, her heart kept pounding against her ribs. Would Redtale hear it? She had to change the subject, even temporarily. "It's still home. Don't you ever go back to the Highlands?"

Redtale shook her head. "No reason to."

"Really? You don't have any family?"

"Oh, lots of kin. Eleven siblings, who knows how many cousins, plus my father and his five wives."

"And you don't miss them at all?"

A wistful look flitted across Redtale's expression. "Didn't say that. I do. It's complicated."

And apparently that was all the guard would say about that. The two of them fell into an uncomfortable silence for the rest of the ride.

The transport pulled up in front of Everys's shop. A small crowd had gathered, most of them press. She frowned. She had hoped for more reporters, if for no other reason than curiosity. But then, maybe a smaller crowd would be a good first step.

One of the guards hauled open the transport's door. Redtale slipped out, then turned to help her exit the vehicle. Everys ground her teeth as she stumbled, the tight fabric of her dress making it difficult to move. This had been the one new outfit she had purchased. Not the fancy, formal attire a queen would normally wear, but a smart business outfit, more in line with a CEO's wardrobe. But the skirt took some getting used to.

Redtale escorted her to the platform that had been erected outside her shop. A simple podium stood at the center, with queen's guards standing on either end of the stage. Everys strode up to the podium and smiled at the assembled crowd.

"Good afternoon," she said. "I realize most of you have only heard about me. Many of you only know me as Everys, the newest queen of the Xoniel Dynasty. But before that, I was a resident of Bastion and, more specifically, of Fair Havens.

"It wasn't until I moved to the palace that I realized how much I thought was normal that shouldn't be. Bastion is supposed to be the crown jewel of the Dynasty, the envy of the rest of the world. When I was growing up, I heard the same things that you likely did: Bastion is a cultural center unlike any other in the world. We are home to so many multinational corporations. In the palace's shadow, wealth and opportunity is available to everyone."

So far, the crowd had behaved as she'd expected. And why wouldn't they? She was simply repeating the usual propaganda, the sort of thing the Dynasty had been proclaiming for generations. She fought back a satisfied smile. Time to kick the legs out from under them.

"And yet Fair Havens is proof that much of what I said simply isn't true."

That got their attention. Several of the reporters' heads snapped back, their surprise clear on their faces.

Everys leaned forward. "Did you know that a child who is born in this neighborhood is twice as likely to wind up in prison than if he'd been born elsewhere? And even those who avoid that fate usually wind up with low paying jobs that make it difficult to break the cycle of generational poverty. We all know this about Fair Havens. Given this neighborhood's rough reputation, it's little wonder so few of your colleagues joined us today."

Several of the reporters shifted uneasily, glancing at each other, like they wondered how she knew.

She gestured behind her toward the building. "Before I became queen, this was my shop. The Broken Sword. I did my best to eke out a living among my neighbors. Fixing broken devices, selling used electronics.

"Now many people would look at me and say I'm a success story. I was able to rise out of Fair Havens and become something more than just a simple shopkeeper and fixer of broken electronics. I think a lot of folks, if they were in the same position as I was, would likely thank the Warrior and put this as far behind them as possible. But I can't do that. I believe when a person rises out of a broken situation, they have an obligation to help others if they can.

"That's why I purchased this building. This will be the first in a network of community outreach centers that will offer financial, social, and educational assistance in the poorer neighborhoods of Bastion. This location will be where we test the concept and refine it. I truly believe that this will be the first step toward a stronger, more stable future for our city and Dynasty."

Now many of the reporters wore skeptical looks.

"And who's gonna pay for any of that?" someone shouted. She couldn't tell if it had been a reporter or not.

"At first, I will. I have reallocated the funds that were to be used for my personal living expenses for this project. Based on my early projections, I will be able to fund this center for half a year, but it is my hope that others of similar means will partner with me or be inspired to provide similar services in other low-income neighborhoods."

Everys glanced at Redtale. She nodded subtly. Good. This was the trickiest part of the day. She wanted to bring her announcement to a dramatic conclusion.

"And to show my intentions, I have an initial gift that I would like to make to the people of Fair Havens."

Sure enough, she could hear the rumble of the approaching engines. And there, three blocks down, the first of the transports made the corner.

"I have taken the liberty of purchasing foodstuffs for the residents of Fair Havens. For the rest of the day, I will be here to distribute these gifts. If you can't make it down here right now, I have made arrangements that the good people at Korga's Market will store the leftovers and make sure they're distributed fairly."

That had taken some doing. Old Man Korga was an honest sort, but when Everys contacted him about helping, he had been incredibly reluctant. But she had appealed to his patriotism and promised she would make sure to give his business a good word or two in exchange.

The first transport pulled into place and the back opened. A number of soldiers spilled out, but most of them weren't armed. Everys smiled at Redtale. More of her help. There were plenty of off-duty soldiers in Bastion at any given time. But it had taken the head of the Queen's Guard to gently "suggest" that their time would be better spent helping their fellow citizens than carousing.

Everys took a breath to continue her speech, but then the cab door on the first truck burst open and Quartus emerged. He smiled, a brilliant flash of teeth, and waved to the crowd.

Her jaw dropped. What was he doing here?

Apparently the reporters wondered the same thing. They quickly swarmed the transport.

He waved for them to quiet down. "My friends, when I heard what our queen had planned, how could I not be here?" He worked his way over to the stage, climbing onto it in one fluid motion. He stepped to her side and put his arm around her. "She has my full support."

Everys fought to keep her frustration from her expression. This was supposed to be her moment, to let the Dynasty know she was a different kind of queen. Instead, Quartus had just brought the focus to himself. His mere presence made her an afterthought, a shadow fading in his brighter spotlight.

But as they stood there, with him waving to the crowd, she realized she couldn't think like that. The reporters looked less skeptical. Folks from the neighborhood were already gathering. Word was probably getting out that Quartus was here. That was bound to bring more reporters, more people, more attention. Exactly what she needed.

He leaned in closer to her. "Smile, Everys. They're going to love this. They're going to love you."

And the way he said those last two words, she couldn't help but wonder if he meant it for just that generic "them," or if he maybe meant it for him too.

13

Within an hour, the streets outside The Broken Sword were packed. Under Redtale's watchful eye, a somewhat orderly distribution process was set up. It had been her idea to pack the different items in different trucks. Everys stationed herself at the last one, making sure to make eye contact and say a word or two with every person who walked by. Things went smoothly until Quartus decided to help the soldiers unload the transport behind her. He distracted the crowd, slowing the line. And, if she was honest, he distracted her too.

Eventually, Everys had to admit defeat. She motioned for the line to wait, then she turned to Quartus. "Why don't you come over here and help me?"

He looked almost genuinely surprised. But he ambled over to her. "If you insist, my queen."

She turned back to the line. A Grerid woman and her three children waited, so she pulled out four money transfers, each good for two hundred blades each. The mother bowed, first to her, then to Quartus, and then scurried off, giggling with her children.

"I must say, this is impressive." Quartus looked back at the building. "Did you really buy this? Or are negotiations 'on-going?'"

"No, I really bought the building. I had to spend a little extra to expedite the property transfer but—"

"Amazing!" He turned to her. "How did you manage in such a short time?"

Everys smiled. Like she was going to share all of her secrets.

Quartus chuckled, a low, throaty sound that sent shivers up Everys's spine. "You truly are remarkable."

Heat painted Everys's cheeks, and she turned back to distributing the food.

"Prince! Queen! Over here!" A gaggle of reporters, newcomers from the looks of them, waved from the other side of the crowd.

Quartus laughed and put his arm around her waist, drawing her close. She gasped, startled, as he pulled her in tight. If he noticed her surprise, he didn't let on. Instead, he smiled broadly and waved to the reporters.

Everys realized she should probably do the same. She tried to copy Quartus's easy smile and casual wave. It probably didn't look natural, but apparently the reporters were satisfied. They moved on.

"Truly amazing," Quartus repeated.

Her heart slammed in her chest. Then she realized it wasn't just her heart she felt, but his. He still held her close, turning her slightly so the two of them faced each other. She looked down into his coppery eyes. His deep, warm, tender...

She took a step back. Inkstains, what was wrong with her? Hopefully no one saw what almost happened. She could already imagine pictures of her and Quartus flashing across the Dynasty's holdings with speculation about them almost kissing and... Wait, had she really almost kissed Quartus? Did he want her to? Did she?

Everys pressed a hand to her head, suddenly dizzy. "Is it okay if I take a quick walk, Redtale?"

Redtale made a quick motion with her hand. Two of the guards in the line responded with signals of their own. Redtale nodded. "Lead the way. Not too far or the snipers will have to shift their positions."

Everys wanted to laugh. Inkstains, she wouldn't want to inconvenience the snipers! She looked around and realized there really wasn't anywhere she could go to get away from the crowd. Then her gaze fell on the building. Well, actually, there was.

She slipped over to the shop's door. It took her a moment to unlock the door—the biometric sensor was out of sync again—but it eventually popped open. She slipped inside.

Once Redtale followed, she pushed the door shut, blocking out the din of the crowd. She pressed her hands against the closed door, drawing strength from the familiar feel of the battered metal. Then she turned and faced the shop.

It felt strange, being there again. Almost like waking from a dream. Or maybe stumbling into one. She wasn't sure. What was real for her now, the palace or the Broken Sword? She drifted forward, running

Before she could leave, though, Kyna snared her wrist and drew her in close. "Do not think you can continue to play the fool, Everys. Far too many of our people have ignored the opportunities placed before them. Open your eyes. Listen! And be ready." She punctuated her words by poking Everys in the forehead.

Everys shook Kyna's hand off of her wrist. "Enough. I need to get back to work."

Kyna laughed. "Or is it that you want to get back to your brother-in-law?"

Everys froze.

"Yes, girl, even an old blind woman can see the way you look at him and he at you." Kyna leaned forward. "A tantalizing distraction, I'll admit, but that's all he is."

That was enough. She had wasted enough time. She turned to leave the room.

"Oh, Everys. I believe you forgot something."

Everys spun around, ready to finally tell the old crone off once and for all. Instead, she paused when she realized what Kyna held out to her.

Two pens. Her mouth went dry. If Redtale saw this, would the guard realize the significance? Everys snatched the pens and tucked them in a pocket. "I'd appreciate it if you left, Auntie."

Kyna smiled. "Of course. An old deaf woman isn't needed here, is she?"

With that, Kyna picked up the bandana. This time, though, she wrapped it around her eyes, once again making herself look blind. Then she retrieved her staff and walked out of the back room, heading through the display area.

Everys followed her out. Kyna brushed past Redtale, sweeping her staff in front of her. As soon as the old woman had left the shop, Redtale turned back to Everys.

"Wasn't she deaf just a moment ago?" she asked.

Everys shook her head. "It's a long story."

"I see." Redtale motioned for the door. "Ready to go back out, Blessed? I think the reporters are looking for you. The prince too." From the way she spat Quartus's title, it was clear that the guard shared her auntie's opinion of him.

Everys forced herself to smile. "After you."

Redtale nodded and led the way, opening the door then stepping through. She signaled for Everys to follow. She did and worked her way back to Quartus's side.

He glanced at her as she approached. "Is everything all right?"

"It is," she said, then offered him a smile of her own. "Especially now that I'm back out here with you."

He looked surprised, but the dazzling smile he offered her was definitely worth it. If Everys had to be here, the least she could do was enjoy her time. And somehow, Kyna's disapproval of the situation made the whole thing that much sweeter.

14

“Your Strength?”

Narius groaned at the sound of his assistant's voice. From Urett's tone, Narius knew he had news he didn't want to share.

He tossed the scriber onto the desk in front of him. It skittered and came to rest against the others. Masruq's financial forecasts would have to wait, along with the reports about the Dynasty's construction projects in the southern reaches, the tax estimates from Maotoa, and the dozen or so other documents that demanded his immediate attention.

"Duke Brencis insists on seeing you immediately," Urett said.

Of course he did. "Show him in."

As Urett stepped back out of the office, Narius glanced around the room. He hated being in the Amber Office. This was the nerve center of the Dynasty, where decisions were made for the glory of the Dynasty. And yet Narius never felt comfortable here. This space never felt like it belonged to him. Like he was an impostor, an intruder who would be chased away when the real king arrived. Truth be told, he would rather be in his private study. But that wouldn't do. It wouldn't be proper for the king to hide himself away in his private residence for hours on end.

Besides, then he'd have to allow Brencis to invade his private sanctum, and he wasn't about to do that.

The door opened, and Brencis barreled in, his cheeks already flush and the veins in his neck bulging.

"What seems to be the trouble today, Duke?" Narius forced himself to keep his annoyance from his voice.

"Six hours ago, a squadron of Dalark recon skimmers crossed into our airspace."

"Oh?" Narius asked. "Just recon? Any fighters?"

"Just recon," Brencis said.

"Where did this happen?"

Brencis stepped over to one wall and plugged his scriber into a large vidscreen. A map of the Dynasty's western border sprang to life, and then the view shifted to show the southwestern border. The Plotan Expanse. Narius frowned. Nothing but farmland down there, along with a few midsized cities. Nothing strategically important.

"What happened?" Narius asked.

"Upon detecting the intruders, Viscount Wexxik scrambled fighters to intercept. They made contact and demanded they leave our airspace immediately."

"And?"

Brencis scowled. "They did. The Dalark claimed they experienced a navigational glitch and 'accidentally' crossed the border."

Narius frowned. "So what's the problem?"

Brencis spluttered, then jabbed a finger at the screen. "Don't you see, sir? Dalark is testing us. First it was the firefight in the Demilitarized Zone. Now this incursion. They are gauging our reactions!"

Narius quirked a brow, and the duke's face turned several shades redder. Narius knew that Brencis hated it when he looked at him like that, which was why he made sure he did at least once every time they talked. He picked up one of the scribers, scrolling through its information until he found the appropriate report.

"I have here an after-action report from the squad involved in the 'firefight' you mentioned," Narius said. "Do we really have to go over this again?"

Brencis's scowl intensified, but he nodded once, curtly.

Narius started reading. "'After interviewing those involved, it was determined an inexperienced recruit got separated from his patrol. When he heard the patrol in the vicinity, he believed they were Dalark soldiers and engaged. The resulting firefight lasted ten minutes and several soldiers were injured by friendly fire.' Dalark wasn't even involved."

"I read the report as well, sir. I've examined the maps, the radio logs, all of it. I do not believe the soldier was in error. I believe he did catch the Dalark transgressing the zone and responded appropriately. And now they tried it again, but at the opposite end of our border. Don't you see what's happening? They're looking for the best place to invade."

Narius rolled his eyes. Not this old song again. "We've been over this before, Duke. Tormod's spies haven't found any evidence of this supposed invasion you're so convinced is going to happen. And Alezzar keeps reminding us the only reason Dalark maintains so many troops in the Beachhead is because we—or rather, you—refuse to withdraw our troops from our side."

"So you won't do anything?" Brencis demanded.

"I didn't say that. I will send a message to Emperor Devroshan through Alezzar reminding him of the sovereignty of our airspace. I will tell him that we understand these sorts of mistakes happen—after all, we've made similar, yes?—but that we will be monitoring the situation to make sure this doesn't happen again. And that will be the end of it."

Except he hoped it wouldn't. Maybe Devroshan would make an issue of it. If he did, then maybe Narius could insist on a face-to-face meeting. If they had the meeting here, he could invite the Emperor's family to accompany him. And then he could see Innana again.

Brencis laughed, a harsh bark. "Except it won't, Your Strength." He jabbed another finger at the map. "Look at what the Dynasty holds right now. Since our rise, we have forged a mighty nation through conquest. Your predecessors have always met every threat with force. Your father would have ordered the Dalark aircraft shot down. Your grandfather would have dropped incendiaries on the Beachhead."

"And that would have resulted in months of fighting that would gain neither side anything," Narius said.

"Except proving that we are worthy heirs of the Warrior!" Brencis roared. "But the weaker we appear, the more people forget we are to be feared. Why else do the Cold Light defy our authority?"

Narius crossed his arms. "'Just as there are many kinds of weapons, there are many kinds of strength. Knowing which to use in battle is the beginning of true wisdom and assured victory.'"

Brencis's lips twitched into a snarl. "I know what the Warrior's Meditations say and—"

"Do you? Then I don't need to remind you what he said about insubordination, do I?"

Brencis looked ready to say something but apparently decided against it.

Narius blew out a tense breath. "I understand your frustration, Duke. It very well could be that Dalark is trying to provoke us. And yes, my father and grandfather would have gleefully accepted the invitation. But I can't do that. Not from a lack of conviction or courage. Should Dalark give us a genuine reason to fight, I will send our troops into battle and, if need be, lead the charge myself. But I feel that, if the Dynasty is to endure, we must not throw away our troops' lives needlessly. Do I make myself clear?"

Brencis ground his teeth, but he nodded. "Forgive my impertinence, sir."

Narius forced himself to smile. "It is not impertinence to speak your mind with such passion. I appreciate your desire to keep us secure. It is a goal that I share."

The door to the office banged open. Paine rushed in.

Narius swallowed a groan. From the look on the vizier's face, he brought more bad news. Narius offered up a quick prayer to the Warrior that it wasn't a Dalark invasion. He did not want to hear Brencis's smug "I-told-you-so."

"My apologies, Your Strength. Duke. But I fear we have a situation on our hands." Paine crossed over to the vidscreen and adjusted the controls.

The map disappeared, replaced with a live news feed. It was an aerial shot of a city street. Narius frowned at the image. People thronged the streets with an urgency and underlying anger he could practically feel. Information scrolled across the bottom of the screen identifying it as... Bastion? Here? So close to the palace?

"A riot?" he asked Paine.

The vizier shook his head. "Not yet, although some reports suggest it might be soon."

"Why? What caused it?" Narius asked.

The image on the screen changed. A line of people snaked through the streets, jostling one another, pushing, shoving. Narius could read the tension, the simmering anger, in their postures and expressions. Paine was right. It wasn't a riot yet, but it would be soon. The camera panned along the crowd, revealing... Were those royal guards standing watch over the crowd? He frowned.

Then the camera settled on two people. Narius recognized the first immediately. His brother. He sighed. Quartus could give the Trickster a run for her money, that was certain. And standing next to him was...

His eyes widened. Everys.

Quartus whispered something to Everys. The two of them laughed and her eyes shone.

"You were saying about rebels, sir?" Brencis asked quietly.

Narius ignored the verbal jab. Apparently the duke had been correct. Only he hadn't realized that the problem was within his own palace.

15

The line never ended. By the time the sun dipped, Everys was convinced she had seen every resident of Fair Havens. She suspected she had seen some of them twice. Not that she could blame anyone if they had done so. The Dynasty had ignored them for so long, they probably figured they were owed that little extra.

Just as Everys was wondering if they should stop, Redtale touched her elbow.

"Got a situation brewing, Blessed," she whispered. "Another visitor."

"Who?"

"Your brother."

Everys sighed. She hadn't seen Legarr yet. But she knew he'd want to take advantage of this somehow. Redtale led her toward the back of the building.

Sure enough, Legarr slouched against the wall, his expression sullen. Two of Everys's guards minded him, their expressions stern. When he saw her, though, he smiled lazily.

"Hey, Everys! Sorry I'm so late getting here." He opened his arms as if expecting a hug.

Everys crossed hers. "What do you want, Legarr?"

"Is it so wrong that I wanted to congratulate my sister on her marriage? That's what families do, right?"

She winced at the barbed question. When Legarr married Tilash, nobody had attended the wedding. Partly because Mama and Papa and Galan were getting ready to leave Bastion. Partly because no one believed the marriage was legitimate. But Legarr and Tilash had been married five years, and she had never met her.

"Thank you," she said, taking a step toward him.

"You know, I always knew you'd do well. Everyone thought so. Why do you think Papa left you the shop in the first place? He knew you would make us all proud. And look at you! Queen! Amazing."

Everys resisted the urge to smile. Sure, Legarr sounded sincere. He had lots of practice offering empty compliments. She knew what was coming.

"And now I'm the queen's brother. That makes me nobility, right?"

Redtale grunted. It may have been a laugh, but Everys couldn't tell for sure.

"Look, I'm not wanting much. No mansions or lands or titles—although if you have some sitting around, I wouldn't say no! Instead, I'm hoping you might be able to help me out. You've clearly got access to some impressive funds. Maybe you'd see clear to helping your brother launch a business venture?"

Everys chuckled. "Let me guess. It's a 'can't go wrong' sort of deal, guaranteed to make everyone involved rich beyond their wildest dreams?"

Legarr chuckled. "Well, I wouldn't have put it so sarcastically, but yeah, that's accurate."

"So what's this great business venture?"

Legarr's face lit up. "I have a connection who can get me some surplus military transports, amphibious ones."

"Why would you need those?" Everys asked.

"See, I've got this great idea. I get a fleet of about half a dozen or so, and we can take people out on the Melgor River."

Everys gaped at him. Why would anyone want to do that? The Melgor was horribly polluted by factories upstream from Fair Havens. While she couldn't smell it from her shop, its rank odor permeated the neighborhood along its banks. There was no way anyone would willingly pay for a river tour in military surplus vehicles. "That is the dumbest idea I've ever heard."

"Not really, if you have a bit of imagination," Legarr countered. "We all know that there are people who want to clean up Fair Havens and rehabilitate it. And once people figure out you're from this neighborhood, Fair Havens is suddenly going to become the trendy neighborhood to live in. Within a year, we'll have rich folks lining up to move here. And when they do, I'll be the first person to take advantage of it."

Redtale grunted. "That's if you can actually get the transports. The good stuff wouldn't go to someone like you."

"I've got my connections already, thanks for worrying. And especially now that I have an in at the palace too. Right, sister of mine?"

Everys rolled her eyes. "I'm not giving you any money, Legarr."

His face froze. "But... but..."

She held up a hand. "I know how this works. I'll give you the money, and you'll promise to pay me back. But then you'll encounter some unforeseen problem. Maybe your supplier won't have the transports after all. Or they'll be in worse shape than you anticipated. Or the river will never be clean enough. Or, or, or. You'll keep promising that I'll get my money back, but eventually, you'll just encourage me to move on because it just didn't work. Does that sound about right?"

As Everys outlined Legarr's scheme, his face grew redder and redder. Soon he was shaking with barely restrained fury. "That's not true! I *do* have connections. Powerful ones, and they're going to make sure I get what I need."

Everys waved away his words. "I've heard all this before. You used to tell Papa the same thing, remember? And he never believed a word of it."

"But Papa would still give me the money. But he's not here anymore. Instead, I'm left with a sister who has never even met my wife and probably didn't even give me a second thought once she got into the palace." He took a step back. "Forget I asked you for anything. I don't need your charity. By the Spear, nobody here does. None of us need your pity!"

With that, he stormed away, shoving past one of the guards.

Everys's eyes stung. Sure, Legarr was a con artist and definitely not to be trusted, but he was the only family she had left. She was suddenly aware of how alone she really was.

Redtale cleared her throat. "Blessed, why don't we head back home? Nobody would mind if you made a gracious exit."

She wanted to laugh and cry. She was supposed to be home. This was her building now, after all. But Redtale gently steered her out of the alley and toward the military transports.

The moment she emerged from the alley, a shout went up from the gathered crowd, cheers and laughter. People waved. Everys returned the gesture half-heartedly. The crowd shouted even louder.

Everys drank in the happy faces. Everyone seemed so grateful and that buoyed her mood. Why shouldn't she be thanked? Regardless of what Auntie Kyna or Legarr said, she'd have a positive impact on the community.

Her gaze hitched on a man at the front of the crowd. He didn't seem happy to see her at all. Instead, he glared at her, pure hatred shining in his eyes. Once she spotted him, though, he ducked his head as if trying to hide. But as he did, she noticed something odd. Green lines spread across his cheeks from his ears, looking like vines or branches twining along his skin. Why hadn't she noticed them before?

The man suddenly snapped upright and leveled a finger at her. "Death to the royals! Freedom for the oppressed!"

And then black smoke erupted from the man's body.

Everys froze in place as the cloud rushed toward her. Then she noticed similar plumes of smoke quickly overtook the crowd, panic following in their wake. People stumbled and screamed as they tried to stampede away. As the smoke rolled over them, they collapsed to the ground, coughing and heaving.

But then a change came over the crowd. They stopped struggling and coughing. Instead, they attacked each other, roaring and screaming in a complete rage. And the brawl only got larger as the smoke swallowed the crowd, the citizens of Fair Havens driven to an absolute frenzy.

"Everys, *move!*" Redtale ripped a weapon from her belt. Two other guards dragged her toward the transports.

"Wait, where's Quartus?" she shouted. "Where's—?"

And then she saw him. Quartus was surrounded by his own guards, but he didn't seem to need them. Instead, he wrestled one of the rioters to the ground, trying to subdue the screaming man as best he could. He looked up in her direction, worry painted across his face, but he nodded grimly, then went back to the fight.

Everys started to say something, but pain exploded across her forehead. Someone had thrown something at her. A rock? A bottle? She had no idea. Pain swam behind her eyes, and she wanted to collapse into a ball. But the guards wouldn't release her. Instead, they dragged her the last few feet and unceremoniously tossed her into the back of a transport. Redtale dove in behind her, firing into the crowd as she did. As soon as she was inside, she yanked the door shut and pounded on the wall to the cab. With a roar of the engine, the transport lurched forward. It sounded like it smashed through something almost immediately, but it didn't stop, didn't even slow down.

Within minutes, the sound of the riot faded from around her. Redtale relaxed, but then her gaze landed on Everys. Her eyes widened and she rushed to her side.

"The queen's been hit!" she bellowed.

Everys tried to wave her off, but Redtale wouldn't leave her alone. Instead, two more guards surrounded her and pressed a bandage to her forehead, peppering her with questions. Was she hit anywhere else? Did she feel any other pains? Was she okay?

She wanted to cry at that last question. No. No, she was not okay. What should have been a victory had just crumbled around her.

16

As soon as they made it back to the palace, the guards hurried her to the palace's private hospital. Doctors and nurses rushed to her side, ushering her onto a nearby bed. She tried to tell them she was okay, but they didn't listen. As two of them worked on her forehead, the others poked and prodded, making sure she wasn't injured anywhere else.

While the medical team worked, the guards hovered outside the door. At one point, Redtale sent one of them away, and when the young man came back, the guard commander's expression turned positively grim.

"Blessed, I hate to bother you, but I have to ask. Did you see any of the agitators?" Redtale asked.

Everys nodded, which elicited a grunt of frustration from the doctor trying to bandage her forehead. "I did, yes."

"Can you describe him?"

"Definitely a man. Human. Looked... Kolvese, maybe? But there was something strange about his face."

"Oh?" From Redtale's tone, it was clear that she wasn't surprised.

"Yeah... there were these... lines on his face. Green lines."

The room went silent. Redtale nodded grimly.

"What?" Everys asked. "What's wrong?"

"A Cold Light thrall?" one of the nurses whispered.

Then Everys understood everyone's shock. A chill trembled through her. "Those are real? I thought they were just a rumor."

Redtale shook her head. "Unfortunately, they are all too real."

The strength drained out of Everys's body. Everyone in the Dynasty whispered about the threat of the Cold Light: sentient trees whose Hearth had been conquered by Narius's grandfather, King Vetranio.

According to rumors, the trees could overpower a person's mind and brainwash their victims into serving their every whim. Everys had always discounted them as mere rumors or tall tales.

"What's going on in Fair Havens right now?" she whispered.

Incredibly, Redtale's expression turned grimmer. "A riot. Biggest one Bastion's seen in decades."

Everys closed her eyes and groaned. That only made things worse. "Where is she?"

Everyone snapped to attention. Narius stormed into the room. His gaze latched onto her forehead, then skittered across the medical devices and personnel before finally landing on one of the doctors.

"Can she walk?" he barked.

The doctor nodded.

"Good." Narius jabbed a finger in her direction. "You. Follow me. Now."

Who did he think he was, talking to her like that? But from the expression on everyone's faces, no one would stand up for her if she refused. So with a heavy sigh, she lowered herself off the examination table. Narius left, not even checking to see if she was following. But she did. The day had turned sour so quickly. Might as well end it in the worst way possible, with her new husband.

He led her to the throne room where, unfortunately, they were not alone. Vizier Paine, Duke Brencis, Governor-General Zammit, and half a dozen other advisers waited for them.

"If it isn't our resident rabble rouser!" Brencis snarled. "The night is still young, Queen Everys. Shall we call the Dalark Imperium? Perhaps you can spark an international incident."

Everys gaped at him. How could he speak to her like that? More infuriating, Narius didn't object either. Well, she would have to do it herself.

But before she could, Narius snapped an open palm up in her direction, cutting her off. "Report, Vizier."

"The situation continues to deteriorate," Paine said. "Latest reports indicate the rioting is spreading into surrounding neighborhoods. The constabulary are doing their best to contain the violence, but I fear they will need reinforcements, and soon."

"I concur," Zammit said. "If we can keep the violence contained, nothing of importance will be lost."

Everys bristled at his words. "Except for the people of Fair Havens and their property."

Brencis fixed her with a fiery glare. "They would have been safe if you hadn't stirred them up."

"They wouldn't be able to be stirred up if they didn't live in abject squalor!" Everys shot back.

"They could leave at any time," Brencis said.

"And go where?" Everys asked.

"Enough!" In spite of his shout, Narius still looked composed, every inch of him king. "Governor-General, Duke, send enough troops to assist the constables. Use what force is needed to end the rioting as quickly as possible."

Everys started to object, but Narius ignored her. He turned his attention to Paine. "Vizier, I want regular updates until the violence is over, understood?"

Paine nodded.

"Now leave us," Narius said.

Zammit and Paine bowed to Narius but ignored her as they left. Brencis cast a snarl in her direction before storming out. One by one, the rest of the advisers retreated.

Leaving her alone with Narius.

At first, she didn't meet his angry gaze. He simply sat on his throne, his face an expressionless mask. He looked more like a statue than a living person, the carved effigy of an angry god considering how best to smite a pitiful mortal worm.

But then she realized that she couldn't back down. The riot wasn't her fault. The distribution had been orderly up until the end. And she wasn't about to cower. So she straightened and met his glare with one of her own.

They stared at each other until Narius broke the silence.

"Explain yourself."

"The people are in need. I was trying to help them."

"By starting a riot? Yes, I'm sure that will be very beneficial."

"I didn't do that. There were Cold Light thralls in the crowd who started the violence."

Narius's lips twitched into a sneer. "Indeed? How convenient."

"One of my guards saw them as well."

That took him by surprise. Then he shook his head. "It matters little. If you hadn't gathered so many people in one place, this riot would not have occurred. So I say again: explain yourself."

She opened her arms. "What is there to explain? I told you already. In spite of all the lofty promises about prosperity and peace, there are still those in your own capital city who go to bed hungry and scared every night."

"And it is my responsibility to change that?"

"Yes!"

"What would you like me to do? Go from door to door? Tuck them into their beds?"

Heat shot through her cheeks, and her fingers curled into fists. "There's no need for sarcasm."

"Oh, I disagree." His facade cracked, his lip twitching ever so slightly. "Where did you get the money for this disaster?"

"Don't worry, I didn't spend your money. I spent mine."

He frowned. "What do you mean?"

"I used the queen's discretionary budget."

"The queen's—" He laughed, a clipped outburst. "That is not what it's intended for!"

"Really? Do you think I need that much money for dresses?"

"Yes!" Narius responded. "Do you know how many formal functions you will be expected to attend? You can't simply show up in the same outfit twice. It would cause a scandal."

"Then let it!" Everys pointed toward one of the walls. "There are people out there who will starve to death tonight, yet I'm expected to waste millions of blades on dresses that I only wear once? Where is the wisdom in that?"

"I never said it was wise. It's what's expected. You're not supposed to go around making policy!"

"I never did."

"Didn't you? I heard your little speech, where you practically accused the Dynasty of neglect. You admitted, in public, that we weren't doing what we could to help our citizens."

"You're not, though!"

Narius's hands clenched into fists, and he looked away. When he started speaking again, his tone was measured, but Everys could practically feel the tension bleeding through it.

"We have other priorities we need to focus on. Could we spend money on making sure everyone has enough food to eat? Yes, I suppose we could. But then what would happen? We wouldn't be able to defend our borders. Our citizens would come to rely on us instead of taking care of themselves."

"I'm not saying we should take care of everyone."

"Oh no? I assume you made sure everyone who received your gifts were truly deserving?"

She blinked. No, she hadn't. Then she shook her head. "Maybe not today, but in the future, we will."

"There will not be a future. You've done enough damage! Just stay in the palace and don't get in the way. That is what is expected of you as queen!"

"Well, I never wanted to be queen anyway."

"Do you think this is what I wanted?"

"Then why did you choose me?"

They glared at each other. Everys's skin practically blistered beneath his gaze, but she wasn't going to back down, not now. If he hadn't chosen her in the first place, none of this would have happened.

"I have my reasons, which I am now calling into question."

"So why don't you just get rid of me?" she shot back.

He glared at her, his jaw clenched.

She smiled viciously at him. "You can't, can you? Paine told me you need to be married for your reign to be valid. Is that why you abducted me off the streets to—"

"We never abducted you!"

"Oh, I forgot. It's only a crime if the Dynasty isn't the one doing it." Everys turned to leave the throne room.

"I have not dismissed you yet, woman!" Narius hurled that last word like an insult.

Everys fixed him with what she hoped was a withering gaze. "Watch your tone, *husband*. Don't forget, I'm the one who has all the power here."

He laughed. "Are you delusional? I am the king of the Xoniel Dynasty. I am the successor of the Perfected Warrior. And you are just... just..."

"What?" Everys prompted. "Finish the thought. Come on."

He shook his head. "I will not deign to stoop to your level."

"Why? Because I'm from Fair Havens? A commoner? A Siporan? All of that may be true, but I still have all the power. Because here's the important difference between us: you need me more than I need you. And if you're not careful, I'll leave you like Viara, and you'll have to start all over again!" She punctuated her last point with a jab of her finger and stormed out of the room.

Redtale was waiting for her outside. She eyed her critically. "Didn't hear him dismiss you, Blessed."

Everys glared at her, and the guard raised her hands in surrender.

Back at her room, Trule and the other girls were waiting for her, and they immediately fussed over her the moment she entered. It was the last thing she needed. She dismissed them, sending them all away. They didn't want to leave, but eventually, they all did, leaving her alone in blessed silence.

As she stood in the middle of the room, finally alone, she could feel the tears well up within her. But she wasn't going to give in to self-pity. Instead, she would go to bed, set aside the disaster, and figure out what she would do tomorrow.

She walked into her bedroom and headed for the armoire. Maybe she'd find some comfortable pajamas in there. That was all she needed right now. She opened the door to the armoire, then froze.

Someone had painted something on the inside of her armoire, a crude message, slashed in a hasty script: *I know what you are, scribbler.*

She stared at the message, dumbfounded. Who had done this? One of the girls? No, that didn't seem possible. They were all too timid. A guard? Maybe, but none of them seemed outwardly hostile. Had Narius done it? No, if he suspected what she really was, wouldn't he have said something?

Everys stumbled away from the message and bumped against the bed. Then she collapsed onto it, wrapping her arms around herself and hoping that sleep would take her soon.

17

S leep eluded her the entire night.

As she lay in her bed, she was sure she could hear sirens and gunfire in the distance. Objectively, she knew she couldn't hear the chaos, but still, the imaginary noise echoed through her mind. Every time she closed her eyes, she saw the people tearing the neighborhood to pieces. By the middle of Fourth Watch, she considered using one of the pens Kyna gave her. She could easily draw a sleeping rune and force herself into unconsciousness. But no, that wouldn't be wise, given the message someone left her in the wardrobe.

When the sun rose, painting her room with warm colors, Everys groaned. Might as well face the day. She rolled out of bed and stumbled for the door. But she stopped when she stepped through.

Redtale stood just outside her bedroom door, facing the large window where morning light streamed in. Tears glistened in Redtale's eyes, and she hummed a haunting melody. Everys paused as Redtale moved her arms with fluid grace, crossing them over her chest, reaching up to touch the stubs of her horns, then dropping them to her side, only to repeat the pattern several times. Then she covered her face and dropped to one knee. Everys felt distinctly uncomfortable, like she was intruding on a very private moment. It wasn't right for her spy like this.

Just as she started to clear her throat, though, Redtale rose and turned toward the door. When she saw Everys, she froze in place, a stricken expression flashing across her face. But just as quickly, it was gone. "Good morning, Blessed."

"I'm sorry for interrupting."

"You weren't."

They stood in uncomfortable silence. Questions bubbled through Everys, but she wasn't sure how to ask any of them.

"Blessed? Are you all right? Should I get the medics?"

That broke the reverie.

"No, I'm fine." She touched the stitches in her forehead and realized that, without meaning to, she was mirroring Redtale's actions. She forced her hands to her side, grabbing onto her pajamas to keep her hands still. "Do you mind if I ask what you were doing just now?"

Redtale's eyes hardened. "That's a very personal question."

"I-I'm sorry, I didn't mean to—"

"But you have a right to be curious." Redtale pursed her lips and looked at the floor, as if the answers were written there. "You may have noticed I don't have my horns."

That was an understatement. Everys had seen Ixactl in Fair Havens, and all of them took inordinate pride in the size and shape of their horns. Some of the male Ixactl she knew even decorated them with paint and jewelry. It was still jarring to see Redtale with her stumps.

"To my people, broken horns are a sign of defeat. If one clan defeated another in combat, it was expected that the victors would break the horns of the losers."

"So you were defeated in combat?" Everys couldn't picture Redtale ever being defeated in anything.

She smiled ruefully. "I broke off my own horns."

Everys cocked her head. Redtale's tone suggested that this should be scandalous, but she couldn't understand why.

Redtale must have picked up on her confusion. "I was young. Idealistic. And angry. So very angry."

"At who?"

"The Dynasty."

Everys gaped at her. Redtale chuckled and nodded.

"My grandmother was our clan's archivist, charged with remembering our culture and our ways. She was training me to take her place, and she filled my head with stories of our people's past glory. How we claimed the Ixac Mountains and Highlands as our domain, guarding it from interlopers. How the clans would clash, sharpening each other so we could defend our home better. And at the heart of our society was the *ma-se-kranna*."

"The what?"

Now Redtale's smile turned wistful. "It was a sacred item, a relic from ancient times. No one quite remembers what it was exactly, but it was the one thing that could unite our people. The clans would fight over just about anything, but never the *ma-se-kranna*. It occupied a prominent place in our hearts, minds, and imaginations. It was held as a common trust for the Ixactl people."

"What happened to it?" Everys asked, even though she already suspected the answer.

"The Dynasty. When the Xoniel overran the Highlands three hundred years ago, we fought against them until they captured the *ma-se-kranna*. We surrendered, thinking the Dynasty would return it. They didn't. They broke no horns. Instead, they took our young warriors for their armies, the strength of our bodies giving their reign steel and stone." Her voice had changed tone, like she was reciting something she'd memorized many years earlier. She shook her head, as if clearing it. "The clans eventually accepted the loss. But when I was young, I couldn't. So I broke my own horns in protest."

Everys tried to imagine Redtale with that much passion. She couldn't imagine her losing control. "So how did... I mean, if you hated the Dynasty that much..."

"How did I wind up as a member of the royal guard?" She chuckled. "Penance. Breaking off my own horns brought shame and dishonor to my family. I could no longer serve as the clan's archivist given my condition. And I was an outcast among my people. So my grandmother decided I could reclaim my honor by serving in the Dynasty's military. I was forced to enlist the next day, leaving the Highlands behind. Like I said yesterday, I haven't been back since."

"Why not?"

She shrugged. "At first, shame. Then resentment. Now, though, there's really nothing left for me there. Most of my kin don't miss me, and to be fair, I don't miss them either. So why go back?"

"They're your people. Your family!"

Again, she shrugged. "By blood, I suppose. But I've found my place here. I haven't forgotten what made me break my horns, though. That's why, every morning, I face the rising sun and perform the Kata of Mourning. So I don't forget the *ma-se-kranna*. So I never lose track of who I am at my core. I may wear the uniform of a guard, but I am first and foremost an Ixactl."

Silence fell on the room. Everys didn't want to break it, understanding what Redtale had shared was too sacred to sully with anything she might say. Finally, she settled on saying the only thing she could think of: "Thank you for sharing that with me."

Redtale nodded. "If I'm to protect you, you need to be able to trust me. There can't be secrets between us."

And suddenly, the moment was broken. At least, it was for Everys. Redtale had just shared an important part of who she was. And she was right about trust. Should she reciprocate? Should she reveal what she was capable of? Would Redtale understand? Would she still protect her? Or would the guard turn her in to the Dynasty?

But before she could decide what to do, Redtale spoke, "According to Challix, the king has 'suggested' you remain in your quarters today."

Everys sighed. No surprise there.

"But if you wanted to take a walk around the gardens or see more of the palace, I could make some quiet arrangements." Redtale quirked her brows at her.

Wait, was Redtale suggesting they defy Narius's orders? That was touching, but given how angry Narius was the night before, given the words they had fired at each other, it was probably better to lie low for the time being. Still, it was sweet.

"Thank you, but I'm feeling a bit too tired to go out," Everys said.

"Then I'll let you rest. Let me know if I can do anything for you."

With that, the guard left her alone. Everys looked out over Bastion and a sense of helplessness crashed over her. What was she supposed to do now? Trapped in a palace, cut off from everyone and everything. What choices did she have left?

"On this glorious day of Advance, we remember how our Perfected Warrior slew the Gravedigger with one blow." Istragon's voice was resonant yet hollow. The Supreme Prelate had clearly memorized this script decades earlier and just spewed the words as his body carried him through the correct motions.

Not that Narius had room to criticize. Most mornings, he didn't focus on what was being said in the armory anyway. It was all empty phrases and gestures, dressing up the Warrior's statue with the day's appropriate weaponry. He knew Istragon insisted this ritual kept the Dynasty rooted in its heritage, but Narius saw it as a wasted half hour.

But this morning, he focused himself on the movements, the words, every little detail. Anything to keep his mind from drifting to the night before.

Even that proved to be a false refuge. After all, the point of the armory service was to remind the spectators of how the Warrior marshaled his strength to slay the gods and win the love of the Water Bearer. Narius's reign was supposed to reflect the Warrior's ideals, including his marriage. As the Warrior cherished the Water Bearer, so the king must cherish his queen. But he doubted the ancient prelates ever envisioned a romantic life like his! Dented Shield, how was he going to untangle this mess now? Wasn't his role difficult enough without so many distractions?

He looked at the mural depicting the Water Bearer on the armory's ceiling. Whoever had created this image had made her a classic Hinaen beauty: long black hair, piercing silvery eyes, high cheekbones, and a haughty expression. Very similar to Viara, truth be told. Narius idly wondered what would happen if he ordered a new depiction of the Water Bearer created, one with Dalark features. Istragon would likely have a heart attack, but at least then, Narius could know his ideal bride watched over him every day.

"Your Strength?"

The gentle question snapped him out of his reverie. He looked around and realized everyone else had left, except for one acolyte who wore a concerned look.

"Is everything all right?" the acolyte whispered.

Narius nodded and quickly rose. "Lost in thoughts... of how the Warrior can inspire me today."

The acolyte beamed at him, clearly buying the lie. Or, at the very least, doing a good job of pretending. Narius excused himself. Not surprisingly, Paine waited for him just outside the door. The Grand Vizier fell into step with him as Narius exited the armory. Much to his surprise, so did Challix.

"Shouldn't you be minding the queen right now?" he snapped at her.

To her credit, Challix didn't flinch. "She is in her quarters having a quiet breakfast, sir."

Narius grunted, then looked at Paine. "The latest?"

"Reports from your advisers are on your desk in the Amber Office, Your Strength," Paine said. "From what I saw, nothing pressing, although Brencis is naturally worried about how Dalark might take advantage of the unrest in Bastion."

Narius snorted. Of course he was. "And the 'unrest?'"

Paine nodded. "It tapered off in the middle of First Watch, but Zammit reports tensions are still running high. She's ordered a curfew for the next four days, but there are already crowds forming around the local armory, in the market, and at The Broken Sword Shop, which was apparently looted last night."

Narius listened to everything Paine said, but with every word, heat built in his chest until he couldn't contain it anymore. "That woman!" he snapped.

Paine quirked a brow at him. "The queen?"

Narius snorted. "Queen in name only. I never should have married her."

Paine nodded sagely, but a faint smile flitted across Challix's face.

"Actually, as messy as this situation may be, the one person who came out of this the best is Everys," she said.

Narius froze. "What?"

Challix nodded. "Several news organizations conducted surveys. And while there's the usual heat-to-light ratio, data shows that the majority of Bastion believes the queen's intentions were good and even laudable. While they aren't happy with the riot, they appreciated the effort. Several indicated they thought such attempts were long overdue. One poll participant said, and I quote, 'It's good we finally have a royal who understands us.'

"Additionally, I've been tracking public opinion of you in the past several days. When Queen Viara left, your numbers declined, especially among traditionalist citizens. But once you married Queen Everys, their opinion stabilized. Not only that, but your perception among the more marginalized subjects of the Dynasty improved, even despite the disturbance in Fair Havens.

"Now, granted, the dust is still settling. Their opinions may change in the coming days, but initial reports are promising." Challix looked on the verge of smiling again. "Say what you will, but it would appear marrying Everys was a smart tactical move, Your Strength."

Paine glared at Challix in an obvious attempt to silence her. But Narius winced, Everys's angry words echoing in his ears. *You need me a lot more than I need you.* It was true. If she walked out on him, the same way Viara had, his reign would be over. Istragon would see to that, and he would likely have those traditionalists at his back.

Narius nodded. "Paine, I am in need of your advice."

"Oh? And what would that be?"

"We have to come up with a good apology."

18

Maybe she should have taken Redtale up on the offer to get out of her room. Everys knew her quarters were huge by anyone's standards, but she felt like the walls were constricting around her. If she stayed there, they would squeeze the life out of her. By lunch, Everys retreated to her bedroom and flopped down, staring at the ceiling. At least she wouldn't see the walls coming this way.

Someone knocked at the door, and Trule popped her head inside. Her scales had paled, and she stammered, "Blessed, can you come out here please?"

Everys frowned. Why did the maid look so flustered? She snared a robe and pulled it on, tying a quick knot. When she stepped into the other room, she was glad she did.

Quartus stood in the living room area.

Her mouth immediately went dry. He wore loose-fitting pants and a shirt that was open at the neck, exposing his broad, muscled chest. His hair was tousled, as if he hadn't combed it. His eyes lit up at the sight of her, and his brilliant smile nearly blinded her.

"I'm sorry to intrude," he said.

Everys caught herself staring at his chest and forced her gaze to his face. He was here. *In her room.* Adolescent Everys would likely have been turning cartwheels in excitement, but now her legs felt like they had been locked in place.

"I knew the guards would get you to safety yesterday. But I wanted to see for myself that you were fine." He took a step closer to her. "You are fine, yes?"

No, not at all. Heat poured through her, from her cheeks into her chest then radiating out to her arms. Those waves of heat were chased by needles of ice that danced across her skin. Everys glanced around and realized that Trule and the other girls had vanished. Just her and Quartus... alone.

"Can I help you?" Without intending it, her voice shifted into shop-keeper mode.

He chuckled, low and throaty. "Only by telling me if you're all right."

She shrugged. "As well as can be expected, I suppose."

"Very good. Then I will—"

Trule scurried back into the room. Her eyes were huge, and she looked on the verge of fainting. Everys frowned. Maybe the girl had a medical condition. She always looked like she was ready to collapse.

But then Narius strode into the room, and Everys understood why the serving girl looked so flustered.

Narius's expression was calm when he walked in, but when he saw Quartus, his features soured. A crease grew between his brows as his gaze skipped between Everys and his brother and back again.

"Good morning, brother! Come to check on your bride as well?" Quartus's tone was light and breezy.

"What are you doing here, *brother?*" Narius practically spit the last word.

"Just trying to be solicitous, that's all."

Fire ignited in Narius's eyes, but he didn't say anything.

Quartus's smirk returned. He stepped over to Everys, snatched her hand, and kissed the back of it. "I'll leave you now, I'm sure you both have much to discuss."

With that, he slipped out of the room. Trule squeaked an apology—at least, that's what it sounded like—then retreated from the room.

Narius watched Quartus's departure, then he turned back to Everys. Questions warred across his features, and Everys could tell he was debating asking them. She glared at him, silently daring him to do so. She was ready for the next round.

But Narius sighed and he seemed to deflate. He held up his hands, as if to block her next words. "I didn't come here to fight. Instead, I have a proposal."

She laughed, a mirthless bark. "The proposal should have come before the wedding, don't you think?"

He blinked, then chuckled. "I suppose it should have, yes."

Everys's next retort died in her mouth. Narius had changed. In that instant, when he'd laughed, his expression had softened. He wasn't the hard-faced warrior, ready for a battle. Instead, he looked—open? Vulnerable? No, that wasn't quite it. She couldn't quite explain it, but in that instant, his features had changed into something that gave her pause.

"Regardless, I hope we can talk." He motioned toward a couch. "Please."

Everys considered it. Narius's tone was more respectful than it had been the night before. He seemed genuine enough. Crossing over to the couch, she sat down and adjusted her robe.

He sat down opposite her, a respectable distance between them. He cleared his throat, looking around the room, before finally risking a glance in her direction. He looked shy, almost painfully so.

"For what it's worth, I am sorry about what I said last night."

"Which part?" she asked.

His face reddened ever so slightly. "Most of it, actually. I kept replaying it in my mind, and I realized you are correct. I do need you more than you need me. And I have treated you horribly. Certainly not the way you deserve to be treated. You are queen, after all."

Everys smiled thinly. "And before that, I was still a person, wasn't I?"

"Of course you were!" he snapped, then sighed. "I don't want to start this again. Instead, I would hope you could be convinced to stay. At least for a little while longer."

"And why would I do that?"

"To help your people." Narius rose, clasping his hands behind his back. He looked every inch a commanding officer delivering a briefing. "I understand your desire to help Fair Havens. I too feel that it is horrible so many of my citizens live in poverty so close to my palace. It is not right or just."

"And yet the situation persists," Everys said.

"And admittedly, none of my predecessors have done much to correct the situation." He continued talking as if she hadn't said anything. "To my great shame, neither have I. But to your credit, in your first week with the crown, you at least attempted a solution. I... commend you for that."

Did he just choke on his own words? She was tempted to point it out, but she saw how serious his expression was and decided not to risk it.

"So I propose a deal." He turned to give her his full attention. "I have significantly more discretionary funds at my disposal. Like you, I'm expected to spend it on frivolous things like attire, decorations, and other luxuries. I have spent very little of it, and the amount has been accruing."

After seeing his quarters, she believed him.

"If you would be willing to stay here in the palace as my..." He frowned, as if searching for the right word. "...spouse, I would pool my resources with yours to continue your efforts. I believe we can have a lasting impact."

Everys narrowed her eyes as she studied him. Just the night before, he had lectured her on how improper it would be to do just that sort of thing. "What's the catch?"

"Excuse me?"

"Last night, there was no way you would have ever agreed to this. Now you're suggesting it? Why the change?"

Narius mouthed a few words then sighed and sat down on a chair opposite her. "Can I be honest with you?"

She laughed. "If you can't be honest with your spouse, who can you be honest with?"

He actually smiled at her. "I must admit, I don't have a lot of experience with that." He took a deep breath. "I face a lot of pressure in my position, and—"

"No."

He blinked at her. "Excuse me?"

She was just as surprised as he was. The word had slipped out without her intending to speak. But she leaned forward. "You sound like you're talking to the press. That's not honesty. That's carefully worded stock answers. Be honest."

He met her gaze and nodded once. "My life is spinning out of control. Things were bad enough when Viara left. I'm... I'm not sure I'd be able to hold on to my throne if another wife left me."

Everys stared at him, surprised. Once again, Narius's demeanor had changed. Gone was the stiff, formal soldier, ready to do battle. Instead, he was a young man, worried, maybe even scared. Vulnerable.

As much as she hated to admit it, she felt sorry for him.

"But it's not just my personal life. There's been increased... friction between the Dynasty and the Dalark Imperium lately. The tension could escalate into a full-scale war."

"That's not what you want?" Everys asked.

He glared at her. "Of course not!"

She held up her hands. "Sorry. But you're supposed to be the embodiment of the Perfected Warrior. Isn't that what warriors do?"

He nodded reluctantly. "I suppose so. My father would have. And that's what Brencis wants too."

"But you don't?"

He shook his head. "The Dynasty grew by conquest. War made us who we are. But there comes a time when you've conquered more than you can control. I fear we may have reached that point in the Dynasty and possibly even passed it. A war with Dalark may capture their Beachhead, but I fear that will be a short-term gain leading to a larger defeat."

She almost called him on using stock answers again, but she realized that he was still being honest.

"Hence my offer. Things are barely in balance now. I worry that, if you were to leave me, that would be the tipping point. And no one would fare well if that were to happen."

That wasn't entirely true. The nobility would likely do okay. Those with wealth and influence usually did. The people who would be hit hardest would be the folks like her, those trapped in the slums of Bastion and the Dynasty's other cities.

"That's why I'm asking you to please stay." He was practically whispering. "You have no reason to, and quite frankly, I wouldn't blame you if you didn't. And I won't try to persuade you by talking about doing it 'for the good of the Dynasty' or anything like that. Just... please. Stay."

She frowned. She shouldn't. There was no reason to.

And yet...

She nodded. "All right. I will."

He smiled, a genuine smile of relief that lit up his features. Everys sucked in a surprised breath. Quartus may have been gorgeous, but in that moment, Narius wasn't all that bad either. She winced at the thought. The last thing she wanted to do was find her husband good looking.

"Very good," Narius said. "I'll have Paine start drawing up some plans that we can go over when I get back."

"Get back?" she asked. "From where?"

Narius rose. "A base along the Demilitarized Zone. There was an unfortunate accident there recently. Brencis thinks it'll be a morale booster if I go there."

"Do you want me to come with you?"

He gaped at her, and she couldn't blame him. What was her problem? She seemed to talk first and think later. But even as she wanted to curl up and die for saying it, she kept on talking.

"I mean, if one royal is a morale boost, think what two would do. And it'd probably be good if the two of us were seen in public, wouldn't it? There are going to be people who think you're mad at me after what happened in Fair Havens, and this would show them that everything is okay. Well, not okay, but—"

Shut up, Everys. She clamped her mouth shut.

Much to her surprise, he nodded. "I would appreciate the company. We leave tomorrow morning at the beginning of Second Watch."

"I'll be ready."

He nodded again, a gesture that almost looked like a salute.

"And thank you, Everys. I appreciate your help. With all of this."

Then he was gone, his words hanging in the air.

Everys let out a long, stuttering breath. Then she stood up. "Trule, get back in here! I need your help!"

If she was going to go to a warzone, she wanted to at least look the part.

19

Redtale was not happy when she learned of Everys's travel plans. "No queen has ever gone to an active military base. Especially not one in the Demilitarized Zone," she said.

Everys examined herself in the mirror. Trule had found a great outfit for her, a pants and tunic combination that was a simple tan color. But there was brilliant blue piping along the legs and arms to make her stand out. Trule had assured her the clothing represented the most recent fashions out of Ksann, wherever that was. Everys thought it was perfect. No frills, but still regal.

"Besides," Redtale continued. "I couldn't make the proper arrangements for your security. The only guard from your detail going is Kevtho, and he won't be enough."

"Redtale, the king's own guard have arranged the security. If they're allowing him to go, it must be safe."

Redtale shook her head. "Not the same thing, Blessed. The king served in the military. He'll know what to do if the situation becomes dangerous. You won't. Plus, if Dalark learns you're both across the border, they're liable to get frisky."

Everys considered the back of the outfit. The tailor had stitched a pattern across her shoulders that resembled camouflage but didn't cause the material to bunch up. "I'll be fine."

Redtale grunted. "If Matron Halis were here, she'd make you see reason."

Everys frowned. "Any word on where she went?"

She shook her head. "We know she went to the Bastion airhub and boarded a skimmer for Olecc. Her family lives there. We have footage of her leaving the Olecc hub, but then she disappeared. Local constables have been turning Olecc upside down but haven't found a trace of her."

Trule sniffled from her perch by the mirror. Everys couldn't blame her. Since Halis disappeared, Trule had stepped in to do Halis's work as well as her own. The girl was doing fine, but it was a lot of responsibility for someone so young.

"Did we find out who was sick?"

"That's the thing. Mother's fine. Father too. And they both claim that they hadn't spoken with Halis for a month."

Now that was troubling. If that were true, why did Halis leave the palace at all? Everys's stomach twisted.

Redtale must have read the worry on her face. "We're doing our best to track her down."

The door to her quarters banged open, and a squad of guardsmen marched in. Unlike Redtale and her troops, these guards wore patches marking them as part of Narius's detail. Their leader gave Everys a cursory examination, then sneered.

"She's not ready yet?" His voice was harsh with a northern highlands accent. "Expected better of you, Redtale."

Redtale bristled. "I wouldn't be too worried, Zar. My lady's a lot tougher than some of the ones in your squad."

Everys froze. Why would Redtale say something so nasty to her fellow guards? Her gaze darted to the king's guards and braced herself.

Much to her surprise, their leader just guffawed and shook his head. Then he turned to her.

"Skimmer leaves in an hour, Blessed. And don't worry. You'll be in good hands." Zar gave Redtale a pointed look. "Unlike now."

With that, Zar left, followed by his men.

"Friend of yours?" Everys asked.

Redtale chuckled. "Not especially. There's always been something of a friendly rivalry between the queen's and king's guards. They yank our horns, we drop a rock on their heads, that sort of thing."

Everys's eyes widened. Were those Ixactl idioms? She hoped so. She didn't want to dodge any falling rocks.

"Now if you'll excuse me, Blessed, I'm going to give the skimmer a once-over before you leave. Not because Zar didn't do it right, but to make him think that I think he didn't."

She strode out of the room. Everys let out a shuddering breath and turned back to the mirror. One hour. One more hour before she would head for a warzone.

One more hour before she'd be that much closer to her ancestral home.

Eventually, Redtale led her to the landing field behind the palace. A large cloud skimmer sat on the tarmac, and soldiers milled around the skimmer. Then one of the soldiers turned, and Everys realized it was Narius. He wore a simple uniform, one without rank, but with a small cluster of ribbons on his right shoulder. Wearing that uniform transformed him. He wasn't the same man she married. This wasn't the angry man who confronted her in his bedroom. This wasn't even the apologetic man she spoke with the day before.

This was the Dynasty's king.

She actually slowed down enough that Redtale had to nudge her from behind. "Military doesn't like it when royals make them tardy."

Everys nodded absently, still studying her husband. This couldn't possibly be the same man. Instead of appearing aloof, he was stoic, the calm in the storm, the bedrock upon which the Dynasty would stand or fall. In that moment, she understood how he had been able to hold on to power in spite of his youth. This was not a man to trifle with.

She shook her head, trying to clear it. Inkstains, what was wrong with her?

Then Narius's gaze met hers and her mind locked up. Those golden eyes swept over her from head to toe, like a military officer inspecting a soldier. And as much as it annoyed her, she found herself hoping he'd approve.

He must have. A faint smile flickered across his lips, but he nodded once, curtly. The approval of a commanding officer.

She strode up to him and offered a smile of her own. "Husband."

His head jerked back as if she had slapped him. Then his smile reappeared, sticking around a bit longer. "Wife." Amusement bled through his tone. "Are you ready to go?"

"Whenever you are."

He motioned for her to go first. She strode up the ramp into the back of the skimmer. The room—was that the right term? She was going to have to do some studying if she didn't want to sound stupid—was mostly empty, with seats along both walls. Rows of hooks hung down the center of the ceiling. The interior was a uniform white with black highlights.

Narius stepped up beside her. "This way."

He led her deeper into the transport and through an open door. Zar and two of the king's guards waited on the other side. They snapped to attention, saluting Narius as he passed.

The room they entered looked like it belonged back in the palace. There was a cushy-looking couch along one wall, a vidscreen opposite that. A small desk with a data terminal was tucked in one corner, and two doors led to a tiny bathroom and a kitchenette.

Narius slid behind the desk. "Feel free to watch whatever you want on the vid."

"How long will it take?" Everys asked.

"Zar?" Narius asked.

Zar cleared his throat. "Current estimates suggest a three-hour flight, sir."

Everys started around the desk. "Is there anything I can help you with?"

Narius turned in his chair, blocking her view of the terminal. "No, nothing important. Thank you, though."

Even though he had blocked her vision, she had still caught a glimpse of the seal for the Constabulary of Bastion. Official reports about the riot in Fair Havens? Apparently he wasn't in a mood to share. At least, not right now. So, she went back and sat down on the couch.

A few moments later, the skimmer shuddered. She started and braced herself, her eyes wide.

"Are you okay?" Narius asked.

She scrunched up her face. She didn't want to admit it, but... "I've never flown before."

Narius's smile grew warm, and it looked like he almost laughed. "Nothing to worry about. Our pilot has logged hundreds of successful flights."

"That may be, but I've logged significantly fewer," Everys replied. Her fingers dug into the couch as the room tipped, threatening to throw her against the far wall.

Much to her horror, Narius got up and came around the desk. The slanting floor didn't seem to bother him, and he sat down next to her.

"It's going to be fine. Why don't we find something to watch together?" He activated the vidscreen.

"Don't you have work?"

He shrugged. "Nothing that can't keep. What are you in the mood for? Comedy? Action?" He smirked at her. "Or are you a closet romantic?"

She snorted. "Not exactly."

"Didn't think so." He settled on a drama program, something she had heard customers in her shop talk about from time to time. "Will this do?"

She nodded and forced her focus on the images that played out on the vid. Anything to forget the way the room lurched and bucked. Anything to distract her from the man who sat dangerously close to her.

20

S omeone jostled her shoulder. "Everys?"

She winced and opened her eyes. Narius stood over her.

Bolting upright, she almost collided with his head. "What's going on?"

"You fell asleep an hour ago," he said. "I didn't want to disturb you."

She fell asleep? She looked around the cabin. Two of Zar's men stood at attention near the entrance. The vid still played episodes of that drama. No wonder she had fallen asleep.

Then Narius took her hand and gave it a gentle squeeze. The sudden contact shocked her. She looked down at their joined hands, then up at him. A smile shone in his eyes.

"Sorry. The landing is usually worse than the takeoff. Thought you might want someone to hang on to."

She pulled her hand free. "Thanks, but I'm fine."

If he was offended by her action, he didn't let on. Everys rubbed her hand absently, wondering if—

Then the cabin seemed to drop out of the sky. Her stomach lurched, and she bit back a scream. Maybe she should have held on after all.

Narius chuckled. "It's all right. I felt the same way the first time I flew to the front."

A bone-jarring thump shook the entire skimmer. Everys worried she was going to be tossed out of the couch, but somehow, she wasn't.

"What was that about?" she asked.

"Standard procedure, I'm afraid," Narius said. "The Dalark have missile batteries pointed in our direction, so our skimmers have to drop for the dirt the moment we approach the base to avoid getting shot down."

"Has that ever happened?"

"Not in... what, twenty years?" If he was asking someone, no one answered. Narius shrugged. "But on the off chance it would happen, the military keeps the old procedures in place. Institutional inertia is extremely difficult to overcome."

A few minutes later, the skimmer jerked to a halt. The guards stepped out of the office, and Narius rose, straightening his uniform.

"A few words of caution," he said. "While many people think we're at peace with Dalark, technically, it's only a ceasefire. We are technically still at war with Dalark, so this is an active military base. Stick close to the guards and do what they say."

That didn't do much to untwist the knot growing within her. Narius held out a hand and smiled warmly. "Don't worry. We'll be fine."

She recognized the promise in his words and, much to her surprise, realized he meant it. Even more surprising, she believed him. This time, she gratefully took his hand and allowed him to escort her out of the cabin.

The soldiers waiting in the back of the skimmer snapped to attention as they passed. Narius let go of Everys long enough to salute, then tucked her arm back into his. They strode down the ramp.

A clutch of military officers waited for them. One of them stepped forward and nodded curtly to them.

"King Narius, good to see you. Queen Everys, my name is Viscount Orsin. Welcome to Firebase Forward Two-Seven. If you'd follow me, please?"

Everys studied the man. He was Hinaen, but that didn't surprise her. It was hard for non-Hinaens to rise to command posts. The Dynasty did have its "institutional inertia," as Narius put it. The viscount was older, most likely close to retirement, but still fit. He had the look of a fighter, not a strategist, someone who wouldn't object to rolling up his sleeves and brawling if he had to. Orsin smiled, but it didn't reach his eyes, and he motioned for them to follow.

"What's the situation presently, Viscount?" Narius asked.

Orsin launched into a report, one punctuated with additions from the other officers. Everys lost track quickly. Too much military jargon delivered at too high a speed. So she took the time to examine the base.

There wasn't much to see. A row of military vehicles were parked to her right, a cluster of buildings to her left. The perimeter was surrounded by a high fence and beyond that...

Everys's breath hitched. The Demilitarized Zone. Or, as her people knew it, home.

She stared at the forests beyond the fence, thick vegetation as far as her eye could see. Just centuries earlier, that land had been the heart of the Siporan Ascendancy. She knew the old maps well enough. From this base, they should have been able to see the spires of Ylida, the easternmost fortress city. Tribute from the Xoniel and other kingdoms flowed through Ylida to Nekek the Bright. She could almost imagine the gilt buildings and sparkling towers rising over the trees, but it was just a figment of her imagination.

She hoped she was also imagining the way fire seemed to pulse through her veins. The old-timers at conclave told of how a toratropic mage's strength grew the closer they came to the homeland. She had always assumed such stories were legends, but standing here, closer to their shattered home than she had ever been, she couldn't deny the way that—

"My queen? Are you all right?"

Everys blinked and turned to Narius. Everyone stared at her, questions on their faces. Inkstains, had she completely focused on that distant wilderness?

She forced a smile and nodded to Narius. "Quite all right. I apologize. This is..." What was a good excuse? "...the first time that I've ever been outside Bastion."

He studied her face, his golden eyes narrow, then he patted the back of her hand. She had no idea if he actually believed her, but at least he wasn't going to make an issue of it.

The assembled officers led them toward the buildings at one end of the compound. The soldiers, a mix of the Dynasty's races, trotting through the base gave their group a wide berth. Everys chuckled under her breath. What must they be thinking, seeing this many officers and royalty among them? She tried smiling at some of them, but they ignored her.

Eventually they stepped into a building marked as the infirmary, one large room filled with orderly rows of cots. Most of them were empty, thankfully, but there were half a dozen soldiers clustered together. No, wait. She frowned. There was another soldier in the infirmary, halfway across the room from the others.

"So what happened?" Narius asked.

She glanced at him, surprised. Shouldn't he know this already?

One of the officers stepped forward anyway. "As you know, sir, according to our cease fire arrangement with Dalark, we take it in turns to patrol the Zone."

Narius nodded sagely. "I remember those patrols quite well, yes."

Everys resisted the urge to gape at him. He had been within the Zone? He had been closer to her homeland than she ever had been.

"Vanguard Harset was on lead when he got separated from his unit. He believed he heard movement in the woods behind him," one of the officers said.

Ice gripped Everys's heart. Movement in the Zone? Had they seen someone? Had someone not been careful enough?

"He claims he called for identification but received no answer. When he repeated the demand, something rushed him, so he opened fire. In the confusion, several soldiers were injured. Once the squad overseer regained control, he called in a med evac."

"Did he hit whatever rushed him?" Everys was surprised she was able to keep her voice so calm.

Viscount Orsin shook his head. "No, Blessed. There wasn't anything there."

Everys swallowed her relief. Hopefully that was true. But she couldn't keep asking questions. They'd get suspicious.

Narius surveyed the room. His expression twisted into a scowl. "I'm afraid there's one part of this I don't understand. Was Vanguard Harset hit in the firefight?"

The officers hesitated, just for a fraction of a moment, but Everys noticed. Then one of them cleared her throat and said, "Uh, no, Your Strength. He was not."

"Then why is he in the infirmary as well?" Narius asked.

That same officer cleared her throat again. "The night after the incident occurred, several of Vanguard Harset's compatriots... expressed their displeasure."

Narius's eyebrows rose. "Physically?"

"Unfortunately."

Everys took a step closer to the injured soldier. Harset was young and, much to her surprise, Plissk. His sallow, scaly skin and dusky hair, along with his sharp angular features and reptilian eyes, clearly marked his heritage. It also made the large bruises across his face all the more visible. Harset took one look at her, then turned away, shame painted across his face.

"And were his attackers punished?" Narius continued.

"Ah, no, Your Strength."

Narius turned to the officers. "Why not?"

"Because... ah, because there were no witnesses to the incident."

"I see." Narius's tone was cold enough to flash freeze the room. "Get out."

"Your Strength?"

"You heard me. All of you. I wish to speak to the squad. Then call a general assembly of the troops. Immediately. No exceptions."

The officers bolted, rushing out of the room. So did most of the medical personnel, although a few nurses stayed behind to monitor their patients. Narius waited before stepping forward. He looked at the rest of Harset's squad, tucking his hands behind his back.

"Before I say anything else, I have to know: how many of you have gone on patrol through the Zone before?"

Most of the squad raised their hands.

"Do you remember what it was like? The shadows? The way the history of the region grew heavier with every step you took? The feeling that, at any moment, you could stumble into a toratropic snare or some other arcane trap?"

Everys bristled at the last question, but those who had raised their hands nodded, their faces grim.

"I assume that, for the rest of you, this patrol was your first time in the Zone as well?"

Those soldiers nodded. One of them spoke up. "I won't lie to you, Your Strength. I was just as jumpy as Harset. If I hadn't been hit, I likely would have opened fire too."

"I thank you for your honesty, soldier." Narius took a step closer to Harset. "The rest of you. I assume you understand what happened was an accident, yes?"

The other soldiers all nodded, although a few of them didn't look happy having to admit it.

"I want to tell you all a story, if I may. Seven years ago, shortly before my father's death, I served in the military. My father offered me any assignment I wanted. I think he assumed that I would seek out the safest, most comfortable posting. Instead, I came out here. Not this base, mind you, but one like it.

"And I remember what it was like, that first night in the Zone. I was sure I saw ancient horrors lurking in every shadow. Convinced that at some point, scri... Siporan mages would come out and carve their runes into me." He offered Everys a weak smile. "No offense, my queen."

She was still so shocked at his story that she didn't realize she should have been insulted until after he started speaking again.

"And that first night, I wound up firing my weapon too."

That got Harset's attention. The rest of his squad's too. "You, Your Strength?" one of them asked.

He nodded with a rueful smile. "I thought for sure I saw someone and, just like Harset, called for identification. When they didn't answer, I opened fire."

"Did anyone get hurt?" Harset's voice was surprisingly high pitched.

Narius shook his head. "Chaos must have been sleeping. It turned out to be a chakrut."

Everys snorted. She had heard of chakruts. In the ancient texts, they were depicted as nuisances, chattering little furballs that got underfoot more than anything else.

The soldiers looked horrified, but Narius laughed as well. "No, it's all right. It is funny. My squad thought so too. Turns out I had managed to shoot the chakrut right between the eyes. Once we returned from patrol, dead chakruts turned up in my bunk, in my boots, just about everywhere. They wouldn't let me forget."

The other soldiers chuckled as well.

"But there was one thing that my squad did that I appreciated most of all: they understood I made a mistake. Now, in my case, no one was injured, and I suppose that made things easier. But you are all soldiers of the Dynasty, part of the larger whole. When one of you suffers, you all suffer with him, yes?"

The soldiers nodded.

"Vanguard Harset caused your suffering, and I know he suffers with you. Why are you excluding his suffering from yours?"

No one had an answer for him.

"Now I cannot order you to do this, for no one can control another's spirit, but I would suggest that, as soldiers of the Dynasty, you work together from here on out. Or do I have to start stuffing chakruts into your bunks?"

As the soldiers laughed, Narius crossed over to Harset and sat next to him. He patted the wounded Plissk on the shoulder. "I know you've faced difficulty fitting in here. Not many of your people enlist in the military. I appreciate your service, and I'm sorry that this happened. Take heart in the fact that none of your squad were killed. You made a mistake, and I have no doubt that you will make a fine soldier for the Dynasty."

Harset sat up in his bunk a little straighter and nodded gravely. "Thank you, Your Strength."

Narius patted Harset on the shoulder again, then moved on, stopping by each bunk to share a quiet, personal conversation with the soldiers. Everys watched him, surprised at the growing respect that welled up within her. This was no act. He looked more relaxed here than any of the other times she had seen him.

But then the door to the ward banged open and an officer stepped inside. "The company is assembled and waiting for you, Your Strength."

Narius nodded curtly. He faced the wounded soldiers and offered another smile. "Continue to heal, soldiers. Your Dynasty needs you."

Those that could offered salutes. Narius nodded to Harset one more time, then turned toward the door. As he did, his features hardened into a grim mask. He once again looked every inch a king.

"Shall we, my queen?"

While he may have phrased it like a question, Everys knew it wasn't. She took his arm. As she walked, she couldn't help but wonder: who was her husband really?

21

Heat slapped Narius in the face as he stepped outside. His blood burned at the thought of the wounded Harset. He knew the military had their traditions. But to beat a fellow soldier until he wound up in the infirmary? And for the commanding officers to act like it was normal? No. Not in his Dynasty.

He surveyed the gathered troops. Most of the soldiers were human, although he spotted three Ixactl and, much to his surprise, a Weyfir. Why one of the coast-dwellers would enlist in the army and not the navy was beyond him. He held up a hand. The buzzing whispers died almost immediately.

"Before my arrival, I reviewed reports concerning the recent 'incident' in the Zone," Narius said. "But as we know, an after-action report rarely conveys the complete truth."

That observation earned him a few muted smiles.

"And now that I have uncovered the truth, I must share how disappointed I am."

Several of the lower ranked soldiers visibly flinched, and he thought he heard a few of the officers suck in sharp breaths.

"What did I learn? No Dalark incursion, just a scared recruit making a mistake. Soldiers who decided to 'discipline' said recruit. And no one has tried to find the culprits." Narius frowned. "And that causes me grave concern. Is this how soldiers behave? Is this the Perfected Warrior's honor on display? I am sorely tempted to reset all of your progress toward becoming citizens."

This time, the soldiers struggled to hide their reactions. Anger mixed with shock rippled through the crowd. Good. Let them stew. For most of them, military service was their only path to citizenship. But now he had their attention.

He tucked his hands behind his back and glared down at the soldiers. "I suggest the persons responsible for beating Vanguard Harset step forward for appropriate punishment. If I learn that no one has done so by this time tomorrow, I will void the progress of every soldier serving in this base toward citizenship." He fixed his attention on the officers. "*Every* soldier."

An angrier, louder rumble rippled through the crowd. Narius stood up straighter. "Do you think I'm being unfair?"

Much to his surprise, some of the enlisted soldiers actually nodded.

"Would your kin back home be proud of your behavior? Beating a vanguard for making a mistake. How brave!" He swept his gaze over the assembled troops one last time. "We expect better of you. *I* expect better of you. Prove that you belong here. Prove that you belong in the Dynasty. Prove your honor. Dismissed."

The troops didn't look happy, but they filtered away from the infirmary. Narius fought to keep from smiling. Not too bad, if he had to judge. His father might have even approved of his performance. Maybe. Father could strip the hide off a recalcitrant soldier at a hundred paces with only a glance. Narius didn't quite have the gravitas yet, but maybe within a few years.

"That's it?" a voice asked. "That's what you came here to do? Demoralize the troops?"

Narius turned. Viscount Orsin glared at him, and his subordinates shied away from him.

"Viscount?" He forced himself to keep his tone civil.

"You dare talk about honor? You dare talk about duty? You, who are slowly stripping our military of the funds we need?" Orsin stabbed a finger at the Zone. "Beyond that wilderness lies the Dalark Beachhead, and they would like nothing more than to overrun this position and devour our territory. And you're doing nothing to prepare for it. Worse, you weaken our military and insult our troops!"

Heat painted Narius's cheeks. His gaze twitched toward one of his guards. Jarha, his swordbound. All he had to do was say the word, and Jarha would hand him his ceremonial blade. A formal challenge to a duel might be enough to get Orsin to back down. After all, Narius was decades younger, clearly in better physical shape, and had spent years training for duels. This would resolve the issue decisively. His palm itched at the idea of having his sword in hand, teaching the viscount some respect.

But no, that wasn't the direction he wanted to take the Dynasty. Besides, he understood Orsin's frustration. Falling Sword wasn't ready yet; revealing details of his new plans for the Dynasty's future wouldn't be prudent. He forced his fingers to unclench.

Apparently Orsin considered Narius's silence permission to continue. "Your father would be ashamed of you! When he died, the Dynasty was strong. It was feared by Dalark and all the lesser nations. But now, in just a few short years, you have brought us to the brink of ruin."

"I hardly think that's true. Our economy is the strongest it's ever been. Our borders are secure—thanks in no small part to your own efforts." The compliment almost stuck in Narius's throat, but he had to try to placate the belligerent officer. "And—"

"That's not what I'm talking about! How do you explain that?"

He pointed, and at first, Narius thought he was pointing at Jarha. Had the swordbound drawn the weapon already? But no, Jarha was standing just behind him on his right and the viscount was pointing to his left.

At Everys. Her eyes were wide with surprise, and her mouth popped open.

Narius whirled on the viscount. "You go too far, Orsin."

Orsin laughed. "I could say the same for you. To marry one of *them*. To make her your queen. To... to take her into your bed! Have you no pride? No understanding of history?" He jabbed a finger toward the Zone. "Don't you remember what once stood out there? Their precious Ascendancy! The Dynasty has bled to ensure that the Siporans can never rise again. And yet you married one! How can we trust someone who has clearly been bewitched by this scribbler?"

That last question was directed more to the gathered crowd of officers. Narius spluttered, unsure of how to answer. For a moment, he considered telling the viscount that he hadn't actually taken Everys to bed yet, but he doubted that would make things any better. And while the viscount was being insubordinate, from the looks on his officers' faces, it was clear that they agreed with him.

But Everys brushed past him. It took him a moment to realize that she was headed straight for Orsin.

"Kevtho?" she said, her voice cool. "Draw your sword, please."

Silence fell across the gathered officers, which made the gentle sigh of metal brushing against metal all the more noticeable. Everys's swordbound stepped forward, his weapon at the ready, his expression grim. Everys stared down at Orsin, who had gone pale.

"What's the matter, Viscount?" she asked. "Don't you have your sword ready? Maybe one of your subordinates will loan you theirs."

Orsin stammered, his eyes wide. "M-my queen, I am not... that is to say, if you demand this, I will fight, but there's no need to—"

"No need? You call me a scribbler. You accuse me of using witchcraft to seduce the king. And you behave shamefully in front of your officers. You're lucky I'm the one challenging you to a duel. I would think Narius would have every right to demand satisfaction, yes?"

The viscount still wouldn't meet her gaze. Even Narius was tempted to take a step back. He could practically feel the fury radiating off Everys.

"What's the matter, Viscount? Not so bold now? Aren't you so brave, strutting around in the ashes of my people," Everys snapped. "So brave, watching over ruins and wreckage. If you're so keen on your history, let me ask you: in the centuries since the Ascendancy fell, have the Siporans ever rebelled against the Dynasty?"

Orsin glared at her, but he shook his head. "That's probably not for lack of trying."

"Really? That's what you're resorting to? Hypothetical rebellions? You'd think that sorcerers—no, I'm sorry, *scribblers*—would have come up with *something* in the past four hundred years." She walked a circle around him. "So what is the Dynasty spending all those blades on? Keeping the ghosts of my people in check? Glaring at our former allies across an uncontrolled wilderness? Maybe that's why you're so frightened. If my husband continues to defund you, people will realize what a bloated mess the military actually is, how useless it is. That's certainly the impression I'm getting."

Orsin stiffened and whirled on her. "How dare—"

And then Kevtho was there, his sword against the viscount's neck. Orsin froze. Everyone did.

"Ready for the duel now, are we?" Everys whispered.

Orsin's mouth moved, as if he were chewing on his words. Then he looked down, his face bright red, but he shook his head. "No."

She glared at him, then turned her attention to Narius. He sucked in a breath. She was radiant. Her eyes were alight, passion burning within them. And she had been transformed by the fire.

"Am I allowed to void someone's citizenship?" she asked.

Narius's mouth had gone dry, and he couldn't quite comprehend what she had asked. But then the words sunk in. He shook his head. "No."

"Pity." She turned back to Orsin. "You'd best hope my husband has that for you, Viscount, because I promise you that every day, every morning, every evening, every time I draw breath in his presence, it will be to suggest that he not only void your citizenship, but that he demote you so far it'll take you four hundred years to even start dreaming of earning your rank again."

With that, she turned and offered Narius a sweet smile. "I think I've seen enough. Have you, husband?"

Narius shook himself out of his reverie. "I agree. Shall we return to Bastion?"

She nodded and took his offered arm. "I can't wait to get out of here."

Neither could he. But as they walked back to the skimmer, he couldn't help but wonder: who had he married after all? He hadn't expected that. He knew that, had he been able to marry Innana, she would have never accompanied him to a military base, let alone threaten a military officer's citizenship. While he hadn't anticipated that Everys would do so either, he found himself impressed. And he had no idea how it made him feel.

22

Everys's nerves practically sang. So many thoughts! Standing up against that racist viscount, seeing those injured soldiers, and just being *there*, so close to what should have been home. So close to Papa and Mama and Galan, even if she didn't see them. It was all too much.

The skimmer bumped and shuddered as it came to a halt on the tarmac. As soon as it had come to a complete stop, Narius practically bounded out of his chair and headed for the exit.

But before he left, he turned to her. "Everys, I..." His cheeks flushed and his gaze dropped to the floor. Then he coughed and looked up at her. "Thank you for coming with me. That's... that's..."

Apparently that's all he had to say, for he turned and fled out of the cabin. She chuckled. How many people could say they had seen the king looking like a flustered schoolboy? It was almost cute.

Redtale squeezed through the cabin door. "You ready to head back to your quarters?"

She motioned ahead of her. "Lead the way."

Redtale hesitated. "Kevtho told me what happened. Did you really challenge Viscount Orsin to a duel?"

Everys nodded and then braced herself for a scolding.

Instead, Redtale regarded her with a thin smile, then snorted. "Wish I could have seen that. After you."

By the time Everys emerged from the skimmer, Narius had disappeared. She headed for the palace, going over a mental checklist as she walked. Now that they had returned, she'd have to corner Masruq again to see if she could find new funding for the outreach center. Then what? Maybe a report on the current situation in Fair Havens? Was the neighborhood under control? Would Challix be able to find out for her? Maybe she'd see if she could pull some reports from the local constables and see what they said. And then—

"And where are you off to in such a rush?"

Everys jumped, startled by the sudden question. She turned and found Quartus jogging after her, a lazy smile on his lips.

"I tried calling your name several times, but you didn't seem to hear me." He glared at Redtale. "I would have thought your guard would have told you."

Redtale sneered. "I figured she had more important matters to worry about."

Quartus bristled.

Everys quickly stepped between them. "It's all right. I'm sorry I didn't hear you. What can I help you with?"

His features softened, and he smiled again. "I heard you had gone to the Demilitarized Zone. I'm impressed. You are full of surprises, aren't you?"

He stepped closer to her, and she could smell his musky scent. It was nice, earthy and warm, enough to tease a bit of heat from her cheeks. "Well... you heard correctly. Now, if you'll excuse me, I have a lot to consider—"

"Ah, yes. Your grand plans to improve the lives of the Dynasty's people." His smile broadened. "You are certainly making quite the impact. I like that about you. And I'd also like to help."

"Y-you would?" Everys winced as her voice caught. Inkstains, get it together! Yes, the man was handsome, and the way he looked at her was enough to make her knees knock together, but she should be more composed than this!

"As a matter of fact, I have some ideas I'd like to share with you regarding your initiative."

Redtale cleared her throat.

Quartus's smile turned brittle, then relaxed again. "That is, if you don't have any other pressing matters to attend to right now."

Everys looked down in surprise. When had he taken her hand? His was strong yet soft, warmth enveloping her fingers. It felt good. It felt nice. It felt...

Inkstains, it felt *right!*

"No," she mumbled. "I don't have anything else right now."

His face lit up, practically shining with excitement. "Excellent. This will only take a moment."

He led her toward the palace, and Redtale fell into step after them.

Quartus paused, turning toward her guard. "Really, Redtale? We'll be in the palace. She's safe with me, I promise."

Redtale's mouth puckered into a scowl. She looked from the prince to Everys.

What could it hurt? "It's fine, Redtale. Really."

Redtale looked ready to argue, but didn't. Instead, she saluted, then tromped away, muttering under her breath the whole time.

Quartus set out again, leading her inside and through unfamiliar hallways. She chided herself for not knowing where they were. They were still within the private residence, she was sure of that much. Eventually, he popped open a door, pulling her inside.

The room beyond was small by the palace's standards but still overly large by anyone else's. They stood in a living room with pristine couches and an empty bar. An archway to her left led to a bedroom. It didn't appear as though anyone had occupied these rooms for a while. So where were they?

"Guest quarters for visiting family," Quartus explained. "When our cousins come in from the outer provinces, they have to stay somewhere."

"So why are we here?" Everys asked.

Quartus chuckled, a low, throaty sound, and rubbed the back of his neck. "Well... Sometimes I want to disappear. Get away from the prying eyes of servants and guards. So, every now and then, I'll get away from it all in one of these rooms."

"And you can really find privacy here?" Everys asked.

He nodded. "Absolutely. There are forty of them. It'd take them a while to search every single one of them."

She started and turned to look at him. Forty?

He laughed. "Royals are expected to have big families, and we've outgrown the ancient ways of dealing with unwanted relatives. So we have to find someplace to store them when they invade the palace."

Everys looked around the room again, trying to picture it. Forty rooms like this, sitting unoccupied most of the time? Heat flashed through her. Couldn't they find a way to use that space better? Somehow?

She shook her head. Not now. Focus. She turned to Quartus. "So what did you want to talk to me about?"

"Like I said, I want to help with your charity outreach project."

"You do?"

He nodded. "I meant what I said in Fair Havens. You are an amazing woman. What you did there was truly remarkable."

"Starting a riot?"

He brushed aside her words. "We always stumble as we learn to walk, yes? Keep attacking the problem, from new angles, and learn from your mistakes. That's what it means to be Xoniel, after all. Before long, you can conquer even the gods themselves." He favored her with another warm smile. "I have no doubt you could challenge even the Perfected Warrior himself."

She blushed at the compliment.

"That's why I want to help you," Quartus continued. "I've heard Narius has offered to help as well. He may be giving you funds, but I doubt he'll give you the time or attention you truly deserve. I'm willing to not only give you money, but something far greater as well: myself."

The breath hitched in her throat.

"Not to be immodest, of course, but I understand the way the Dynasty thinks. I can help you navigate the bureaucracy without getting entangled by it. I can rally my friends in the nobility. And I have a special relationship with the press. I can ally them to your cause. Why, within a few short weeks, you could be making a bigger impact than you ever dreamed, not just here in Bastion, but throughout the Dynasty's holdings."

That did sound nice. She hadn't thought of how to handle the bureaucracy or the press. And having nobles on her side would help. But... "What do you get out of this?"

He chuckled. "The satisfaction of knowing that I've made a difference. Knowing I helped my queen do what she knows is right. And just being with you, Everys."

Again, her breath stuttered in her throat. The way he said her name, like a whispered promise...

"I don't want you to think I'm doing this out of obligation." He stepped even closer to her. The heat from his body washed over her, chased by that delicious scent of musk. "I want to be your partner."

"M-my partner?"

He chuckled again, a low and throaty sound. "And maybe more than that."

In one fluid motion, he pulled her into a tight embrace and kissed her.

She couldn't breathe. Couldn't think. Couldn't process his lips pressing into hers, his hands pulling her against his chest. And then her body responded. Her arms snaked around his neck, her fingers tangling in his hair. And the taste of his lips, so full of promise and desire and heat and...

"It's a shame you're not wearing the lingerie I sent you," he murmured against her ear. "You would look radiant in it."

The lingerie he sent—

Her mind caught up with her body, and she realized what was happening. Yes, she wanted him. Smudges, she wanted him! He was handsome and charming, and she had daydreamed of an encounter like this when she was growing up. But he had sent her the lingerie? Not Narius? Her mind frantically replayed her wedding night. Trule hadn't said who'd sent the lingerie. Could it have been Quartus?

"Everys?" Quartus asked. "Darling, what's wrong?"

She looked at Quartus. He looked confused, but she could still see a predatory glint in his eyes.

"Why did you want me to go to Narius's quarters wearing that outfit?" Everys asked.

His face went blank, but then he smiled that flirtatious smile. "Oh, that. It was... kind of a joke, I guess."

A what? Her cheeks burned at the memory of being caught by Narius, of the rage in his golden eyes. "A joke?" She pulled herself free from his grasp.

"I knew neither of you were exactly happy about the situation, and so I... well, I thought it would be funny..."

"To strip me down and send me to your brother's bedroom?" Her voice was cold.

He squirmed under her scrutiny. Good. "Maybe it was in bad taste."

"Maybe?"

"But that was before I got to know you! Had I known what I know now, I would have never done it."

"And that makes it all right?"

He stammered, clearly unable to come up with a good answer. Not that she expected him to.

She looked around the room again, then noticed the way the light danced on the bedroom walls. She frowned and brushed past him. He called her name, but she ignored him.

Unlike the rest of the suite, the bedroom had obviously been occupied recently. Seven candles burned on a dresser, casting their flickering light through the room. And rather than the scent of neglect and disuse hanging in the air, the room smelled like flowers. And the bed...

Her eyes widened. A corner of the blankets had been pulled back, revealing satin sheets beneath.

She turned back to Quartus. He had planned this. Any desire for him snuffed out, extinguished in a burst that chilled her heart. How many times had he hidden out in these rooms? Had he been alone every time? Probably not.

"Everys?" His question was soft. For the first time, he looked uncertain.

"What kind of woman do you think I am?" she asked. "You would offer me some money, your friends, and then we'd just tumble into bed together?"

"No!" But his expression contradicted his denial. His smile faded, and he stumbled back a stcp.

In that moment, she saw the truth. He didn't take her seriously. Her fingers twitched, and she wished she had some ink. A quick rune, sketched near Quartus or better, on him, and he would learn. Oh, he would *learn* to respect her.

But no, that wouldn't help. Better to just leave rather than exact any sort of revenge, especially revenge that would reveal what she was. She marched out of the room, brushing past him while shooting a withering glare in his direction. She made it to the door.

"Everys, wait!"

She paused but didn't turn.

"For what it's worth, I wasn't trying to hurt anyone."

"Really? With that present? With what you've tried to do?"

Silence. "I wasn't trying to hurt you."

She wanted to laugh. From his perspective, he probably wasn't trying to hurt her, just use her as a weapon to humiliate his brother.

Sending her to Narius's room in lingerie. Flirting with her. Making people think that something was happening between them.

Everys turned back to him. "Stay away from me."

He nodded. "I will. I promise. I just... I just..." He gestured vaguely, then his shoulders slumped. "Don't tell Narius. Please. My problem isn't really with him. My life is a prison. I can never be my own person. In many ways, I'm just a prop for Narius's reign. An afterthought." He looked up at her, his eyes wide. "You can understand that, can't you?"

The question tugged at her heart and she almost wanted to comfort him. But she recognized it for what it was: A line. Another lie. Another attempt to use her. Smudges, how stupid did he think she was?

But at the same time, he did look genuine. And she did understand. The cage may have become more bearable, but it was still a cage. She couldn't really blame Quartus for feeling that way.

"All right," she said. "I should, but I won't. Just stay away from me."

He nodded, raising his hands in surrender. "I will. By the Sword, Shield, and the Warrior's entire armament, I promise to leave you alone."

And he meant it. She recognized that in an instant. With a nod, she slipped past him into the hall, hurrying away from the room. With any luck, she'd be able to leave all of this behind her.

23

"She really threatened to revoke the viscount's citizenship?" Paine's words dripped with skepticism.

Narius fought the smile that tugged at his lips. "She did indeed."

Paine paced along the edge of the Amber Office, but Narius didn't pay him much attention. He knew his friend well enough. Paine would spend the next several minutes parsing out the potential threats and advantages from that verbal clash. Within an hour, Paine would formulate a dozen strategies that would not only protect the throne, but gain Narius significant advantages with someone in the Dynasty, be it the military, the nobility, or the public. But it was best to let him walk through his process, spinning his thoughts.

While Paine mumbled to himself, Narius read through his incoming correspondence. Most of it was fairly routine: various reports from the ministers, invitations to parties and galas from members of the nobility, petitions from the Ethnarch Parliament and those they passed on from the Hall of All Voices. He would have to read through it all eventually, but he sifted through the virtual stack, looking to see if anything stood out from the rest.

And there it was. A short message, forwarded to him through a number of cutouts and false fronts: "From across the seas, the Bearer sees and weeps with you."

A thrill shot through him. Years earlier, Narius had Tormod set up a network of backchannel couriers so that, once in a great while, he and Innana could share messages with one another. They always used phrases and images from the other's mythology. She would speak of the Perfected Warrior and the Water Bearer. He would compare her to the spirits and potentates. This obscure line, taken from the Warrior's Meditations, was easy enough to decipher. Innana knew what he was going through and sympathized with him. Just knowing she hadn't forgotten him relieved some of the pressure. Hopefully, someday, he would finally find a way to marry the woman he truly loved.

As he thought about that glorious possibility, his terminal beeped softly. Another incoming message, this one from...

He groaned when he saw the sender's ID. "Clarinda Gaines," he muttered.

That stopped Paine midstride. "What about her?"

Narius scanned the message. "It's another invitation to TelleGlin's factory in Dropport so we can discuss our 'future relationship.'"

Paine snorted. "The woman remains incorrigible, I'll give her that."

That was one way of putting it. From the moment he met her, Narius had recognized Gaines for what she was: an inveterate ladder-climber. Oh, she was impressive. She had taken her family's company and turned it into a financial giant that loomed over the Dynasty's economy. But that hadn't been enough for her. She'd set her sights, first on the nobility, and then on the throne. The moment Viara left the palace, Gaines had made a nuisance of herself, sending invitations to dinner and what she probably thought were coy presents to entice him. But it hadn't worked. While Narius had wanted a willing partner, Gaines had been too eager, too hungry. It was off-putting. He wanted nothing more than for her to leave him alone.

But he couldn't, for one simple reason: he needed what TelleGlin could offer. Falling Sword depended on it. He knew he would have to speak to her eventually.

"Shall I send your usual regrets, Your Strength?" Paine asked.

Narius groaned and mopped a hand over his face. "No, we'd better not. It'd be rude to refuse her yet again. I just can't stomach the thought of spending any time with her."

Paine froze in place, and Narius could practically hear his mind tumbling through different calculations. Then a predatory glint shone in his vizier's eyes, and Paine took a careful step forward.

"Then may I suggest we take a middle path? One that will satisfy her desire to meet with a member of royalty and send her a clear message of your unavailability for her machinations?"

Narius frowned. "What do you have in mind?"

"Why am I going to this factory again?" Everys asked.

Challix twisted around to face her. "Because your husband asked you to represent him to Clarinda Gaines."

Well, if she was going to put it like that...

The buildings of Dropport crawled by. This neighborhood had been Bastion's port on the Melgor River until a team of military engineers rerouted the river. The neighborhood had decayed, the same way Fair Havens had, until a number of companies moved their facilities into the neighborhood, a move spearheaded by TelleGlin. At least, that's what Challix had told her during their morning briefing. Everys had only half paid attention, mostly because she didn't want to come face-to-face with Clarinda Gaines again.

The transport pulled up outside a building that appeared to be a museum. Or a social club. It didn't resemble a factory, at least none Everys had ever seen. Instead of a dingy brick or stone box, TelleGlin's facility had a soaring glass front, an architectural work of art. They parked on a clean, well-maintained drive which circled a magnificent fountain.

Clarinda Gaines strode out of the building, surrounded by a cloud of aides and assistants. Gaines wore a sharply tailored suit, the dark colors complimenting her Weyfir complexion. Her bright hair was twisted into a tight bun that made her almost as tall as Everys. While she looked friendly enough, Everys could easily see how fake her smile was. But she plastered on her own fake smile and strode forward.

"Mistress Gaines, so good of you to host me," she said. Hopefully that would satisfy protocol.

"I was so glad to be given the opportunity. After all, I've been hoping a royal would visit my facilities." A bare hint of disappointment hid in her voice. "And please, call me Clarinda. I insist."

"Only if you'll call me Everys."

For half a heartbeat, everyone froze, each of them wearing shocked expressions. Then Gaines chuckled. "I appreciate the informality, but that just wouldn't do, Blessed. Shall we begin?"

Gaines started for the building, and as Everys fell into step with her, her guards and Gaines's entourage quickly formed a shell around them. Everys idly wondered how they would fit through the building's doors, clumped together as they were, but they somehow managed. As they stepped through the large glass doors, Everys once again marveled at how different the TelleGlin facilities were from her expectations. This appeared more like a resort than anything else. Gaines chattered amiably as they crossed the spacious lobby, past a curved reception desk made of expensive hardwood, then through a set of double doors into a gleaming white hallway.

Everys turned to Gaines, who motioned for them to step into a small room to their right. Inside, there were racks of baggy white jumpsuits. The TelleGlin personnel donned the outfits over their clothes. Everys's guards followed suit, although two of them helped her get into one of the jumpsuits first.

"I apologize for the inconvenience, Blessed," Gaines said. "But we're going to inspect some very delicate devices, and we don't want to contaminate them."

That made sense, but Everys still felt self-conscious, shrugging into the brilliant white clothing with everyone watching. She adjusted the fabric several times, convinced it wasn't draped properly. But no one seemed to care.

Once again, Gaines led the way, out of the room and down the hall. Large windows looked into immaculate rooms, all made out of gleaming white tiles. People in similar outfits moved carefully, working on different projects. While a lot of different technology came through Everys's shop, she didn't recognize anything the technicians were working on.

"This is TelleGlin's R&D lab," Gaines explained. "The devices under development will one day be manufactured at our various facilities throughout the Dynasty's holdings before they'll reach our citizens and residents. I suspect that your friends in Fair Havens will eventually enjoy what my technicians are working on today."

Everys frowned. While Gaines's tone was light and friendly, she still imbued enough condescension in the word "eventually" to sting. Clearly Gaines didn't care one way or another if the people in Fair Havens got her tech. But she chose to let it pass.

"And what are they working on here?" Everys asked.

"A trade secret, I'm afraid." Gaines's smile widened. "But I suppose I can make an exception for our new queen. Come with me."

Gaines opened the lab's door and motioned for Everys to enter. But as her guards and Challix tried to follow, Gaines blocked their path.

"I'm afraid that invitation was for the queen only."

"But—" Challix started, anxiety painted across her face.

Everys held up a hand. "I'll be fine. After all, I'm in Mistress Gaines's facility. She will take that responsibility seriously, yes?"

Gaines's smile faltered, just for a moment. But she brightly replied, "Of course. She'll be perfectly safe with me. And you'll be able to observe everything from the hallway."

Challix and the guards didn't object, even though they looked like they wanted to. Gaines nodded and stepped into the lab.

"If you'll follow me please?"

They walked over to one of the tables, where a technician fiddled with a number of components. Based on what Everys was seeing, it looked like the technician had laid out the basic components needed for a vidscreen. She had worked with those parts numerous times. But she thought some vital components were missing.

"Is something wrong, Blessed?" Gaines asked.

Everys realized that she was frowning. She quickly eased her features and said, "No, everything is fine. It looks like you're working on a vidscreen."

That statement seemed to take Gaines by surprise. But then the CEO laughed and said, "Oh, yes, I forgot your background. A third-hand electronics vendor, yes?"

Once again, Gaines's words were shot through with condescension. And once again, Everys ignored it. Challix had emphasized how important TelleGlin was to Narius's long-term plans, although she was maddeningly vague on how or why.

"Something like that, yes." Everys frowned as she mentally pieced together the components. The parts were small, as if they had been designed to create a screen as thin as possible. Not only that, but it appeared as if much of the connecting materials were made to bend. Her eyes widened. "Are you creating a flexible display screen?"

The technician actually dropped the tool she was using, and Gaines gaped at her. Everys resisted the urge to look smug. Not bad for "a third-hand electronics vendor."

"Wh-why, yes. We haven't quite gotten all the kinks worked out yet, but we hope to have several working prototypes within two weeks, maybe a month at most."

Everys nodded. "Very impressive, Mistress Gaines. You must be quite proud."

"Well... yes, I am." She motioned for Everys to follow her into the next room. "TelleGlin has been a part of my family for three generations. I'm sure it would come as no surprise to hear how difficult it was for my great-grandfather to create something enduring. The Dynasty has never really trusted Weyfirs."

Everys cocked her head to one side, considering it. While that was probably true, Weyfirs had never faced the kind of discrimination that Siporans had. The Weyfir Commerce Union had willingly allied themselves with the Dynasty before being integrated into the Dynasty's holdings. As a result, most Weyfirs were well-off, especially compared to the other non-human races.

"But I have accomplished much. When my father left me the company, we were mostly known for transport engines. In the last fifteen years, I've repositioned us for the future. TelleGlin won't just be a forerunner of new technologies, but will be the cutting edge itself. For example..."

Gaines led her to a large device, one covered in conduits and tubes. Everys frowned, trying to piece together what she was seeing. It looked like...

She sighed. She had no idea. Everys turned to Gaines and shrugged.

Gaines's eyes shone triumphantly. "This is the prototype for a revolutionary ion thruster, which could propel robotic probes into the furthest reaches of our star system."

Oh. Everys didn't have any experience with rocket engines—no wonder she couldn't piece together what this was. She glanced at Gaines again and froze. Why was the CEO looking at her so expectantly?

"...very nice," Everys offered.

Gaines's prompting expression faltered. "There are more things to see."

They came to a halt next to what looked like an end table with a robotic arm. The table itself was made out of metals and plastics. The arm was threaded through with tubes, which ran back to a mechanism tucked behind the table. That had a large control panel on it, along with a few large tanks.

Everys glanced at Gaines, who regarded her with a challenging expression. Was she supposed to guess again? Was this a way for the CEO to feel superior to the queen? Fine. She'd play along. If she had to guess, something from the mechanism would be pumped into the arm, and then... sprayed onto the table? Why would they want to do that?

"I'm afraid I'm not familiar with this technology," Everys said.

Gaines's look of triumph soured Everys's stomach. "This device is going to revolutionize medical procedures in just a few short years. It is a tissue fabricator. We can take a sample from a patient, use their DNA to clone the necessary tissues, then craft a new organ to be transplanted into the patient."

Everys stared at the machine. "That is incredible. Absolutely incredible!"

Gaines smiled, and this time, the expression seemed genuine.

"I can see why my husband considers you such a valuable partner for the Dynasty," Everys said. "Why, with one of these devices in every hospital in the Dynasty's holdings, we could save so many lives!"

At the mention of Narius, Gaines's smile turned brittle. "Yes, well, it would have been nice if *your husband* had been here to share that sentiment."

Everys froze. Where had this venom come from? "I'm sorry, Mistress Gaines, have I done something to offend you?"

Before Gaines could answer, the door to the lab opened, and a technician walked in, carrying a large box. He struggled to maneuver it through the room, looking like he almost dropped it several times. The technician walked to the other side of the room and set to work unloading the box into a cabinet.

Gaines actually laughed. "Have you done anything? No, not at all. Not consciously at least." She rested a hand against the fabricator, then fixed Everys with a hard stare. "Do you know how many noble families there are in the Dynasty right now?"

Everys had no idea, so she shook her head.

"According to the last census, there were forty-five major houses and three times as many minor ones, all of them with their property holdings, subordinates, and income. Every single one of them is human, the vast majority Hinaen. No surprise there. But do you know what is truly galling?" Gaines ground her teeth before she spat out the answer. "If you were to consider TelleGlin a 'noble house,' we are wealthier than all of the minor houses combined. We own more property than half of the major houses. And yet my family has been denied a place within the nobility. Now, I ask you, is that fair?"

Everys didn't know how to answer that. She had no idea how a person became nobility. Was there a limited number of titles?

"No, it isn't." Gaines clearly wasn't expecting her to answer. "While I was building TelleGlin into a global giant, I was also petitioning first King Girai, then King Narius, to grant my family a title. Do you know how King Girai responded? 'There is no room in the heights for a Weyfir scuttler.'"

Everys winced at the slur. She even checked to see if the technician had heard it. Didn't appear he did. The Dynasty was certainly fond of insulting people based on their ethnicities.

"So you decided to try for queen instead?" Everys asked.

Gaines gave a half-shrug. "I thought that, maybe, if I offered to become queen, Narius might take my petition more seriously. I thought I would finally be the first Weyfir noble. But instead, he made history in a completely different way." Her gaze sharpened, and suddenly, any pretense at friendliness evaporated. "So yes, *Blessed*, you could say that you are in my way. And I don't appreciate it."

The full intensity of Gaines's anger slammed into Everys, and she stumbled back a step. Her gaze hitched on the technician, who had glanced in their direction. Everys straightened, trying to maintain her composure.

"Nor do I appreciate the many demands that King Narius has been making of me of late. So I would appreciate it if you delivered a message. Until he is willing to grant me a title that befits my position within the Dynasty, we will not offer any further assistance with his... special project."

His what?

"For the Cold Light! Freedom for the Hearth!"

Everys whirled in time to see the technician charge at them, wielding a—was that a *sword?* With a savage cry, the technician raised the blade over his head.

Gaines shrieked. Everys felt rooted to the spot. But then the blade dropped toward her head.

She ducked, the sword slicing into her protective suit. The attacker growled and spun on her. Everys snatched the closest thing she could find, a small metal tank, and hurled it at her attacker. He swatted it out of the air with the flat of his blade and advanced on her.

"Death to all tyrants! Death to the Dynasty!"

She frowned. There was something off about his expression. His features were slack, his eyes hollow. If he wasn't wielding a sword, she wouldn't have felt threatened at all. But he was armed. And he wasn't stopping. He raised the sword over his head.

Everys stumbled backward, only to slam into a table. Her hands groped behind her, hoping to find a weapon or something else to throw, but she found nothing. And he was so close, so—

"Blessed! Get down!"

The shout jolted her but she dropped to the floor.

There was a series of loud clicks, then red stains blossomed on the technician's chest. Surprise flickered across his face, but he dropped to one knee, the sword slipping from his fingers. Then more pops, more stains, and he pitched forward onto the floor. Everys had to scramble to her left to avoid him falling on her.

Everys stared at him, her mouth working but no sound coming out. What happened? Had he been shot? By whom?

Then her guards swarmed around her, quickly hustling her out of the lab, and she realized it must have been one of them. Challix shouted an apology for cutting the tour short, but Gaines didn't seem to hear.

Within minutes, the guards shoved Everys into the transport, and they peeled away from TelleGlin's facilities. It wasn't until she was absolutely sure she was safe that the trembling started, first in her stomach, then radiating into her arms and legs.

"Blessed?" Challix asked. "Are you all right?"

Physically, yes. But mentally? Emotionally? She couldn't be sure which had been worse: the tension between Gaines and her or the attack in the lab. Either way, she was glad to leave it behind her. Hopefully she wouldn't have to face something like that again anytime soon.

24

Much to Everys's chagrin, Narius and Paine waited for them at the palace. She barely made it out of the transport before they hurried to her side.

"Are you all right?" Narius asked.

"Guards, report!" Paine snapped.

One of Everys's guards—she thought his name was Apilsin—snapped to attention. "A tech got a sword into the facility and attacked the queen."

Everys took a deep breath. "Before he attacked, he said something about the Cold Light. Freedom for the Hearth."

"Chaos's fickle heart!" Paine muttered.

"Oh, I'm fine, by the way." She directed that comment to Narius.

He actually looked relieved. "I am so sorry that this happened. I thought you would be shown some new technology. I thought you might enjoy it!"

Everys gaped at him. He thought she would have fun? Being thrust into an awkward social situation with a woman who had been a rival for his hand? He thought that would be *fun*?

"I would suggest the guards debrief the queen immediately. I will sit in and—" Paine said.

"No. That's not going to happen," Everys said.

Paine blinked at her. "Excuse me?"

"There's not going to be a 'debriefing.' I already told you everything I know about the attacker, everything he said and did before one of the guards killed him." She turned to the guards. "Who did that, by the way?"

Kevtho took a step forward. "I did, Blessed."

Everys laughed mirthlessly. "Protecting my life as well as my honor? You should have challenged him to a duel. You've got that sword for a reason."

Paine sputtered, but Kevtho offered her a wry smirk.

She turned back to Narius. "As for what I saw while on the tour, not all that much. Gaines showed me some impressive technology, and she had a message for you."

"Oh?" Narius asked.

"She won't help you with your 'special project' until you give her what she wants."

At least Narius looked surprised. "She said that? Specifically? Any other details?"

Everys's gaze narrowed. Why was he so worried? Did he think that Gaines said something she shouldn't have? Revealed details about this unknown project? But she was queen. Why couldn't she know?

She wobbled, but caught herself before anyone noticed. Exhaustion slammed down on her. All of this was too much. Gaines's attitude, the attack, the inkstained secrets upon secrets! She wanted nothing more than to take a nap.

Apparently that wasn't going to happen, not if Paine could help it. He cleared his throat. "Regardless, we should still develop a strategy on how to proceed with Mistress Gaines and TelleGlin. Given their importance, we should placate her."

"I assume you have a suggestion?" Narius asked.

"I do. In two days, we will have the grand gala to celebrate the Night of Shards. We should invite Mistress Gaines, perhaps even seat her at the main table with you and the queen. That way—"

Everys didn't hear the rest of Paine's suggestion. A harsh buzzing filled her ears. They couldn't possibly expect her to participate in a Night of Shards celebration. There was no way. *There was no way!* How could Paine be so cold? How could Narius be so clueless? How could either of them expect her, a Siporan, to celebrate the destruction of Nekek the Bright? How could they expect her to listen to people singing the praises of King Heronus, the Xoniel king who brought down the Ascendancy? How could they expect her to play political games on a night that the Siporans mourned? Her knees went weak, and she almost collapsed onto the pavement right there.

The Xoniel called it the Night of Shards. The Siporans knew it as Downcasting. And there was no way that she would play along. Not this time.

To his credit, Narius caught on before Paine did. He started to say something, but she took a step back.

"That's not going to happen," Everys whispered. "I will not be there."

"But you must!" Paine insisted. "It's your duty as queen!"

She snarled at him. "I don't care. There is no way that I will be able to sit there and pretend like I'm happy about what your Dynasty did to my people. Don't you get it? I may be queen, but I was Siporan first."

"But what will we tell the guests?" Paine asked.

"I don't care. Tell them I'm sick. Tell them I've gone home to spend time with my family. Or you could do this crazy thing known as 'telling the truth!'" She glared at Narius. "You might try it some time."

She didn't wait for him to respond. Instead, she turned and headed into the palace.

"The king did not dismiss you!" Paine thundered after her.

She stopped long enough to turn back to Narius. "Anything else, *husband?*"

He stared after her, his expression stricken. He shook his head.

"Then if you'll excuse me, I'm heading to my quarters. I'm afraid I'm coming down with a cold, and I don't think I'll recover for the next few days."

With that, she headed for the palace and left them behind.

25

Everys spent the next two days hiding in her quarters. A childish strategy, sure, but she didn't want to see Narius or talk to him. She knew that, if she did, he'd try to convince her to attend the so-called Night of Shards party and that was the last thing she wanted to do. So she spent her time going over plans for her outreach center, coming up with a list of possible donors she could approach for their support.

The night of the actual party, though, Everys dismissed the girls at sunset and ordered her guards out of her quarters. When they objected, she insisted. Thankfully, Redtale wasn't there to argue; the head guard had been missing all day. By the time darkness fell, Everys was alone. She looked over the room and nodded. Narius could observe the night his way, and she would do it hers. A smile tugged at her lips. If only the scriveners back at conclave could see what she was about to do.

Once the door was securely locked, Everys set to work. She crossed to the fireplace and, using a glass from the kitchenette, scooped out darkened ash. She hadn't been able to burn the correct kind of wood—ceriton oak only grew within the Ascendancy's former borders—so she hoped regular ash would do. The real challenge had been having ashes at all. The girls were too efficient at cleaning out the fireplace, but it looked like she had enough.

Next, she moved the furniture away from the room's center, then rolled up the rug and tucked it in one corner. That left her an empty area to work with. Once she had enough space, she got another glass filled with water. Then, after wetting her finger and dipping it in the ash, she set to work drawing out the proper runes. She had to draw fifteen of them, and according to the rites, they were supposed to be done right after sunset. Thankfully, she knew them by heart. Her masters had used the Downcasting runes to teach her the basics of toratropic magic. The circles, bisecting lines, the swirls, accent marks, and hash marks, she easily sketched them onto the floor.

Once the runic ring was finished, she stepped back and looked them over. A bit sloppy, but neatness didn't matter for Downcasting. As a matter of fact, some scriveners encouraged those who observed the vigil to be deliberately messy as a sign of deep mourning.

So what was next? Her memory was a little fuzzy on this point. She had to keep vigil among the runes until sunrise, that much she remembered for sure. But there was something else. Oh, right. She was supposed to keep a relic of the Ascendancy on hand as a focus for her meditations. Some Siporan families had heirlooms from the Ascendancy, little trinkets they kept hidden away just for Downcasting. Papa or Mama might have had something at one point. Everys couldn't quite remember. She definitely didn't have anything that would qualify in her room.

Or did she? She found one of the pens Kyna had given her. A little unconventional, but then the rampant misuse of toratropic magic had brought about Downcasting. It seemed an appropriate selection.

Once she had retrieved the pen, she sat down, cross-legged, in the center of the ring. She set the pen in front of her, took a deep breath, and closed her eyes. She wasn't entirely sure what to do now; she had never kept vigil during Downcasting before. Mama and Papa had tried to get her to, but she had always refused, and they had never forced her. She vaguely remembered her masters saying that Siporans were to call to mind their history. The hubris of the Siporan mages who built the Ascendancy into the cruel empire it was. The way they ignored the Singularity's repeated warnings. The eventual justice when the Singularity used the Xoniel and Dalark militaries to overthrow the Ascendancy and humble His people.

But it had been so long since she had been to conclave, she could barely remember the texts, the stories, the traditions about what happened. She could only remember little snippets. *The Singularity opposes those who are proud and haughty. Those who misuse His gifts to glorify themselves; those who overlook the needy, the oppressed, those who have nothing. Return to His way before He casts you down and reminds you who you are.*

Everys shifted, not because of physical discomfort. She had been so focused on the Dynasty's injustice, yet she had overlooked the injustice in her own history and heritage. The Siporans had been just as guilty as the Dynasty. Worse. They knew better. They knew the Singularity's expectations, and they had ignored them. As a result, they had lost so much: their power, their prestige, their home. For four hundred years, they had lived as exiles under the Dynasty's heel. And Downcasting was the time to remember that history.

Another line from the ancient texts floated through her mind. *How long? How long will You forget about us? How long will we languish in obscurity? How long will our enemies gloat over us? Answer me. Assure me. Let us know that You are still there, that You are still sovereign, that You are still near. Let me see how You will paint our futures in runes of light.*

An uncomfortable weight settled on her. She looked down at the pen. As much as it may have seemed like the Singularity was gone, He obviously wasn't. He still bestowed His gifts on His people. He still rebuked them when they misused them. As much as it pained her to remember, she still had her abilities. She had her ink. And now, for whatever reason, she was here, in the palace.

Her gaze fell on the door to her room, where she had traced the runes when she'd first moved in. She remembered the odd echo she'd felt. Somewhere in the palace, there was toratropic magic at work. She had wanted to try out some tracking runes to see if she could locate the source, but she had never had the time or privacy to do so.

But Downcasting? Nothing but time. Once the runic circle was drawn, all that was expected of her was to stay awake for the entire night. Why not put that time to good use? She briefly considered using the pen, but she didn't want to waste such good ink on what could turn out to be a wild chakrut hunt. She still had lots of soot and plenty of water. That would have to do. Pulling the bowls close, she set to work.

It didn't feel right to be at the gala by himself. Narius took a sip from his wine and looked over the gathered nobles. They had come from all over the Dynasty's holdings for the Night of Shards. They dressed in their finest regalia, packed into the palace's main ballroom, and he, as king, had to play dutiful host, providing the food, the drink, the entertainment. A band played classical music, popular when the Ascendancy fell. The nobles paired off on the dance floor, spinning and twirling. From Narius's estimation, there were at least three scandals brewing from those pairings already, and the night was still young. By morning, gossip reporters would buzz about all the new dalliances of the Xoniel nobility.

It was all so stupid.

Narius forced himself to smile. He was on display. People would parse his expression, his posture, his dress.

The fact that he was at this celebration alone.

He did his best not to frown, even though he wanted to. Everys's defiance still rankled. Maybe he had been insensitive, but what would people think? The queen, missing from one of the most important celebrations in the Dynasty's calendar? Surely they could have come up with some sort of compromise.

But she wasn't here. And neither was Innana. The latter could have been. The Dynasty extended an invitation to the Dalark every year. After all, the Imperium had allied with them to bring down the Ascendancy. They should have been there to commemorate that victory. It would have been an excuse to see Innana again. How long had it been? Five years? Six? He couldn't remember. Too long. He closed his eyes and pictured her on his arm. No, out on the floor, dancing together. Trying to remember all the steps for those complicated dances no one actually used anymore. Laughing as they stumbled. Enjoying the jealous glances from the noblemen. Then slipping out into the garden...

"Your Strength?"

Narius stifled a groan. He peeked out of the corner of his eye. Paine stood a respectable distance away, his hands behind his back.

"What is it?" Narius asked.

Paine stepped forward and whispered, "I hesitate to disturb you. But Duke Brencis insists on speaking with you. Immediately."

Narius frowned. What could the duke possibly want in the middle of the party?

Paine led him through the ballroom. As they passed the dancing partygoers, most of them acknowledged him with a bow or a nod or, in some cases, salutes. He spotted Clarinda Gaines off to one side, in an intense conversation with a knot of nobles. Narius frowned and scanned the crowd. Where was Quartus? Had his brother already found a new lover and slipped off to the guest wing with her?

So why would Brencis want to speak with him? More warmongering against Dalark? Not good timing, in the middle of a celebration of the two kingdoms' shared victory.

Brencis waited for him out on a patio that overlooked the gardens. He wore a formal uniform rather than civilian attire, and his hands were clenched behind his back as he surveyed the gardens. As Narius approached, he turned to face him and nodded, his face severe.

"Duke? You don't seem to be enjoying yourself tonight," Narius said.

"Hard to relax when Dalark prepares for war and no one seems ready to do anything about it," Brencis said.

Narius clenched his jaw. So predictable. Before Narius could respond, Brencis continued, "Is it true? The queen challenged Viscount Orsin to a duel?"

"She did, yes."

Brencis snorted. "Unbelievable! Kerrik has served with honor for thirty years! She has no right!"

"Except she does," Narius shot back. "And, quite frankly, Viscount Orsin instigated it. And the way he allowed what happened to Vanguard Harset—"

Brencis nodded sharply and looked back out over the gardens. "Shameful, without a doubt. But sire, I want you to think about what you did."

"What I did?" Narius repeated

Brencis fixed a fiery glare on him. "You brought a Siporan woman to the edge of the Demilitarized Zone mere days before the Night of Shards. You've been redirecting our funds to that secret project of yours for the past year. It's not difficult to understand why Kerrik was... concerned about what her presence meant."

"What her presence..." Narius's frown deepened. "Do you have something to say to me, Duke?"

Brencis straightened, clearly recognizing the challenge in Narius's tone. "Permission to speak freely?"

"Always."

"You could have married anyone within the Dynasty. As a matter of fact, I suspect there are at least ten to fifteen young women in the ballroom right now who would kill for the chance to be your queen. But instead of choosing someone from the nobility, you chose a commoner. And a Siporan! Why?"

Narius's jaw tightened. He could have explained that very few of the noble families had responded to Paine's inquiries, that Istragon was getting so upset about Narius's continued singleness that he had to act swiftly. But he didn't owe that to the duke. Not like that.

"My affairs are my own," Narius said.

Brencis shook his head, then took a step closer. "I like you, Narius. I always have. I've watched you grow into a young man who exemplifies the qualities the Perfected Warrior held dear. But threatening your officers, cutting the military's funding, marrying a *Siporan*. I worry you may be sending unintentional signs of weakness to Dalark and our other enemies."

Narius laughed. "The Dynasty doesn't have any true enemies anymore, Duke. The world has changed."

"Not as much as you think, sir. Oh, yes, Dalark honors our truce, but mark my words, they are only biding their time. You can't afford to alienate anyone right now. To do so would be to court disaster."

Narius studied the duke's face. Brencis was so earnest, almost desperate. "What would you have me do?"

"Take a firmer stance against Dalark. You keep dismissing their incursions as misunderstandings, but I tell you, they are testing us! You believe Vanguard Harset's actions were a mistake, but I'm positive he saw something. Dalark scouts, maybe."

Perfect. First Harset had jumped at shadows, and now Brencis was as well. This madness was infecting every level of the military! "What else?"

"Restore our funding. Assure our troops that the king is committed to providing them with the most state-of-the-art weaponry and armor so that, when war comes, we will be able to crush our adversaries."

He should have predicted that as well. "Anything else?"

Brencis nodded. "Divorce Everys. I don't know what kind of spell she's put you under—"

"She isn't a toratropic mage! We wiped them out centuries ago."

"A poor choice of words, but you have to admit, marrying her is unprecedented."

"Maybe, but so is the head of the Dynasty's military giving me marriage advice."

Brencis flinched. "If I've overstepped, I'm sorry, Your Strength."

Narius patted him on the shoulder. "No need to apologize. As the Warrior said, 'A duel between friends leads to sharper blades.' I know you just have my best interest at heart."

"Always."

"Then let's return to the party and try to enjoy ourselves, shall we?" Narius gestured toward the palace. "It's supposed to be a celebration, after all."

Brencis smiled and nodded. "That sounds nice."

Narius motioned for Brencis to go ahead of him. With one last glance at Paine, Narius fell in step behind Brencis, marching back into a celebration that felt all too hollow.

26

Everys blew a stray lock out of her eyes. She had spent the last five hours drawing rune after rune with the ashes. The impromptu ink worked fairly well, all things considered. And she knew how to draw these runes. They were some of the earliest she'd ever practiced.

But the results were maddening. She had hoped that she wouldn't have found anything. Or, if she did, she'd get a strong enough impression she'd be able to search it out in the morning. But she got inconsistent results. A tug to the left, a strong impression to the right. Then a feeling there was something below the ground outside the palace and, at one point, far above the palace.

She frowned at the mess on the floor, then considered the pen. Maybe that was the solution. Ash-and-water paste was decent, but maybe it wasn't enough. If she used the pen's ink, she could get a good fix on whatever she had detected.

But should she? The moment she broke open the pen, the distinct stench would fill the room and be impossible to cover up. It would lead to questions she wouldn't want to answer. Satisfying her curiosity probably didn't justify breaking the pen.

She sighed and looked around the room. It almost looked as if the Downcasting runes glowed faintly in the dark, but that had to be a trick of her sleep-deprived mind, because the failed runes appeared to glow too. That was a lot of ash, and it would take a while to clean it all up. Trule would have a fit if she saw it. Maybe she should just give up and clean the floors.

But the vigil wasn't over yet, and the girls wouldn't be in for hours. Aside from the guards patrolling the palace grounds, she might have been the only person still awake. Narius's party ended a few hours earlier; she had heard the guests' transports leaving. She dipped her finger in the ash and started doodling random lines on the floor. Maybe she should have gone to the party after all.

A wistful smile tugged at her lips. She drew a young woman in a ball gown. Then she added a young man in formal attire. The illustrations were simplistic, probably unrecognizable to anyone else. But they were good enough for her. The rest of the spell was a simple enough rune; Galan had taught her when she was seven. A few quick strokes and swirls, a tap to bring it to life, and...

Two figures sprung up from the floor, each of them a foot high. They were little more than moving shadows, outlines vaguely shaped like people. The male stepped forward, sweeping into a dramatic bow. The female responded with a bow of her own. Then the two of them glided around each other in an intricate dance. The woman flourished her dress with each turn. Then the two figures came together, their faces closing in for a delicate—

Everys's eyes widened. She quickly dismissed the spell, the two ashen figures collapsing. Her heart slammed into her rib cage. Did she actually *want* that to be real? The spell was designed to act out the caster's thoughts, both conscious and unconscious. So is that what she thought would have happened if she'd attended the gala? She shook her head, trying to dislodge the image of the dancing couple from her mind. No, that couldn't be right. What would Papa think of her?

Worse, what did the Singularity think of her? She scrunched her eyes shut and braced herself for what she knew was coming: the rebuke for misusing her power on something so frivolous. If she ever deserved it, it was now.

Only nothing happened.

Everys pried one eye open and peeked around. What was going on? The Singularity couldn't possibly approve of what she was doing, could He?

Or was it because... Her eyes widened.

Was it because He wanted her to feel that way about Narius?

She shoved the thought aside as quickly as it formed. No! Narius was a nice enough man, but totally wrong for her. How could she, a Sipo-ran, stay married to the man who represented the empire responsible for her people's destruction?

Except the Xoniel were just a tool in My hands.

The thought—a paraphrase from the ancient texts—floated through her mind. A reminder of what Downcasting was all about.

She shook her head to clear it. She was being silly. Or maybe it was exhaustion. She hadn't drawn this many runes in years. Normally the mere thought of using the forbidden magic caused her endless waves of anxiety. To have drawn dozens of runes in such a short time frame... well, she hadn't done something like that since her training. She was surprised she hadn't been rebuked at all that evening.

That thought caused her frown to deepen. Why hadn't the Singularity rebuked her? So much of what she had been doing was frivolous, chasing shadows that clearly weren't actually there. Shouldn't the Singularity have objected to her taking such incredible risks, drawing runes in the middle of her floor in the palace? That violated at least half the vows she had taken to protect her people's secrets from those who would destroy them. So why hadn't the Singularity rebuked her even once?

Unless...

Unless He didn't mind. Or could it be that He wanted her to do this? To use this forbidden magic in the heart of the Dynasty's power? That couldn't be right. Didn't using her gifts like this make it all the more likely that her people would face reprisals from the Dynasty? Wasn't this kind of recklessness what got the Ascendancy destroyed in the first place?

Was it recklessness? Or was it disobedience? Reckless disobedience is one thing. Reckless use of My gifts is still another.

She froze. That wasn't a quote from the ancient writings, at least not one that she recognized. And yet it felt like it could have been. She glanced around the room. Where had that thought come from?

Everys forced herself to laugh. Sleep deprivation. Maybe it would be best if she called it a night and tried to get at least a little sleep. She should just clean up the mess and be done with it.

It would probably take her a long time to clean up and she'd need to get started right away. Did the girls keep any cleaning supplies in her quarters? She didn't think so, but then, she didn't know for sure. She frowned. Maybe she should have paid better attention.

Well, she'd be able to get what she needed quickly enough. She walked over to the door and pulled it open.

The two guards snapped to attention as soon as it was open. "Is there something you need, Blessed?"

What were their names again? She was pretty sure she had never met them before, which made sense. She usually wasn't up this late. "I'm just looking for a broom. Could you get one for me?"

To their credit, the guards didn't seem at all surprised or suspicious by her request. One of them nodded.

"Not a problem. I'll just—"

The guard stiffened, his voice choking in a strange gurgle. Then he slumped to the floor.

Something swished through the air, and the other guard gasped before he too collapsed. Everys stared down at them, her eyes wide. Was that *blood* pooling underneath them? What had happened?

She looked down the hall, and her blood turned to ice. Two men dressed in black clothing crept through the shadows, both holding weapons at the ready. They must have realized that she had seen them, because one of them made a slashing motion in her direction. The other raised his weapon and—

The same swishing sound, followed by a *thunk*. A metal flechette was embedded in the door frame next to her head. She quickly slammed the door, locking it, then whirled around, staring at the room.

What could she do? Call for help? How? Hide? But where? They were right outside. But she had to do something quickly. If she didn't, they'd kill her, the same way they killed her guards.

27

Something heavy slammed against the door. Everys pressed herself against the door, hoping she could lend her strength to the wood. But it was already buckling. She whimpered. What could she do? She didn't have any weapons. She was helpless.

No, wait. The bowls of water and ink. The pen! Her heart seized in her chest. Maybe she wasn't so helpless after all, but should she draw more runes?

The door bucked, shoving her away. Her attackers were almost through. She didn't have any choice. She had to do something!

As she ran through the room, she paused long enough to scoop up the bowls of ashes, water, and the pen, then retreated to her bedroom. Once she had closed and locked the door, she assessed her surroundings. A window that overlooked the palace gardens, the door to her living quarters behind her, the doors to the bathroom and her large closet to her right. Given that she was several stories up, if someone came for her, they'd have to come through the door. She could work with that.

She knelt by the door and set to work, drawing her first defensive rune with the ashes. It couldn't be too fancy. Her hand was shaking too much for anything complex, plus the impromptu ash ink wouldn't be powerful enough to do serious damage. A snare rune? Seemed like a good call. Setting the rune's parameters were easy enough: the trigger radius, the length and nature of the hold.

Maybe she should use the pen? No, not yet. Yes, this was an emergency, but hopefully the ashes would do the trick.

Once the snare rune was done, she considered he next step. Should she retreat to the bathroom? The closet? No, she didn't want to be cornered more than she was. What else could she do? More snare runes? She glanced at the ash ink. Not much left.

A crash came from the living room. Her attackers had kicked down the door. Everys crawled behind the bed. She didn't feel safer, but maybe it would buy her a few moments.

For several minutes, nothing happened. Then the door-knob rattled.

Everys tensed, dipping her finger into the ash ink. She still couldn't remember any combat runes, but she'd have to improvise if—

The door burst open, and her attackers rushed through. Their appearance barely registered; she was too focused on their weapons. Sleek, black metal, large and threatening. Those weren't civilian firearms. No, those appeared to be military weapons.

As the intruders crossed the threshold, the snare rune flared. A band of white light flashed across the doorway. Everys held her breath. Once the spell took hold, the men would be paralyzed for several minutes, giving her time to call for help. But instead, the light sputtered, then winked out. The men hesitated in the doorway, but then they opened fire. Everys dropped behind the bed. Flechettes embedded themselves in the wall, and thanks to the adrenaline surging through her, she fumbled the bowl. It shattered, spilling the makeshift ink. No!

That left her no choice. She snapped the pen in half, and a rancid odor gagged her. Her mind raced, different rune configurations tumbling through her thoughts. She remembered what one of the masters said about the ancient rune warriors, how they had tubes of ink on bandoliers when they went into battle, and that, as they fought, it appeared as if they were dancing. How did that help her now? She needed the actual runes, not—

Something fluttered past the window. Two ropes, and the way they danced in the night, something—or someone—was sliding down both of them.

Concentrate, Everys! She had to come up with something immediately!

Then she remembered. Combat runes were simple, designed to be drawn in the heat of battle. Master Igway had shown her and his other students a half-rotten book he had smuggled out of the Demilitarized Zone. He had allowed them to look over one of the pages, and for a brief moment, she remembered two of the runes with crystal clarity. Hopefully it'd be enough.

Everys daubed some ink on her left hand, then jumped from her hiding place. As she did, she slashed her fingers across the back of her left hand, a zig-zagging line that doubled back on itself, then swirled around the rune in a circle. She jabbed her open palm toward the soldiers.

Nothing happened.

Everys dropped behind the bed again, looking at the rune. She had drawn it correctly. The jagged lines, the enclosing circle, the—

Plaster burst from the wall as more flechettes tore through the air. Everys bit back a sob and scrubbed at the ink. It only smeared, staining the back of her hand black. Why hadn't it worked?

Then she realized: she had forgotten a bisecting line through the circle and lines. She redrew the rune, then jumped to her feet, praying that this time, the rune would activate.

The combat rune flared blood red as electrical bolts erupted from her palm. The blue lightning danced between the soldiers and arced to the floor. Their bodies convulsed.

Everys winced as pain sliced up her arm. She should have remembered that too. Toratropic magic could be used as a weapon, but the rebuke came quickly. But what choice did she have?

The lightning tapered off as the spell consumed the ink. She shook out her hand, trying to dispel the rebuke's pain. The soldiers collapsed, smoke rising from their clothing. They looked to be either dead or unconscious. Either was fine. She turned to face the window just as two soldiers slid down the rope.

More ink from the pen, and she swiped her fingers across the back of her hand, three curling lines that she once again enclosed in a circle. When she thrust her hand at the window, flames burst from her palm and washed over the soldiers. They flailed, but the fire sliced through their ropes. Their shouts turned to cries as they tumbled away from the window.

The moment the flames died, agony raced up both of Everys's arms. It started as a simple throb at her wrists, but soon, it felt as though her skin was peeling from her arms all the way up to her shoulders. She choked back a sob and pulled her arms in. She had never experienced a rebuke this strong before. Why?

She stumbled over to the window and looked over the edge. The two soldiers lay several stories below, their arms and legs twisted at unnatural angles. Neither of them moved. They had to be dead.

One of the men in the doorway groaned. She glanced at them. What was she going to do about them? She wasn't going to kill them, that was for sure. But how could she explain what happened here?

One of the soldiers clawed at his mask and eventually pulled it off. He rolled onto his side, and Everys got a good look at his face. His reptilian features, his sallow skin, his—

Vanguard Harset.

She stared at the young man, horrified. Angry welts covered his scalp, his cheeks, his forehead, and blood dribbled out of the side of his mouth.

Harset groaned and pushed himself up on his knees. His eyes fluttered open, and he looked up at Everys.

She gasped and took a step back. Liquid darkness swirled over his eyes. Could he even see anything?

"Blessed?" His voice was hoarse as he frowned up at her.

He didn't seem hostile, but she still kept her distance. There was something oddly familiar about his eyes, but she couldn't put her finger on what.

"F-forgive—" Harset whispered, but his words turned to a hiss as his body went slack.

Everys knelt next to him and checked for a pulse. Nothing. Harset was dead. And so was the other soldier, apparently.

She blew out a shuddering breath. Now what? Her gaze landed on the failed snare rune. Inkstains! She quickly scuffed at the rune with her foot, smearing the pattern. The flechettes they shot at her were still embedded in the wall behind the bed, and the ropes from the other two soldiers dangled outside the window, swaying in the wind.

Was she safe? Probably not. She checked the pen—there wasn't much left—and knelt. She sketched out another tracking rune, adding a bit more details. Instead of looking for toratropic magic, she focused on hostile intent. This time, she worked carefully, trusting that the pen's ink could carry the complexity of the rune.

Once she was done, she braced herself and activated the spell. A distinct pull in her chest, upward and to her right. More soldiers on the roof? Maybe. She closed her eyes, trying to remember the layout of the palace. What was in that direction?

Her eyes snapped open. Narius. His quarters. The soldiers were standing on the roof above his room.

She ran into the living room. The room was in shambles. Harset and his partner must have come through here before entering her room. The couches and other furniture had been shoved out of place, one table flipped over. The remnants of her failed runes were smeared over the floor, as were the Downcasting runes. That was a small blessing, but she had to focus. She had to do something. She had to—

What could she do? How could she explain any of this? Even if she alerted Redtale, the guard would want to know how she defended herself. And by that time, the soldiers could have attacked Narius. No, she had to do something.

She glanced at the pen. Empty. She rushed back into her room and found her other pen. She hated to use both in one night, but what other choice did she have?

So how to get to Narius's room? Going through the halls didn't seem wise. For all she knew, there could be more soldiers in the hall.

Her gaze fell on the hidden entrance to the passage that led to Narius's chamber. That was her best option. Granted, he hadn't been too happy when she'd used it last time, but hopefully he'd be more understanding this time.

She yanked open the door and rushed down the passageway. It felt like it took an eternity to get to the door to Narius's quarters, but finally, she was there. She tried to push it open.

It was stuck shut.

She tried again. It still wouldn't budge.

She threw herself against the door. Nothing.

She pounded against it, shouting Narius's name. Had he locked it? Why wasn't he answering? Her mind filled with pictures of the soldiers rushing into his quarters, killing him without warning. She had to get in there. Now!

She held up the pen and grimaced. "Sorry, husband. I need to do some renovating."

28

Narius couldn't sleep, even though exhaustion pulled at him. His mind wouldn't slow down, ricocheting from one thought to another to another. After lying in his bed for two hours, he finally moved to the living room. At first, he had tried doing some work, reviewing reports from the riot in Fair Havens, checking on projections for Falling Sword. But he eventually realized that wasn't helping. So he set it all aside, stretched out on the couch, and put on some soft music. Unfortunately, even that didn't help.

His gaze drifted toward the sealed off passageway to the queen's quarters. Not for the first time that night, he wished Innana was on the other side. But she wasn't. Everys was.

What was she doing?

The stray question caused him to frown. This deep into Fourth Watch, she had to be asleep. But why would he even wonder that at all?

He rolled so his back would be to the entrance. He needed sleep. Elamek wanted to meet about agricultural export projections in the morning, and Brencis would have something new to gripe about.

Wait. What was that?

Narius sat up. There was a cracking sound, like wood splintering under a heavy load. Large cracks appeared in the wall, radiating from a spot halfway up the secret door. Then, with a loud pop, the wall shattered, dust roiling through the room. He gagged as a horrendous stench clawed up his nose. What was that?

Before the dust settled, someone rushed into the room. Everys! She was an absolute mess. Her hands were stained black. Her hair was disheveled, and strange light gleamed in her eyes.

"What are—how—how did you do that?" Narius demanded.

She didn't answer. Instead, she dragged him toward the bedroom. He tried to stop her, but she was much stronger than he had imagined.

"What is going on?" he demanded.

She shushed him, pushing him deeper into the room. Then she shut the door and motioned for him to step away. He did so, a tremor worming through him. Was she going to attack him? Given how wild she looked, possibly.

But then she knelt, waving her hand over the door and... No, wait. She was painting the door, thin lines of black...

Narius's eyes widened. A cold knot twisted in his chest. Drawing. With ink. A rune.

He stumbled backward, hitting the bed with the back of his legs. That was what he smelled. Ink. For the past four hundred years, the Dynasty had mixed chemicals into their inks to render them magically inert. They also added a noxious odor to alert people if a Siporan was using toratropic magic. He had a weapon stashed in his bedside table. Could he reach it before Everys attacked him?

Her work apparently complete, Everys turned to him. "Narius..."

He held up a hand. "Don't come any closer!"

Pain flashed across her face. "We don't have time for this. There are assassins in the palace. They attacked me, and now, they're after you."

What? Her words didn't make any sense. His gaze flicked to the door. Swirls and slashes of black ink glowed softly. He had never seen an actual Siporan rune before, but from the historical accounts he had read, just being in their presence was supposed to sap a warrior's strength and cloud his mind. Yet Narius didn't feel any weaker. Confused, yes.

Everys grabbed his arm, squeezing. "Narius! Do you have a weapon? The rune won't keep the doors sealed forever!"

Is that what it was doing?

She growled, then hurried to the window. She set to work, drawing another series of runes along the sill.

"What—" His voice caught, cracked. "What are you doing?"

"They might come down from the roof. They did in my room."

"Your room?"

She glanced over her shoulder. "Narius! I can't do this by myself. Will you help me or not?"

The steel in her voice cleared his mental haze. He dashed to the night table and pulled the weapon, a military flechette pistol, out of its hidden holster. Hopefully it would be enough.

His gaze flicked toward Everys. She had said enemies were coming. Was one standing before him already?

She finished her work on the sill, then tapped the runes in quick succession. They blazed brightly for a second. Then she turned to face him. "Are you ready?"

The gun wavered in his hands. A Siporan witch. He had married a Siporan witch, brought her into the palace. How could he know that she wasn't trying to trick him? How could he trust her?

And yet...

And yet she hadn't attacked him. Moons' shadows, he had given her plenty of opportunities. Why toy with him like this if all she wanted to do was kill him?

Risky to trust her, but as he studied her face, he didn't see a trace of deceit. She was genuine. She looked truly frightened but ready to fight.

He raised his weapon, ready to aim at either the door or window. "Ready."

They waited. Sweat stung his eyes. He resisted the urge to swipe it away. Instead, he checked the door, the window. A glance at Everys. Her entire body seemed tense, coiled, prepared. She held a small tube in her hand, a drip of black along its rim. So many questions bubbled through his mind. What could she do with it? Was it made of human blood, like the old stories suggested?

Then the door handles rattled. Something thudded against it from the other side. Whoever it was bit off a curse, then there was a loud bang as something slammed into it. Much to Narius's surprise, the doors didn't budge. There was movement by the window, ropes dropping into view. Four soldiers rappelled down the lines.

Narius's eyes widened. Each of them wore special ops uniforms, armed with military-grade weaponry. But his training took over. He pivoted, bringing the pistol to bear on one of the targets. The soldier in his sights hit the sill and worked to bring his weapon around...

Then brilliant blue light flashed along the length of the windowsill. The soldier flailed, his feet apparently stuck, and he thrashed, as if trying to free himself.

Narius fired. The pistol made a soft *chuffing* sound. Flechettes sliced through the soldier's armor. The man staggered, firing an errant shot that whizzed past Narius's ear. Then he toppled backward off the windowsill, his rope snapping taut a second later.

The other three soldiers touched down and readied their weapons. Narius snapped off a shot but missed the one on the left. Shattered spear, not good! He would have to—

Brilliant flames engulfed the three soldiers. They shrieked, but they couldn't douse the fire. Everys stepped forward, fire coursing from her open palm. Sweat slicked her brow, and her face twisted into an agonized rictus. Then she swiped her right hand across the back of her left, and brilliant lightning burst out of her palm, dancing between the soldiers. They convulsed, then fell off the windowsill, their singed ropes snapping as they did.

Narius gaped at her. Had she been capable of this the whole time? How could he have...

She staggered, falling to one knee. Her skin had gone pale, waxy. Going into shock? Narius rushed to her side and helped her lie on the floor. "Are you okay? What can I do?"

She curled into a ball, shaking her head and mumbling something he couldn't understand. Should he get a medic? No, that would probably lead to too many questions.

Something slammed against the doors again. He glanced up. The pattern Everys had painted on the door flared with a deep red light, then faded. A second later, there was another collision, followed by another flare of light. How long would the spell last? The lines of the rune were slowly fading, as if unraveling from the edges.

He pulled Everys across the floor, tucking her behind the bed. Then he knelt next to her, keeping the bed between himself and the door. Not good cover but better than nothing.

Whoever kicked the door kept trying, and the pattern flared with eerie light. But each time, the flare was less intense, and more of the ink vanished. Narius steadied himself, aiming for the door. Any moment now.

With one last flash, the pattern vanished, and the door splintered inward. Three more soldiers stumbled through. Narius fired and took down two of them with headshots before they could fire. That was better. The third, he purposefully aimed for the knee. The soldier tumbled to the floor, clutching at his leg and screaming. Narius vaulted over the bed and kicked the soldier's weapon away from him. He then knelt and ripped the tactical mask from the man's face.

He didn't recognize him—not that he really expected to—but the man's face was twisted in pain.

"Who sent you?" Narius shouted.

The soldier started to answer, but his expression twisted even further, as if something was burning him from the inside out. Strange crackling light danced across the man's temples, darting into his eyes and out of his mouth. Then the man convulsed, his back arching. Black jagged lines clawed across his skin. Within seconds, the soldier had been completely consumed, and his body crumbled to ash.

Narius stumbled backward. He couldn't be sure, but those strange lights looked a little like the glow from Everys's rune.

Everys! He hurried back around the bed. She wasn't writhing anymore, so that had to be good, right? And the color seemed to be returning to her cheeks. But she was still unconscious.

Footsteps thundered through the other rooms. Narius spun, training his weapon on the door, and—

Zar and his team rushed into the room, their weapons drawn and ready. The guards quickly scanned every corner of the bedroom, one of them rushing to the window. As soon as they were assured the threat was gone, Zar stepped forward.

"Your Strength, are you all right?" he asked.

Narius almost laughed. No, not at all. Assassins in the palace? Defended by a Siporan witch? No, he was most definitely not "all right."

Zar glanced down and froze. He looked between Everys and Narius, a question burning in his eyes. At least Zar didn't ask it.

Like his guardsman would believe him if Narius told him.

But Zar quickly got over his confusion. He launched into a status report: palace in lockdown, guards patrolling the halls and roof, perpetrators being hunted down.

Narius tuned him out. He trusted that his men had things under control. Instead, he regarded Everys carefully. Who exactly had he brought into his home?

29

G uards filled the room, but Everys didn't feel any safer.

Zar had half a dozen of his men in Narius's bedroom, a dozen more in the living room. The palace was in lockdown, the guards were scrambling to figure out how the attackers breached the palace, and Vizier Paine was already crafting a statement for the press. All of that should have reassured her, but none of it did.

Because she wore a nightgown stained with ink and ashes.

Because she had used her powers in the palace, killing her attackers.

Because she had used her powers in front of the Xoniel king.

She risked a peek at Narius. He stood silently in one corner, his face neutral, but she could feel the anger radiating off him, the frustration, the aching need to act, to do something. He never looked at her. Did he not trust himself enough to make eye contact?

There was a commotion outside the room, but then Vizier Paine bustled in. Even though it was the start of First Watch, the man looked like he was fully awake and alert. Did he even sleep?

Paine bowed, first to the king, then to her as well. "Your Strength, Blessed, I have put out a preliminary announcement to the media that there was an attack on the palace and that you are both safe. I declined to answer further questions until we have more details."

Narius nodded. He turned to the guards. "Has Zar found anything yet?"

As if on cue, the lead guardsman marched into the room. "Apologies for the delay, sire. There were some... oddities about the attack we're having trouble reconciling."

Much to Everys's surprise, Narius didn't look in her direction. Was that good or bad?

"What sort of oddities?" Paine asked.

"Lack of corpses, for one. Don't know what happened to them, but something turned the assassins to ash. Even damaged their uniforms and weapons. Never seen anything quite like this before."

Everys's head snapped up. How had that happened? And when? Harset's body had been there when she'd left her room.

"We've also been working to reconstruct the attack. Near as we can tell, they hit the queen's quarters first, killing her guards. Two secured the door while two others came down from the roof."

A pit opened in Everys's stomach. She had been so worked up, she had forgotten about the dead guards. Who were they? Was Kevtho okay? Redtale?

Zar didn't supply any answers. "We think they hoped the attack there would draw our attention. We're not sure what kind of attack occurred, though. The queen's quarters are... kind of a mess."

Ice filled Everys's chest. Would they be able to figure out what she did?

"But someone killed the attackers?" Paine asked.

Zar hesitated, then nodded. "Hard to say for certain what happened with the lack of bodies. But based on what I saw, the king did a pretty good job of protecting himself and the queen." Zar glanced down at Everys. "Good thing you were in here, Blessed. Although I am curious, seeing as the king sealed up the passage between your quarters."

Was Zar expecting her to say something? Confess? His gaze intensified, boring straight into her. She could feel the truth clawing its way up her throat, about to escape...

Then Zar frowned and held a hand to his ear. "Don't worry, Redtale, we've got her and—"

Everys sat up straighter. Relief chased away the dread, and for a single moment, she felt better. Redtale was still alive.

Zar's frown deepened. "Not gonna happen, Redtale. Don't know what you've been up to all night, but most of us have been working and—" The guard fell silent again, his frown deepening. His gaze flicked from Everys to Narius and back again. Then he nodded curtly. "Understood."

"Is there a problem, guard?" Narius asked.

Zar's scowl turned positively toxic. "Not at all, sir. It sounds as though Redtale has made an important discovery about tonight's attack. Specifically, who is responsible."

"Who?" Narius asked.

"According to Redtale, Prince Quartus," Zar said.

Fire swept over Everys, chased by absolute numbness. *Quartus? Why would he have done this?*

Narius straightened even taller. His face turned stony, unreadable. "Where is my brother now?"

"Redtale has him under arrest, and they are waiting for your judgment in the throne room."

Narius nodded once. He started for the door, but halfway there, he paused and turned to Everys. "Go with my guards and clean yourself up. I will see you in the throne room in fifteen minutes."

Everys hesitated. She couldn't read his expression. There was no warmth, no familiarity in his gaze, nothing welcoming in his posture. Did he want her along for moral support? Or was he going to put her on trial as well?

She swallowed once. His words hadn't been a question or a suggestion. She could feel the undercurrent of command in his tone. She forced herself to stand. Her legs wobbled, but she managed to catch herself before she stumbled. Two of the king's guards flanked her as she left Narius's room and headed for her quarters.

With every step, she was convinced she was marching to her own execution.

30

S he had just enough time to scrub the ashes and ink from her hands and slip into a clean outfit before the guards hustled her to the throne room. Narius led the way inside, Everys trailing behind him. They were surrounded by Narius's guards, and objectively, she knew that she was as safe as she could be. But she had a hard time convincing her heart of that. How long would Narius stay silent about what he had seen?

She gasped when she saw Quartus. The prince lay in a heap, unconscious, a metal gag covering his mouth and manacles on his wrists and ankles. His clothing was disheveled and torn, like he had been in a fight. Two members of the queen's guard stood on either side of him. Redtale stood at attention by the throne, but she moved the moment her gaze landed on Everys. The guard hurried up to her, holding out a hand like she wanted to comfort her but not making contact. For a split second, Everys wished she could hug her if only to draw some of her seemingly endless supply of calm.

"Are you all right, Blessed?"

"I am now. Where were you?" She winced at the venom in her own voice.

If Redtale was stung by her tone, she didn't let on. "I'm sorry. My men and I... well, we had a situation." She gestured in Quartus's direction.

"Why is he gagged?" Everys asked. "And unconscious?"

"The gag is standard procedure." Redtale snorted. "The Xoniel love their traditions. When a blood member of the royal family is accused of treason, they're not allowed to speak at their trial. As for his current physical state, well, he celebrated the Night of Shards a bit too hard."

"He what?"

Redtale shook her head. "Can't talk about it right now. Traditions, like I said. I can't lay out the case until the full tribunal is here."

Tribunal? What? But Redtale didn't explain further, instead stepping back to her station and assuming a stiff-backed posture.

Narius sat on his throne. He didn't even look in Quartus's direction. Instead, he studied the opposite side of the room before his gaze landed on Everys. His features tightened, and he nodded toward her throne.

Everys didn't want to move, but she forced her legs to carry her up the dais and sit on her throne. This was the first time she ever had. It wasn't all that comfortable, the seat as hard as a rock, the back pushing into her shoulders like it was trying to force her to hunch over. She wiggled, trying to get comfortable, but gave up.

Narius nodded at her, but his expression didn't soften at all. An uneasy silence fell over the room. Everys didn't even want to breathe too loudly lest she attract attention to herself.

Duke Brencis stormed into the throne room. From the way his uniform was rumpled, he had apparently dressed in a hurry. Two of his aides scurried in after him, whispering frantically, but he jabbed a finger at an empty corner of the room and they quickly retreated to that safe space.

A few minutes later, the doors opened, and Vizier Paine and Minister Masruq hurried inside. Masruq also looked like he had been woken from a deep sleep, but worry was painted across his face. He rushed toward the dais.

"Your Strength! Blessed! I am relieved to see that you are both unhurt," Masruq said.

Everys managed a shaky smile, but she could feel her lips quivering and knew that if she wasn't careful, she'd start crying. Narius, for his part, simply nodded.

Masruq scurried to his place, folding his hands over his belly.

A few more ministers filed into the throne room, but Everys couldn't remember any of their names. Once they had taken their places, Narius cleared his throat.

"Let us begin." His voice was hollow.

Redtale cleared her throat. "As ordered, Your Strength. I have uncovered evidence that Prince Quartus orchestrated the attack on the palace this evening. Not only that, but I have further evidence that he is responsible for the death of Matron Halis."

Everys's head snapped back as if she had been struck. What?

"Really?" Duke Brencis snapped. "You think Prince Quartus is capable of such things?"

Redtale didn't wince at the rebuke. Instead, she turned to face the duke. "If I may explain?"

"Please do." Brencis's voice was a warning growl.

"Earlier this month, Matron Halis of the queen's staff disappeared under unusual circumstances. At the request of the queen, I investigated and learned Matron Halis traveled to Olekk to supposedly see a sick relative. Once there, she disappeared without a trace. Yesterday I was contacted by the Olekk constabulary. They found Matron Halis's body. Apparently someone killed her a while ago and hid the body"

Everys gasped. A few of the tribunal members glanced in her direction. Redtale did too, sympathy blazing in her eyes.

"Are you saying Prince Quartus traveled to Olekk and murdered Matron Halis?" Brencis asked.

Redtale shook her head. "No. The constables determined she was the victim of a simple mugging and already have the perpetrator in their custody."

Masruq clucked his tongue before speaking. "Then pardon me for asking, Guard, but how is any of this relevant to these proceedings?"

"Because Matron Halis's relative wasn't sick. Someone lied to get her to leave the palace." Redtale turned to look right at Quartus. "And based on evidence found on her body, the person who lied to her was Prince Quartus."

Again, Everys felt like she had been slapped across the face.

"Why would he do that?" Paine asked.

Redtale shrugged. "I couldn't say for certain, Vizier. We all know the prince loves to torment the king."

Everys's stomach twisted. The pieces fell into place: the lingerie, the cryptic orders on the wedding night. Quartus must have wanted to embarrass Narius, so he engineered what happened. But he must have known Matron Halis would have never gone along with the plan, so he got her out of the way and used Trule to act as his patsy instead. She looked at Narius, then the other members of the tribunal. Should she speak up? Try to fill in some of the blanks?

Apparently not, since Redtale kept on talking. "Upon learning this information, I decided to speak with the prince. I discovered he left his guards behind and disappeared into the city. So my squad and I went into Bastion to find him.

"It took us a while to piece together the reports, but we finally managed to track him down to... well, a pleasure palace in Beyond-the-Wall."

Murmurs swept through the throne room, and Everys's cheeks heated. She had never been to Beyond-the-Wall, but everyone knew that neighborhood was filled with bars, brothels, and gambling dens.

"We found him in the arms of a woman who bore a striking resemblance to the queen." Redtale's features twisted into a scowl.

Now Everys's cheeks practically blazed, especially as some members of the tribunal looked at her. She risked a glance at Narius. His jaw clenched tighter, and his eyes flashed, but that was it.

Redtale gestured to the prince. "He was unconscious when we found him. The girl couldn't tell us what he had taken. We tried to rouse him, but as you can see, we were unsuccessful."

"How does any of this relate to tonight's attack?" Paine asked.

"While we were searching for the prince, I had some of my men check the outgoing comm reports. I had hoped that I would find something connecting the prince to Halis's murderers. Instead, they found encrypted communiques to Firebase Forward Two-Seven."

A chill swept through Everys. Viscount Orsin's base. Was that why Vanguard Harset had been one of her attackers?

"And those messages said what?" Brencis demanded.

"My apologies, Duke. We haven't breached the cypher yet," Redtale said. "If I were to hazard a guess, it would be to set up this attack."

Quartus's chains clinked as the prince stirred. His eyes fluttered, then snapped open. He thrashed once against his bonds, and it sounded like he tried to shout, although the metal gag muffled the sound. His gaze ricocheted from person to person until it landed on Narius.

"Welcome back to the land of the living, brother." Narius's voice was ice. "For however short a time you may have."

A pit opened in Everys's stomach. What did that mean?

"We have heard convincing evidence of your crimes, Quartus," Narius said. "Starting with your deception of Matron Halis, which resulted in her murder. That would be bad enough, but to consort with traitors who then tried to assassinate your king and queen? Father would be so ashamed of you."

Quartus tried to say something, but again, his voice was unintelligible. His gaze roamed across the others in the room, then his body collapsed. Like he had given up.

"Prince Quartus of the Xoniel Dynasty, you have been brought before your king in the manner fitting traitors," Narius said. "And as such, I sentence you to the traditional punishment. Your name shall be stricken from our genealogies. Your name shall not be heard on our lips and will instead be treated as a curse and byword. Your estate shall be given to the poor. You shall be beheaded, and your body shall be incinerated and dumped into the Melgor River."

A sharp sting danced up Evereys's arms, similar to the rebuke she felt when she killed the attackers earlier. She gritted her teeth, but another rebuke came, stronger than the first. She entwined her fingers and squeezed as the pressure built.

Why? I haven't performed any magic!

Another rebuke, hard enough that her arms spasmed. Her face pinched.

Okay, I know! All life is precious to You. But I'm not the one who's doing this.

But she was queen, and that meant she could stop this.

"Wait." The word slipped through her clenched teeth.

Narius paused in mid-sentence, his expression still stern and foreboding.

Everys took a steadying breath. "The prince hasn't been given a chance to speak in his defense."

Brencis snorted.

"With all due respect, Blessed, this is traditional," Masruq said.

"But that doesn't make it right," Everys said. "Anyone in the Dynasty's holdings are guaranteed a right to speak at trial. The Dynasty's citizens are given even greater privileges. So why are these rights denied to the family that rules over them?"

"We are held to a higher standard," Narius said.

"Then let us also show a higher standard of mercy," Everys countered. "Don't kill him. Confiscate his holdings. Erase him from your genealogy if that's needed. But spare his life."

Narius's gaze tore into her. Had she just taken a step too far?

"By the Spear, the man tried to have you killed!" Brencis said. "And you would spare his life?"

Everys didn't look away from the king. She held his gaze with hers. "Please," she whispered.

Narius blinked, looked down. Then he turned to face his brother again.

"Who am I to deny my queen?" His voice was empty. "Very well. Quartus, former prince of the Dynasty, you are hereby banished. We declare you to be outside the protection of lawful society."

Wait, how was that better? If Everys understood what Narius had said, he might as well have ordered Quartus's execution! She braced herself for the Singularity's rebuke, but surprisingly, it didn't come.

Redtale stepped over to Quartus and hauled the prince to his feet. She released him from his chains and gag. Quartus glared at the guard, then rubbed his wrists and jaw. But finally, he turned to his brother and bowed. "As you wish, Your Strength."

When Quartus straightened, he looked at Everys. He appeared as devious as ever, but there was an undercurrent to his expression. Gratitude, maybe? Whatever it was, it vanished as two guards clamped onto his arms to force him out of the throne room.

As soon as Quartus was gone, Brencis sighed. "I hope no one takes this as a sign of weakness, Your Strength. Compassion for family is one thing. Showing weakness is entirely another."

Narius didn't answer. Instead, he turned to Zar. "Keep the palace under lockdown until the cryptographers have finished with those messages. Increase patrols as well. We will reconvene at the end of First Watch to learn of any new developments. Dismissed."

Each member of the council bowed to Narius and Everys, and while they tried to mask their emotions, Everys could read the frustration in some of them, Brencis especially. The duke was stiff and clearly upset about the way the trial went. Masruq offered some flowery praise for her compassion and mercy. Paine said nothing, simply stalking out of the room.

Everys checked on Narius out of the corner of her eye. He still sat on his throne, rigid and obviously seething. That was a storm that would have to break soon. Maybe it would be best if she put some distance between her and the inevitable explosion. She rose.

"Guards." Narius's voice was quiet but still carried the snap of command.

Everys froze in place, and her gaze rested on the chains in Redtale's hands. She would have to use them on Everys, wouldn't she? She would be bound, gagged, and put on trial for her illegal magic. He probably dismissed the council to save face. It wouldn't do for them to learn how she had duped the king. Fine. If he wanted to get rid of her that way, he could, the ungrateful little...

"Leave us."

The guards looked just as surprised as Everys felt, especially Zar. The commander stepped forward. "Sir?"

"I want a moment alone with my queen."

Was that a good thing? His face was still composed, but his expression bordered on anger. At least, she thought that was anger. It was so hard to tell.

The guards saluted and filed out of the room. Redtale cast one last look at her, and Everys offered the guard a nervous smile.

Once the doors to the throne room had closed, Everys turned to face Narius. He didn't move. Didn't even look at her. She braced herself, ready for whatever might come.

"So. A toratropic witch?"

She flinched in spite of herself. "That's not how we refer to ourselves."

"Oh." He finally looked up at her. "Thank you."

"Wh-what?"

"You heard me. I realize you took a tremendous risk... doing what you did. We both know how this should end. But you exposed your secret to save my life, and that is something I cannot overlook."

"So I'm not going to be dragged out of here in chains?" Everys asked.

He chuckled. "Now wouldn't that be a great way to end the night? All of Bastion is probably already buzzing about the attack. When they learn of Quartus's banishment, that buzzing will turn to murmurs. And if I were to reveal that my Siporan queen actually is a toratropic mage like so many people have suspected? The resulting sonic blast would level the palace. No, I think it best if this remains our secret."

Oh. So it wasn't really gratitude that fueled this decision but self-preservation. She should have expected that.

"I do suggest that you be more careful in the future," Narius said. "While I appreciate what you did, your actions are going to raise questions. If anything else unusual were to happen... well, I'm not sure I'd be able to do much."

"Don't worry, I'm good at hiding what I can do."

"Glad to hear it." He sighed again, running a hand through his hair. "And now I suppose we have to find places to not sleep, eh? I doubt the guards will let us use our quarters, seeing as they're both battlegrounds. I'll have my staff set you up in visiting dignitary quarters for now. Not as lavish as the queen's, but it will do for tonight."

A weight settled in her stomach. She knew about those rooms already, but she didn't dare tell him. He might change his mind about Quartus. "What about you?"

"Concerned for your husband?" He smiled wearily. "I'll head down to the guards' barracks and pretend to sleep on one of their cots. Maybe. Good night, Everys."

She startled at the tender tone of his voice as he said her name. He levered himself out of the throne and started for one of the side doors.

Before she could really think about what she was doing, she took a step after him. "Narius, wait. One more request?"

He paused and turned back to her. "Still feeling bold?"

She shrugged. "You do owe me your life."

"A debt that I thought I repaid by sparing Quartus. Believe me, I won't be able to explain that decision to anyone."

No, she supposed he couldn't. "I'm sorry."

He waved away her apology. "One more request."

"Have dinner with me?"

His head snapped back, surprise painted over his face. "What?"

"I mean... I just thought that since we're, well... and after tonight... maybe we could spend some time together and..." She flinched at how silly she sounded. "I just thought maybe we could..."

"I would like that."

Her words caught in her throat. Had he really just agreed?

"Y-you would?"

He nodded. "It probably couldn't be for a few days, given the chaos in the palace right now. But say three nights from now?"

"Absolutely. My quarters?" She smiled nervously. "If they're repaired, that is."

"I'll make sure they are." He bowed. "Good night, my queen."

She returned the gesture. "Good night, my king."

With that, Narius left the throne room. A moment later, the main door opened and Redtale stepped inside.

"I've received word that the staff is moving you to the dignitary's wing and..." Her voice trailed off, and she studied Everys's face. "Blessed? Are you all right?"

She nodded absently. She was, wasn't she? She had survived an attack on the palace, revealed her secret to the one man in the Dynasty who was honor-bound to destroy her kind, and yet somehow, she felt like she had only just now made a dangerous mistake.

And yet, at the same time, she couldn't deny the little thrill that danced through her as Redtale led her from the throne room. Somehow, she doubted she would be able to sleep, and it wasn't just because of the attack.

31

S he had asked him to dinner. And he had said yes.

Even though Redtale had brought her to one of the guest rooms, too much had happened for Everys to sleep. Especially as the memory of her asking Narius to dinner and his answer kept chasing through her thoughts. After trying—and failing—for four hours to rest, she eventually decided to check on her quarters. As Everys stumbled through the hall, she couldn't quite wrap her mind around the final events of the night. The attack was a hazy blur. The trial, a half-forgotten dream. But she had asked him. He had agreed. Those memories were crystal clear and oh so confusing.

What had she been thinking? Maybe the result of exhaustion? She was coming down from the rush of battle, mentally drained from the numerous rebukes. Her skin still burned slightly, like she had laid out in the sun for too long.

"Are you all right, Blessed?" Redtale asked.

Not at all. How could she be? She had invited the descendant of her people's destroyer to dinner. And he had accepted! How could she be all right after that?

But she couldn't go into that with Redtale, so she smiled and said, "I'm fine."

Redtale snorted. "Don't believe that for a second, but I won't press it now. Let's get you back to your quarters and—"

As she said that, they stepped into her foyer and came face to face with the wreckage. Ash had been smeared all over the floor, but thankfully, Everys noted, the runes had either burned away or been scuffed over. The furniture had been shoved out of place, and there was definite signs of the attack: military bootprints made from the ash, flechettes stuck in the wall, spatters of blood. Everys froze in the doorway, not wanting to enter.

But then Trule bustled into the room, followed by several of the other girls. Trule snapped orders at them as they went. "...and wash the floor. We want this back in order by the time —" Trule's gaze landed on Everys, and her eyes widened. "B-Blessed! I'm sorry that things are still such a mess! We did our best, but the guards wouldn't let us get to work while they were documenting everything and—"

Everys waved away her apology. "It's all right, Trule. Really. I'll help you clean up."

Trule's eyes bulged and several of the girls gasped.

Redtale cleared her throat. "That's not expected."

"Maybe not. But some physical activity might help. Besides, my parents taught me to clean up after my own mess." She winced at her words. Hopefully Redtale wouldn't catch the confession.

If she did, she didn't let on. "As you wish, Blessed. I'll have four guards outside your doors. You feel at all unsafe, we'll move you to somewhere secure."

She nodded. Then, without really thinking about it, she rushed forward and hugged Redtale. "I'm glad you're back."

The guard stood stiffly in Everys's embrace, like she was frozen. But then she wrapped one arm around her and patted the top of her back. "So am I."

Everys turned back to the mess. "So where should we get started?"

At first, Trule seemed positively sick that Everys was helping, but as Everys got to work and did what she was told, the servant loosened up. They didn't dare touch the flechettes still embedded in the wall, and some of the furniture would obviously need to be replaced, but for the most part, the room was back in order. And as near as Everys could tell, none of the girls suspected what she had been up to the night before. They were obviously curious about the ashes, but they didn't ask about it.

Finally, after eight hours of hard work, Trule declared the job over. "Go and get some rest, girls," she said. "We'll have to finish the last details tomorrow."

The girls bowed to Everys, who thanked them individually. Then the servants left the room, exchanging greetings with the guards as they passed. Everys watched them go, then realized that Trule was lingering by the door.

"Is something wrong, Trule?" she asked.

Trule pursed her lips, then shook her head. But Everys could still read the lurking question in her expression.

"What is it?" she prompted.

"The attackers. The guards said one of them was Plissk. Is that so?"

Oh, no. Everys should have thought of that already. "Yes, he was. Vanguard Harset." She took a step closer to Trule. "Did you... did you know him?"

Trule laughed, a bitten off hissing sound. "Do you know every Siporan, my lady?"

Everys winced, but not from the mockery. She should have known better.

But Trule shook her head and kept talking. "I didn't know him, but I know what the reaction of the Dynasty will be. There are not many of us who leave the sands to join what they call 'civilization.' Those who do are usually regarded with suspicion, if not hostility. After all, 'the Dynasty has a long memory,' yes?"

Everys nodded. It did indeed.

"They all remember how the Plissk fought the Dynasty, how we were 'brutal' in defending the sands. And so, when they hear of stories of Plissk being violent or doing something... well, like this—" She waved a hand toward the room. "—they assume all Plissk could be just as violent, to spill blood for sand."

"I'm sorry," Everys said. "That isn't right and I—"

She caught herself. She was about to say she understood what Trule was going through. After all, many within the Dynasty still considered all Siporans to be witches and would-be tyrants. How many times had she confronted that kind of hatred on the streets of Fair Havens?

But while she might have been able to sympathize with Trule's experience, it wasn't her place to speak but to listen, to hear what Trule had to say.

"Can you tell me more?" Everys asked.

Trule shook her head. "No, my lady. It is not proper. But I thank you all the same. Good night."

Before the serving girl could get back to work, though, Everys snatched her hands. Trule's eyes widened again, revealing how truly different they were from Everys's: sandy-colored irises that bordered a narrow slit of darkness. The servant's hands were cool in Everys's, and her skin had a rough texture that didn't feel right. But Everys squeezed them anyway.

"I appreciate everything you're doing for me," Everys whispered. "And I promise, if you ever need help, I will."

Trule mouthed some words, then slipped her hands free and scurried away.

As soon as she was alone, Everys felt a crushing weight descend on her. It felt like her arms were suddenly made of iron, dragging her toward the floor. She stumbled as the exhaustion consumed her, and she barely made it to the couch before she collapsed. She stared up at the ceiling as sleep soaked through her body. And within seconds, she had mercifully left the twisting emotions behind.

She had asked him to dinner. *She* had asked *him*. Yes, he and Viara had spent time together, but out of obligation, and she had rarely initiated. But Everys had. And he had accepted. Gravedigger's ashes, what had he been thinking?

"Your Strength?" Paine's quiet words snapped Narius out of his reverie.

Narius looked up from his desk. Instead of letting him try to get some sleep, Paine and the other advisers sequestered Narius in the Amber Office. Partially that was to keep him updated on the ongoing investigation, but part of it was to keep him safe as well. Normally he would have objected. A king shouldn't hide, especially during a time of crisis. He definitely shouldn't cower behind the guards. But he hadn't slept for a day and a half. And his head was still spinning from everything. Viscount Orsin a traitor? Quartus conspiring with him? The cryptographers had confirmed it, decoding the messages between the two. Quartus had specified the time, Orsin the attack vectors and personnel involved. That alone was too much for him.

But Everys protecting them both with illegal magic... He might never sleep soundly again.

"Your Strength?" Paine asked again.

Narius forced himself to focus on the vizier. "Do we have any more word on how the assassins breached our security?" He winced inwardly at how hoarse his voice was.

Duke Brencis nodded toward the display screen that filled one wall. On it was projected a real-time image from an orbiting satellite, showing the palace grounds. Narius could pick out the individual soldiers manning the walls, the watchtowers, the roof. He even thought he saw some of the hidden emplacements for snipers, anti-aircraft guns, and other defenses. The display wavered, replaced with a computer-generated wireframe model.

"At the end of Third Watch, a military cloudskimmer came in from the southwest. Bastion air command challenged their approach, but they responded with the appropriate clearance codes, claiming they were a part of a training exercise. As the skimmer approached the palace, someone inside cut our exterior communication lines and disabled our advance warning systems."

As the duke narrated the events, the image of a bright red cloudskimmer appeared over the palace. Brencis pointed at the display.

"Using silenced flechette throwers, they killed the sentries on the roof and dropped troops at these four points." Red dots appeared on the palace roof. "Two teams descended into the palace for the frontal strikes on the king's and queen's quarters while the other two teams prepared to rappel into the rooms. We believe their intention was to cause a distraction by attacking the queen first."

Narius frowned. So clinical. Dozens of soldiers had died that night, but Brencis described it like they were wooden pieces on a game board.

He started to ask a question, but it blossomed into a yawn.

Masruq cleared his throat. "Friends, while this is fascinating, let us be reasonable. Much of what we're learning is still preliminary and could change as more details emerge about motivations and tactics. For now, I suggest we let our king get some rest, yes?"

Brencis looked ready to object, but a glare from Paine silenced him.

"Excellent." Masruq turned to Narius. "Rest assured, Your Strength, the Dynasty will be waiting for you when you wake."

Another yawn escaped Narius's control. He nodded. "Very well. But wake me if you learn anything."

Zar and several other guards escorted him from the office. As they walked, Narius spotted Tormod lurking in one corner. Not a surprise. The Master of Shadows tended to stay on the edges to observe. He motioned to him, and Tormod nodded, slipping along the wall and falling into step with the king as Narius left the room. Narius wouldn't have been surprised if no one had noticed the spy had left, or if they had not even been aware he had been there to begin with.

"Your Strength?" Tormod asked, his voice a bare whisper.

As soon as they were in the hall, Narius turned to him. "As the reports come in, I want you to sift through them for the mention of anything... unusual."

"Unusual?" Tormod repeated, his features twisting into a confused look. "In what way?"

Narius caught himself. He was about to say something about how the assassins died. It had to be related to toratropic magic, he was sure of it. But if he said anything to Tormod, the spymaster would want to know why Narius thought it was Siporan magic, and then he'd have to admit what Everys had done. And it definitely didn't feel right to expose her like that, not after she had risked herself to protect him.

"Just anything that... well..." Narius sighed. "Never mind, Tormod. Just keep an eye open."

"I'll keep both open. My ears as well. And never fear. I'll remain vigilant as always."

Narius nodded his thanks, then followed the guards as they led him to more secure quarters for some rest. But then a thought occurred to him. He may not have been able to ask Tormod about toratropic magic, but he was supposed to have dinner soon with someone who could probably give him all the information he needed.

32

Everys didn't know what was worse: the knot twisting in her stomach, the smell of the food she was pretty sure she was ruining, or the way the girls had giggled at her all day before she dismissed them.

She ran a hand through her hair. Where had the time gone? She should have had plenty of time to get ready, but somehow the time had slipped away. Figuring out the menu had been a pain. This meal was too important for just anything. She wanted to serve significant food. So she had spent hours poring over recipes before she settled on a dish called "karabek." Apparently it was a traditional Xoniel dish served when ratifying a new diplomatic arrangement. A good fit.

But that had led to an argument with the kitchen staff. They had been horrified at the idea of the queen cooking for herself. It had taken close to an hour to convince them to relinquish the ingredients she needed.

And then the question of what to wear! Nothing too formal, obviously. But she didn't want to be too casual either. How to strike the proper balance so he—

Someone knocked at the door.

She whirled away from the kitchenette, her breath catching. He was here already? No! Dinner wasn't ready yet, she hadn't had the chance to change and—

Another knock.

Everys cast a wild glance around the room. It was mostly ready, just a few stray items that she would have tucked away if she'd had the chance. She swiped her hands down the front of her shirt, then winced and checked for stains. Nothing, thankfully.

He knocked a third time. She swallowed hard and hurried over to the door, painting on what she hoped would be a friendly smile.

Zar glowered once she opened it. "Oh, so this was to be a truly casual dinner."

If only she had some ink she could use to paint a rune that would bar the guard from entry.

Narius pushed past Zar. "See, Zar? I arrived at my wife's quarters without incident. You and your men can stand down."

Zar's glower turned positively radioactive. "I'd rather one of us remain at your side, Your Strength."

"Duly noted." Narius patted Zar on the shoulder. "Your caution is commendable. But we can look after ourselves, can't we, Everys?"

Everys jumped, startled to be drawn into the conversation. "Uh, yes. We can."

"But—"

"Dismissed," Narius said.

Zar's jaw clicked shut. He nodded before retreating, his posture stiff and angry.

Narius turned his full attention on Everys, and the breath caught in her throat. She finally noticed how he was dressed: a simple brown shirt and slacks, an outfit that struck a fine balance between casual and dressy. And here she was, standing in work clothes and...

"Shall we?" Narius motioned toward the room.

Everys nodded and stepped aside.

He paused in the foyer, sniffing at the air. "Are you cooking... Is that supposed to be karabek?"

Supposed to be? That couldn't be good. "Um, yes. It seemed appropriate for tonight and—"

"So this is to be a peace summit between Xoniel and... what, the exiles from the Siporan Ascendancy?"

Her cheeks burned. "Well, no, but given everything that happened—"

"You do realize half the ingredients don't exist anymore, right?" His smile grew broader. "Due to over hunting the karabs to near extinction and the fact that the ikthar plant turned out to be poisonous?"

"That's why I substituted rigthorn nightvale for the ikthar spice and—"

Then she spotted the laughter lurking in his eyes, which became brighter with each passing moment. A laugh bubbled up her throat, and he joined her.

"I appreciate the sentiment, but I hardly think it's necessary," he said. "We're not the leaders of warring factions, right?"

"Wouldn't that describe our relationship so far?"

His laughter died suddenly, and he gave her an uncertain look. It passed quickly, and he smiled again, but it was hard to miss the uneasiness in his expression.

"Maybe this isn't a total loss. I tried to make karabek once a few years ago." He hesitated. "I can help you if you really want to go through with this."

Everys froze. Did he want to cancel dinner? But if he really didn't want to be there, he could have easily come up with a believable excuse. He did have a Dynasty to oversee. Maybe it would be better to focus on the task at hand, like not ruining the meal.

Narius stepped over to the kitchenette and leaned over one of the bubbling pots. He took a deep breath, then flinched.

"Have you actually tasted this?" A chuckle threaded through his voice.

She hadn't had the chance yet, but she had been following the recipe as best as she could. She grabbed a spoon, scooped up a little bit, and licked it.

Fire coursed across her tongue and down her throat. Chasing it was a bitter taste that gagged her. She dropped the spoon and clamped a hand over her mouth, willing herself not to vomit. Everys stumbled back, dropping the spoon. Oh no! She had ruined it! There was no way he would—

Wait, why was he laughing?

Narius picked up the spoon. He examined the sauce and, before she could say anything, tasted it. His cheeks flushed, and he closed his eyes for a few seconds. When he opened them, tears streamed down his face.

"That's pretty close to authentic," he said.

Everys pried her fingers off her mouth. "Wh-what do you mean?"

"Karabek isn't meant for a casual dinner," Narius said. "It was created to test a warrior's fortitude and strength."

Everys gaped at him. "B-but the history texts said the ancient Xoniel kings would serve this during peace talks!"

Narius nodded. "To make sure that the other party was worthy of that peace. Not the wisest diplomatic strategy, unless you count having an iron stomach as indicative of trustworthiness."

Everys turned to the stove. This was a disaster, plain and simple! She couldn't serve this to him! They'd spend the rest of the evening sick to their stomachs or—

A hand touched her shoulder, squeezing gently. "It's all right, Everys. I appreciate the thought."

"Do you think we can salvage the meat?"

Narius laughed again. "If you've been following the recipe, no. The sauce was created to mask the taste of the meat."

Oh. Tears stung her eyes. Smudges, this wasn't what she wanted at all! "So what do we do?"

He smiled, a twinkle in his eye. He pulled his comm out and whispered something into it. About a minute later, the door opened, and half a dozen servants bustled in carrying steaming dishes. Without even a glance in her direction, they set to work, setting out plates and silverware, along with the food.

Irritation flashed through her. So he hadn't trusted her cooking? But then she caught a whiff of the food the servants were setting out. An earthy, hearty aroma with just a hint of sweetness playing underneath, a smell that made her mouth water and her mind wander to simpler times.

Her eyes widened, and she turned to him. "Is that palane stew?"

He nodded, his expression suddenly bashful. "I hope you don't mind."

Mind? It was her favorite food as a child, something Siporans prepared during times of great celebration. Ever since the fall of the Ascendancy, it was a rare treat in Siporan homes. Everys couldn't remember the last time she had eaten it. Not since Papa and Mama and Galan had left.

Within minutes, the servants bustled out of the room again, and Narius motioned for the table. "I'm sorry. If you want to finish the karabek, we can do so, but I don't think it'll pair well with the stew."

"You didn't think I'd be able to make a good dinner for us?" Everys asked.

"Not at all. But one thing the military taught me is always have a backup plan."

That made sense. And the stew smelled so good. She smiled. Maybe this wouldn't be such a disaster after all.

33

She couldn't help herself. Everys dove into the stew, gulping it down so quickly she barely tasted it. But after half a dozen scoops, she realized she was being extremely rude. When she came up for air, she realized Narius was regarding her with a grin.

Her cheeks reddened. "Sorry."

He shook his head. "No need to apologize. It is very delicious. Although I suspect you'll enjoy it better if you slow down."

There was some truth to that. She forced herself to set down her spoon. "So what should we talk about?"

"Well, we could talk about how you practice illegal Siporan magic," Narius said, his tone idle.

Everys's fingers coiled around the spoon as if it were a weapon. "Are you complaining?"

He studied her face for a moment, then smiled. It wasn't a genuine expression; she could easily read the tension in his eyes, the tightness of his lips. "No. But it does raise a number of questions."

"Questions I probably can't answer," she said.

His eyes narrowed. "You would withhold information from your husband and king?"

She leaned forward. "Who's the girl in the picture by your bed?"

Now his eyes widened.

"We both have subjects we'd rather not talk about." Everys forced herself to smile. Hers was just as fake as his, but at least they matched.

"A fair point." He drummed his fingers on the table, then headed over to the kitchenette. He rummaged through one of the cupboards and came back with three small glasses, which he set in a row on his side of the table. He went back and returned with three more.

"What are you doing?" she asked.

"If our partnership is going to be successful, we need to be more open and honest with each other. I obviously have questions about you, and you likely have just as many about me. But, as you said, there are topics that would be off-limits.

"So this is what I propose." He set a glass in front of her with a solid *thunk*. "We take turns asking each other questions." *Thunk*. "And while we can refuse to answer a question, we can only do so three times." *Thunk*.

She frowned at the glasses. Why did they need these? To keep track of the refusals?

He went back to the kitchenette and returned with the pot of the karabek sauce. He ladled some of the thick, brown sludge into the glasses. "But we also have to drink this if we refuse."

Everys's jaw dropped open. He poured the sauce into her glasses as well.

"That's... Well, that's..." She groped for the right word.

"Intriguing? Adventurous?"

"I was going to say childish."

"That too."

She eyed the sauce. She could catch a hint of its putrid stench, which was almost as bad as ink. This was ridiculous. Stupid. But then she looked over at the glasses on Narius's side of the table. She did have questions, and this might be a way to get answers.

"Well?" he prompted.

"So who goes first?"

Everys could read the eagerness in his eyes, but he still gestured toward her. How gallant.

She leaned back in her chair and considered her options. She could go for the jugular right away, but he'd probably respond by drinking. It made more sense to go in slightly sideways.

A smile tugged at her lips. And there it was.

"So why did Viara leave you?" she asked.

Narius's eyes widened in surprise. Then he chuckled. "Oh, so it's going to be like that?"

She shrugged. "A girl can't be curious?"

Narius touched one of the glasses of sauce absentmindedly. Everys could almost read the mental calculations. Should he down a glass now or save them for future questions? After a few moments, he pulled his hand back.

"The truth is, I don't know."

Everys frowned. "She didn't tell you?"

"Communication wasn't really something we did. Ours was a marriage of political convenience."

Everys bit back a teasing comment about how similar that was to their own marriage. It didn't seem like the right time to point out the pattern.

"Father needed to upgrade the weapon systems on our sub-orbital fighters, Viara's father produced the best. Plus, it was a way to keep some of the noble families off-balance. While I'm not happy about the chaos she caused by leaving, I'm relieved she's gone. We were never a good fit."

Everys's mind drifted back to the picture of the mystery girl by his bedside. Was she a better fit? Everys would ask him about her eventually. But she braced herself for his first question.

"So... toratropic magic." He leaned forward in his chair. "The Dynasty outlawed the practice after the Ascendancy fell. And we tainted our ink to make sure the magic wouldn't work anymore."

Everys glanced at her cups of sauce and suppressed a smile. She wouldn't waste one on this, especially since the answer should have been obvious.

"Are you sure about that?" she asked.

He started to answer, then his jaw clicked shut. She could see the answer piecing itself together in his mind.

"When King Heronus overthrew the Ascendancy, he interrogated the mages he captured about how to taint the ink. They said that if we mixed ink with ellay root, it would negate the magic." He let out a low whistle. "They lied to us."

She nodded. "The ellay root only makes the ink smell bad. It doesn't stop the magic from working. Besides, a lot of different substances can be used when a mage doesn't have ink on hand."

His eyes widened. "Zar said ashes were smeared all over your floor. You were using it as ink?"

She nodded.

"So you're saying a toratropic mage could use anything?"

Everys shot a glance at one of the cups. That question was dangerously close to one of her vows. But she thought there was enough wiggle room to avoid actually drinking. "Not exactly. Water doesn't work, for example. And sometimes makeshift ink can't do much of anything."

Narius nodded thoughtfully. "So how does it actually work?"

"Shouldn't I be able to ask a question before you get another?"

Narius's mouth snapped shut, and he blinked. "Fair enough."

"So who's the girl?" Everys asked.

His eyes narrowed, and his cheeks reddened a little. Then, in one fluid motion, he snatched up one of his glasses and downed the sauce in one gulp. Much to Everys's surprise, he barely flinched after swallowing. His only reaction was a small twitch of his eyes and a single drop of sweat that appeared along his hairline. Then he grimaced.

Everys wanted to crow in triumph. She had suspected if she asked about the girl, he'd drink. Now he had one less when she started probing about more sensitive subjects. But she was still disappointed that he hadn't answered the question.

"My turn." He leaned forward. "So how does it work? The magic?"

She nudged a glass. Technically she could answer. If Nekek the Bright still stood, he could have found a philosophical treatise explaining the basic mechanics. But it still didn't feel quite right, sharing this information with him. But his expression was curious, not hostile.

She sighed. "It's hard to explain, but this is an example one of my teachers used. You know computer simulations?"

He nodded.

"When you create a computer simulation, you write code to set the parameters. Well, the same thing is true when it comes to the universe. There's an underlying code that governs everything."

"The laws of nature."

"Sort of? It's not just the physical laws but—" She squirmed. She hadn't talked about this for so long. "—moral and spiritual as well."

Please don't let him ask more about that.

He pursed his lips, his expression thoughtful. Then he motioned for her to continue.

"The runes temporarily tweak the code to speed up a person's healing or to reinforce a door that's about to be kicked in or—"

"Or throw lightning bolts at attackers?"

She swallowed hard, remembering the rebuke from killing those soldiers. "In certain circumstances, yes."

He leaned back in his chair. "So why don't the Siporans rise up again? You still have your magic despite our efforts."

She gritted her teeth. He was straying closer to topics she wasn't supposed to discuss with outsiders. "Because there are rules about how we use the magic. If we misuse our power, we get rebuked."

He frowned. Clearly he wasn't getting it.

Her gaze hitched on a glass of sauce. Could she really answer this? "If there's a code, someone wrote it. We call the writer of the code the Singularity. He taught us the runes and how to use them. If we misuse our magic, we face consequences. We call it a rebuke."

"Is that why you fainted?"

She shifted in her seat, forcing the words out. "Yes. Killing someone with the magic is strictly forbidden."

His frown deepened. "Then how could the Ascendancy exist in the first place? They did that and so much more. Wouldn't that violate these rules?"

Oh, inkstains! "It did."

"So why didn't the Singularity rebuke the mage-kings?"

"He probably did," Everys said. "They may have dulled the pain through narcotics. Or used proxies. And as painful as a rebuke can be, they don't do lasting damage."

"So if there are rules, you have to learn them from somewhere," Narius said. "Where did you learn about how to do any of this?"

Everys swallowed a groan. That question definitely crossed a line. She tightened her left hand into a fist as she grabbed a glass of the sauce and, after taking a deep breath, chugged it.

Fire screamed down her throat, and tears exploded in her eyes. She tried to cough, but her breath caught, and she wheezed. A shudder slammed through her, and she almost fell out of her chair.

"Not too bad," Narius said. "At least you didn't vomit."

She glared at him. "You asked an awful lot of questions just now."

"So I did." He looked at the two remaining glasses in front of him, then pushed them away. "Tell you what. Your next question, I have to answer. No sauce."

Got him. She tried to smile but couldn't. "What is Clarinda Gaines working on for you?"

His eyes widened. Then he chuckled. "Congratulations, wife. How much do you know about Xoniel mythology?"

What did this have to do with anything? "What everyone knows: The Perfected Warrior fell in love with the Water Bearer. When the other gods objected, he defeated them in combat, which not only earned him the Water Bearer's favor but also made him a god in his own right."

"That's the official theology, but there are alternate versions of the story." Narius chuckled. "Supreme Prelate Istragon would have a conniption if he knew I was talking about this, but there's another version that says the Water Bearer was both human and the Warrior's wife. Then the Trickster kidnapped her. The Warrior swore to rescue her, so a lesser god took pity on him and sent him a divine weapon, the Starsword, which fell from the heavens and landed outside the Warrior's home. Using the Starsword, the Warrior defeated the gods and rescued his wife. There used to be a sect that claimed they still had the Starsword in their possession."

Everys frowned.

He must have read her confusion. "About a hundred years ago, the supreme prelate convinced the leaders of that sect to have the Starsword undergo a battery of scientific tests to determine if it was authentic. It turned out that the sword couldn't be the original; it was too 'young.' But the testing did reveal something interesting. It was made out of meteoric iron."

"What?" Everys asked.

"What do you know about our star system?"

Everys wracked her memory. She barely remembered what she had learned in the Dynastic schools: one star, ten planets, they lived on Pedrevor, the fourth. "Not that much, I guess."

"In between Kallistan and Trickster's Abode, there's a large belt of asteroids, along with thousands or millions of others that orbit the sun. A lot of those rocks contain precious minerals, not to mention water ice and other chemicals."

Was he trying to waste her time? "So what?"

Narius leaned back in his chair and looked out the window. "Ever since the Dynasty was founded, it has prospered through war. We conquer and pillage a nation, forcibly integrate their people, then repeat the process. But we've conquered nearly everyone on Ehun.

The only major territory left is Rioka or the Dalark Beachhead, and after the Colonial Uprisings, we can't afford to go overseas. Our system isn't sustainable."

"Not to mention cruel," Everys added.

His cheeks reddened. "A fair point. But without that cycle of conquest, the Dynasty will first stagnate, then crumble. While I know you don't think much of us, imagine the chaos if the Dynasty collapsed. Old grudges, civil wars... Imagine the death toll."

Everys shifted uncomfortably. What he said sounded true. The Dynasty had conquered many former enemies like the Plissk and Dunestriders who now at least coexisted. If the Dynasty were to suddenly disappear, how many of the conquered people would revert to their old hatreds and feuds? Probably more than she'd want to admit.

He met her gaze. "That's why I'm trying to shift our economy from war to something else."

"Asteroids?"

"Mining them. Just imagine: fleets of robotic vessels, harvesting those metals and water and whatever else we find. Imagine if the Dynasty had the controlling interest in that."

Her eyes widened as she thought back to the tour of TelleGlin. "That's why you need Clarinda's ion engines."

He nodded. "I want to use them for my mining fleet."

"But why all the secrecy? If this will benefit the Dynasty, why keep it to yourself?"

He leaned back in his chair. "Because there are too many people trapped in the old traditions and mindsets. Since the Dynasty's birth, our core identity is that of warriors. Remember the old joke? 'There's only two seasons for the Xoniel: war and getting ready for the next one.' There are those who see that as reality, and they will fight to keep it that way."

"Like Viscount Orsin."

"Exactly. But if everything is in place and the system is already working?" Narius waved a hand toward the ceiling. "I don't think we'll meet as much resistance."

Everys considered his words. It wasn't a bad plan. While she wasn't an expert on economics by any means, she knew enough to know that most of the Dynasty's prosperity was built on the military, both in developing weapons and going to war. If they could nudge the Dynasty away from that, that could only be a good thing.

"So my turn now." Narius regarded her. "According to our records, your parents are still alive, and you have two siblings. So why haven't I met your family yet?"

Everys swallowed a groan. She grabbed a glass and downed the sauce. Strangely, it didn't burn as badly. Either she was building up a tolerance or her taste buds had been burned off.

His eyebrows rose. "I'm not quite sure what to make of that."

"Make of it what you will." She squared her shoulders. "My turn. Why did you pick me?"

He froze. Uncertainty flitted across his face. He opened his mouth as if to speak, but then he snared a glass and drank.

"Now I don't know what to make of that." She was surprised at how much that actually hurt.

"Sorry." His voice was a bare rasp until he coughed. "Let's get back to the toratropic magic. You said the ink is like a lens. So it's necessary for a rune to work?"

"More or less," Everys said. "Without ink, we can't direct the toratropic forces to do what we request."

"So you only draw runes if you have ink."

It wasn't a question, not officially, so Everys didn't object to him tacking on another one again. "Not necessarily. For example, there's a Siporan ritual we perform when we take up residence in a new home. We draw runes by our doors to not only invite the Singularity into them, but to also ask for His protection. I did that the day I moved in."

Narius looked toward the door. "But I don't see anything."

Everys smiled. "I didn't use ink. Here."

She cleared a spot on the table. Then she traced the runes on the tabletop, a complex knot of swirls and lines. Narius leaned forward, his eyes intense. Maybe he hoped to see bright lights or sparkles.

"Is that really supposed to work?"

She shrugged. "I suppose. But it's not really about casting a spell. Back in the days of the Ascendancy, Siporans would draw these runes every day with fresh ink. Since it's too dangerous to do that, it's been decided that we can just trace them and that will have to be good enough."

Actually, as she thought of it, there was more to it than that. The masters had decreed Siporans were supposed to retrace the runes daily, but as far as she knew, no one did. She never had. Maybe they hadn't learned the lesson of Downcasting thoroughly enough yet.

"Why not carve them into the wall?" Narius asked. "Wouldn't that be easier?"

She forced herself to smile. "If we did that, people would notice the runes, and it's tough enough to be Siporan within the Dynasty as it is. And that wouldn't work anyway. A carving might have the shape, but without the ink, it wouldn't be able to do anything even if it was supposed to."

Narius leaned forward in his chair. "But that doesn't make sense. If carvings don't work, then why—"

His eyes widened, and he clamped his mouth shut. Like he was about to ask something but didn't want to. But why? Because...

Because he must have seen runes carved into something. But where?

"Narius?" Everys asked. "Why would you ask about carving a rune?"

His lips pushed together into a thin line. His gaze skipped to his last glass of sauce, then he sighed and slumped in his chair.

"Come with me. I have something I should show you."

34

The chilly night air nipped at Everys's arms as they left the palace. Why was Narius taking her to the royal gardens? Sure, it was a nice night and the gardens were lovely, but this seemed like the end of a romantic evening. What did this have to do with carved runes? But he didn't explain. Instead, with a hand on the small of her back, he steered her deeper into the gardens.

She hadn't had the chance to thoroughly explore the gardens yet. From the brief glances she got, they looked pretty. But up close, they were breathtaking. Different kinds of trees lined the path, surrounded by flowers and shrubbery. Little signs along the way explained each section was filled with different plants from around the Dynasty's holdings. Rather than a confusing hodgepodge of plants, though, the effect was one of seamless tranquility. As they meandered along the twisting path, Everys felt like Bastion, the palace, all the cares and worries, slipped away. Like they disappeared into another land, a simpler time. They weren't king or queen, but just two people out for a walk to enjoy each other's company.

But then they came across a barren patch of dirt. According to the display placard, it was reserved for cuttings from the Cold Light's Hearth. That reminder of the Dynasty's history shattered the illusion, and any enjoyment Everys was experiencing vanished. So much for escape.

Eventually, they came across a mound of stones in what Everys guessed was the heart of the gardens. Narius turned to face her.

"Many people don't realize this, but the palace originally stood here. Two hundred years ago, Diradae terrorists burned it to the ground. The king, my great-great-grandfather, rebuilt the palace where it stands today and converted this area to gardens. I think he also did it to hide this." He gestured to the rubble. "Technically, the king can decide whether or not to share this with anyone else. As far as I know, you're the first queen to know about it in four generations."

Know about what? The rubble? Did most queens not make it this far into the gardens?

Narius waved his hands over a broken column that stuck out of the pile. At first, nothing happened, but then the jagged surface lit up. The ground vibrated gently beneath Everys's feet as a portion of the rock pile shifted, revealing a darkened opening. Lights flickered in the depths, and Narius motioned toward the opening.

"Welcome to the Dynasty's archives," he said.

He started for the door, then paused long enough to offer his arm. Everys hooked her hand into the crook of his elbow, and the two of them descended into the shadows.

Once her eyes adjusted to the dim light, she realized that they were heading down a stone staircase that circled lower and lower.

"So you and I are the only ones who know about this?" she asked.

"The only two in Bastion, yes. There is a Master Archivist who cares for what's down here. He comes to the palace once a month. The rest of the time, he lives far away from here. Truthfully, I'm not entirely sure where. And I'm not always sure when he visits. There are tunnels that lead from the palace grounds out into various neighborhoods in Bastion so he can come and go without being noticed."

That struck Everys as an odd arrangement. Why the secrecy?

Eventually, they came out into a small foyer made of rough-hewn bricks. The first thing Everys spotted was a glass display case that held... a stick? She stepped closer. No, it was a large tree branch. But strange faces, elongated and stylized, were carved along its length. A tattered piece of cloth, blue and green and brown, was tied to the top.

"What is this?" she asked.

"According to the archivists' lore, two thousand years ago, a human tribe who lived in the heart of what's now the Dynasty's holdings went to war with another tribe. After destroying the village, the conquerors took this, the defeated tribe's totem. The conquerors eventually called themselves the Xoniel, and since then, we have taken trophies from those we have subjugated."

"So that stick was the first of the trophies? It's the real thing?"

"I don't think so. The archivist says some of the original trophies were destroyed when the palace burned. So they made replicas. I don't know what's what. The archivist does."

As they rounded the totem's display case, Everys stumbled to a halt. Rows of displays spread out before them. Each one was filled with various odds and ends. Some held statues, others what probably were sacred objects from whatever cultures they came from. The most bizarre, though, was a steel column with a lump of misshapen glass perched on it.

"What's this one?" Everys asked.

"I think it's from when my grandfather conquered the Cold Light," Narius said.

Everys leaned in to get a closer look. It was a large, uncut gem, mostly green but shot through with veins of yellow and red. Parts of it were translucent, almost as clear as glass, while other parts looked like clouds roiled within. As Everys stared into it, she got the distinct impression of a presence, something weighing down on her, drawing her closer until...

She stumbled forward, almost tripping over her own feet. Narius caught her and helped her upright. "Are you okay?"

She nodded, then realized she had grabbed onto his arm, holding on to it tightly. She quickly let go and stepped away.

If he noticed her embarrassment, he didn't let on. Instead, he beckoned her to keep walking. "Come on, what I want to show you is in the center of the archives."

She nodded and let him take the lead. She cast one look over her shoulder, haunted both by the way that strange object seemed to call to her and by the way her heart had thrilled, even momentarily, to feel the muscles underneath his sleeve.

If Father knew who Narius had brought into the archives, he would have had a stroke.

It wasn't the first time Narius had thought that. Father would never have supported Falling Sword. He had believed in ruling through strength and fear. Economic prosperity was an afterthought, not a goal to be pursued for its own benefit. No, victory and honor above all else, with the former being the true priority. Military victory. How many times had Father brought Narius into the archives to remind him of those ideals? And not only was Narius ready to walk away from war, but he'd also brought a Siporan to see these trophies?

From the way Everys stared at each display, her eyes wide and her mouth popped open, he thought it was completely worth it.

"Is that a pile of *skulls?*"

"Unfortunately," Narius said. "The Plissk chieftains kept track of their victories with a literal head count. When my ancestor conquered the tribes, he confiscated the Chief-of-Chief's collection. Apparently there was an argument over where to store it. He wanted it in his throne room. His wife insisted it be kept somewhere else."

Everys shuddered. Narius couldn't blame her. According to the archivist, there were at least four hundred skulls in the pile, the majority of them Plissk, but with enough of the other races mixed in to keep things "interesting," whatever that meant.

Everys turned a slow circle. "Why keep all of this?"

He shrugged. "Bragging rights mostly. Although officially it's so each king can teach their heir the Dynasty's heritage. You know, 'Look, my son, at what your forebears accomplished. It is now up to you to carry on this impressive tradition with conquests of your own.'"

She studied his face. "That sounded like a direct quote."

He shuffled to a stop. It had been. Father had said words to that effect every time they had come down here and had forced Narius to recite, with painful specificity, the history of each artifact. He could probably recite most of it if he wanted.

Narius shook his head to clear it. No time for reminiscence. Besides, he doubted that Everys would want to hear any of it. He snared her hand and led her toward their destination.

"Okay, stealing that tapestry makes sense, but what's that giant clay weevil? Was it a divinity or a mascot or..." Her voice trailed off.

And Narius understood why.

Standing before them was a half-circle of five stone pillars, vaguely shaped like curved talons or teeth, their points facing outward. A large rune was carved onto each pillar, facing toward the center. Of all the displays, this was the most impressive. But he knew why she would be speechless.

Everys took two steps toward them, then fell to her knees. She stretched out a shaking hand. "D-do you know what these are?"

He nodded. Maybe Father's history lessons would be helpful after all. "Your people called them the Principalities, yes?"

She nodded absently and clambered to her feet. Then she took a halting step toward the pillars.

"You can see why I was curious about the carvings," Narius said. "Why carve runes onto the Principalities if that doesn't work?"

"Because the carvings are a template," Everys whispered. "Every day, celebrants would enter the Scriptotum and ink the runes. See? There are still traces of the pigment on the edges where it didn't burn off."

Narius frowned and took a closer look. Sure enough, pale blue flecks dotted the runes' edges. He had examined the Principalities how many times and he had never noticed?

"So you do need ink for the spells to work," Narius said.

Everys nodded. "The spell consumes the rune's ink. Once the ink is gone, the spell ends." Her gaze hitched on something else. "Are those... Are those void shields?"

What? Before he could say anything, Everys rushed to another alcove, where shields hung on a wall. She pulled one down and brought it over to Narius, pointing along the top edge.

"See these little holes? There's a cavity inside in the shape of a rune. Before battle, a warrior would pour ink into this hole. Then he could activate the spell, which would give his shield more durability or set it on fire or whatever the rune was supposed to do."

"According to the archivist's lore, those holes proved that Ascendancy blacksmithing was inferior to ours." Narius winced. "Sorry. Xoniel historians can be a tad... self-aggrandizing at times."

"Our texts have nothing but respect for Xoniel soldiers," Everys said. "The mage-kings often hired them as mercenaries and honor guards. Well, before Downcasting, that is."

"So I've been told."

Everys looked at the shield, then back to the Principalities. "When the Dynasty destroyed Nekek the Bright, these were brought here?"

Narius nodded. "As proof of the Dynasty's strength."

Everys started to ask another question, but her gaze caught on something else and her eyes widened. She dropped the shield, which struck the cement floor with a loud clatter, then she raised a trembling hand to her lips and stumbled toward another display.

"Is that... is that...?" she whispered.

Why was she so impressed by that display? Sure they were more Siporan artifacts, but it was just a rack of broken swords. Each one looked as though its blade had been broken in half, the ends jagged. Most were held in rows of three or four, but there was one perched at the very top. He never understood why these would be considered important by the Ascendancy.

"What are they?" he asked.

"*Ur-keleshen.* In Dynastic, that could be translated as 'Never Slaked.' Or 'Always Thirsty?' It's not a clean translation," she whispered. She stepped into the alcove, her hand outstretched. But then she snatched her hand away as if she had been burned. "This is what ruined my people."

Narius glanced at her face to see if she was joking, but her expression was deadly serious. She still wouldn't touch the sword, but her fingers hovered above it.

"'And when the king saw that his blade had broken, he took a shard and carved his wrath, his agony, his revenge, his empty future on the flat. And armed thus, he turned their blood to ink and brought about the curse that toppled the nation.'" She backed out of the alcove, her body trembling. "I can't believe it still exists."

"What?" Narius asked.

Everys took a deep breath. "When the Singularity taught my people toratropic magic, He had us carve eight key runes on the Principalities." She pointed toward the pillars. "Those were the basis of the spells we were allowed to cast. We could experiment with them, but there were very strict limits on how much improvisation was allowed.

"But that changed with *ur-keleshen*. It belonged to a Siporan king named Annaeus. He was a cruel man, self-centered and vain, but a powerful toratropic mage. A rival for his throne attempted a coup and defeated Annaeus in a duel. The king's blade was broken during the fight. Then the rival brought Annaeus's children before him and slaughtered them one by one.

"The king, distraught, took a piece of metal, carved four new runes into the flat of the broken blade, and stabbed his rival. The runes activated, creating a weapon of unimaginable destruction. And this discovery ultimately ruined the Siporans. It encouraged us to experiment with rune-writing beyond what the Singularity allowed. And it revealed the most powerful ink is blood. Shortly thereafter, the Ascendancy was born."

Narius frowned. "And the other swords?"

"Copies," Everys said. "Annaeus had copies of *ur-keleshen* forged for his armies, capable of the same cruelty."

Narius walked up to the weapon rack. Up close, he could see the difference. While all of the swords appeared broken, most had been forged with shorter blades and jagged edges. Each sword had four runes carved into the flat of their blades, but the copied runes had crisp lines whereas the originals were faint scratches. If Narius squinted, he could tell that the copied runes were the same as the originals. He reached out to pick up the original so he could get a closer look.

Everys shouted and knocked his hand away. "What are you doing? Don't touch it!"

He smiled at her reassuringly. "Everys, it'll be fine. I've picked it up before."

She gaped at him, clearly aghast. "Y-you what?"

To illustrate his point, he carefully gripped the broken sword's hilt and lifted it from the rack. The balance was off, but that wasn't a surprise, given that two thirds of the blade was missing. But he still twirled it in his hand before holding it up to show her. "See?"

Her entire body quaked, her eyes wide. "D-don't you get it? This isn't a game, Narius. Taking these things lightly is what destroyed my people!"

He snorted. "I think the Xoniel helped a little."

Narius regretted the joke the moment he said it. Everys's body went rigid. Fire flashed in her eyes, and for a second, Narius considered striking a defensive stance with the sword.

But she didn't attack him, even though it looked like she might. Instead, she stabbed a finger at him. "Only because the Singularity allowed it. If He hadn't, you would have never even dented Nekek the Bright's walls."

Now Narius bristled. "As if we needed some god's help!"

"You don't get it," Everys said. "None of you ever have. The reason the Ascendancy fell wasn't because your army was stronger or your commanders smarter or your tactics or technology better. It was be cause... because..." Tears welled up in her eyes and her voice got very quiet. "Because we didn't listen."

Why was she crying? He took a step toward her, but she shied away, then turned, fleeing back through the archives.

Narius's arm drooped, and the sword almost slipped out of his fingers. What had happened? He had brought her down to the archives to show her the Principalities, to see if she would share more of her heritage and history with him, and instead...

He sighed and set the sword back on to the rack. He shouldn't have been surprised. Viara had predicted once that he would always be alone. Maybe she had been right all along.

35

A week later, the smell of karabek still lingered in her quarters, a reminder of how things had ended with Narius. She had hoped the stench would fade, but it was persistent, and no matter how hard she tried to ignore it, she couldn't.

Just like she couldn't forget the lingering pain from the sharp words she had hurled at Narius.

In the intervening week, she had considered trying to make amends. Maybe not with another dinner, but with a conversation. Or send one of the girls with a note. Something. But no, she just couldn't muster the courage. Plus, she had too much to do. A Queen's Court was scheduled for the end of that week, and as much as she wanted to put it off, she couldn't. Challix had practically imprisoned her in her quarters, going over dossiers for all the potential guests so Everys could memorize as many details as she could.

Only now that the day of the Court had come, her assistant was nowhere to be seen.

"Any idea where she is?" Everys paced in a dressing gown, glaring at the door to her quarters.

Trule, much to her surprise, didn't blanch or even flinch. "Challix said she'd be here by now. Do you want me to send one of the guards to find her?"

Everys chuckled. Just picturing the way Challix would react to being dragged before Everys lightened her mood. But no, that wouldn't be helpful.

Thankfully, Challix breezed in. Even though she was running late, she still looked impeccably put together, her dark hair swept up in a bun that made her sharp features all the more severe. She wore a black business outfit, a knee-length skirt and matching coat. Her gaze swept over Everys, then she sniffed.

Three older women swept into the room, carrying what looked like a large fabric pyramid between them. It took Everys a moment to realize that it was actually a dress, made of cloth that looked like oil shimmering on the surface of water. But why was there so much of it? Trule made a soft gasping sound, then covered her mouth. To keep from laughing? Or maybe crying. Everys wasn't sure what the right response was supposed to be.

Challix positively beamed at them. "Do you like it? It's the latest fashion from Erecone."

Everys's jaw dropped open. *This* was considered fashionable? It looked like someone had stolen a tent from a frontline military unit and turned it into a vastly oversized dress. At least, she thought it was a dress. She still hadn't spotted any sleeves.

"Now, it will take some work to prepare you, but don't worry. These ladies have worked with some of the best noble families in Bastion. They'll more than make up for your girls' shortcomings."

Trule and the other girls gasped. One of them even muttered something under her breath, but whoever it was fell silent at a sharp glare from Challix.

"You can't be serious," Everys said.

Challix's face froze. "What do you mean?"

Everys gestured at the cloth. "I can't wear that! I'm not even sure how you'd get me in there!"

Challix turned to look at the dress and frowned. "That's because you're looking at it upside down."

Everys tipped her head to one side. Oh, that made a little more sense. But still...

"Why would you expect me to wear that?" Everys asked.

"It would be a boon to the Dynasty. You are a trendsetter, after all. You would inspire other nobles to dress in Erecone fashions. And Minister Masruq is currently in negotiations with Erecone. If you wore this dress, they might be more favorably inclined to trade with us."

Everys gaped at her. Seriously? She had to wear a ridiculous costume so a foreign country might be willing to trade with the Dynasty? Was Challix joking? But her adviser's expression remained stoic, earnest even. Best to put a stop to this.

"I don't think so," Everys said.

"It is tradition to—"

"Do I look like a traditional queen?" Everys spat the words at her.

Challix blanched, her jaw clicking shut.

"Maybe this has been the tradition for the past however many generations, but it stops today," Everys continued. "I'm not going to the Court to be some sort of fashion model."

"Oh?" Challix arched a brow. "And what do you think this Court is about?"

"Strengthening connections with the nobility. Trying to get them to support Narius's vision for the Dynasty." Everys waved at the dress. "I don't need to be wearing that monstrosity to accomplish those goals."

Challix pursed her lips. "Perhaps not. But the Court starts soon. Unless you have something else in mind that you can put on right now, I don't see how... what?"

Everys looked her adviser up and down, a grin tugging at her lips. "What size do you wear?"

Why were her hands so sweaty? Everys resisted the urge to wipe them on the suit coat. Granted, doing so wouldn't stain the fabric, but Challix was annoyed enough at losing her outfit. The last thing Everys should do is provoke her further.

Her feet itched, like they wanted to move, but she didn't want the doors to the East Gallery to open and reveal her pacing. She had to be poised. Regal. Challix's final words to her echoed in her mind: *If you're not going to dress like a queen, you had best act twice the part.* As much as Challix annoyed her, what she said made sense.

She could already hear the muted conversations on the other side of the door. According to the girls, the guests had been arriving for the past hour or so. By this point, though, all of her guests would be assembled and waiting for her grand entrance.

Redtale stepped past her, taking up her position by the doors. She wore a dress uniform, all dark blues with red piping along the sleeves and legs. "Ready, Blessed?"

Everys froze. The moment she said she was, Redtale would open the door, revealing her to the guests. She would have to step into the gallery and greet the assembled nobles. Once the doors were opened, she'd be on her own. Challix, Trule, and the other girls wouldn't be with her. And from what she had gathered, Narius wouldn't show up either. A Queen's Court belonged to the queen. If she wanted it to be successful, it was all up to her.

Inkstains, what was she doing? This was more frightening than going to the Demilitarized Zone.

"Blessed? Are you okay?" Redtale asked.

No, of course she wasn't! Her guests wouldn't be fooled. They had seen queens before, real ones. They'd see right through her. Maybe she could play sick. Yes, that was it. They couldn't get upset if the queen became sick. She took a step back, already savoring the relief. She'd send someone in to explain she had suddenly taken ill, that she regretted not being there with them.

"Hey. Everys."

Redtale's use of her name snapped her out of her thoughts. When had her guard stepped so close?

"You will be fine. These women will be petty. They'll be overly polite to your face and snipe at your back, but you're stronger than the lot of them put together. If you can survive a riot and an assassination attempt, you can handle a bunch of bored noblewomen."

That statement knocked Everys out of her fear by replacing it with a new one. What did that mean? Did Redtale know what she did?

"I'll be in there with you the whole way," she said. "And if things get really bad, you just give the signal and my men and I will slaughter the whole lot of them."

A laugh escaped her. "Why not just do that right now and save us the trouble?"

Redtale smiled. "Because that would be more merciful than unleashing you on them. Now go in there and show them why you're queen."

Everys stood up taller, tipped her chin back. Redtale stepped to the door and wrenched it open, and Everys, squaring her shoulders, walked through.

She stepped out onto a stage with a broad staircase to the main floor. Five hundred women, some younger than her, most quite a bit older, waited for her. They wore fashionable dresses, some almost as ridiculous as the one Challix had brought. They stood in clusters, the significance of which she couldn't decipher. But they all turned as one to face her. Most of the older ladies looked positively aghast at her appearance.

"Good afternoon." Thankfully her voice remained calm. "Thank you for joining me. I look forward to our time together."

Her words were received with a smattering of applause. Nothing enthusiastic, but Everys doubted the nobles could do enthusiastic without cracking their facades. She stepped down to the main floor. As she did, servers appeared and circulated through the crowd with trays of snacks and drinks.

Several of the guests moved quickly to be the first to greet her. Everys recognized some of them immediately. There was Lady Oron Pilsin of the Low River Province; her husband was trying to get Narius to annex a portion of his neighbor's estate for its mineral rights. And in her wake were Ladies Hixom and Uwendi; as near as she had been able to tell, both were horrible gossips who would likely hover near her the entire Court to glean juicy tidbits for their stories. And then there was—

Everys lost track as a small cloud of nobles formed around her, each one offering a bow or a curtsy. Everys was able to greet most of them by name—a feat that clearly surprised most of them—and the few she couldn't were outwardly polite enough to introduce themselves. There was Petite Wexxil, who in spite of her name towered over the other guests. And Duchess Wendly of the Right Highlands was probably here to ask her to get Narius to lessen the farming quotas for their province, but she also knew that Narius needed those quotas to stay the same because of the Cold Light rebellion. There was Lady Leedeke and her daughters, Jillson and Jolds who, for some reason, dressed in identical outfits.

And there was...

Everys froze for a split second. Clarinda Gaines, dressed not in formal attire, but a very similar business outfit. She looked like she had just emerged from a board meeting. Her hair was swept up into a rigid style, her crystalline eyes raking over the assembled crowd. But when Gaines noticed Everys, a predatory light shone in them.

Everys gritted her teeth. She had to be polite. For Narius's sake. He needed Gaines's engines for his mining probes. As much as the woman rankled her, she had to at least be friendly during the Court.

She forced a smile and carefully extracted herself from the cloud of well-wishers, striding across the ballroom toward Gaines. If the other woman noticed her approach, she didn't let on. She spoke quietly with some of the other guests, not even pausing as she snared a drink from a passing waiter.

Once Everys had closed the distance, Gaines turned to her with an obviously fake smile. "Queen Everys! It is good to see you again."

Gaines's disdain was only thinly veiled, and not very well. The other women standing nearby exchanged knowing looks, hints of grins on their lips.

Everys forced a smile of her own. "Lady Gaines, so glad you could make it."

Gaines's expression faltered, just for a moment. Everys fought to keep from crowing in triumph. First point to her. Using a noble title was a petty way to needle Gaines, but Everys felt grossly outmatched, like a warrior stepping into battle against an opponent much larger than her with only a stick and a plank of wood for a shield. She blinked at the mental image. Maybe she had absorbed more of the Dynasty's way of thinking than she'd realized.

But then Gaines's smile was back, just as artificial as ever. "I am glad to see that you are in good health. Why, after the attempt at TelleGlin and then on the Night of Shards, I would think that you would be hesitant to be seen in public. At the least, I would be worried about another attack hurting one of your guests."

"A calculated risk, to be sure." Everys forced herself to keep her tone measured and even. "I am so glad that you're here, though. After all, TelleGlin is an important part of the future my husband is envisioning for the Dynasty."

Gaines's gaze sharpened ever so slightly. Everys struggled to keep from smirking. Was it the hint that Everys knew something about the engines? Or was it the subtle emphasis she had put on the "my" in "my husband?" Either way, Gaines appeared to be more on edge.

But any suspicion disappeared from her expression, and she smiled. Genuinely, it seemed. "I have to admit, I almost didn't come. These courts can be really boring, and I've got a stack of work waiting for me back at the office."

A subtle reminder of her status as a CEO? Maybe, but Everys decided to ignore it. "Well, I'm not sure you'll find today that much more exciting."

"Oh, I wouldn't worry." Gaines took a sip from her glass, but Everys didn't miss the twinkle in her eye. "These events often become more dramatic than you anticipate."

Before Everys could ask what she meant by that, Gaines turned to her group of friends, making it clear their conversation was over.

Everys blinked, surprised at the brusque attitude. She could have pressed the point, but she decided not to. After all, she wouldn't be the one to bring drama to the day. The Court had to run smoothly, and she was going to make sure it did.

How long had the Court dragged on? Two hours? Four? Everys wasn't sure anymore, but it had to end soon, didn't it? But no, the servants kept bringing out food and drink and none of the guests were leaving.

She swallowed a sigh and gently rolled her shoulders, all too aware of the knot forming between them. Thankfully, none of the women vying for her attention noticed her discomfort. Not that they would have stopped if they had. They had been blathering about country estates and trips to exotic destinations and how much money they had spent on their various luxuries the whole time. Everys had already forgotten their names. They probably had suitably impressive titles with long genealogies stretching back to the dawn of the Dynasty, but at that point, she didn't care. Her feet hurt, and all she wanted to do was retreat back to her quarters for a nap.

At least the Court had gone smoothly. The small quintet of musicians had played gentle music the whole time. As near as Everys could tell, they did an okay job. The nobles seemed to agree. She had spotted a number of the women discreetly getting contact information from the musicians. And everyone had been unfailingly polite to her, even going as far as to offer her what seemed like genuine compliments on her business attire.

She let her gaze roam across the room. The women were still clustered in their little knots, gossiping, laughing, eating, drinking. So very formal, so very polite, so very—

Wait. Why was Redtale looking so worried?

The guard's eyes had widened, and she had pressed her hand against her ear. She whispered something, her face reddening. She took a step forward, almost rushing, then caught herself. She smiled at some passing ladies, then moved carefully but urgently from her post toward Everys.

Everys turned to the women circling her and excused herself, quickly moving to intercept Redtale. As soon as they had closed the distance, she whispered, "What's the matter? Assassins?"

Redtale shook her head. "Worse than that. I just got word that—"

The main doors banged open, and Everys whipped around. An imposing young woman stood on the stage, a smirk on her perfectly sculpted lips. She was a little shorter than Everys, with black hair that flowed halfway down her back. Her emerald eyes glinted with silent laughter as her gaze swept over the gathered women. Although Everys had never met her, she recognized her instantly. How could she not?

Narius's ex-wife, the former queen, Viara.

36

A pit opened in Everys's stomach. What was she doing here? She hadn't been invited, had she? No, that made no sense. But what should they do now? What was the correct protocol for having the former queen attend the current queen's Court?

"I'm sorry, Blessed," Redtale whispered. "We didn't realize she was in the palace until it was too late. We think she may have snuck in with Duchess Illon's delegation. All those robed servants..."

The rest of Redtale's apology dissolved into a buzz as Everys stared at her predecessor. Viara's gaze drifted across the gathered nobles, her smirk toxic.

"It is so good to see all of you again." Viara's voice was a spoken song. "I regret I wasn't allowed to say farewell to you properly, but, as you know, I had little choice."

Whispers rippled through the room. Everys couldn't gauge what her guests might be saying. Were they amused? Horrified? Some mixture of the two?

Viara fixed a speculative gaze on her, as if reading her thoughts. Everys realized that was exactly what the former queen wanted. To create a scandal. To prove some sort of point. Fine. If that was the game, Everys would play.

She forced herself to turn to Redtale, a smile on her lips. She took a deep breath and spoke loudly enough that those around her could hear. "Thank you for informing me of our guest's arrival. I'm so glad that she was able to join us." Then she turned to Viara. "Although I must admit, I'm a bit surprised to see you here. You'll pardon me, Viara, but since I didn't think you'd want to attend, I didn't send you an invitation."

"Quite all right, *Blessed*." The way Viara spat out the word, it might have been an insult. "I am sure you have been simply overwhelmed. To rise so far above your place, it must be terribly taxing. One of your other guests made arrangements for me to attend."

Did they now? A smile flickered across Gaines's face. Either she was enjoying the spectacle—entirely likely—or she was the one who caused it. The momentary expression of glee was enough to lend steel to Everys's resolve. She wouldn't buckle. She couldn't.

She turned sharply on her heel and fixed a smile on her face. "Well, I for one am glad to see that you're looking so well. You left the palace so abruptly and disappeared from the public view. I know there were many who were concerned."

"Were they now?" Viara arched a brow. "And was one of those 'many' my husband? No, that couldn't be. The man is physically incapable of showing any concern for anyone other than himself."

Now gasps bubbled through the guests. Everys flinched.

Viara chuckled. "Oh, please. You all act so shocked, but you know it to be true. Narius's family is infamous for the coarse way they treat their wives. I knew I was going to be a living decoration when I married him. But you, my dear. Don't you wonder why he chose to marry someone from Fair Havens like you?"

The pit in her stomach swallowed her. To hear that question, asked by someone else... No, asked by *her*. She went still, not even daring to suck in a breath.

"You know, he married me for his family's gain. Not that he had a choice. Our parents made the match and all the arrangements. But why, do you think, did he choose you?" Viara's gaze sharpened. "Demographics. That's all it is. Poll numbers. Everyone knows his hold on the Dynasty has been slipping. He had to do something drastic to hold on. So here you are."

The pit inside her threatened to completely engulf her. Was that the answer? Was it that crass, that simple? She had been the only commoner in line that morning. Well, except for Clarinda Gaines. She wasn't a noble, but she wanted to be one. And she was wealthy.

Everys's gaze darted to Gaines, who stood nearby with a small cluster of noblewomen. While the CEO wasn't gloating openly, Everys could easily read the laughter in her eyes.

"Look, the poor thing is about to cry." Viara leaned forward. "What's the matter? Were you hoping to hide the truth? We all know what you are."

Ice sliced down Everys's back. That phrasing, so similar to the message scrawled in her armoire. Had that been a message from Viara? No, that wasn't possible; she had left the palace long before the message had been sent. But Viara probably had cronies within the palace who would be more than willing to vandalize Everys's room.

If Viara knew about the effect her words had on Everys, she didn't let on. Instead, she took a step forward, her grin positively feral. "You know what you are too, don't you, *katharin*?"

For one insane moment, Everys actually felt relief that Viara hadn't accused her of being a toratropic mage. But then her words registered. *Katharin*, an Old Dynastic word for "commoner," used in the modern Dynasty to describe a nobody, a worthless person, a waste of space and time and energy. While most of Everys's guests gasped at the brazen insult, a few giggled quietly. She resisted the urge to look around at her guests because she knew what she would find. Agreement. Condescension. Sympathy, but not for her. For Viara. For the disgraced queen, now fighting back against the commoner who dared to take her place in the palace. Oh, they had all behaved so friendly, been so polite, but now that Viara was here to speak for them, she knew what they were all thinking. She was a commoner. *Katharin*. Nothing.

Wait. Maybe she was. But she was so much more than that now.

She forced herself to laugh, but soon, real laughter slipped from her throat. "You know, it's been a while since someone called me that to my face. Back in Fair Havens, I was called that at least two or three times a week. Usually more. I'd even be willing to bet that plenty of people have referred to me by that term since my marriage, just not to my face.

"But why stop there? *Katharin* is so tame. Why not use the other terms that I'm sure have been assigned to me? Like 'phony queen.' 'Pretender.' Or how about 'scribbler?'"

The room went silent. Several of the guests stared at her with wide eyes, probably wondering if she was a toratropic mage or if they had called her that recently and couldn't figure out how she knew. Even Viara had gone still, her face an expressionless mask. Everys studied her expression, hoping to catch some hint of guilt that she knew about the message in the armoire. But the former queen's features were too composed.

"But I'm not a *katharin* anymore, am I? I'm the queen," Everys said, forcing ice into her tone. "And that means that there are certain expectations as to how I should behave. Kevtho? Please come here."

The guests looked confused as to who she was talking to until Kevtho strode forward. The moment the other women saw the Sword-bound, though, they started whispering. Viara's eyes widened as well.

"If I'm not mistaken, since you just insulted me in front of witnesses, I can challenge you to a duel. Granted, I'm still new at this, but I think that's how this works," Everys said.

Viara had actually stumbled back a step. Kevtho came to a halt next to Everys, his hand on the sword's hilt.

Everys held out a hand. "Kevtho?"

The guard shot her an uncertain look. Everys steeled her expression and nodded grimly. Kevtho drew the sword and dropped into a ready stance. But it was clear from his expression that he wasn't comfortable.

"Very good. Now please give me the sword."

Now he looked stunned. "Blessed?"

"You heard me. If Viara wants to make this personal, we'll do this ourselves. The sword. Please."

Kevtho shot a look at Redtale, who shrugged. After another moment's hesitation, Kevtho handed the blade to Everys.

Thankfully, she was ready for the weapon's weight. She didn't fumble it like the first time she'd held it. Instead, she swung it around in a short arc, then pointed it directly at Viara. "Well? I'm sure we can scrounge up a sword for you."

Viara's eyes were wide, and she held up her hands in quiet surrender.

Everys turned a slow circle, looking at all of the guests. They looked just as horrified. At least she had their attention. Maybe they'd actually pay attention to what she said next.

Whatever that would be.

"Is this too daring? Isn't this the Dynasty's way? Someone strikes us, so we hit back harder. We defend our honor. We revel in conflict. We spill blood, someone else's or our own, to satisfy that craving. Is that the Dynasty you want to be a part of? Because I don't. And neither does my husband." She turned back to Viara. "I think that's why you left him. You were scared. You heard his talk of changing the Dynasty, making it better, and you realized your perch on top of Dynasty society was threatened, so you tried to humiliate him by leaving him." She gestured to the gathered crowd, careful to use her free hand. She didn't need anyone thinking she was threatening them. "And I know that afterwards, Narius tried reaching out to many of the families who are gathered here, trying to find a new wife. And none of you took him up on the offer. I wonder why that is?

"Because none of you were daring enough to be his queen. So, he finally had to go to Fair Havens and choose me. A *katharin*. A Siporan. A scribbler. And you know what? He even gave me the chance to walk away, just like you. I could have gone back to my home and left all of the whispers and rumors and hostility behind. But I didn't. Do you know why?" Everys's smile broadened. "Because I believe in what he's doing. The king is taking on a monumental task right now, trying to strengthen the Dynasty and ensure that it stands for centuries."

Then her words caught in her throat, not because she was lying, but because she wasn't. She knew she had to say something like that, but in that moment, she realized that she actually meant what she had said. Narius, for all of his faults, for all of his naivete about the Dynasty's legacy, genuinely wanted to make things better, just like she did. They might disagree on how to accomplish it, but they had the same goal.

She turned to face the other women. "But there is still time for bravery, even now. I don't know why all of you came here today. Maybe it was out of obligation. Maybe it was to see your friends. Maybe it was out of morbid curiosity to see how the scribbler is doing. But whatever brought you here, I hope you will join me. Join us. We can work together to strengthen the Dynasty for all of its people."

Everys locked eyes with Clarinda Gaines as she spoke those words. Much to Everys's surprise, the CEO reacted. A small flinch, a flicker of understanding. But then her expression softened. She nodded, barely, almost imperceptibly, but she did.

Everys released a soft sigh of relief. A small victory, sure, but she would still count it. But why not try for a bigger one? She turned back to Viara, then handed the sword back to Kevtho. The guard quickly returned it to its sheath.

"There is no reason for us to be hostile. I can't do anything about what happened to you while here at the palace, but I know we can work together, if you want."

Viara glared at her, then laughed, a brittle sound. She flipped her hand, dismissing Everys's offer. "As if I would sully myself with someone like you. Mark my words, friends, if you stand with this one, you'll be responsible for the downfall of the Dynasty."

"Or they will be part of its transformation into something that will endure for generations to come," Everys countered.

Viara huffed, then spun and stormed off for the door. Redtale and the other guards barely had time to get out of the way before she made a dramatic exit. Redtale looked at Everys, a question painted across her face. Everys nodded subtly. Redtale returned the gesture and stepped into the hallway after Viara. There was no way Everys was going to let the former queen go unescorted through the palace.

Everys turned to her guests. "I understand if any of you want to leave with Viara. I wouldn't blame you. After all, it's awkward when the queen challenges someone to a duel. But if you're willing, I hope you will stay and enjoy the rest of your time with me."

That seemed to be the only invitation they needed. Soon the room was bubbling with friendly conversation, strained at first, but turning more and more genuine as time went on. Everys continued to mix and mingle with the guests. Most of them were simple introductions with hollow flattery and surface-level chatter. But occasionally, Everys saw a flash of respect in a guest's eyes, a subtle nod, or a sincere word of gratitude.

As the Court wound down, the guests started to leave in groups of two or three. As they left, they paid their respects.

One woman, stocky and her hair silvered with age, rushed up to her, her face split with a broad grin. "A truly wonderful event, my queen. You should be quite proud. And since you have extended your hospitality to me, I hope I could return the favor. Would you be willing to join my family for dinner sometime in the future?"

"Absolutely..." Everys's voice trailed off. She knew she should recognize this woman, but the name escaped her.

The woman laughed gregariously. "Oh, you poor dear. Your mind is probably full to bursting with so many names and faces, you'll never keep them straight. I'm Oluna Hishi, Minister Masruq's wife."

"Oh, Madam Hishi, my apologies!"

"'Madam?'" Oluna laughed and swatted at Everys's hand. "I won't stand for that. You will call me Oluna, or I will start calling you 'The Most Effervescent Incarnation of the Water Bearer.' That is one of the ways we're supposed to address the Dynasty's queen, you know."

One of? Everys blanched and Oluna laughed even harder.

"But do come to dinner sometime soon, all right? Maybe we can work on Masruq together to bring about these changes your husband is envisioning, yes?"

"I would like that very much."

And off Oluna went, calling out to some of the other departing ladies to wait up for her. Everys watched them all go, and within minutes, she stood by herself in the ballroom.

"Blessed."

She jumped and spun around. Challix arched a brow at her.

"How long have you been here?" Everys asked.

"The entire time," Challix said. "Ready to assist you if you needed it and... you didn't."

"Is that praise?" Everys asked.

Challix's lips twitched into the barest smile. "Perhaps. We have a long way to go, but today was definitely a step in the right direction."

Everys nodded. This felt like a win to her. And at this point, she was willing to take it.

37

Narius didn't know what was more amusing: that Paine was so annoyed or that he couldn't conceal it.

The vizier paced the length of the Amber Office, his back rigid, his hands jammed behind his back. Although his face was still calm, Narius could easily read the tension in his eyes and around his mouth.

"Bad enough the queen wore business attire, but to challenge Viara to a duel? And suggest the Dynasty needs to change? Thank the Gravedigger the nobility hasn't called for her ouster and yours!" Paine punctuated his statement with a look in Narius's direction.

Narius fought to keep from smiling. "Have any nobles complained?"

Paine winced. "No. In truth, the feedback I have received thus far indicates the nobles in attendance found the queen's enthusiasm refreshing. If naive."

That got his attention. "They actually said she was naive?"

"No. That's my interpretation."

Narius snorted. Figured. "And Challix's?"

Another wince. "She appears to have fallen into the same delusion as the others. She was quite complimentary of your wife."

In spite of the venom in those last two words, Narius couldn't help but smile. Everys wasn't his anything, appearances to the contrary. Well, he supposed they were partners. Friends maybe, although after their dinner he wasn't sure she considered him that anymore. The memory of her anger caused his chest to ache. He shouldn't have waited this long to apologize. Now it would appear insincere.

"It would seem you're the only one who has a problem with her, old friend."

Paine snorted. "I am hardly the only one. Have you listened to any of the prelate's homilies of late? Virtually every message includes a condemnation of the queen, and while he doesn't dare insult you directly, he has become more and more pointed in his criticism of you."

"Really?"

"He says you are ignoring our founding principles by allying yourself with one of the Dynasty's enemies—"

"The Siporans are no threat! They haven't been for centuries!"

"—and that the Perfected Warrior would be ashamed of your actions as well. He is most insistent on that point."

Narius frowned. "Since when have you cared for the Warrior's dictates?"

Paine's shoulders slumped, and he sat down in a chair across from the desk. "You know that I don't. But there are many in the Dynasty who do. They listen to the prelate and they will be influenced by his views. And not just his. We still haven't located Viscount Orsin, have we?"

No, they hadn't. Narius's hands spasmed into fists. Granted, the viscount's attack had brought Everys and he closer together, but it galled him that Orsin was still free.

Narius's comm terminal pinged, indicating a new message. He called it up, then spotted the informational tag. From Clarinda Gaines. Now what did she want?

Will sell propulsion units as requested regardless of title. Want to be part of your future.

He choked on a laugh. They had been trying to secure Gaines's help for months... no, *years*, and Everys accomplished it in a matter of weeks? He swiveled the display around so Paine could read it. Maybe that would be enough to make the vizier smile.

But he didn't. Instead, he muttered something about "unwanted interference" and began pacing again.

The door to the office banged open, and Zar rushed in. The guardsman was pale, sweaty, his eyes wide. "Y-Your Strength. It's... it's..."

Narius's heart slammed into his ribs. He had never seen Zar this rattled before.

"There's a Cold Light thrall in the palace. Right now," Zar whispered.

Dizziness swept over Narius. The Cold Light were attacking? How had they breached the palace's security?

Paine came around the desk and grabbed Narius's arm. "We'll get you to safety, Your Strength. Guard, alert Redtale and have the queen escorted to—"

"You misunderstand, Vizier." Zar swallowed hard, but his body still trembled. "This isn't an attack. The thrall... he's in the throne room. Waiting to talk to the king. He said he's come to... to parley."

They wanted to what? Parley? Not an attack?

"Strange times, Narius," Paine whispered. "As the Warrior said, 'Strange times mean little peace.'"

For once, Narius couldn't argue.

His heart thudding in his throat. The hyper-awareness of his surroundings. Drowning in cold sweat. Narius hadn't felt like this since his days in the military. The assassination attempt had been so frantic, he hadn't had time to marinate in fear.

He hadn't missed the sensation.

Zar, Paine, and he crept toward the throne room. According to Zar's whispered explanation, the moment the thrall showed up at the palace gates, the guards had evacuated this wing of the palace as a precaution.

"But why let it in at all?" Paine whispered.

Zar grimaced. "Said he came under the truce we offered the Cold Light."

"The king hasn't offered any such truce!" Paine said.

Realization dawned on Narius. "No, but my father did. Back when the rebellion first started. He offered the Cold Light safe passage into the city so they could talk terms. They never took him up on it, but we never rescinded the offer."

They passed a portrait of his father and mother, staring sternly at the hallway. His mind ricocheted to Everys.

"Where is the queen?" he asked.

"I had Redtale lock down the residential wing," Zar said. "We've got three squads guarding the hall and half a dozen in her quarters."

Narius nodded grimly. If things got out of hand, at least she'd be protected. Although he was curious what her powers could do to a thrall.

"I don't like this at all." Paine touched Narius's arm. "We should insist on somewhere else for this meeting. Somewhere more secure."

"Like a cell in the dungeon," Zar muttered.

The guard might have meant it as a joke, but Paine nodded. "Exactly. You've heard the stories of what Cold Light thralls are capable of."

He shook his head. "The offer was made in good faith. It would be dishonorable of us to not see this through."

Paine grumbled, but he didn't object. Neither did Zar, although Narius could feel the guard's tension increase.

They turned the corner to the throne room. Four guards had their weapons drawn and ready. When they spotted Narius, they unlocked and opened the doors. The moment they had, an unfamiliar odor wafted into the hall, overwhelming Narius. It smelled like moss, soil, and a few scents he couldn't identify. He staggered, then shook his head, squared his shoulders, and stepped through.

A dozen guards had their weapons pointed at a lone figure in the center of the room. It appeared to be human with russet hair that was a mass of tangles and knots hanging down to his waist. His homespun clothing was simple greens and browns with elaborate vines and leaves woven into the fabric.

No, wait. The vines were moving.

The thrall turned to face him. As he moved, the vines encircling his arms and legs writhed, adjusting to his new position. Narius suppressed a shudder. He had heard stories of the way the Cold Light ensnared their thralls with plant matter, but he never thought he'd see an example of it in person.

"Narius King." The thrall's voice was flat, without any inflection or emotion. Narius could almost hear creaking timbers underneath his words. "So glad that we may speak in the here-and-now."

Narius drew himself up. "And whom am I addressing?"

The thrall imitated his stance. "Tall Reach, the Third of the Yore-root."

Narius settled on his throne. "What brings you to Bastion?"

"It has been many rings since your Dynasty captured the Hearth. Many rings since our saplings have tried to chastise you for it."

Narius frowned. Were rings years? Decades? It could be either, he supposed. "That is true. And the invitation to parley has been open this entire time." Apparently. "So why are you here now?"

"Because we of the Yoreroot wish to extend an invitation to you. Come to our copse. Speak with us. Not through messengers. Stand in my shadow so that we may exchange our breaths."

Narius's mouth went dry. As far as he knew, no outsider had been invited into the Cold Light's forests since his grandfather had conquered the Hearth. Since then, the Cold Light had only communicated through comms or the occasional thrall. He exchanged a look with Paine. The vizier looked just as surprised as he was.

"And what would we discuss?" Thankfully, his voice didn't crack.

"True peace between you and us."

Now Narius almost fell over. An end to the attacks? Restoring the food shipments from the Hearth? And without resorting to a counterinsurgency campaign?

"I-I would be honored to do so, Tall Reach."

The thrall bowed stiffly, almost as if he didn't know how to bend properly. But then he straightened. "There is but one requirement."

Ah, he should have known. "And that is...?"

"The Siporan, Everys Queen, must accompany you."

38

This had to be a dream.

Everys sat in the Amber Office, her body and mind numb. She had been cocooned in shock ever since Narius summoned her. A Cold Light thrall. A request to parley. And a demand for her presence.

She glanced around the room. Paine stood in one corner, glaring at her like this was all her fault. Duke Brencis stood stiffly on the other side of the room, reading something on a scriber. There was a young man, definitely Hinaen, who Everys didn't recognize. And Narius... He sat at his desk, his fingers steepled, his brow knitted into a thoughtful frown. His golden eyes pierced her, but not with any hostility. He was measuring her. Assessing her.

"This is preposterous." Paine practically spat the words. "Your Strength, I can't believe you're even considering the Cold Light's demands."

"Not a demand, Vizier," Narius said, his voice quiet. "A request."

"Request, demand, invitation, whatever you call it, we cannot accept." Paine gestured toward her. "Sending her to a military base on the Demilitarized Zone is one thing. But sending her to the Cold Light's Hearth is reckless. Only seasoned diplomats, protected by our best troops, should venture into those forests. Not some..." The vizier's words caught. "Not her. You agree with me, don't you, Duke?"

Brencis glanced up from his work. "Actually, I disagree. While the Cold Light are technically in rebellion against the Dynasty, there is no active combat."

"You don't count bombs in our own city as combat?" Paine asked.

"Of a sort, yes. But not in the Hearth. Our soldiers patrol the fringes unmolested."

"That's because we don't enter the Hearth itself. We all know what happens to those who do. Enthralled or worse!" Paine said.

Narius held up a hand. "Gentlemen, I appreciate your concerns, but let's be honest. The decision about whether or not the queen goes to the Hearth isn't up to the Cold Light. And it isn't up to either of you. Or me." He looked directly at Everys. "It's up to her. If she decides she doesn't want to go, I will support her and meet with the Cold Light alone. If she decides to go, then I will be glad for the company. Truth be told, if she decides to go, I fear for the Cold Light."

Everys found herself straightening in her chair a little.

"But I do not expect her to make an uninformed decision. That's why I asked Kestonin Ulri to join us today." Narius motioned toward the young man. "He is our foremost expert on the Cold Light."

Kestonin laughed quietly. "Although that's not saying much, I'm afraid. It's a pleasure to meet you, Queen Everys. So, to get started, how much do you know about the Cold Light?"

Everys wracked her brain, then stammered. "They're thinking trees?"

Paine snorted and rolled his eyes.

Kestonin blinked. "That's not technically correct. Is that all you know?"

Irritation flashed through Everys. "No!"

Kestonin ducked his head. "My apologies, Blessed. Please, continue."

Everys crossed her arms. "The Cold Light enslave people who venture into their forests. They were conquered by King Vetranio, Narius's grandfather, so their fertile farmlands could supply the Dynasty, but they've never met their assigned quotas. They've been in revolt ever since, demanding their independence."

Narius chuckled. Even Paine appeared to be smiling.

She looked between them. "What?"

"Unfortunately, Blessed, that about sums up all we know about the Cold Light," Kestonin admitted sheepishly.

Everys blinked at Kestonin. "Really?"

"I'm afraid so. Much of what we believe to be true and factual is based on mountains of conjecture. But here is what little we do know for certain." Kestonin activated the vidscreen, displaying a map of the

Dynasty's holdings. "As you can see, the Cold Light's territory is in the northeast part of the Dynasty and is our most recent acquisition.

"The name of the territory comes from an ancient Plissk travelogue written by a wanderer named Irrke. He spoke of a land that was as bright as his native sands, but where the air was cold. A Cold Light. The name stuck, and soon, everyone was using some variation of it."

From there, Kestonin launched into what amounted to a history lecture, listing off the different references to the Cold Light in ancient texts. Thankfully, he didn't dwell too long on the Ascendancy's relationship with the Cold Light. She could already feel Paine's glare drilling into the side of her head. No need to give the man any more ammunition against her.

She did risk a glance at Narius halfway through the lecture. Even though the king had likely heard all this information dozens of times before, his full attention was on Kestonin. He even leaned forward in the chair, his expression thoughtful.

Kestonin kept droning until Paine cleared his throat. "While all of this is... fascinating, I don't know that any of it is particularly relevant to the current situation."

"With all due respect, Vizier Paine, I disagree," Kestonin said. "Historically, every major empire on Ehun has coveted the Cold Light's Hearth due to the land's incredible fertility. Most ancient empires made conquering Cold Light lands their first priority before moving on to their neighbors. There's only one notable exception—the Siporan Ascendancy."

Everys winced. According to the scriveners, the Cold Light had freely traded with the Ascendancy, although the Siporans considered them a vassal kingdom.

"And yet, in spite of all that, very few outsiders have been inside the Cold Light's forests, correct?" Narius asked.

Kestonin hesitated. "That's not entirely true, Your Strength. The Cold Light Hearth is actually filled with non-vegetative inhabitants."

He fiddled with the projector, and the image shifted, overlaid with colors. The verdant green dimmed, and large red patches, each of them almost perfectly circular, appeared in the middle of the dense forests.

"While we've heard rumors, it wasn't until we were able to take satellite images that we were able to confirm their existence. There appears to be at least a dozen city-sized settlements of outsiders within the Cold Light lands. And based on our observation over the past few decades, we're convinced that the population growth within is not simply a result of procreation. Instead, there appears to be growth from emigration."

Everys frowned. "How would they get in? I thought the forests were impassable."

"They should be," Brencis said. "Everyone who's ever invaded the Hearth has come to regret it. Whole armies go into the forests and rarely return. The trees themselves fight against any invading force, and it's so thick inside the forests that you can't see the attacks coming."

"Then how did the Dynasty conquer the Cold Light?" Everys asked.

The room fell silent. Then Narius cleared his throat. "Incendiary bombs, dropped from low orbit."

A chill swept over Everys, pooling at the small of her back. At first, she thought she misheard Narius. But then, as she realized there was no mistake, she imagined what that must have been like. Fire falling from the sky, destroying so much of the forest. She met Narius's eyes. While his expression remained neutral, she could see the hint of shame lurking in his gaze.

"The Cold Light surrendered almost immediately." Narius's voice turned grimmer. "But Grandfather wasn't done. He had his honor guard burn a swath through the forests, until he reached the heart of the Hearth, where the yoreroot met."

Kestonin pulled up some footage on the vidscreen. A long column of Dynasty soldiers marched through the smoldering remains of a forest, the trees burned to stumps. They marched into a circular clearing, where a handful of tall trees stood. Humans stood next to the smoking stumps, looking distressed, but they bowed before the soldiers. No, they were showing respect to one man in particular, an imposing figure who bore a striking resemblance to Narius. That had to be Vetranio.

"I know it sounds brutal, Blessed," Brencis said. "But the tactics were effective."

That didn't excuse anything. She suppressed a shudder.

"According to the terms of the surrender, the Cold Light would provide regular shipments of food to the Dynasty," Kestonin said. "In return, the Dynasty agreed not to occupy the forests. Instead, the military maintains a perimeter along the Cold Light's border but doesn't venture into the Hearth."

Everys's jaw popped open.

Narius chuckled. "Grandfather did not like those terms, but when he realized that the Cold Light wouldn't budge, he grudgingly agreed."

"For the rest of King Vetranio's reign, the Cold Light provided the appropriate amount of food," Kestonin said. "But when King Girai took the throne, they provided less and less. When King Girai demanded to know why, the Cold Light asked for the return of the Hearth. When that demand was refused, the Cold Light began a terrorist campaign that intensified when King Narius took the throne."

It looked like Kestonin was going to continue, but Narius held up a hand. "The point is, Everys, there is much we don't know about the Cold Light. No one would blame you if you decided to not accompany me to these talks. But what do you think?"

She glanced over at Paine. His lip twitched into a sneer. Clearly he didn't expect her to go. From Brencis's expression, the duke didn't either.

And she shouldn't. She knew that. This was deep within hostile territory. She could easily remember the way everyone in Fair Havens worried that they were going to be targeted by a Cold Light attack at any time. She remembered what it was like when the thralls sparked the riot outside her building. Even if she was with Narius and Redtale and all the rest, she knew how dangerous this was.

But she couldn't forget the fear that permeated Fair Havens. If there was a way she could stop that, she had to take it, didn't she?

Before she could think about it further, she nodded. "I'll go."

Paine actually blinked. Brencis nodded thoughtfully. But Narius...

He favored her with a smile, a genuine one, filled with warmth and... affection? Maybe? And that was almost enough to still the flutter in her stomach.

Almost.

39

The next couple of days were a blur. So many preparations. Challix kept asking if Everys wanted to speak to the press about the upcoming journey. She didn't. Trule kept fussing over her wardrobe. She didn't care. Redtale was the only one who stayed out of her way, but Everys also noticed that ever since she decided to go, more guards seemed to follow her around the palace.

Most frustrating, though, was how her mind drifted. Everys found herself wanting to be in Narius's presence. She tried to busy herself by reviewing plans for her outreach efforts. So far, the plans had stalled. Her building had been destroyed in the riot, and no one was sure when anything could be rebuilt. Some of the media wags suggested that she was likely to have children before her outreach center would be finished.

Securing funds proved a headache as well. After the Court, some nobles agreed to contribute, but that created a flock of new problems. The nobles saw this as a new way to jockey for position, squabbling over who would get credit or make announcements to the press. Every step forward only reaped more frustration.

But try as she might, going over these details didn't really distract her from their looming departure. Every hour, every minute, brought her closer to the Cold Light's forests.

Then the day arrived. Even though she hadn't slept the night before, Everys forced herself out of bed to get ready. Instead of wearing something fashionable, she opted for a simple, utilitarian outfit: khaki pants and a loose button-down top. It vaguely resembled a military uniform, and that wasn't a coincidence. Everys knew she would soon enter hostile territory. Best to look the part.

She chose to skip breakfast, especially since her stomach twisted at the thought of food. She was stressed enough; she didn't want to add vomiting to the list of the day's possible outcomes.

Then, surrounded by four of her guards, she marched through the palace to the landing pad. Narius waited, flanked by his own protectors. He smiled thinly, then held out a hand toward her. She frowned. What was he doing? Why so stiff and formal?

He jerked his head subtly to the right and upwards, his eyes darting in that direction as well. She peeked where he indicated and realized what was up there: press drones. The unmanned cameras hovered just outside of the palace's no-fly zone, probably trying to capture this very moment. No wonder Narius behaved the way he did. They had an audience. The whole Dynasty could be watching, wondering what this parley with the Cold Light would mean.

Fine. She could play along.

She smiled broadly and took his hand, allowing him to sweep her closer and escort her toward the waiting skimmer. She laid a hand on his bicep and giggled.

He arched a brow. "Laying it on a bit thick?"

"I could kiss you, really give them something to talk about."

Narius coughed. "I don't know if that would be... appropriate."

His cheeks actually reddened! That made the idea all the more enticing. So what would it be? A quick kiss on the cheek or she could grab him by the lapels, pull him to her and—

When did it get so hot on the tarmac?

Mercifully, they clambered into the skimmer. But even though they were out of the drones' gaze, Narius didn't release her hand. He lingered as the guards rushed onboard, sweeping through the craft. Even though they were deep within the palace, they clearly weren't taking any chances. Only when Zar returned and reported that everything was clear did Narius let go.

"I know that Paine will want to go over our bargaining positions while we're in the air," Narius said. "Want to join us?"

Everys smiled. She was tempted. Seeing the consternation on the vizier's face would be worth it. But as the skimmer's ramp retracted and the door ground shut, the lack of sleep caught up with her. Her whole body drooped and grew heavier by the moment.

She shook her head. "I'm going to try to get some sleep. How long of a flight will it be?"

"About five hours."

"Perfect. Wake me before we land?"

A wistful expression flitted across his face. Was he disappointed?

He turned to leave, but then stepped in closer, so close she wondered for a moment if he had decided to kiss her after all.

"I should have said this right away," he whispered. "I'm sorry for how I behaved after the dinner. How we argued. I should have been more willing to listen. Please forgive me."

She gaped at him, stunned at his quiet earnestness. Her mouth went dry, and she stared into his eyes, suddenly uncertain what she should or even could say.

But then he motioned for one of the guards to escort her deeper into the skimmer. They led her to a lushly decorated room, one that appeared to have been ripped straight from the palace. Everys sank onto a plush couch, rolled onto her side, and was gone before the skimmer even took off.

He didn't want to wake her. Even though the skimmer was mere minutes from touching down at Vetranio's First Stand, the military base that watched over the Cold Light border, Narius didn't want to wake her. He had slipped into the skimmer's lounge and found Everys curled up on the couch, a peaceful expression on her face. He was so used to seeing Everys scowling or smirking or staring right through him that he didn't expect to ever see her features so soft, so gentle. He found all he could do was stand awkwardly by the door and stare. Why had he never seen her like this before? So calm, so vulnerable, so—

The skimmer lurched. Any moment, it would touch down. She'd probably wake up on her own. Did he really want the first thing she saw to be him staring at her?

He cleared his throat. "Everys?"

She sat up, swiping at her face. "...time is it?"

"Half through Second Watch. We're actually about to land."

She straightened, ran a hand over her hair. "What's the next step?"

"Strategist Overturn, the commanding officer of Vetranio's First Stand, has a platoon of soldiers ready to escort us into the Hearth, along with the necessary ground transportation. But from the preliminary reports, we're not sure how we're supposed to get into the forest itself."

Everys frowned. "What does that mean?"

"The Cold Light have the ability to shape the forest, to move the trees as they wish. It's part of the reason why it's so difficult to conquer them. As of right now, Strategist Overturn is reporting the roads into the Hearth are impassable."

"They're not going to let us in? We made the trip for nothing?"

He ground his teeth. "Maybe. The Cold Light could have changed their minds. Or they were testing us. But even if we don't get to travel into the forest itself, it'll be a boost in morale for the troops at this base. That's valuable in and of itself, even if it isn't why we came out here in the first place."

Everys frowned, her eyes narrowing, and she studied his face. He shifted uncomfortably at how penetrating her gaze had become. She probably saw how frustrated he was. As much as he tried to put a positive spin on the situation, he still felt a gnawing sense of disappointment and, yes, even anger. He should have known better.

A *bing* sounded in the lounge, and a light blinked on the wall. They were coming in for a landing. Narius sat down next to Everys. A few moments later, the skimmer rattled and bumped, and even though they didn't have any windows in the lounge, he knew they had landed. Narius ran through the post-flight checklist. Zar and his team would exit first to sweep the area. Then they would confer with the military staff on the ground, confirming that the area was secure. Probably another sweep after that, just to be sure. Whatever the case, they wouldn't be able to disembark for a few more minutes.

Everys rose from the couch and stepped over to a mirror, checking herself. She didn't have to. While her hair was slightly mussed, he doubted any of the soldiers would notice. She may not have been born into the nobility, but Everys practically radiated calm assuredness, a steadiness he envied.

"Thank you."

She turned, surprise painted across her face. He was just as surprised. He hadn't actually meant to say that, but now that the words were out there, he realized how much he meant them.

"For what?" she asked.

"For being here." His voice came out quiet, as if he were trying to keep the words inside. He swallowed hard, then decided it would be best to charge forward with the truth. "I'm terrified right now. No one from the Dynasty has been inside the Cold Light's Hearth since my grandfather. I'm not sure I'd be able to do this alone. But it helps. That you're here."

The confusion on her face dissolved into a small smile. "Truth be told, I'm just as afraid as you are."

"At least we can be nervous together."

She hesitated, then took a step forward, holding out a hand. "Together."

He took her hand and she gently tugged, helping him stand up. But as he did, the transport lurched. Academically, he should have known it was coming, but the sudden motion was enough to throw them both off balance. He staggered just as she stumbled into him.

Their heads collided, a sharp pain radiating from his forehead through the back of his skull.

She groaned and stumbled backward, clutching her head and laughing. He laughed as well, rubbing at the impact spot. Wouldn't that make things all the more impressive, to have the Xoniel royalty enter the negotiations with matching bruises?

His gaze met Everys's. Her smile broadened.

Then the door to the lounge banged open and Zar stepped in. "We're clear, Your Strength."

Everys's shoulders sagged. "I guess it's time to go."

He nodded and headed for the door, but he had a nagging feeling that he had missed something, and he wasn't sure how he felt about that.

40

Everys squinted as she exited the skimmer. How could the sun be so bright? But in spite of the blinding radiance, she didn't feel much heat. As a matter of fact, chilly air caressed her cheeks, her skin prickling. Cold light indeed.

She surveyed the base. In many ways, the layout resembled that of Firebase Forward Two-Seven. That made sense; it probably made things easier for the Dynasty's troops. But beyond the fence, stretching as far as she could see, was forest. No, a green and brown wall, packed tightly like one colossal structure than individual trees. She shuddered, this time not because of the cold.

Narius stepped next to her and cleared his throat. "I don't know if you've ever read any of the accounts of Grandfather's war, but I'm starting to understand why most of the soldiers in the campaign respected the forest."

Respected was a good word for it. There was an unnatural stillness that flowed into the base. Normal sounds were dull, almost muffled. Even stranger, there was no motion from the trees. It was like staring at a moment captured in time, unmoving, unchanging.

As they stood at the top of the ramp, inspecting their destination, a man with strategist's insignias strode up to them. He was an Ixactl, broad in the shoulders, his face looking as though it had been carved from gray rock. His most prominent features, though, were his horns. They pointed straight out before curving back on themselves. How could he stand upright with that much weight? Wouldn't he constantly be off-balance?

He saluted sharply. "Welcome to Vetranio's First Stand. I'm Strategist Overturn. If you'd come with me, please."

He started down the ramp. Everys didn't move. It felt as though she had been rooted to the spot. But Narius placed a gentle hand at the small of her back and prompted her down the ramp.

The strategist eyed Everys appraisingly. "My cousin seems quite taken with you, Blessed."

Everys stared at him, his words not registering, before the pieces came together. "Redtale?"

"She may not claim it. Old grudges within a clan die hard. But yes, we are cousins on my mother's side." Overturn faced Narius. "We've kept an eye on the perimeter ever since you notified us of your arrival. Things have been quieter than usual and we're not sure why. Nothing on thermal scans, nothing on the long range mics. Near as we can tell, whatever is normally moving along the border pulled back a few days ago. I'll be able to provide you with an update on recent activity, but I'm afraid there isn't much to report. We haven't seen a grain convoy in the last twelve weeks."

"What would normal be?" Everys asked.

Overturn snorted. "That's the thing of it, Blessed. There is no 'normal.' According to the terms King Vetranio set, we should receive shipments at least once a week, possibly more depending on the weather. But that hasn't been the case for the last forty-five years."

Everys looked over the base and frowned. "Please forgive my ignorance, Strategist, but is yours the only base on the Cold Light border?"

He nodded. "Yes, ma'am, it is."

Her frown deepened. While she wasn't an expert on military deployment, to her eye, this base looked smaller than Firebase Forward Two-Seven and didn't appear nearly as busy. But if this was the only base along such an important border, shouldn't it be bigger? More active?

Overturn nodded sagely. "I wondered the same thing when I first arrived. Wouldn't I need more troops? More equipment? More bases? But here's the thing: the forest doesn't tolerate intruders. There's a reason we never enter the forest, Blessed. Our patrols never stray into the trees, and even then, we have dozens of soldiers disappear without a trace every year. Do you know why?"

She shook her head.

"Because the trees take them," he whispered.

Everys gasped, then looked to Narius. Why did he look so annoyed? And was the strategist... was he *laughing?* Not out loud, but his eyes shone. Her nerves gave way to displeasure.

"I'm sorry, Blessed, but there's a tradition here that we try to spook the new arrivals by telling them the forest will eat them. You're perfectly safe," Overturn said.

"But I'm not a soldier," Everys said.

Overturn waved for them to follow. "We don't need many soldiers here because not much ever happens. Truth be told, we have very little to do. We're more of a formality than an actual occupying force."

As they walked toward the barracks, Overturn pointed out various buildings and points of interest, although the latter really didn't live up to the term. Maybe someone with military experience would find the process by which they fine-tuned their satellite communications interesting, but to Everys, the words were just noise. She tried to pay attention, but her gaze kept drifting toward the forest. The longer she stared at it, the more unnerved she became. There was an aura of unreality that seemed to roll off the tree line, and—

She blinked. Did one of the trees move? Not by much, but she could have sworn that one of the treetops had shifted ever so slightly.

"Blessed?" Strategist Overturn asked.

She couldn't look away from the forest. There! Another tree, closer to the front, swayed just a little bit, slipping to the left.

"Everys?" Narius's concern was plain.

And then she heard it: the sound of timber creaking, soft at first, but growing louder. And the trees! Not just random tops moving a little, but a great wave. It almost appeared as if something huge slammed through the forest, knocking over the trees. No, wait. The trees didn't actually fall. It was more like they bent out of the way, leaning to one side or the other. Then the trees righted themselves again, but not where they had originally stood. What was going on?

Strategist Overturn barked an order. Dozens of soldiers raced toward the disturbance. They fell into orderly lines, their weapons at the ready. Two tanks rolled forward, aimed squarely at the forest line. Narius grabbed Everys's hand and started to drag her away.

But she planted her feet, yanking away from him. "No, wait!"

The trees at the very edge of the forest swayed and shifted. An opening formed. As the trees bowed out of the way, a small group of people emerged. They appeared to be human at a distance, but even from so far away, Everys could spot the vines and leaves woven around their arms and through their long hair. Thralls. Half a dozen thralls shuffled toward the soldiers.

"Ready!" Overturn shouted.

Tension flared through the Dynasty troops. Everys could feel death drawing near, ready to be unleashed with just a word, just a breath, just a—

Narius stepped forward, raising his hands. "Hold!"

Overturn's head snapped around, anger plain on his face, but he repeated the order. The soldiers lowered their weapons, but to Everys's eye, they didn't stand down. Not really. They were still wound tight, ready to snap. But at least they weren't overtly threatening anymore.

Something else emerged from the forest behind the thralls. Vehicles, three of them. Everys frowned. They appeared to be military, splashed with camouflage paint, all greens and browns. But they were oddly broken, big chunks of their walls torn out and covered over with wooden beams and patchwork metal.

"Ancestors' wrath!" Overturn's voice was a bare whisper. "Are those what I think they are?"

Narius, who had gone pale, nodded.

"What are they?" Everys prompted.

"Troop transports, old ones," Narius whispered. "From my grandfather's war. I'd have to get a closer look, but I'd be willing to bet that it's from the initial invasion force, the one that was..."

His voice trailed off as the thralls approached. Most of them hung back, but two strode forward. They were surprisingly young, maybe in their late twenties. The man was broad-shouldered and appeared to be Dalark. The woman was human, but Everys couldn't quite place her race. They both bowed to Narius, then to her.

"King Narius, Queen Everys," the man intoned. "We greet you on behalf of the Yoreroot. We apologize for our delay. This section of forest is being particularly stubborn. It didn't want to grant us passage, but we have been able to mollify it."

Everys and Narius exchanged a look. The forest was being stubborn? But then trees normally didn't move, so she supposed that made some sense.

The woman cleared her throat. "My name is Yllana, and this is my companion, Lesarl. We have been given the honor of escorting you to Tall Reach's shade. If you would accompany us, please?"

She gestured toward the waiting vehicles.

Strategist Overturn stomped forward. "Absolutely not! We have transportation for the king and queen and will escort for them into the forest."

He gestured behind them. Everys turned and saw half a dozen modern troop transports waiting, along with dozens of heavily armed soldiers.

"I am afraid the Yoreroot does not approve of so many intruders," Lesarl said. "The king and queen will be quite safe in the trees' shadows. The Cold Light do not intend them any harm."

Everys wanted to laugh. The terrorist attacks in Bastion suggested otherwise. Narius crossed his arms, his brow furrowed. He wasn't going to agree to that, was he?

"How many would you allow to accompany us?" Narius asked.

"The invitation was but for you and your queen," Lesarl replied.

"Be that as it may, if we proceed alone, it will make those we leave behind nervous," Narius countered. "If you were to allow some of our own soldiers to accompany us, for their own peace of mind, it would be a great gesture of trust."

Lesarl frowned, then his features went slack, his eyes staring at nothing. Or maybe he was staring at something a long distance away. It only lasted for a moment or two, but once it passed, he smiled.

"A dozen soldiers. Any aides you might require," Lesarl said. "That is how far we may accommodate you."

Narius bowed. "And we thank you for it. We will join you momentarily."

Lesarl and Yllana both nodded, then stepped back toward the vehicles.

Overturn whirled on Narius immediately. "Your Strength, I don't like it. Duke Brencis made it very clear—"

Narius held up a hand. "The Duke isn't here. Even if he was, he would understand the need for a gesture of trust. Pick six of your most trusted soldiers, Strategist. They'll escort us into the Hearth along with my personal guard."

Overturn fumed, but he nodded sharply, then turned toward the soldiers and started barking orders.

Yllana motioned for Narius and Everys to join her, leading them to the first transport. Lesarl took charge of Paine, Kestonin, and the rest of their entourage, escorting them to the other transports. Narius offered Everys his hand to boost her into the vehicle.

There was a distinct musty odor to the interior, which was sparse, only long benches lining the side walls. But there had been obvious modifications as well. Large sections of the walls had been torn out, boarded over with planks of wood that had been painted to match the rest of the interior as closely as possible. And were those throw pillows on the benches? Everys poked one of them, a rainbow-colored square, and sure enough, that's what it was. Everys sat down on the bench, trying to keep her heart from slamming out of her chest.

Narius clambered into the transport and froze in the entrance. His gaze roamed over the interior, then he nodded thoughtfully. "I see they discarded the weapon rack, which I suppose isn't much of a surprise, given how they removed the rest of the armaments."

"Are we doing the right thing?" Everys whispered.

Narius blinked at her, clearly surprised. But then he sat down next to her and patted the back of her hand. "Maybe not, but at least I have my secret weapon with me."

She tried to scowl at him, but a sob hiccupped out of her. He squeezed her hand.

Yllana climbed into the transport, then froze. "I-I'm sorry. I didn't mean to intrude."

Narius laughed. "Not at all. Are we ready to depart?"

Yllana nodded as she sat down on the bench across from them. "We will not arrive at Tall Reach's shade today. The journey is slow-going due to the condition of the roads. It will take at least three days to arrive. I hope that is acceptable."

Narius nodded. "Of course."

With a lurch, the transport started rolling. Everys craned around to peek through a narrow slit as they moved out of the military base and into the forest.

It was only then that she realized that Narius's hand was still on hers. And even more surprising, she found that she really didn't mind.

41

The first few hours of the trip passed in near silence.

Everys spent part of that time staring out the narrow window. At first, she hoped that she would be able to spot animals or something interesting. But she quickly realized all she would see were trees, trees, and still more trees.

But what else could she look at? She didn't want to even glance at Narius. He had removed his hand a while ago, but she could still feel his warmth on the back of hers. She wasn't sure where her mind might drift if she so much as peeked at him, so she carefully studied the interior of the transport. Unfortunately, there wasn't much to examine. The benches were well worn from use but otherwise unremarkable. Simply put, the interior was too empty to be all that interesting.

That left Yllana. Everys tried to be subtle, stealing quick glances to catalog small details. Yllana didn't seem to notice, so Everys let her gaze linger. She quickly realized Yllana might not actually be younger than her after all. She appeared youthful, but there were subtle lines around her eyes and lips, and her hair was a riotous mass of brown tangles streaked with white. But Yllana's most noticeable feature was the plant matter twisted around her and woven through her hair. Vines with tiny leaves were intertwined in tight braids, and thicker tendrils wrapped around her arms and chest. Some had even stabbed through her skin, near her temples, along her arms. Most of the time, the vines only moved when she did, but every now and then, Everys was sure the leaves twitched on their own.

"Did it hurt?" She blurted the question.

Yllana turned from the window. "Excuse me?"

Flames danced across Everys's cheeks. "I-I'm sorry. It's just... The vines. Did it hurt?"

The other woman smiled. "No. Not at all."

"Even when they... well..."

"There was some initial discomfort, but more because of my nervousness than the actual bonding process," Yllana said. "Now I don't even notice them."

"Really?"

"Everys!" Narius whispered.

Yllana smiled. "It's quite all right."

"How old were you when you were enthralled?" Everys asked.

Yllana smiled wistfully. "Eighteen autumns."

Narius leaned forward. Apparently his curiosity had gotten the better of him too. "Is that normal?"

She nodded. "Quite. Some are chosen earlier, but that is rare."

"Is Tall Reach listening in on us right now?" Everys asked.

Yllana shook her head. "No, Tall Reach has bonded with forty-seven others. While he has long experience, not even he is capable of splitting his attention so many times. I could attempt to summon him if you wish."

Narius shook his head. "That won't be necessary. I'm sure he's very busy preparing for the parley."

Yllana settled back on her bench.

Everys frowned. If there were forty-eight thralls serving Tall Reach, that meant there could be just as many serving other Cold Light. There could be tens of thousands, maybe even hundreds of thousands of people living within the forest. Of course, there had to be. How else would the Cold Light farm their land? But where did all the people come from?

"Were you born here?" Narius asked the question on the tip of Everys's tongue.

"Some of us were born within the forest. My family has lived in the Cold Light's shade for ten generations."

"Is that why you were chosen to be a thrall?" Everys asked.

Yllana grimaced, which turned into a brittle smile. "Please, we do not like that term. It makes it sound as though we have no choice."

Everys winced. She knew what it was like to be called a term she didn't like. She should have been more sensitive.

Narius held up his hands as if in surrender. "My apologies. We didn't mean to offend. What terminology would you prefer?"

"We are given the opportunity to serve the Cold Light. We are joined with their presence, grafted to their minds."

Everys frowned. "So 'grafted,' then?"

Yllana tipped her head to one side, her expression thoughtful. Then she nodded. "Yes. That seems appropriate. To answer your original question. While the Cold Light take a family's history into consideration, it isn't the only factor."

Silence hung in the air as Everys digested those words. Then she leaned forward. "If you don't mind me asking, why did your family come here?"

Yllana looked down at her hands. "From what my parents have told me, my ancestors crossed the Spineridge Mountains to escape persecution."

Narius's eyebrows rose. "The Spineridge? What would make you..." His voice trailed off, his gaze narrowing.

Yllana squirmed on her bench, her eyes down.

Then Narius sucked in a sharp breath. "Your family were practitioners of the Elderreach, weren't they?"

Everys's mouth went dry. The Elderreach? According to the sacred texts, the Elderreach was an abominable belief system, the stuff of nightmares. While some of the ancient mage-kings had dabbled in the belief, mingling the blood sacrifices with toratropic principles, most of them had done their best to eradicate the Elderreach and its followers. It was one of the few things the tyrants were commended for.

Yllana grimaced. "It is true. My family held to the Elderreach. But my ancestors abandoned those beliefs shortly after they came here. The Cold Light, while welcoming, do not tolerate those that would disrupt the Hearth's peace."

That didn't give her a lot of comfort.

"And we were glad to do so," Yllana continued. "Most of my family did not survive the journey. But there are many secret routes into the forests that the desperate may find when they need them most."

"I suppose having our military on the border complicates matters," Narius said with a chuckle.

It looked like Yllana was about to say something, but instead, a smirk flitted across her face.

"What?" Narius prompted.

"I mean no offense, Your Strength, but in spite of your many technological advancements, the Dynasty is not as omniscient as they believe."

The transport's interior brightened. Everys glanced out the window. They had emerged into a clearing. No, not a clearing. A massive farm, fields stretching into the distance. People picked their way through the crop. Were they weeding the field? Maybe. She frowned. Why would anyone put a field here? There was a hill in the middle of it all, a large grayish lump that...that...

The hill was moving.

Everys's eyes widened as she realized what she was actually seeing. A massive creature, the size of a house, slowly tromped through the field on four thick legs. A long, whip-like tail trailed behind it, brushing through the plants. A barrel-like head with four large, glassy eyes perched on a thick neck. Like the other beings, it worked the fields, although how it was able to handle the plants with such massive hands, Everys couldn't guess.

"Is that..." she whispered. "Is that really..."

Narius craned around to see what she was looking at. He spat out a curse and whipped around to Yllana. "Is that a shessu?"

Yllana's lips twitched into a grin. "It is."

Everys couldn't believe her eyes. A real, living shessu! The plain giants had supposedly gone extinct six hundred years earlier. At one time, the shessu herd caravans wandered far from their heartland, traveling as far as the Ascendancy, creating trade networks, enriching all parties involved. But they had proven too tempting of targets for not only bandits, but the old empires as well.

"How many are still living?" Narius whispered.

"Far too few. At last count, only a few hundred."

Everys gasped. A few hundred? How was that possible? How could the Dynasty have missed so many in a territory they supposedly controlled? Sure, the Cold Light never allowed Dynasty troops into the Hearth, but overlooking something that big? No wonder Narius had fallen silent. He had to be wondering what else the Cold Light were hiding. She was too, but she was too nervous to ask and learn some horrible truth, so she kept silent.

Yllana did as well, closing her eyes and leaning her head against the transport wall, silence descending on the transport as they rode on.

42

A few hours later, the transport rolled into a village. At least, that's what Yllana called it. It took Narius a few moments to actually spot the buildings. They blended into the trees and hills, and even the streets were little more than footpaths through the grass.

As soon as the transport came to a halt, Yllana opened her eyes. "We're stopping here for the night, Your Strength, Blessed. We'll depart for Tall Reach's shade after first light. The locals have readied a hostel for you."

As soon as the transport's door opened, Narius slid out. He knew he had to keep his expression neutral, his steps even. Regal. But try as he might, he knew that some of his anxiety bled through as he walked to the other transports.

Paine extracted himself from the second transport. Good. When the vizier spotted Narius, he strode to meet him halfway.

"You saw it then?" Narius asked.

Paine nodded grimly. "It was hard to miss."

"And you understand my concerns?" Narius continued.

"Entirely, Your Strength."

Narius crossed his arms with a satisfied nod. Of course Paine would see the problem. While learning there were still living shessu had excited him at first, he quickly realized the implications. No wonder they had such a difficult time locating the Cold Light in Bastion. If they could hide something as large as a shessu from the Dynasty's eyes, evading the authorities would be a simple matter.

"Did your guide suggest there were secret ways into the Hearth?" Paine asked.

That was troubling as well. While it explained how the rebels infiltrated the rest of the Dynasty's holdings, it was also disturbing they hadn't heard of such hidden pathways until now. Maybe he would have to schedule a long talk with Tormod after this parley was over.

"Can you believe we're here?" Kestonin's exuberant shout cut through Narius's tense thoughts. The specialist practically skipped over to Narius and Paine. "Your Strength, thank you for including me in this trip. I've already learned so much from speaking with Lesarl."

The thrall—er, *grafted*—who rode with Kestonin slipped out of their transport. He did not look nearly as enthusiastic as Kestonin. If Narius had to guess, the specialist had likely kept up a barrage of questions the entire ride.

Thankfully, Zar hopped off the lead transport and jogged over to Narius. He whispered into his comm unit, then nodded. "The guard's about fifteen minutes behind us, sire. Some of 'em stopped to gawk at the shessu. Once they're here, I'll have them secure the perimeter." Zar looked around the buildings. "Wonder where all the people are."

Narius hadn't noticed that, but now that he thought about it, the village did seem strangely abandoned. He hadn't seen any activity since they'd pulled in.

Yllana emerged from the transport, followed by Everys. Everys took a look around at the village, but when her gaze met his, her smile brightened considerably. He couldn't help but mirror the expression. Even though she had been on the same long journey with him, she didn't look any the worse for wear. For a moment, he wondered if she had used a rune to rejuvenate herself when no one was looking. But no, that didn't seem likely. There was no way she would risk it with so many potential witnesses.

The two women crossed over to Narius and Paine. Yllana smiled broadly, if a bit vacuously. "We hope you'll find the accommodations here acceptable, Your Strength."

"I'm sure they'll be fine," Narius said. "But I am curious. Where are the residents of this village?"

"They've been evacuated," Yllana said.

They were... what? He couldn't have heard that correctly. "Excuse me?"

Yllana nodded. "The residents of this village were asked to shelter you for the night. The Yoreroot requested they temporarily relocate."

"And they were okay with that?" Everys asked.

Confusion clouded Yllana's face. "Of course. Why wouldn't they be? The Yoreroot requested it."

That answer clearly didn't sit well with Everys, the way her expression froze. He couldn't blame her, but he was more surprised at how effective that "request" had apparently been.

Yllana motioned toward the buildings. "There is room enough for all your troops to bunk down for the night. Vizier Paine, Specialist Kestonin, you are each going to be given your own home. As will the king and queen. But now, before I show you to your quarters, we have prepared a meal..."

She led them to a large pavilion bordered by thick pillars that held up a peaked roof. Dozens of tables were set out in orderly rows with enough seating for at least two hundred people. One long table was covered with all sorts of different foods, at least half of which had steam rising from their platters. Narius frowned. No sign of cooks or servers. Who prepared the meal?

No answer was forthcoming. Instead, Yllana and the other grafted escorted the Xoniel delegation into the shelter and started serving them. Shortly thereafter, the troops from Vetranio's First Stand arrived and sat down to eat as well. Soon the pavilion filled with laughter and chatter as the soldiers devoured the feast. The food was delicious, well prepared, and flavorful. And it seemed to fuel the noise. Kestonin peppered their hosts with innumerable questions about Cold Light society, biology, and whatever other topics popped into his head. Even Paine wound up in a quiet conversation with Yllana, although Narius couldn't hear what the two were talking about.

But Narius kept to himself. It had been a long journey, and questions weighed heavily on his mind. All he wanted to do at that point was sleep, and maybe escape the nagging curiosity, if only for a little while.

An hour later, Yllana stood up and motioned for silence. "We thank you for enjoying our hospitality. We will now show you to your quarters. Your Strength, Blessed, if you will follow me?"

Narius frowned. Who was going to clean up after dinner? But then the other grafted stepped forward, taking his plate and cup. His frown deepened. That didn't seem right. He motioned to Zar and signaled that the soldiers should help. Zar acknowledged the unspoken order.

The rest of the Dynasty's delegation followed Yllana deeper into the village. Narius studied the buildings as they walked past. They were tucked into the trunks of trees or nestled in the side of hills, blending in almost perfectly. He suspected if they checked the satellite imagery, it would be difficult to pick out the village. Plus, as he considered the paths between the buildings, he realized how difficult an assault would be. He spotted half a dozen places where troops would be caught in crossfires, places where civilians could hole up, and places where the defenders could stage a counterstrike.

He blinked. No, this line of thought wasn't helping. He shouldn't be looking at this like a soldier. He should keep his mind focused on the task at hand.

As they walked, Yllana pointed out the houses where Paine, Kestonin, and the troops would stay. Finally, they came to the largest house in the village, one carved into the trunk of a massive evergreen tree. Stairs circled the trunk, leading to a balcony fifteen feet off the ground.

"This is where the village's grafted normally lives. It seemed appropriate to house you here." Yllana opened one side of the grand double doors and gestured for Narius and Everys to enter.

Narius did so, but stopped short in the entrance. The interior was simple, rustic. The walls were rounded and unpainted, showing off the grain of the tree. There was a small kitchenette with what appeared to be a wood-burning stove to his right, a sitting area with long wooden benches and simple chairs to his left. Doors led off to the other rooms. Given that this was the residence of the village's grafted, he had assumed that the residence would be more stately, more lavish.

Everys scooted past him and nodded approvingly. "This is very lovely. When you get the chance, please thank the grafted for his or her hospitality."

He winced. He should have thought to do that right away.

Yllana beamed. "Of course. I bid you good evening. Please do enjoy your stay." With that, Yllana withdrew.

The moment the door shut, it felt as though Narius's body turned to jelly. He wobbled on his feet, then laughed.

"What's so funny?" Everys asked.

Narius motioned around the room, toward the door. All of it. All of it was so strange. To stand in a Cold Light village, the first king to have ever been invited there peacefully. A feast with no cooks. A modest home for the village's most important individual. But as he grasped for the words, he realized she probably understood, so he just shook his head. "I'm just tired. That's all."

"Me too," Everys said.

They both started for the hallway, almost colliding. He took a step back and motioned for her to go first. She took the door to the left, so he headed to the right. The hallway proved to be more like a tunnel bored through the wood. The walls were rounded, worn smooth. He ran his hand along one of them, surprised at how glossy the wood was. But the tunnel ended in a small, spherical room he had to duck to enter. There was a shelf, or maybe a bench, in one wall with a hole in the middle. A grate, a foot in diameter, was set in the middle of the floor. Narius frowned, twisting around to examine the room more closely. What was this? He leaned over the hole, and a musty smell wafted up and caused him to gag. It smelled like...

His eyes widened. Was this what passed for a grafted's bathroom?

In the distance, Everys started laughing. Then she called his name. He hurried out of the bathroom, checking the main room. No, she wasn't there. He swung around the corner, wound through the smooth tunnel that led to a bedroom where Everys stood laughing next to...

The only bed in the room.

He stared at it. It made sense, he supposed. After all, how would the Cold Light know their marriage was a sham, that they had never slept in the same room together?

Everys kept laughing, and soon, he was chuckling as well.

"Figures," she said.

"I suppose so." He sighed. "Well, enjoy the bed. I'll sleep on the bench in the common room."

Her head snapped back, and she frowned. "What? No! Narius, you need your rest!"

He smiled. "I appreciate the sentiment, but I've slept on far worse than a wooden bench. You take the bed. I insist."

She looked ready to argue, so he fixed her with his sternest gaze. She met his glare with one of her own, but after only a few moments, she wilted and nodded.

"Thank you," she whispered.

Narius nodded and headed out to the sitting room. He looked over the bench. It looked like he could stretch out on there. No problem.

Small problem: the bench proved a lot more solid than he expected. He was sure he had slept on more comfortable rocks. How did the grafted who lived here even sit on it without getting a cramp?

Narius groaned. His right arm had gone completely numb, so he flipped onto his other side. His shirt, which he had balled up into a makeshift pillow, unwound and almost slid off the bench. He sighed. At this rate, he wasn't going to get any sleep.

Then again, the bench wasn't the only problem. His mind simply wouldn't shut down. The more he thought about secret routes into the Hearth, hidden shessu, all of it, the more anxiety twisted in his stomach, ricocheting through his thoughts. Could this all be a trap? Get the king, queen, and the vizier in their land, then the Cold Light would storm out those hidden paths and decimate the Dynasty.

No, he couldn't think like that. This was a chance to make a real difference. He could end the hostility between the Cold Light and the Dynasty. And if he succeeded with Falling Sword... He could completely recreate the Dynasty for generations. Maybe even centuries.

Oh, yes. Those kinds of thoughts really helped him settle down.

He flipped onto his back and stared at the ceiling. Whatever process had been used to carve the room left the tree's rings clearly visible. He vaguely remembered what he had been taught about tree growth in school, something about the ring's thickness indicating how that particular year had been in terms of rainfall and other growing conditions. Something like that? That could explain the pattern that he saw: thick rings interspersed with narrow, creating a hypnotizing wave pattern.

But then he heard soft footsteps in the hall. He sat up.

Everys stood in the doorway, wearing a satin night outfit that covered her from her neck to her wrists and ankles. It looked comfortable. They stared at each other for a few heartbeats. Her gaze flicked down toward his bare chest, then skipped down to the floor. He considered grabbing his shirt and pulling it back on, but would that make her more uncomfortable? He didn't know what to do or even why she had come into the room.

Finally, she cleared her throat. "Don't read anything into this, but come with me."

She stepped into the room and took him by the hand, pulling him off the bench then leading him to the bedroom. His mouth went dry. *Don't* read anything into it?

She pulled him into the bedroom and gestured toward the bed. "There's more than enough room. We're both tired, and we *are* married."

Without another word, she clambered back onto the bed. He stood there, staring at her, his mind going blank repeatedly. Anytime he had imagined sharing a bed with a woman, he had always pictured Innana being that woman. But what Everys said made sense. They were married, so why hadn't they ever...

Everys poked her head up. "If you're going to, get in already."

That snapped him out of his reverie. He slid into the bed, which turned out to be surprisingly comfortable. There was a bit of tug-of-war over the covers as he and Everys tried to get comfortable, but then they both fell still and the shadows crept in. Everys, it turned out, gave off a fair bit of heat and soon, Narius's body melted and he was drifting... drifting... drifting...

"Narius?"

His eyes snapped open. Everys's voice was a gentle whisper. Chills swept across his arms. "Yes?"

She didn't say anything, and for a few moments, Narius wondered if he imagined her speaking.

But then she spoke again: "I'm proud of you. I know you're nervous. But this is a good thing."

He lay there in the darkness, stunned at the power of her words, the power they had over him. He stammered, then said, "Thank you. And thank you for being here."

She rolled in bed, sighed, and it sounded like she fell right to sleep. Narius tried to as well, but found that once again, sleep eluded him. But this time for an entirely different reason.

43

Daylight tickled Everys's eyes, and she groaned, burrowing deeper into the sheets. Why was it morning? The mattress was so comfy, the bed so nice and warm, and it felt so good to be curled up next to...

Her eyes snapped open, and she lifted her head. Sometime during the night, she had drifted across the bed to Narius. He was still asleep on his back, an arm draped over his eyes.

Everys's cheeks burned. Had they cuddled?

"Someone shut off the sun, please," Narius groaned.

She giggled in spite of her embarrassment. "I don't think we can."

"Nonsense. I'm the king. That has to count for something." He offered her a sleepy smile. "Good morning. Did you sleep okay?"

"I did. You?"

"Better here than on that bench." He sighed. "I suppose we had better get up."

Her stomach soured. Did they have to? The thought of having to ride in that transport again was enough to make her want to disappear under the covers and never emerge again.

But then she heard someone tromping down the hallway. "Your Strength? Are you—?"

Zar walked into the room and stopped short. He stared at Narius and Everys, his mouth popping open in surprise. Then he whipped around, his back to the bed. "My apologies, Your Strength. I didn't... That is... Yllana says they'll be serving breakfast at the pavilion in a few minutes. Thought I'd come to tell you and—" He coughed and retreated from the room.

Narius watched him go, then burst out laughing. "I've never seen Zar so flustered." He rolled out of the bed and headed over to their luggage.

"I suppose we should prepare for the day. I'll see if I can figure out how to use the bathroom, okay?"

Then he left as well, leaving Everys in bed. She knew she should have been worried that Zar saw them in bed together. But for some reason, she didn't mind as much as she thought she would.

Everys thought they'd never arrive. It took another two days of careful driving through the forest to reach the parley. Two long, boring days. Occasionally the monotony was interrupted by picturesque scenery: rolling plains, a spectacular waterfall, a cliff overlooking a misty valley. And the nights proved interesting. Every place they stopped, there was only one bed for them. After that first night, they agreed to share the bed without a word. Was it strange she found herself looking forward to sleeping next to Narius?

Toward noon on the third day, their small caravan rolled into a larger town. This one wasn't abandoned. Dozens of people milled through the streets, all from the different races of Ehun. As Everys slid out of the transport, the activity around them stilled. Many of the villagers stopped to gawk at her and Narius. They weren't hostile. At least, they didn't appear to be. Zar, Paine, Kestonin, and the rest of the delegation joined them. The guards started to form a protective ring around them, but Narius motioned for them to stop.

"A posture of fear will only create a divide," he explained.

Zar didn't look happy, but he silently ordered the troops to stand down. Soon Lesarl and Yllana approached them, their smiles relaxed.

"The actual parley will begin in two hours," Lesarl said. "Tall Reach has ordered you be provided a place to prepare yourselves."

The grafted led the delegation deeper into the town. The crowd parted for them. Everys didn't think they were hostile, merely surprised. The only people who recovered from their surprise were the children. They waved and smiled as she passed, and she returned the gesture.

Eventually, they entered a large building at least twenty stories tall. Like all Cold Light buildings, this one appeared to be organic, flowing lines and shapes, like it had been grown instead of built. It appeared as if dozens of trees had been woven together to form the walls. If anyone could do that, the Cold Light could, but given the sheer size of the building, it would have taken them decades, if not a full century.

The interior was breathtaking. The floors were highly polished wood that blended into towering walls. Irregularly shaped windows were spaced, seemingly at random, constructed of stained glass. But much to Everys's surprise, the rooms they passed were mostly empty, just large, cavernous spaces, as if waiting for someone to move in. When she asked Yllana why that was, the grafted didn't explain. Instead, the grafted led them to a back room, one with a low counter covered with food and drink. Yllana pointed out a bathroom through a back door, then she and Lesarl excused themselves.

Paine started to say something, but Narius held up a hand, watching the door. After several tense moments, Narius lowered his hand and nodded.

"Well, this is all very dramatic," Paine said. "Why do you suppose they brought us here? To intimidate us?"

Kestonin shook his head. "Doubtful. Based on my conversations with the grafted, the Cold Light won't care."

Narius frowned, looking around the room. "Who do you suppose lives here?"

"Given how empty the rooms are, no one," Paine replied. "But that mystery will keep. We should review our positions, Your Strength."

They huddled together, Paine quizzing Narius about various facts, figures, and statistics with Kestonin "helping." When Everys tried to step into the circle, Paine closed ranks with the others to block her out.

Really? That was... that was... Everys sighed. Typical. It was typical. Well, if they didn't need her...

She slipped out of the room. She waited just outside the door to see if anyone noticed. Much to her disappointment, they didn't.

Everys wandered down the hall, peeking into different rooms. Sure enough, all empty. What had they been? She couldn't really figure it out. Bedrooms? Offices? Living spaces? One could easily have housed all four transports from their caravan.

But the further she wandered, the rooms changed. They were just as empty, but dust coated the floors and windowsills. The last few rooms appeared to have been unused and untouched for years. Maybe even longer, given how thick the dust was.

Eventually, Everys realized she would have to go back to the others. But before she did, she decided to peek in one last room.

Like all the others, this one was undecorated and covered in dust. But something caught her eye. There was a small pile in one corner. Given the thick layer of dust, she couldn't tell what it was; at first glance, it appeared to be a rock. But as she approached, she realized it was actually fabric, tossed in this corner and probably long forgotten. Even though she knew she shouldn't disturb it, she couldn't help herself. This small lump was the only thing she had found in the entire building. She nudged it with her toe, gently at first, then with more force, just to make sure nothing had made that corner its lair. Satisfied, she knelt and tugged at it.

Her efforts kicked up a cloud of dust that caused her eyes to water. Everys waved her hands to clear the air. As she pulled more of the fabric away, though, she realized it couldn't have been that old. As dirty as it was, it held together remarkably well. Only a few areas seemed tattered and worn.

After she had pulled about six feet of material out of the pile, she felt foolish. She hadn't found anything important. While the fabric felt like it had been heavily embroidered, she couldn't tell what kind of pattern the stitches made. She sighed. This was silly.

Something heavy *thunked* onto the floor at her feet.

It was a thick book with a stained leather cover.

Everys gaped at it. An actual, ink-on-paper book? She hadn't seen one of those in years. Modern scribers made paper books extremely rare. She carefully picked it up, expecting it to crumble into dust, but it didn't. She brushed off the cover, hoping to find some clue as to what she had found. But the cover, while mottled from age, didn't have any writing on it, no decorations, nothing.

The pages were covered with a flowing script, written in a language she didn't recognize. At least, she thought it was a language. The looping patterns appeared to be more like vines unfurling. But she had no idea what any of it said. There were no illustrations, just row after row of the flowing lines. Sometimes they were horizontal, sometimes vertical.

No, wait! As she flipped through the pages, she thought she spotted a few that had drawings. At the very least, it wasn't the same writing as before. She flipped back and... Yes! There was a drawing, of eight curving stone pillars, like talons, creating a circle with their points facing outward. Surrounding those pillars were crudely drawn human figures, carrying what appeared to be pots and brushes. The strange vine-like writing surrounded the drawing, and she got the feeling that the lines were explaining something about the sketch.

But she didn't need to read the language to recognize what was depicted. The Principalities, standing in the Scriptotum before Nekek the Bright was destroyed. Hovering over the plinths was a cloud... or was that a ball of fire? Or was it... A shudder wormed through her. A depiction of the Singularity?

A chunk of ice lodged in her chest. Why did the Cold Light have a book with a drawing of the Siporan's most sacred space?

She turned the page with trembling fingers. Another drawing of the Principalities, only this time, a human figure stood in their midst. This person, whoever it was, had runes drawn on his or her arms. She squinted as she examined them. Were those... yes! She recognized them! The runes Siporans drew on their doorframes, inviting the Singularity's presence. Why would this person have drawn those on his or her arms? And the Singularity's fire, rather than hovering over the Principalities, seemed to flow down over the figure, entwining him or her.

Her finger traced the drawing, and a longing rose in her heart. A tug, like a rebuke, only pleasant. Inviting. Enticing.

Someone called her name in the distance.

Her head jerked back. How long had she been gone? The others must have noticed and started looking for her. Inkstains, Narius must have been beside himself!

She considered taking the book with her, but she knew that wasn't a wise idea. Everyone would want to know where she found it and why she wanted it. After shoving it back into the pile of fabric, she got up and dusted herself off. She jogged out of the room and almost collided with Lesarl.

He looked her up and down. His eyes narrowed. "Are you all right, Blessed?"

She willed her heart to slow, but it didn't listen. She nodded. "F-fine. Sorry if I made anyone worried."

"No need for apologies. The yoreroot has given your delegation the run of the embassy. I was sent to find you as the parley will begin soon." His gaze fell to her dirty hands, her stained clothing. "Did... Do you have any questions?"

She froze. His eyes were piercing. He almost appeared hostile. So she shook her head. "No, not at all."

She barely got the words past the questions that tried to blurt from her lips.

Lesarl hesitated, then nodded. "Very well. If you'll follow me, please?"

They walked silently until they arrived where the rest of the party were waiting. Narius and the others had already changed into their finery.

Paine glared at her. "Perhaps it would be best if the queen were to prepare herself. We don't have much time."

She resisted the urge to spit back some venomous taunt. Instead, she walked over to her luggage and pulled out her outfit, looking around for somewhere to change.

Narius must have noticed her hesitation. "Gentlemen, let's give the queen some privacy."

The others complied, but before he left, Narius stepped closer. "Are you all right?"

She forced herself to nod. She couldn't admit how off-center she felt. Not right then. But the sooner they finished talking to the trees, the better.

44

Something had shaken Everys. Narius could tell she had withdrawn into herself. She said she was fine, but he knew better. When she emerged from the room, dressed in her simple yet elegant outfit, he could practically feel the tension rolling off her. But with the soldiers, Paine, and Kestonin hovering around them, he couldn't ask. He filed away the concern. He'd ask when they were alone.

Several of the grafted waited for them nearby. Lesarl and Yllana bowed formally. "The time has come. The Yoreroot will assemble soon. Please, if you will, follow us to Tall Reach's shade."

The grafted led them back through the palace—that was how Narius identified the building—and out into the streets. Much to his surprise, they were empty. Granted, they had been inside for an hour or two, but the streets were so quiet that he could have easily believed they were in a long-abandoned city, that the people he saw earlier had been hallucinations. Or maybe ghosts. He didn't know which possibility would be more disturbing.

Eventually, they left the city itself. The border was stark. One moment, they were in an urban area. The next, they had entered a dense forest. The grafted led them on a winding path that wove between the trees. With each step, Narius grew more unsettled. Why leave the city? This was feeling like an ambush. From the way Zar and the other guards crept through the underbrush, their weapons lowered but their eyes up, they suspected the same thing. Even Kestonin walked silently, pressed close enough to a soldier that the trooper could have worn him as a backpack.

The only one who didn't appear overwhelmed by the sudden change was Everys, but that was only because she seemed so distracted already. She walked along with the rest of them, her arms wrapped around herself as if she were cold. Or frightened.

An urge to put an arm around her shoulders welled up inside him. He frowned. This wasn't the time for such sentimentality, even if he was eager for some human contact. Anything to reassure himself they weren't doing something incredibly stupid.

Well, they *were*, but it would be a convenient lie.

Within fifteen minutes, they passed between two thick trees into a clearing. Narius stopped just inside and stiffened. While they were deep in the forest, there was something deeply unnatural about this space. The ground was perfectly flat, and while it was covered in grass and low-lying shrubs, the clearing had a cultivated feeling. But at the same time, Narius's skin prickled, as if he were standing in the presence of a barely tamed beast.

He took several steps into the clearing, turning a slow circle. He realized that the trees he walked between weren't the only of their kind in the clearing. There were at least two dozen of them, forming two concentric rings. Each tree trunk was forty feet around, stretching high overhead, their branches interweaving into an impenetrable roof. It reminded him vaguely of some ancient temples he had studied, like they were pillars that should have held up a dome or rotunda or some architectural wonder. In the center of the clearing was the oddest feature: A patch of bare dirt, ten feet across. Roots snaked out of the soil, forming a low barrier around the open area. A ceremonial space of some kind, but what did it mean? What was any of this?

The grafted ushered them toward the empty patch before splitting off, each one going to stand next to one of the large pillar-like trees in the inner ring. As one, they turned inward, toward the delegation. Yllana offered Narius a small smile, then she bowed her head. They all did, in perfect unison.

Narius was about to say something when every grafted in the clearing suffered a seizure.

At least, that's what it looked like. Their bodies contorted, as if their limbs were trying to tie themselves into knots. Oddly, they didn't cry out, even as their bodies twisted. Several of the soldiers took a step toward them, but Paine motioned for them to stop. A wise precaution, especially since they didn't know what was happening.

As quickly as the strange convulsions started, they stopped. The grafted froze in their contorted positions, then once again in unison, straightened up. Narius frowned. They appeared... Taller? Larger? Fuller? He couldn't quite put his finger on it, but they had all changed.

Everys gasped. "The trees..."

The what? Narius looked past the grafted. The trees were glowing. It wasn't much, a bit of light seeping through cracks in their bark. But once he spotted it, he couldn't miss it. The light thrummed to an unheard rhythm, brightening and dimming like an ocean tide. Narius looked around the circle. Each tree a grafted stood in front of pulsed in different rhythms.

Yllana stepped forward, an expansive smile on her face. "Narius King, Everys Queen, honored guests one and all. I am grateful you agreed to stand in my shade."

Narius frowned. Her voice had changed. Not in pitch; it was still high and girlish. But now there was a resonance, as if someone—or something—spoke along with her, just underneath her words, a voice he didn't hear so much as feel.

Might as well hazard the guess. "Tall Reach, I presume?"

She nodded, then opened her arms. "Welcome to the Yoreroot. We have not welcomed outsiders into our presence for many branches of autumns."

"At least, not willingly." Lesarl's voice had also changed.

"Firestruck, hush," Yllana said. "Such commentary is of the Below, not the air." She turned back to Narius. "My apologies for my seedmate. There are many who question the wisdom of this meeting. But we have found that we cannot abide the rift between us and you any longer. Fire and death, sown in our name. It must cease."

There was a pause, and the grafted looked at Narius expectantly. Was it time for him to speak? He cleared his throat. "Esteemed members of the Yoreroot, I thank you for the invitation to speak with you. I agree that we should seek peace between the Dynasty and the Cold Light. That is my greatest wish."

Lesarl snorted. More probably, the Cold Light speaking through him. Narius chose to ignore the outburst.

"I am grateful for this chance to travel so deeply into your forests. We have already learned much about you, and I hope you have learned an equal amount about us as well. There is no reason for the antagonism that currently exists between us. It is my dearest hope that we will be able to forge an agreement that will allow us to coexist peacefully."

"With us as your supplier of cheap food for those you have subjugated?" a different grafted asked, the derision in his voice plain.

This time, Yllana—no, *Tall Reach*—didn't rebuke the other speaker. Instead, she arched a single eyebrow and waited.

"If I recall, that was part of the peace agreement that was reached between my grandfather and the yoreroot, was it not?" Narius forced himself to smile. "And who do I have the pleasure of speaking to?"

Tall Reach clucked her tongue and laughed. "Of course. My apologies, Narius King. We, who are so used to the Below, forget ourselves and the needs of flesh. I, of course, am Tall Reach, third of the Yoreroot and he who has been chosen to invite you and to speak for the root. Firestruck is he who defends the forest from interlopers."

The introductions continued, with each grafted stepping forward as Tall Reach mentioned the Cold Light controlling them. Evergreen, the Knowledge-Keeper. Seed Cluster, the Liaison of Fields. Stunted Root, the second of the Yoreroot. And on it went, each grafted stepping forward one at a time and acknowledging Narius's presence with varying degrees of respect. He quickly lost track of them all, despite his efforts to keep track of the names and the faces. The one thing he did notice was that there wasn't a "first" of the Yoreroot. Stunted Root was second, Tall Reach third. So who was the first?

Once Tall Reach finished the introductions, she and the other members of the Yoreroot stepped away from the trees. As they walked, roots burrowed out of the ground, weaving together to form benches in a ring around the central bare patch of dirt. The grafted gathered on one side of the circle, seating themselves in no discernible pattern. Narius and the rest of the Xoniel took their places on the other, although Narius hesitated, hoping that he understood what they should do. When none of the grafted objected, he sat down, as did the rest of his party.

Then silence fell over the clearing. Narius exchanged an uncertain look with Paine. What happened next? Tall Reach smiled pleasantly, his head cocked to one side.

"Once again, we thank you for your hospitality," Everys said. "Speaking for myself, I have been amazed at the wondrous things we've seen on the way here."

One of the grafted—Evergreen?—giggled. "The road to Tall Reach's shade can hardly be said to contain wonders, Everys Queen. Why, there are such sights in the deep forest that—"

"Shall we tempt them thus?" Firestruck retorted. "You know how the humans are. Always hungry for that which is not theirs. Little sense of Below, even less of what overarches. Show them the deep forest? They would burn it all in their ignorance."

Heat flashed through Narius, even though he recognized some of the truth in Firestruck's words. "With respect, while we would be honored to see the 'deep forest,' I feel it best we not lose sight of what brought us here in the first place: fostering peace between our two peoples."

The trees surrounding them creaked as if being blown by a strong wind, but not even a breeze ruffled Narius's hair. The grafted nodded thoughtfully.

"Let us be forthright," Narius said. "We have come to find a way to end the attacks on our holdings by the Cold Light."

The trees around them creaked again. The noise sounded angrier.

"It is not the Cold Light who do these things but—" Firestruck leaned forward, punctuating his words with a pointed finger.

Tall Reach held up a hand. "That is our fondest wish as well. And we are ready to help bring about that desire. We only request one thing."

Narius braced himself. Paine and he had gone over the various concessions the Dynasty could feasibly make. They could reduce the number of soldiers posted at the border, provided the terrorist attacks actually stopped. They could grant the Cold Light more independence in governing themselves, although that seemed like an empty gesture. Given how many non-Cold Light apparently lived within the Hearth, maybe they could work out some sort of deal to bring in trade goods and other luxuries they couldn't get otherwise. But he remembered what he had learned so many years ago: in any negotiation, the opening ask would be extreme but would contain a seed of the eventual compromise.

Tall Reach smiled. "Return the Hearth to us. If you do, we will ensure that the attacks stop."

45

Apparently the Cold Light shouldn't have asked for that.

Everys understood why. Return the Hearth? How was that a compromise? She understood the Hearth's importance to the Dynasty. If they could get the Cold Light to meet the agricultural quotas, there wouldn't be any food shortages in the Dynasty's holdings. There was no way that Narius could give them the Hearth.

Could he? While he hid it well, she could read the tension in his expression. He was holding back his thoughts, trying to remain calm. But clearly his mind was racing.

Maybe she could help. "Tall Reach, forgive me for speaking out of turn, but I grew up in Fair Havens in Bastion. There has been a lot of Cold Light graffiti in my neighborhood, and they all say the same thing: 'Return the Hearth.' Now you are saying essentially the same thing. How is your position any different than the terrorists?"

Firestruck bristled and almost looked ready to leap out of his seat.

Once again, Tall Reach held up a hand to stop his colleague. "I can see why you would think that, Everys Queen. Those who strike at your home do not do so with our consent. But just as competing trees may share the same root in the Below, so too, we of the yoreroot and those saplings share similar desires. We do not condone their methods, but we do understand their motives."

Narius's lip twitched, almost into a snarl, but his expression returned to neutral. "It would be easy for us to assume collusion with that admission."

"What admission?" Tall Reach asked, his arms open. "That we long for the Hearth's return? It has been so since your grandfather first conquered our land." Tall Reach leaned forward. "Have you noticed how the forests you have traveled through are so lush?"

Everys frowned. What did this have to do with anything?

"This is some of the land that was targeted by your grandfather's incendiary bombs. My shade barely survived the onslaught. But the fire cleared away dead brush and timber, allowing new growth. Those trees that survived came out on the other side stronger. My seedmate, for example." Tall Reach nodded toward Firestruck. "Even from the ashes, life persists. While I regret the pain that has been strewn among your kind, it has brought us to this moment, has it not?"

"It has," Narius said hesitantly.

"Then perhaps something good shall come of it, yes?"

Paine cleared his throat. "While we can sympathize with your request, you must admit that it is a bit extreme. While we understand your desire, given our history, that would be difficult to do. Perhaps if you made a gesture to show good faith?"

Stunted Root frowned. "And what would you suggest, Paine Vizier?"

"Remove your agents from Bastion. Allow us to put some of the perpetrators of the worst attacks on trial."

The grafted shifted as the trees creaked and groaned around them.

"That will not be possible," Stunted Root whispered.

Zar sucked in a sharp breath.

Narius held up a hand, stilling the guard. "You can understand why that is problematic. It would almost appear you are issuing an ultimatum rather than negotiating."

Tall Reach went still, his eyes vacant. Then he shook his head and sighed. "You deserve the truth, Narius King. The reason we cannot is because we are cut off from them. They are no longer part of the Below."

"We believe they have smuggled themselves out of the forest and into your territory," Firestruck added. "We suspect that they may have created their own grove somewhere near Bastion."

"How do you smuggle a Cold Light into Bastion?" Everys raised an eyebrow. How was that even possible?

"It is difficult, but not impossible," Evergreen said.

"Then if helping us contain the attacks isn't possible, perhaps you could meet your agricultural quotas. With extra." Paine held up his hands. "Again, as a sign of good faith."

Tall Reach sighed and shook his head. "No, I'm afraid that will not be possible either. Not until you return the Hearth. Then we would be more than happy to not only meet but exceed whatever quotas you might suggest."

"But why would you meet any quotas if we return the Hearth?" The anger in Paine's voice practically blistered Everys's skin.

"We will not be able to until you do," Firestruck said.

"That was part of the agreement between the Cold Light and the Dynasty," Narius pointed out.

Stunted Root snorted derisively. "We have withstood the rise and fall of many fleshling empires. We have had different understandings with all of them. We have outlived them all."

"Is that a threat?" Narius's voice was glacial.

"An observation," Stunted Root replied.

The conversation fell apart from there. Soon, both sides were reciting talking points without discussion or negotiation. Narius and his team reminded the Cold Light of their agreement with King Vetranio, while the Cold Light insisted the Dynasty would have to return the Hearth. The polite argument lasted for what felt like days, although Everys knew it had only been an hour or two. They just kept going round and round with no end in sight.

As Narius repeated his stance once again, Everys levered herself off the bench. She had been sitting for so long her back and legs had gone numb. She just needed to stretch. Narius shot her a concerned glance, but she waved him off. She carefully slipped to one side of the ring, out of the line of fire, so to speak, but not so far that she couldn't keep up with the discussion. Not that anyone had said anything new or interesting.

She wandered toward the pillar-like trees that ringed the clearing. As she approached, she realized that not all of them were glowing. A quick count confirmed that there were twenty-three trees in the two concentric rings, but only eight of them appeared to be thrumming with weak light underneath their bark. Everys turned and realized that there were eight grafted speaking for the Yoreroot. Were the trees individual Yoreroot members?

Everys frowned. Did that mean the Yoreroot always lived here? Being trees, that made a certain amount of sense. But then why hadn't the trees been glowing when they arrived? And everyone referred to this clearing as "Tall Reach's shade," implying it belonged to him. But how was that possible? How had Firestruck and the others arrived?

She wandered toward one of the pillar trees, the one that seemed thicker and taller than the others. She settled her palm against its bark, surprised to feel a fair amount of heat bleeding through the wood. Up close, she could see the steady pulse of light that danced within the tree's trunk, almost feeling the rhythm in her bones. She turned back toward the central circle, startled to find Tall Reach staring right at her. Their gazes locked, and the grafted smiled ever so slightly.

Everys turned back to the tree. "Tall Reach?" she whispered

The air shuddered around her, several leaves drifting down from the tree's high branches. Everys winced in surprise, but when she realized that it was only a rain of leaves, she relaxed and turned to continue her wandering.

Something *thumped* into the ground next to her, something a whole lot more solid than a mere leaf.

She looked down, startled to find a brown object the size of her head at her feet. It looked organic, a seed maybe. She knelt and poked at it. Definitely part of a tree. Should she bring it over to Kestonin? The Cold Light expert would likely have a better idea of what it was.

But as she pulled her hand back, she realized that there was something sticky on the end of her finger. She rubbed her pointer and thumb together, frowning. Some sort of amber liquid coated her skin, not quite as thick as tar, but still pretty viscous. A strange tingle wormed up her fingers. She shook out her hand, gritting her teeth. Probably not the best idea to smear unknown tree sap on her fingers.

Then her eyes widened, and she gasped. She knew what it was.

"Are you all right, Blessed?"

Zar's quiet question caused her to jump. She looked up and realized that the guard loomed over her.

She forced herself to smile. "Just taking a closer look at the local fauna."

He studied her face, as if searching out the lie, then nodded and wandered back to Narius's side.

Everys watched him go, then turned her full attention on the seed pod. Her mind raced, trying to dredge up everything she had been taught about ink production before Downcasting. The ancient mages used a lot of different ingredients in creating their inks. They debated the best recipes and ratios endlessly. But aside from blood, which the Singularity completely forbade, they all agreed sap from a Cold Light seed pod made the most potent of inks. Some of the most powerful runes could only be cast using sap like this. Wars had been fought over the amount that had just fallen at her feet.

She struggled to breathe, heady with the possibilities. Could she somehow smuggle this back to Bastion? She imagined bringing this back to a conclave gathering, showing off her good fortune. Her fellow mages would be beside themselves.

Wait, what was that? The bark on the tree shifted, the pattern moving ever so subtly. The lines rearranged themselves, twisting around and doubling back until...

Her eyes widened. The lines had formed themselves into the rough shape of a rune, one that she knew. An insight spell, one she could cast to pull information from her surroundings and decipher it. Some of the small details were wrong—a misplaced flourish or a line that ended too abruptly—but the pattern was too obvious to be anything else.

Did this mean that Tall Reach wanted her to paint this rune on his trunk? Right now? What else could it mean? But there was no way that she could do so, not with so many people nearby. Someone would see!

As if reading her unspoken objection, the pattern in the bark moved, flowing along the trunk until it disappeared around the other side. Everys carefully followed it. The pattern stopped when she was out of sight. She waited a few moments to see if anyone would come after her or notice her absence. Nobody did.

Her hands trembling, she found the seams at the top of the pod, exactly where the ancient texts had said they'd be. She carefully pried back some of the fibrous outer wrappings, revealing a small pool of sap within. She dipped her finger, then cast a nervous look toward the negotiators. No one seemed to notice what she was doing. Hopefully it would stay that way.

She quickly traced the insight rune against Tall Reach's trunk. She had rarely used this rune, so having the pattern helped. After a few minutes, she rocked back on her heels, studying her work. It looked right, but then again, she was operating on faded memories. She sucked in a deep breath. Only one way to see if she got it right.

She activated the rune, then pressed her hand against the trunk.

Heat flared against the bark, stabbing up her palm. She bit back a startled cry.

And the bottom dropped out of Everys's mind.

Darkness slammed down around her, almost with a physical force. But then, in a heartbeat, she realized she wasn't alone.

A towering being of light stood in front of her.

She stumbled back several steps, a scream clawing at her throat. But the being didn't move, didn't so much as flinch. Once she realized she was safe, Everys examined the colossus. It wasn't human, although it was vaguely human-shaped, with a featureless head, broad shoulders, and arms that ended in what appeared to be small flippers. From the waist down, though, the being's body blended into a long streamer of light that disappeared into the darkness below.

Everys reached out a trembling hand and tried to touch the being's leg, but her hand pressed up against a solid but invisible barrier. Thankfully, the being didn't seem to notice. It reminded her of a statue made of glowing fog.

A soft light caught her attention out of the corner of her eye. She turned and realized that this giant wasn't alone. There were seven others, standing like pillars in a semi-circle. Everys frowned. Eight total? And their placement...

Her eyes widened. The luminous beings stood in roughly the same places as the pillar trees in Tall Reach's shade. She was seeing the Cold Light for what they were. All of them faced the same point in the center. She turned to see what they were looking at.

Eight more beings of light sat on unseen benches. Unlike the Cold Light, these eight were her size with distinct features. She could recognize each of the Cold Light's grafted. As her eyes adjusted to the dimness, Everys realized that a barely visible thread connected each grafted to one of the larger beings.

She turned back to the being she stood next to. Light danced gently through this ethereal body, a mix of greens and blues, bright motes tumbling through what looked like smoke. The effect was hypnotic. But as Everys traced his body with her gaze, she noticed once again how the bottom half of his body didn't turn into legs but instead trailed off into the darkness beneath her. She leaned in to get a better look...

...only to suddenly tumble end over end, falling through a void.

A scream caught in her throat as she fell. She dropped for what felt like days before she jerked to a halt. It was so dark around her that—wait, she had her eyes closed.

Everys pried her eyes open and gasped. A vast web of sparkling lights spread out below her. Glowing orbs of every color zipped along the gossamer lines. It almost reminded Everys of pictures she had seen of Bastion at night, taken from a skimmer. Only here, the lines weren't as straight as city streets. Instead, the lines wove back and forth in an organic pattern.

She turned in midair and realized that a shaft of light stretched into the darkness above, then down into that network of light. As a matter of fact, there were seven other streamers, presumably the other Cold Light in Tall Reach's shade, all of them connected to whatever that was below them.

As she studied the pillar, a globe of green light rushed past her, fast enough that wind tugged at her, almost dragging her with it. A few moments later, a red ball of light shot back up the shaft. She looked at the other streamers and realized that there were similar back-and-forths happening with the other Cold Light as well. Some sort of communication?

She thought about what the Cold Light had been saying during the talks. They kept speaking of "the Below." This was probably it, but what was the Below? A network? She shook her head. No, it had to be more than that. When they'd arrived in the clearing, those pillar-like trees hadn't been glowing. But then, after the delegation arrived, it was like the Cold Light took possession of the trees and the nearby grafted. But they had also spoken of the Below as if it were a communication network. Could it be both? A way for the Cold Light to communicate across long distances and travel throughout their forest?

Everys looked down at the network, spread out so far. What would she see if she could travel along those lines? She opened her arms, trying to bask in the dance of the lights, soak it in, absorb it. Anything she could learn, anything she could understand.

But as she hovered there, she became acutely aware of... a void? A lack? A wrongness permeated her, like there was something out there trying to suck her in, devour her. An emptiness that clawed at her mind.

Her gaze was drawn back up toward where the Cold Light were meeting with the Dynasty's delegation. The sensation was coming from there, tugging at her mind, trying to draw her closer. She gave in, floating up and up, faster and faster, until she returned to the clearing.

She hovered behind the grafted, frowning. The sensation was stronger here, clawing at her mind. She could even sense it bleeding through the grafted, the Cold Light, through every bit of the clearing. The wrongness was bitter, cloying. It was the scent of death and decay, sucking the life out of everything in its presence. But where was it coming from?

She opened herself up again, and this time, the sensation dragged her forward. She fought, but it was no use. She couldn't break free. Everys tried to grab the grafted as she slid past them, but her fingers passed through them like fog. Then she twisted around and realized that somehow, she could see a vast pit yawning open in front of her, just in front of the grafted, a deep chasm filled with that gnawing emptiness that was going to consume her and everything else if it had the chance. She slid closer and closer...

With a gasp, she blinked, and the world refocused. She looked around wildly, startled by the colors and the light and the smell of wood and grass and leaves. She was back. Back in the clearing. Leaning against Tall Reach. How long had the vision lasted? In some ways, it felt like hours, but as she focused on the voices of Narius and the others, she realized it couldn't have been more than a few minutes.

Everys stumbled away from Tall Reach and headed back toward the benches. As she walked, she tried to clear her mind, shake the strange sensations loose. She settled onto the bench next to Narius with a thud. He glanced at her out of the corner of his eye, then turned his full attention back to the grafted who was speaking. What was his name? Oh yes, Evergreen.

She tried to focus on the conversation, but even that proved to be too much. Even though her vision had cleared and she was back in the real world, she could still feel the strange tug on her heart, that clawing void that still wanted to devour her and everyone around her. It was like death. No, not death. More like the absence of life. A drain on it. Like the life was being siphoned from the woods around her.

Her eyes fell on the bare patch of dirt at the center of the benches. She frowned. If she remembered correctly, that's where that strange chasm had been. Right there, where nothing was growing. In spite of everything else growing around them, that dirt remained bare. Black. The only sign of life were the roots poking up out of the soil.

Without realizing what she was doing, Everys stood and moved to the edge of the clearing. Paine muttered something under his breath about her sitting still, but she ignored him. With every step closer to the clearing, the sensation grew stronger. Soon she stood right at the edge of the bare patch, staring down at the dirt. Her gaze roamed across the surface, taking in the mottled texture and color. No life. None. Just a depression in the dirt, as if something heavy had once sat in the middle, held in place by the surrounding roots, connected to—

Inkstains! Smudges! How could they have been so stupid?

"We'll give it back to you," she said.

Her voice sliced through the conversation. She was painfully aware that everyone was staring at her. But she tore her gaze from the dirt and looked up at Tall Reach's grafted.

"The Hearth. We'll give it back to you."

46

S he didn't just say that. She couldn't have.

Narius felt like he had been submerged in ice. No, the entire clearing had been frozen. No one moved. No one even dared breathe. Because there was no way Everys could have said—

Everys repeated herself. "We will give you the Hearth."

He exchanged a look with Paine. Hours of careful negotiating, building a framework for a workable compromise, all of that time wasted!

Paine cleared his throat. "I believe, what the queen is trying to say is—"

Everys whirled on the vizier, her eyes blazing. "*The queen* can speak for herself, thank you very much."

"For herself, perhaps, but not for the Dynasty!" Paine shot back.

The grafted didn't seem to have heard Paine's statement. They looked broken, like something had severed their connection to the Cold Light. Then Yllana blinked and the eerie demeanor of Tall Reach settled on her once again.

"Everys Queen, we knew that there had to be someone within the Dynasty who would understand. Thank you for your promise!"

Narius had to get this back under control again. Once he had the grafted's attention, he forced himself to smile. "I'm sure that my wife has misspoken, my friends. Could we have a break so that we can regroup and make sure that—"

"Except your wife hasn't misspoken," Everys snapped.

Narius grabbed her hand and squeezed as hard as he dared. He didn't want to hurt her, just make sure she was listening. She tried to shake her hand free, but he wouldn't let go. When she glared at him, he shot back a toothy smile, hoping that the hard expression in his eyes would convey his message.

She sighed. "Maybe a break would be good. If only to talk some sense into these men."

Thankfully, Tall Reach nodded sagely and motioned for the rest of the Cold Light delegation to withdraw. They fell into a line and strode out of the clearing.

As soon as they left, Narius rounded on Everys. "Why did you do that?"

Paine popped to his feet as well. "Clearly it was a mistake bringing her along."

"Except it wasn't," Everys shot back. "As a matter of fact, if I hadn't been along, this whole trip would have been a waste."

Narius held up a hand to silence them. "You have to admit, this does seem like we are capitulating."

"Don't you get it?" Everys asked. "They're not asking for much!"

Kestonin gaped at her. "Pardon me for saying it, Blessed, but they are. Are you really suggesting we return the entire forest to them? Grant them their independence?"

"But that's not what they're asking for! Haven't you listened to what they've said? They're willing to meet any agricultural quotas we set."

"An empty promise," Paine replied. "Besides, they promised the same thing when King Vetranio conquered them, and look how quickly they broke that promise."

"But why did they break the promise? Was it really a negotiating tactic or was it because they didn't have any other choice?" Everys's voice was insistent.

Narius frowned. "What are you talking about? Why wouldn't they be able to meet the quotas?"

She turned to him, her eyes alight and excited. "Because they don't have the Hearth. Your grandfather stole it."

His frown deepened. What was she talking about?

She took a step closer to him. "Haven't you noticed? The Cold Light haven't used the word 'Hearth' to refer to their territory. They always refer to it as the forest or the shade. We've just assumed the Hearth means the territory. It actually refers to something else entirely. Something we can return and only two or three people would ever miss."

"What?" Kestonin asked.

Everys bit her lip and looked from Paine to Kestonin, then back to Narius. She leaned in even closer and whispered, "Something your grandfather put in the basement."

Put in the...? What was she talking about?

But then he remembered. The gem in the archive. His mouth popped open. Was that it? Could it be that simple?

Everys, as if reading his mind, nodded. "That's what they're after. That's what they've always wanted."

"What are you two talking about?" Paine demanded.

Narius stumbled back a step, his mind reeling. He replayed the conversation from the parley, trying to remember if what Everys had said was true. He thought it was. But how could she have possibly figured this out? He looked at her, about to ask the question.

But her expression stopped him. Scared. No, absolutely terrified. She made a small, scribbling motion with her fingers, her hand tucked away so the others couldn't see it. His eyes widened. Was that what she had been doing by that tree? Using toratropic magic? What if someone had seen what she was doing? Thankfully, she had gotten away with it, but they'd have to have a long talk about it later.

Or maybe they wouldn't. If she was right about this, it would be the second time she had used her magic to help him. Maybe, if this all worked out, he'd have to revisit the Dynasty's ban on the practice.

He shook his head, dislodging the thought. Stay focused on the task at hand.

"We can't be certain," he mumbled.

"Your Strength?" Paine asked. "You can't seriously be considering this."

He stared at the vizier, his mind racing. Yes, he could consider it. He was. But at the same time, he knew he couldn't simply back Everys's suggestion. It would seem too sudden, too abrupt, if he simply agreed to hand the gem over. He couldn't just skip to the conclusion. He had to lead the others down the right path, if only to cover Everys's tracks. He knew how much Paine distrusted her. No need to add fuel to that particular fire.

Narius turned to Paine. "We won't agree to anything yet, but would it hurt us to ask a few clarifying questions? We've always assumed that the Hearth referred to the land. What if the queen is right? What if we've misunderstood this the entire time? It's worth asking. Kestonin, will you please ask our hosts to join us again?"

The expert nodded and trotted off in the direction the Cold Light had exited the grove. Narius touched Everys's elbow and motioned for her to step away from the others.

"How certain of this are you?" he asked.

For a brief moment, uncertainty flickered across her face. That was answer enough for him.

"If you're wrong—" he said.

"I'm not."

"But if you are, you just made a promise as the queen of the Dynasty to capitulate to terrorists. That sets a dangerous precedent."

"No, I am trying to make amends for a grievous wrong. Even if I'm wrong about what the Hearth is—which I'm not—wouldn't it be a good gesture to return what your grandfather stole? Wouldn't that lead to a greater peace?"

It would. By all the weapons in the Warrior's arsenal, it would.

Kestonin jogged back over to them, already out of breath. He bent over, his hands on his knees. "Th-they're on their way back, Your Strength."

Although Zar snorted at Kestonin, Narius chose to ignore the display of weakness. "Thank you. Shall we?"

He led their delegation back to the benches just as the grafted returned to the clearing. Tall Reach appeared wary as Narius approached, uncertain.

"Narius King, we understand that the ways of the Dynasty are different than that of our own," Tall Reach said. "While we appreciate Everys Queen's offer, we understand she may not speak with necessary authority."

"I must admit, her offer took us by surprise as well," Narius said.

"We will understand if you must uproot her words."

Narius held up a hand. "Let's not be too hasty. I cannot commit to what she said just yet."

That took Tall Reach by surprise. He shifted, looking at the others, before turning back to Narius. "Indeed?"

"First, I must ask a question I fear will expose a gulf of ignorance between our people." He ground his teeth, forcing the words out. "What, exactly, do you mean when you ask us to return the Hearth?"

The grafted exchanged puzzled looks with each other, then Fire-struck spoke. "We mean that which your grandfather stole from us—"

Narius shook his head. "With all due respect, Firestruck, that isn't helpful. My grandfather, in his zeal to conquer the Cold Light, took many things from your people. The land in which you grow, a portion of your harvest each year—"

"Our autonomy. The lives of many of our grove." Firestruck spat the words at Narius.

"Also true. So, when you say the 'Hearth' is something that the Dynasty took from you, that could refer to many things. What specifically does that word mean to you? What specifically is it that you want returned?"

Once again, the grafted exchanged uncertain looks. Then Evergreen took a step forward. "We must admit to some confusion, Narius King. What does 'the Hearth' mean to you?"

"We had assumed that it referred to the land. The territory." Narius made a sweeping gesture around him. "We thought that the Hearth referred to all of this."

Similar stunned expressions radiated across the Cold Light's faces.

"Y-you thought... You thought it meant the forest?" Tall Reach said.

Narius nodded. Everys straightened up, her eyes shining.

"It does not," Tall Reach said. "Instead, the Hearth is the heart and soul of the forest. An object of immense power through which the life of the Cold Light and our forest flows."

"It helps bind us together in the Below. It grants the blessing that makes our fields so fertile," Evergreen added.

"It is that which your grandfather stole as a trophy," Firestruck added.

Tall Reach motioned toward the empty patch of dirt in front of them. "For many branches of autumns, the Hearth rested here, in what is now my shade. It was the honor and duty of my lineage to safeguard it on behalf of the Yoreroot. My great shame is that, when Vetranio King burned his way to my shade, I relinquished the Hearth at his demand."

"So the Hearth is actually... what?" Paine asked.

"A gemstone. A large one. Vetranio King took it from this clearing after he conquered the forest," Tall Reach said.

Paine turned to Narius. "Your Strength? Were you aware of this?"

Narius swallowed, and it felt like his throat was full of razors. "I knew my grandfather had taken a gem as a trophy at the end of the war. I didn't know its significance. I doubt he did either."

Paine gaped at him.

"So the reason why you haven't been meeting your agricultural quotas?" Everys asked gently. "You were trying to get the Dynasty to return the Hearth?"

Seed Cluster shook her head. "No. Our shortfalls have been an unfortunate side effect. Without the Hearth in its rightful place, the land bleeds. What once was fertile land, good for crops, will eventually become used up."

"But if the Hearth was returned?" Everys prompted.

"The fertility would return as well. We would gladly provide the Dynasty with our bounty," Seed Cluster said.

Everys turned to Narius, triumph shining in her eyes. And she had every right to gloat, even if she did so silently.

"Your Strength?" Paine whispered. "Do you know what they're talking about? I've never seen this gem before."

"I have," Narius replied. "We still have it."

A gasp rippled through the grafted. "Narius King, we must ask again. Will you return the Hearth to us?"

Narius straightened to his full height, trying to project a regal air. "Yes. As soon as we can, the Hearth will be returned to the Cold Light."

Firestruck looked positively stunned. But Tall Reach beamed. "We thank you, Narius King, for your understanding."

He wanted to laugh. His understanding? His? No, it wasn't his to claim at all. As a matter of fact, it had been the Dynasty's lack of understanding that had led to this in the first place! But he couldn't dwell on that. Focus on the now and what it would mean for the future.

"What will happen when the Hearth is returned?" Narius asked. "What about the rebels who have attacked our holdings?"

"We will gladly work with you to uproot them. Yes, Firestruck?" Tall Reach asked.

The question seemed to jolt Firestruck back to reality. He nodded sharply.

"They won't seek Cold Light independence anymore?" Paine asked.

"Some will," Firestruck allowed.

"But such desires are a weed," Evergreen said. "The Cold Light have ever been dedicated to helping. With the Hearth restored to its rightful place, most Cold Light will be willing subjects to the Dynasty."

The other grafted nodded.

Then that settled it, as far as Narius was concerned. He rose to his full height, trying to project a kingly aura as best he could.

"Your Strength? Perhaps we should discuss this further..." Paine said.

"No. There is no need. As king of the Xoniel Dynasty, I hereby promise that we shall return the Hearth to the Cold Light as swiftly as possible."

Pure elation rippled through the grafted. Tall Reach appeared to be on the verge of tears.

"How soon will that be, Narius King?" Firestruck asked.

Narius thought about it. If they had to travel back to Bastion the way they came and return with the Hearth by the same route, it could be a several days. Maybe a week or two. But maybe he could speed things up.

"Would it be possible for us to land a military skimmer within the forest?" Narius asked.

The grafted glanced at each other, but Firestruck nodded. "We will make it possible."

Narius turned to Paine. "If we contact the Dynasty's archivist, he'll know what we need and where to find it. If we load the Hearth on a skimmer, they could have it here in less than two days."

Paine's jaw clenched, but he nodded. "As you order, my king."

Narius turned back to the grafted. "Could we impose on your hospitality for a little while longer, Tall Reach?"

Tall Reach nodded. "Of course, Narius King. While we wait for the Hearth's return, we will show you the wonders of the forest. And we thank you for your understanding. May this day forge a new and lasting peace between the Dynasty and the Cold Light."

"Then if you'll excuse us, we will begin to make the proper arrangements," Narius said.

Tall Reach bowed, as did the other members of the Yoreroot. But then they shuddered, their bodies twisting and twitching. When the strange fit passed, the grafted blinked and looked around, as if uncertain of where they were. The pillar trees that ringed the clearing stopped glowing, all but one.

Yllana stepped forward. "Is it true? The Hearth will be returned?"

"As soon as it can be, yes," Narius said.

Yllana laughed, clapping her hands. Her joy was infectious. Narius found himself smiling and wanting to laugh as well.

"We will show you back to your quarters," Yllana said. "Whatever we can offer you, please let us know."

As they walked away from the clearing, Zar fell in step with Narius. "So we've had this Cold Light thingy all this time, huh?"

Narius nodded. "We have."

The guard gave Narius a look out of the corner of his eye. "Makes me wonder what else the Dynasty may have been keeping from its people."

Before Narius could respond, Zar stepped away, ranging ahead of the group. Narius swallowed hard. Why did he get the feeling that they had defused one problem only to trigger a new one?

47

When morning dawned three days later, Everys could feel the weight of what was about to happen. Even though the skimmer wasn't scheduled to arrive for hours, she listened for it anyway. She couldn't eat much for breakfast, her stomach a quivering ball. Narius didn't appear to be doing much better. He barely touched his food either.

The Cold Light had kept them busy while they waited. Yllana and the other grafted took them on a tour of the surrounding forests, showing them breathtaking vistas that left Everys shuddering with awe. And every night had ended with a lavish dinner.

But the time had come for them to make history. They dressed in the finest clothes they had with them. Half a dozen grafted escorted them through Tall Reach's shade to a larger clearing, one surprisingly devoid of trees, the ground perfectly level. Firestruck, controlling Lesarl, waited for them.

"Will this space be large enough for your skimmer, Narius King?" Firestruck asked. "If not, we could clear more area for you."

Everys hoped Narius would say it wasn't so she could see how they would do that, but Narius graciously said it would be fine.

Soon the drone of the skimmer's engines cut through the forest's noises. Then the vehicle dropped out of the sky, skidding across the ground with a muffled thud. A few seconds later, the skimmer's ramp slid open, disgorging a number of soldiers. Much to Everys's surprise, their leader was Redtale, who trotted over to Narius and saluted.

Then she turned to Everys, her expression grim. "I hear you caused a bit of a ruckus, Blessed."

In spite of the guard's gruff tone, Everys wanted to hug her. But the reunion would have to wait. Six Dynasty soldiers tromped down the ramp, rolling a wide cart between them. Narius and Everys fell into step in front of the cart, acting as the lead escorts from the makeshift landing pad.

The Yoreroot's grafted waited for them, dressed in elaborate robes. Each was a riot of bright colors, mostly horizontal slashed with some perpendicular stripes woven in. There was no mistaking the pure joy and delight that shone from their faces as the Hearth rolled closer.

"I have dreamed of this day for so very long, Narius King," Tall Reach said through Yllana.

As the procession came to the grafted, they stopped, and Narius launched into his speech. He reminded the gathered people about the war between the Dynasty and the Cold Light, about how his grandfather had taken the Hearth as a trophy. He then reiterated the Dynasty's desire for the Cold Light to be a peaceful part of their society, culminating with how he hoped returning the Hearth would forge a better peace between the Dynasty and the Cold Light.

Everys tried to focus on his words, but she had heard it numerous times before. Narius had spent all morning composing the speech and asked her to help him tweak it. It turned out she didn't have much to contribute. He had done a good job the first time. But then he had rehearsed it over and over again, so much so that she probably could have given the speech for him.

As he spoke, she glanced over her shoulder. A small cadre of reporters under Challix's watchful eye recorded the proceedings. Even though they never got along that much, Everys's heart still surged with simple joy at the sight of her assistant. Challix glanced in her direction and offered a tight smile. Did that mean she'd missed Everys too? Everys chuckled to herself. Challix was probably saving up a lecture about not returning the spoils of war.

A smattering of applause wrenched Everys's attention back to the matter at hand. Apparently Narius's speech was over, and he was stepping out of the way of the cart. Everys moved as well.

The Dynasty soldiers passed the cart to the grafted, and once the grafted had full control of the cart, they continued rolling it through the woods. Everys and the others followed. It almost seemed like the forest was already responding to the Hearth's presence. The further they went, the brighter the sunlight was, the louder the birdsong, the taller the plants, as if everything were suddenly filled with more life.

Then they entered Tall Reach's shade. Hundreds of the nearby town's residents stood in a loose circle around the central patch of dirt. The crowd parted as the grafted approached, a reverent whisper rippling through the air. They allowed Narius and Everys to follow the cart into the center, but then closed ranks, separating them from the rest of the Dynasty's delegation. A few days earlier, Everys might have panicked at being surrounded, but she could feel the barely restrained joy and excitement. More than that, she could feel the presence of the Cold Light looming over them all. She was safe. She was fine. She was at Narius's side and that was enough.

The grafted gently, reverently, lifted the Hearth from the cart and slowly carried it past the benches and into the bare patch of dirt. They spent a few moments getting the large gem situated into the right spot, then they all backed away slowly.

At first, nothing seemed to happen. Everys was disappointed at how anticlimactic the moment turned out to be. Given the sheer amount of fuss the Cold Light made over the Hearth, she would have expected its return to be more spectacular

But then a burst of light erupted from the center of the clearing, washing over the gathered people. Everys gasped, throwing her hands over her eyes to try to block out the light. Narius shouted next to her. A chill blasted through her, chased by a sense of strength and peace that seemed to soak deep into her from the ground up.

Silence fell over the clearing, then the crowd around her erupted into cheers and shouts. She risked a peek. The Hearth sat in its place, glowing softly, patterns of light dancing and twirling in the gem's murky depths. She even thought she saw some sort of liquid light condense on the exterior of the Hearth, dripping off the sides only to be absorbed by the soil.

She stumbled forward, sliding past a number of dancing townsfolk who spun around her. She came up to the railing surrounding the Hearth and leaned heavily against it, mesmerized by the tumbling colors inside the gem. The closer she got, the more she realized that it wasn't swirling clouds of light, like she first thought. Instead, she could see distinct lines and patterns coming into and falling out of focus, the glow pulsing with the rhythm of a heartbeat. She could almost feel the gentle thrum in her own chest.

As one of the patterns became clear, she froze. It was a toratropic rune, a powerful healing rune she knew all too well. It was too distinct to be anything otherwise. And as she stood there, transfixed by the patterns, she saw other runes spin through the gem, some of which she recognized, many of which she didn't.

"Are you okay?"

Narius's gentle question jolted her out of her trance. She stumbled backward, and he quickly steadied her.

She smiled at him weakly. "I-I think so."

"Are you sure?"

His hand was still on the small of her back, even though she was fine.

She nodded, her cheeks burning, then motioned around the clearing. "Quite the celebration, huh?"

Narius smiled and nodded. "Shall we join them?"

Everys forced herself to nod. He led her away, steering her with his hand on her back. Even though she wanted to continue studying the Hearth, she allowed him to draw her into the cheering crowd.

48

The Cold Light's celebration lasted four days. There was singing, dancing, and feasting. At first, Everys had been swept up in the excitement, but as the days-long party dragged on, she found herself wanting nothing more than to fly home.

Much to her surprise, she realized "home" had come to mean her suite in the palace.

Regardless, that gnawing ache grew stronger by the hour. But Narius wouldn't hear of leaving. He insisted they stay for the entire celebration, where they were seated in a place of honor each day. Citizens of the forest came and went, everyone offering enthusiastic thanks for the Hearth's return. Several of them carried messages from outlying settlements for people unable to attend, including a herd of shessu who apparently couldn't leave the fields. The fields were already responding to the Hearth's presence, and the shessu couldn't abandon them now.

But eventually, the party had to end. The Cold Light and their citizens had to return to their duties. And the Dynasty's delegation had to as well, as Paine reminded them every other hour.

Thankfully, the Cold Light had left the makeshift landing pad open for them, so they wouldn't have to make the multi-day trek back through the forest. But as the Dynasty delegation arrived at the landing pad, Everys was surprised to see Yllana and the other grafted waiting next to a large sled loaded with boxes and... was that a sapling?

Yllana bowed low as they approached. "Your Strength, Blessed, we thank you for gracing us with your presence. The Yoreroot is thankful for your openness. As a sign of their appreciation at the return of the Hearth, we have a number of gifts we would like to present to you."

Narius shook his head. "That is unnecessary."

"It may well be, but they are most insistent, and when you learn what they are offering, I believe you will be satisfied with their choices." She gestured toward the cart, and one of the grafted picked up a box and brought it over to Narius.

As the grafted set the box in Narius's hands, she pulled open the sides, revealing a window. Narius grunted in surprise, and Everys twisted around to peek through the window. The box was filled with bugs? Hundreds of them, maybe thousands, with green bodies, translucent blue wings, and large horns. Each was no bigger than the size of her thumbnail.

"Uh... We are honored." Narius's voice was tentative.

Yllana smiled. "Perhaps if I explained. These are bark beetles, a species of insect that has developed a symbiotic relationship with the Cold Light. Their primary diet is fungus that grows on the Cold Light's pillar trees, and regrettably, the grafted who have bonded to them. The Yoreroot believes the rebels who have attacked your people have smuggled pillar trees from the forest into your territory. If you release these beetles, they will seek out the nearest source of fungus—"

"—leading us straight to the rebels?" Narius's eyes were wide.

Yllana nodded. "Indeed. We are sending six boxes of the beetles and will gladly provide more should you need them."

Narius handed the box to Zar and took a step toward the cart, his expression eager. "We are very grateful for this gift. But, if I may ask, why is there a sapling in the cart?"

"We understand the royal garden has a patch of ground reserved for plants from the Cold Light forest," Yllana said. "We offer this pillar tree sapling to be planted there, along with a sliver of the Hearth itself. You may plant both, and within a generation, a mature pillar tree will grace your gardens. In spite of the great distance, the piece of the Hearth will allow the tree to connect to the Below. This will allow the Cold Light to visit your shade, should you wish it."

Narius's jaw popped open, and it sounded like he was trying to say something. Finally, he managed to stammer, "W-we are, indeed, most honored by this grand gesture."

Yllana laughed and waved away his words. "The gesture is not so grand as you might think. In ages long past, the Cold Light would send pillar tree saplings to various kingdoms to speed communication."

Paine frowned and cleared his throat. "If that is the case, why don't we have one of those trees in Bastion? Why didn't the Cold Light ever make the offer to the Dynasty before now?"

It was the most Everys had heard Paine speak in days, and it was easy to pick up on the anger that flowed through his voice. Redtale tensed next to her.

Yllana regarded Paine with an arched brow. "In truth, we have not made this offer to any kingdom in the last four hundred years due to the fall of Nekek the Bright. When the Dalark and Xoniel burned the city, they destroyed the pillar tree in their royal gardens while a Cold Light was still inhabiting it. After that, the Yoreroot placed a moratorium on sending out more trees. Until now."

Silence fell over the clearing. Everys felt like she could be knocked over.

"W-we are sorry for the loss and are most—" Narius started to say.

Yllana waved away his words again. "There is no need to apologize. In truth, Lightdrinker was partially to blame for his death. The Yoreroot tried to recall him many times, but he believed the Siporan's defenses would stand. It seems many were mistaken about the Ascendancy's supposed invulnerability."

That last statement was directed, not at Narius, but Everys. Chills crawled up her back and settled at the base of her skull, but in spite of the cold, she still broke into a sweat. There was understanding in Yllana's eyes, a conspiratorial expression like she *knew*. She knew exactly what Everys was.

"There is one more gift we wish to bestow, but it must be done in private." Yllana didn't look away from Everys.

Narius and Paine exchanged puzzled glances, but the vizier refused to acknowledge Everys's presence. Narius nodded and made a gesture toward Everys.

Yllana stepped close to Everys and took her gently by the elbow, steering her away from the others. As they walked, Yllana shuddered, and suddenly, her grip was tighter, her steps measured. When the grafted turned to look at her, Everys couldn't miss the alien presence lurking in her eyes.

"Everys Queen." Even in a whisper, Yllana's voice had grown more resonant.

"Tall Reach?"

He nodded. "We are particularly grateful for the role you played in these negotiations. While the Yoreroot was hopeful, we did not truly expect this outcome. At least, not this quickly. If it weren't for your intervention, we might still be mired in fruitless discussion."

"It was my pleasure," Everys said.

Tall Reach led her over to the cart where he subtly pointed to one of the boxes. "In that box you will find several bolts of grass-silk cloth, the finest we produce. And, tucked in the middle of it all, a jar of sap harvested from the seed pod I dropped."

Everys's eyes widened, and she glanced over her shoulder to make sure no one had overheard.

He chuckled. "Never fear, Everys Queen. We understand the need for discretion. We Cold Light are very good at keeping large secrets. Just think of the shessu."

That didn't do much to relieve the knot in her stomach. "How did you know... what I am?"

"In truth, we did not. Long has it been since the Ascendancy fell to ashes. We heard of the Dynasty's reprisals against Siporans, and we feared that those with your abilities had vanished from Ehun. We mourned that loss, especially given the long history between our peoples. Your people helped shape ours in ways that you may never fathom."

"The Hearth?" Even though she had seen the runes tumbling within the gem, she was surprised to hear confirmation of her suspicions.

Tall Reach nodded. "Yes, that is but one way that Siporan mages have helped us. While many do not share this opinion, we of the Cold Light have longed for Siporan royalty to return to Ehun. When we heard of your coronation, we hoped those dreams had become reality."

Everys glanced back at the cart. The Dynasty troops were already unloading the crates and carrying them into the transport. She winced. All it would take is for one of them to open the crate with the sap in it.

"Do not fret, Everys Queen. We are not so foolish as to reveal what you are to your people. The crate is protected by a rune that makes the jar appear to be nothing more than another bolt of cloth."

What? How could the Cold Light produce such a powerful rune? She hadn't done much experimenting with glamour spells—those runes belonged to a different family—but she knew enough to know that disguising the jar as something unlike it took a complex rune. It felt as though the ground was about to open and swallow her.

"How?" she whispered.

"As Yllana told you on your journey to my shade, the Cold Light have long offered sanctuary to those that the outside world deems troublesome, disposable, or dangerous. This offer has stretched back through centuries, and many have taken advantage of it." His voice drifted off, but there was deeper meaning in his expression, as if confirming the thoughts that already brewed in her mind.

If that were true, if they had offered sanctuary to many, then that meant... Her breath hitched. "You mean, there are..."

He nodded. "There are those who fled the mage-king's heresies at the Ascendancy's height. There are those who sought refuge as the Xoniel and the Dalark tore down Nekek the Bright. And there are those who found living in the midst of their destroyers too onerous."

Her head was spinning, overwhelmed by what he was saying. "C-can I... Can I meet them?"

Now Tall Reach shook his head. "I am afraid that is not possible at this time."

"Why not?"

"When we extended the invitation to you to come to my shade, we suggested that the Siporan communities within our forests meet you. They all declined, some more insistently than others."

"Oh." Why wouldn't they want to meet her? The question twisted her heart into a painful knot.

Tall Reach patted her shoulder. "Do not take it so personally. It is not you that they distrust. It is the government you represent. A time may come when they may be more willing to reveal themselves. And while I may not violate their privacy, I will tell you this: you have met some without realizing it."

He paused, his head tipped forward, his eyes prompting.

Did he mean that Yllana was Siporan? No, that wasn't right. She'd said her family were practitioners of Elderreach. But that had been before they came to the forest. Had they converted? Could she ask?

But before she could, Narius stepped closer. "Is everything all right here?"

Tall Reach brightened, then his features shifted, becoming more youthful and open. Yllana blinked several times. "Everything is just fine, Your Strength. There were some private matters I had to discuss with the queen, but I think we have finished."

Everys clamped her jaw in frustration. She could still ask, especially now that it was Yllana and not Tall Reach. After all, Narius knew what she was, and learning that there were other Siporan mages shouldn't bother him too much. But she still hesitated. If Yllana really practiced toratropic magic, if that was something she wanted to keep herself, it wasn't up to Everys to violate that privacy.

So she smiled and turned to Narius. "We are. Shall we go, husband?"

Narius studied her face, as if trying to read the secret. But when Everys didn't say anything else, he motioned for her to lead the way back to the skimmer. Back to the palace. Back to home.

49

"I still can't believe you went there, Blessed!" Trule kept watch on the other girls as they cleaned the room.

"It really wasn't that bad," Everys replied.

"You don't have to keep up the brave front," Trule said. "Being so far from civilization, in the heart of the Cold Light's forest? It's the stuff of horror vids! But at least your parley was successful. I can hardly believe we'll see peace!"

Trule wasn't the only one who felt that way. When Everys and Narius returned to Bastion two weeks earlier, they hadn't realized how their extended absence had played out in the Dyansty's holdings. While Paine had shared with the press that Narius and Everys were going to the Cold Light's forest, he had made it sound like they would be gone from the capital for only a few days at most. And while Zar had kept Duke Brencis updated as to what was happening, those updates hadn't been shared with the public. As Narius and Everys's absence dragged on, the public became more and more nervous. Rumors circulated through the press, stating the Cold Light had captured the king and queen, enthralled them, or assassinated them. By the time they had actually emerged from the forest, the news outlets were reporting that the Cold Light, after killing the Dynasty's delegation, were preparing for an all-out war. When Narius and Everys returned, unharmed, the sense of relief was palpable.

It was also short-lived, especially as the story of what happened started circulating. The common citizens had their doubts about the promise of peace. And why wouldn't they? Even though Paine had written a careful account of what had happened that circulated throughout the Dyansty's holdings, it had only been two weeks.

The food shipments hadn't resumed. The terrorists were still at large. Nothing had really changed.

But Narius planned for that. He and Paine went on a publicity tour to the far reaches of the Dynasty's holdings. They held rallies, gave interviews, praised the Cold Light for their generosity, and did their best to stoke the public's confidence. They had to sidestep questions about where the Hearth had been, since answering those questions would only raise more about what other cultural treasures were hidden.

At the same time, Challix had Everys doing the same thing, only from Bastion itself. Every day brought a new interview with a different reporter. At first, the process had been nerve-wracking. Everys had braced herself for verbal ambushes. But Challix kept things on track. By the fourth day, Everys had been able to relax and regaled the reporters with what she had seen and experienced—leaving out the toratropic vision, of course. Much to Everys's frustration, the reporters didn't ask questions about the negotiations. Instead, they focused on what they saw as Narius's exploits. Their questions suggested she had been a damsel in near distress protected by the brave king. She played her part, but with her teeth clenched the whole time.

Thankfully, their divide-and-conquer strategy quickly allayed the public's fears, and according to the latest polls, the public's opinion of the king and queen had never been higher. As a matter of fact, Everys was finding more and more interest in her outreach center, with messages piling up from potential corporate sponsors, nobles who were finally ready to partner with her, and other interested parties. Sadly, she had been so busy she hadn't been able to answer any of them.

They would still have to wait. Oh, Challix was getting after her to sort through them all, but they had kept this long, what was one more day? Besides, with both Narius and Paine gone on their goodwill tour, the palace staff had turned to Everys for direction. Plus, she had to start laying plans for the next Queen's Court, and half a dozen other projects were springing up in her imagination. There was just so much to do and so little time in each day.

Everys cleared her throat, catching the girls' attention. "Make sure the table has the best lighting, please."

The girls giggled, exchanging glances that they probably thought Everys couldn't interpret. Yes, she was being picky, but she wanted things to go well.

"Uh, Blessed? The soup is starting to boil..."

Everys hurried into the kitchenette and looked over her preparations. Jeslin, the serving girl she had tasked with watching the stove, scurried out of the way. Everys tasted the soup—which was turning out to be more of a stew, much to her consternation—and decided to add a bit more salt. Then she checked the rolls in the oven, which were turning a nice golden brown next to the rack of ribs. She nodded to herself. At least this time, she had stuck to dishes she was confident she could make.

There was a gentle knock at the door.

Everys whirled around. He was here? Already? But dinner wasn't ready yet! Could she insist that he stay out? Maybe ask him to run an errand?

No, that was silly. Why should she be so nervous? This was no big deal. They had agreed to dinner before he left. But still, a little more warning would have been nice!

"Do you need me to stall him, my lady?" Trule asked.

Everys's mind leapt at the possibility. She should have thought of that right away. With Trule distracting Narius, she could slip into her bedroom and change into something more appealing.

Then she spotted the silent laughter in Trule's eyes. She was teasing Everys? That probably shouldn't be encouraged, but in that moment, Everys didn't mind. That simple act of friendship was enough to snap her out of her panic. She ran her hands down the front of her outfit, smoothing away wrinkles that were probably imaginary. Then she cast one last glance over her quarters. Definitely messy, but not embarrassingly so.

So why was she still hesitating?

Time to stop being so flighty. Everys squared her shoulders and stepped forward, pulling open the door.

And there he was, not wearing his military uniform. Not wrapped up in palace finery. No, there was Narius, dressed in simple khaki pants and a loose-fitting white shirt. She could read the exhaustion in his expression, but that seemed to melt away as their gazes met. He held up a bottle of wine.

"Courtesy of the Viceroy of Maotoa," he said.

Everys found her throat dry, so much so that she couldn't speak for a second. But then she managed to croak, "Oh?"

He nodded, then sniffed at the air. "That smells wonderful."

Everys turned toward the room, ready to shoo away the girls, but discovered that they had not only finished setting up the table and served the meal, they had also vanished as well.

"Why don't you come in and tell me about your tour?" she suggested.

Narius smiled and brushed past her, so close she could swear that she felt the heat from his body. That had to be why she was feeling so flush, right? Or she was coming down with something. Maybe she should cancel. Postpone. She didn't want to get him sick.

But then he settled into his chair at the table and favored her with a wide grin, and she decided that maybe it would be worth the risk.

Narius regaled her with stories of his press tour, and as hungry as she was, Everys didn't eat. Instead, she soaked up each word, each image, each idea that Narius shared. While she had seen pictures and videos of the different regions controlled by the Dynasty, somehow Narius's descriptions were more vibrant, imbued with life and warmth and a surprising amount of love. As he told each story, Everys came to realize how much Narius truly cared for the subjects in the Dynasty.

"Everys? Are you okay?" Narius asked. "You've barely touched your food."

She blinked, snapping herself out of her reverie. "No, it's just..." She clamped her mouth down on the words that almost slipped out. How would he respond if she admitted that she missed him?

He stirred the stew with a spoon and offered her a warm smile. "This is delicious, by the way."

"Thank you," she mumbled.

"I've monopolized the conversation," he said. "I've probably bored you half to death."

She shook her head. Not at all. She could have listened to him for the rest of the evening. Again, she couldn't bring herself to admit that out loud, so she shook her head and laughed. "It's fine."

"You're very polite to say so, but it's not." He set down his silverware and leaned forward, folding his hands on top of the table. "What about you? How are plans going for the outreach center?"

"N-not as well as I'd like." Inkstains! Why was she having so much trouble concentrating? "I think I've secured about a dozen partners with various corporations and noble houses, but the real obstacle right now is the building. It was pretty much destroyed during the riot, and while the rubble has been cleared away, construction is stalled. Challix insists we have to secure bids from multiple construction companies and examine each offer thoroughly before even one brick can be laid."

Narius blanched. "Unfortunately, she may be following instructions from Paine. I'll see if I can't smooth things over."

"That would be wonderful," Everys said.

"But that may have to wait. We do have the state dinner to plan for."

The what? "State dinner?"

He nodded. "It's traditional that after peace has been won, the Dynasty celebrates with a state dinner to celebrate those who made peace possible. In other words, we need to have a state dinner to honor you."

She stared at him, not sure she had heard him. Then she sputtered. "B-but there's no new treaty, and it really isn't the end of a war—"

"The Dynasty doesn't see it that way. They've been living in fear and uncertainty. And an argument can be made that we were still at war with the Cold Light because of the terrorist attacks." He shrugged. "I don't have an option. We need to celebrate you."

She frowned. On the surface, his voice sounded happy and light. But she picked up an undercurrent of frustration in his tone.

He briefly met her gaze, then turned his attention to the stew, scooping up another bite. Avoiding her eyes.

Everys studied his face carefully. Although he was doing a fair job of hiding it, she could still read the tension in his eyes, in his jaw. Something was bothering him, and he was trying desperately to hide it.

She leaned forward. "Narius, what's wrong?"

He froze, spoon halfway to his mouth. Then he grimaced and waved toward the table. "We don't have glasses of karabek sauce at the ready."

"Do we need them for you to be honest?"

Another wince, but then his expression crumbled. "I'm sorry. The past few days have been filled with a great deal of latent hostility."

"From the press?"

He shook his head. "No. From the nobility and the ethnarchs. As much as we tried to sidestep the issue of the Archives, the story is starting to spread. Some of the ethnarchs are not-so-quietly wondering if their people's cultural treasures still exist. I'm worried this will turn into a major scandal, especially if the ethnarchs press the question."

Heat flashed up Everys's spine. Shouldn't they? It wasn't right for the Dynasty to have stolen anyone's cultural heritage. If the Siporans had an ethnarch, she'd want that individual to press for the return of the Principalities. It was a small thing, maybe only a symbolic gesture, but true justice could start there.

But he looked so upset. That tore deeply at her own heart. She reached across the table and caught his free hand in hers, giving it a quick squeeze. "I'm sorry."

He looked up at her, surprise splashed across his face. "For what?"

"Isn't this my fault? If I hadn't said anything about the archive to the Cold Light—"

"This is not your fault. This is my people's fault. If my ancestors—no, if *we* hadn't taken those trophies, if we hadn't been so arrogant as to decide everyone had to live under our control, I wouldn't be in this bind. But many in the nobility won't see it that way. Even though they just learned of the archive's existence, many have decided that the objects in the archive belong to the Dynasty and should never be returned. Some of them are suggesting we build a museum to house them all as a 'common trust for the Dynasty's peoples.' If I don't navigate this situation carefully, I'll lose their support and they could even try to overthrow me."

He went back to eating, but Everys's appetite had vanished. In that moment, she realized what a good person Narius was. Maybe he represented the Dynasty with all of its oppressive history and policies, but he was trying. Things would have been easier if he had married Clarinda Gaines or that girl from the picture, someone who understood politics. Someone who could actually support him and not make so much trouble.

"Why did you even pick me?" The question made it past her lips before she could really think about it.

Once again, Narius froze. He looked up at her, and she could read the conflict in his expression. Confusion, sorrow, surprise, they warred against each other across his face.

Everys decided to press on. "Please. I have to know. You could have chosen any of those other women. Someone who understands the nobility. Someone who would bring allies and influence to the table. But you chose me. Why?"

He set down his silverware and took a deep breath. "Traditionally, the queen is supposed to be an embodiment of the Dynasty, representing our collective past and future. Past queens have approached the role in different ways. Some have seen their job as being a passive symbol. Others have been more like you and have tried to take a more active role in the government. But they've all had one thing in common: every single one of them has come from the nobility."

"Wouldn't that have been better?"

Narius shrugged. "Viara was from the nobility and look how that turned out." He fiddled with one of his utensils. "Truth be told, when I was in that moment, I wasn't thinking of breaking with that tradition. I was thinking the same sort of thing that you are now: my next wife had to be a noble."

"Then why did you choose me?" Everys pressed the question.

"Because Tormod insisted."

She frowned. "Who?"

"Tormod, my Master of Shadows."

Everys frowned, running through all of the bureaucrats and government functionaries she had met in the last several months. There were dozens, hundreds, but she couldn't place the name with any faces. As a matter of fact, she wasn't sure she had even heard that name in the past.

But then she remembered the day she had been chosen to be queen. The stumpy man who had stared at her. She had almost forgotten about him. Was that Tormod?

"What did he say that convinced you to pick me?" she asked.

He poked at his food idly. "He knows about many of my plans for the Dynasty and how I want us to move in a new direction. He's very supportive and wants to see the Dynasty change too. He said if I were to marry a noble again, I would be signaling that the Dynasty would remain stagnant. If I married Clarinda Gaines, yes, that would be a departure, but her status as a wealthy entrepreneur already makes her quasi-nobility so it wouldn't be as strong of a statement. But if I were to marry you, a non-citizen, a commoner, and a Siporan? I couldn't make my intentions for the Dynasty any more clear. He was very persuasive. Very insistent."

But *why* had he been so insistent? She remembered the way he had looked at her, as if they were both in on the same joke. How had he known anything about her in the first place?

Her eyes widened. There was one way she could find out.

"Can I meet him?"

Narius blinked, clearly surprised at the question. "Why?"

She shrugged. "Why not?"

He hesitated. "Queens haven't met with the Masters of Shadows in the past."

"And that would stop me why?"

Narius blinked, then guffawed. "All right, I'll arrange it. And I'll warn Tormod to brace himself."

Good. Because maybe, just maybe, she could finally get some of the answers she needed.

50

H er breakfast was getting cold. She should have been eating, but Everys couldn't. She could feel the sketches staring at her, demanding her attention.

The last few days had been consumed with preparations for the state dinner. And although Challix tried to keep Everys shielded from most of the preparations, she still found herself inundated with planning details. First Speaker Zolkin had sent her a message, requesting two dozen seats for prominent members of the Hall, but that wouldn't be possible due to the sheer number of guests expected, especially since the Flail, a powerful coalition in the Hall wanted fair representation as well. Every ethnarch was expected to attend, and each would have a sizable retinue. Nor could they forget the nobility. There was no way to invite them all, so each invitation was an exercise in strategy of who to include and who could bear the snub. And then there was the matter of the foreign delegations. Protocol demanded Narius extend invitations to Dalark, Elscontin, Tomma, and the other major superpowers. Even though Challix said it was unlikely that any of them would send representatives, they had to be prepared should any come.

As if Everys's dark thoughts had summoned her, Challix bustled into the room. "Have you made a decision yet, Blessed?"

Everys fought to keep from wincing. She focused on her breakfast, which suddenly tasted bland and unappealing.

Challix sighed. "You can't keep putting it off. They're going to need time to get everything ready and..." Another sigh. "Fine. If you're not even going to look at me, at least look at these."

Another stack of designs plopped down on the table next to Everys. The sudden impact startled Everys enough that her gaze flicked over to them. The top few sketches were covered with bold lines, splashes of color. The drawings barely looked like anything at first, but then Everys picked out sharp lines that denoted arms and legs, the gentle curve of hips. The topmost sketch looked like a straight dress, sleek with sharp lines and a riot of colors, like a rainbow had vomited across the fabric.

She quickly pulled her gaze away from them and forced herself to take another bite of her breakfast.

"I'm sorry to keep pressing, Blessed, but the dinner is in less than four days." Challix glanced at her scriber. "I have to go. Just let me know when you've decided."

With that, Challix left.

Everys sighed and set aside her spoon. Her gaze drifted too close to the stack of designs, so she turned away from them. She didn't even want to think about it. Up until now, she had managed to sidestep decisions about fashion. While Challix had tolerated her choice of attire at the Queen's Court, she had also made it quite clear that business attire would be wholly inappropriate at the dinner. Every time Challix breezed through the quarters, she inevitably dropped off more sketches and suggested designs for Everys's evening wear. Each of those was accompanied by a pointed reminder that whatever Everys chose would become the standard for dynastic fashion for the next year or two, so she had to pick wisely and carefully.

Little wonder, then, that Everys did her best to ignore the sketches. She knew that she'd have to pick soon. The designers would need time to sew the dress and make sure it was perfect. Nothing less would do for the living embodiment of the Dynasty.

A shiver danced up Everys's back at the thought. So many eyes looking at her, judging her, and not just for what she was wearing. But who she was. Who and what she represented. Judgments made that would shape the Dynasty's future, not just for months but maybe for years.

She shook her head. Ridiculous. She was being ridiculous. All she had to do was pick one, right? Obviously not the top one, that was clearly too garish. But maybe if she took the time to sift through the dozens of possibilities, she'd find one that...

Or she could go prepare herself for the day. There was no reason to sit around in her pajamas. Yes, a bath would help clear her mind and make the decision a whole lot easier.

She lingered in the tub for a lot longer than she should have. But the warm water felt so good, and she knew how stressful the day would be. Yes, relaxing in a hot bath was the right thing to do. As she emerged from the water, she decided she wouldn't signal for Trule and the other girls to help get her dressed. They were all too busy with preparations for the state dinner as it was. She would just take her time to make sure she was truly ready for the day.

Finally, an hour later, she started back toward her sitting room. She knew she should look at those sketches, but maybe it would be better to send a few messages to Minister Masruq and his staff. They still hadn't come up with the promised funding for the outreach center. And there were a number of leads within the business sector and the nobility she hadn't pursued yet. It wouldn't take too long. She would still have plenty of time to—

She almost slammed into Redtale and another guard.

Everys almost screamed in surprise, but caught herself just in time. She smiled warmly at Redtale. She hadn't seen her that much since their return from the Cold Light's territory. She had been perfectly safe the entire time, but she had missed seeing her.

But when their gazes met, she found only coldness in Redtale's eyes. She stood at stiff attention, nodding curtly at her approach.

"Ma'am. This here is Bulwark Rewether."

Everys frowned as Rewether snapped to attention. He was a clean-cut, middle-aged human male. His skin was a dusky gray, his eyes beady. He might have had some Weyfir blood in his heritage. "What can I help you with, Rewether?"

Confusion flitted across Rewether's face. "Uh, actually, Blessed, I'm here to serve you. I'm the new head of your personal guard."

Her what? Everys looked to Redtale, but she wouldn't meet her gaze.

"Don't worry, Blessed, the transition will be seamless," Rewether said. "I've already spoken with the other men in your detail. Redtale has done an admirable job, and I don't foresee any complications. I was hoping you and I could spend some time this morning so we can get better acquainted and you can outline your expectations for me."

"Rewether?"

"Yes, Blessed?"

"Can you give me a moment with Redtale?"

Rewether faltered, but only for a moment and he recovered quickly enough. "Of course, Blessed. I'll be just outside."

Even as Rewether retreated, Redtale still wouldn't meet her gaze. As the door snapped shut, she actually turned away as if she too were going to leave.

"What's going on, Redtale?" she demanded. "Are you being punished?"

Redtale bowed her head. "No, Blessed."

"Then who do I talk to? I don't want a new commander."

"I requested this."

Her words were like a slap to Everys's face. "You what?"

Redtale studied the floor. "I've resigned my commission. Returning home to the Highlands."

"Why? Why would you do that?" Tears stung Everys's eyes. "Was it something I said? Or did?"

She finally looked at Everys, and the anger in her eyes was almost enough to knock Everys backward. "You have to ask?"

Everys shrank back. She didn't think that Redtale would physically attack her, but in that moment, she could feel the force of her rage. Redtale's hands balled into fists, and her jaw worked, clenching and grinding. Finally, she forced her arms to her side.

"Permission to speak freely, Blessed?" She somehow managed to say the words through clenched teeth, and they sounded like the growl of a predator.

"Please."

She reached up, touching the stumps of her horns. "I shared with you why I broke my horns. I told you about the *ma-se-krana*, how important it is to my people."

Everys nodded.

Redtale looked up again, but this time, it wasn't rage that burned in her eyes, but tears. "And then, a few weeks ago, while you were with the Cold Light, I was summoned to the royal gardens. I was met by an official I had never heard of, who opened a secret door I knew nothing about. Then he emerged with the Cold Light's Hearth. In the past few weeks, I've heard the rumors. Of the archive, of what the Dynasty has hidden away down there, precious relics and trophies that were sacred to the peoples the Dynasty has conquered. And I couldn't help but wonder: Is the *ma-se-krana* down there? Has it been so close this whole time?"

Everys started to say something, but Redtale held up a hand, cutting her off. Redtale's scowl deepened. "And then I found out that you knew."

She *what*? How could she accuse her of that? "I didn't!"

"Didn't you? According to the stories your husband has been telling, it was your idea to return the Hearth to the Cold Light. That means that you not only knew about the Archives, but you knew that's where the Dynasty's been stashing their subjects' relics." She crossed her arms and glared at her. "I'm guessing there's some fancy Siporan stuff down there?"

Her mouth went dry, but she nodded.

"And you figured that meant that the Cold Light's Hearth was down there too?"

Another nod.

"And yet it never occurred to you to tell me yourself that the *ma-se-krana* might still exist, that it might be stored in this very building?"

Her question was like a slap to Everys's face. The truth stung more sharply than any physical blow.

"No," she admitted in a bare whisper.

Redtale nodded. "That's why I have to resign. For all of your vaunted words about looking out for the people of the Dynasty, you've become one of *them*."

Everys bristled. "That's not true!"

"Isn't it?" She waved a hand around her room. "Where are the plans for your outreach center? What about the funding?"

"It's complicated! I've been trying, but I've been fighting some bureaucratic resistance. I've made some valuable inroads in the last week, so—"

Redtale snorted. "Trying. Excuses about resistance and troubles and inroads. What happened to the queen who bought a building without anyone realizing? Why have you become so timid?"

Everys's mouth clicked shut. More reasons, more explanations, more rationalizations sprouted in her mind, which could easily dismiss Redtale's observations. But she realized that no matter how she dressed them up, they were still what Redtale called them. Excuses. Flimsy excuses.

"I don't blame you, Blessed," Redtale said, her voice quiet and grim. "It's not entirely your fault. That's the thing about power. When you don't have it, you're so sure you know what to do if you did. But the moment you get power, it changes you more than you expect. I've seen the same thing happen to my fellow guards. Even happened to me. When we're newly conscripted, so many of us were sure we saw how to make things better. But then, once we got promoted a couple of times, that youthful exuberance was gone. It happens, even to the best of us."

"So why are you leaving?" Everys hated the way her voice quavered.

"Because a person has to take a stand at some point or another." She touched her forehead again, her fingers grazing her broken horns. "I knew I had to when I did this. And I realized this was another time too. Don't worry. You'll be in good hands with Rewether. Solid ground, Blessed."

With that, Redtale turned on her heel and quickly marched from the room.

The moment she left, the strength drained out of Everys's legs. She barely made it to a chair before she collapsed. Her body and mind felt numb, wrapped in a haze. The truth of what Redtale had said stabbed into her. She had known how important Redtale's heritage was to her. She could have asked about the Ixactl's treasures. And she hadn't.

She'd have to do better.

Her gaze fell on the stack of designs. If she was going to make a change, she'd have to start right away. An idea started to stitch together. If the Dynasty was going to change, she would have to nudge it in the right direction. And she knew just how to do it.

Where was she?

Narius fidgeted, smoothing the front of his formal uniform. Dressing for the state dinner was easy for him. The king was expected to wear military regalia and a simple crown. He understood a queen had many difficult choices in regards to her outfit and makeup and entire appearance, but all of that should have been arranged far in advance. So why was Everys so late? The dinner was supposed to start!

He glanced at the ornate doors to the palace's main ballroom. On the other side were the guests: ethnarchs, nobility, politicians, business leaders, people from all over the Dynasty's holdings. And they were waiting. Yes, Narius and Everys could make them wait. According to family legends, his great-great-great-grandfather had once made his guests wait for two whole weeks before making his grand entrance. But that wasn't a tradition Narius wished to revive. So what was taking her so long?

Footsteps clattered behind him and Narius turned. A flock of serving girls rushed forward, clearing a way for... Everys? Narius froze, surprised at what he saw. Everys's dark hair had been swept up into an elaborate hairstyle, studded with small gems. Her makeup accentuated her features, making her look like she belonged in a masterpiece.

But what was she wearing? Such a plain and oddly shaped dress! The skirt swept the floor, but the off-white material hung in odd clumps, with silver strips woven into the fabric from her hips to the bottom edge. The top was a little bit better but was also shot through with the silver strips. Were those wires? He had seen some bold designs out of Erecone, but he had never seen anything quite like this. Was she trying to play an elaborate prank?

Then he looked up and saw her nervous smile. No, this wasn't a prank.

"You look very..." She swallowed hard. "Very handsome, Narius."

His mouth went dry, heat flashing through his body. He mouthed several possible responses, but his mind just couldn't get past the dress. Paine was going to have a conniption!

Then Challix scurried up next to Everys, an impish smile on her face. And Narius paused, because as far as he could remember, he had never seen Challix smile, and definitely not with such a mischievous glint in her eyes. No, wait, he had. After the riots, when she had reported on the positive bump in poll numbers. Did that mean she knew what Everys was doing? And she actually approved?

"I do have a favor to ask you," Everys said. "Can you go through the doors first?"

He frowned. It was a violation of protocol, but Challix's smile broadened, so he found himself nodding. "As you wish, my queen."

Everys blushed, then turned away from him.

Narius straightened, took a deep breath, and strode forward. As he did, the stewards on either side of the doors pushed them open, their timing perfect so they swung open in perfect sync. As Narius strode through the door, the high steward announced his name and full title. That took several minutes, as there were a number of traditional honorifics that had to be included.

As the steward explained that Narius was the "Heir of the Shattered Spear, Subduer of the Proud" and so on, Narius looked over the gathered guests. He could easily read the usual fault lines between guests. There, in one back corner, the nobility who sequestered themselves from their lessers. There, the cadre from the Hall who had been chosen to attend. He spotted six or seven ethnarchs and their coteries. Clarinda Gaines and a number of her fellow businesspeople formed another knot near the food and drink. Why was Clarinda smiling so broadly, so expectantly? Was she on the hunt again?

Eventually, the steward made it through Narius's titles and started on Everys's. Hers wouldn't take nearly as long, so Narius forced a thin smile and continued to face the guests.

"Queen Everys, Embodiment of the Water Bear—" The steward's voice cut off suddenly with an audible gasp.

Narius frowned as a ripple of surprise flashed through the assembled guests. The murmured conversations stopped, and all eyes were on Narius. No, not on him. On something behind him.

He turned and his breath caught.

Everys had stepped through the door, but her entire appearance had changed. Instead of wearing the misshapen dress from just a few moments earlier, she wore woven light, which flowed like water to the floor. But as she stepped forward, the radiance faded. Instead, it was replaced by... Was that a desert? Now it appeared as if she wore sand dunes underneath a crystal blue sky. No, not just any desert, Narius realized, but those were images of the Plissk Sanctuary Oasis. As soon as he realized what the image was, though, Everys's dress shimmered, and the sands were replaced by a mountain vista. The Ixactl Highlands! Another shimmer, and Everys wore the cityscape of Bastion itself.

Narius gaped as she glided forward, stretching out her hand to him. She wasn't the embodiment of the Water Bearer. She had transcended the Water Bearer, a divine figure in her own right, her face radiant, her eyes alight with silent laughter. A wave of pins and needles washed over him, chased by a delicious shudder as she slipped her hand in the crook of his elbow and squeezed. A haze fell on his mind, but thankfully, his body knew what to do. He lurched forward, and the two of them descended the stairs. Every fourth step, Everys's dress displayed a different vista: the coasts of Maotoa, the ruins of Elregan, even Tall Reach's shade. The announcer recovered and continued the litany of Everys's titles, but Narius knew that no one was paying attention.

They reached the bottom of the stairs. Everys released him and took a step forward, dipping into a formal curtsy for the guests.

"My friends, thank you for joining us." If she was nervous, her voice didn't betray it. "May we celebrate the foundation we have built for the Dynasty, one of peace, stability, and mutual cooperation. I believe I speak on behalf of my husband when I invite you to enjoy yourselves as we celebrate a new day dawning for all of our people."

The smattering of applause shook Narius out of his reverie. He joined in, then realized he wasn't supposed to. Blunted sword, what was wrong with him?

Everys leaned in closer and whispered, "I need some food. I haven't had anything to eat all day!"

And with that, she headed toward a table laden with food. She didn't make it far, because guests swarmed in to speak with her or to simply stand in her presence. He took a long, stuttering breath. Focus, Narius. He couldn't lose himself now. The dinner was a celebration, yes, but there was plenty of work to be done. Ethnarchs to mollify. Alliances to strengthen and build.

But every step Everys took away from him opened a wider gulf inside him, one that made his mind itch.

52

The dress had gotten the reaction she'd hoped for. If only the smudging thing wasn't so inkstained *heavy!*

It was her fault. The modified display panels were bad enough, but it turned out the battery packs needed to power them tripled the weight. And her secret additions made the rig even heavier. Just walking from her quarters to the ballroom had almost been too much, but the reaction more than made up for the inevitable sore back and chafed shoulders. The look on the guests' faces were reward enough, but the way Gaines's face had lit up when she saw Everys was even better.

And then there had been the expression on Narius's face...

Everys shook her head to dislodge the thought. Focus. Stay focused. She had to finish making the rounds through the ballroom before Trule and the other girls met her for the change. As much as she would have liked to wear her creation for the rest of the night, she knew she couldn't. Not only was it too heavy, but the panels could only display a limited number of vistas and the batteries would run out of power. It had been good for shock-and-awe, but not a sustained campaign. By her estimation, she had another fifteen minutes, maybe twenty, before she'd need to change, and she had covered—a quick look around the room confirmed it—three quarters of the guests. She'd have to pick up the pace.

"My queen, you look radiant!" Clarinda stepped into her path.

Everys suppressed a wince. She had to be polite. After all, if Clarinda hadn't been willing to donate the prototype displays, her dress would have never come together. Granted, Everys had promised to credit TelleGlin in the press, but it would be rude to ignore her unless—

Her gaze caught on a dignitary she hadn't been able to speak to yet, Ethnarch Rockflow of the Ixactl Highlands. Everys swallowed a groan. Given how upset Redtale had been, she had planned on spending some time talking to the ethnarch while she was wearing this dress. Maybe the ethnarch didn't share Redtale's opinion, but at least she could take a few steps in smoothing things over.

But no, it wouldn't be polite to ignore Clarinda. She fixed a smile on her face and said, "It's all because of your technology."

Clarinda laughed. "Be sure to tell the press, won't you? And maybe a few more words about how TelleGlin will help shape the Dynasty's future? Or is that too much to hope for?"

Everys managed to keep her face stoic, even though she wanted to scream at Clarinda to stay quiet. The last time she heard, the launch of the first Falling Sword prototype was at least two years away. But if the wrong noble or ethnarch overheard Clarinda's idle comments, the entire plan could be in jeopardy. But if she called attention to that, Clarinda might speak louder.

Change the subject, maybe? "Tell me, have you ever had the chance to take a stroll through the royal gardens?"

Clarinda's smile broadened. "I can't say that I have, but to be perfectly frank, you're not the royal I hoped would take me on such a walk."

Everys's mouth popped open. Was she still upset about what happened so many months ago?

But then Gaines laughed and playfully swatted at Everys's arm. "Thank you for the offer, but I'm afraid I'll have to decline. Although I would like to set up a time to speak with you regarding some other new technologies we're developing. I was thinking that maybe you could help us come up with a new and innovative way to showcase them. Sort of like what you did with this dress!"

Everys fought the urge to gape at her. What did she think she was, some sort of PR consultant?

Before she could respond, though, Narius stepped up next to her and placed a gentle hand on her arm. "I'm sorry to interrupt, ladies, but I'm afraid I need the queen to speak to someone with me."

Clarinda nodded. "Of course, Your Strength. Blessed, we will be in touch."

And how Everys looked forward to that! Once they were out of earshot from Clarinda, she whispered, "Who do you want me to talk to?"

"Just me."

"What?"

"I've seen that sort of look before. The 'someone rescue me' look," Narius said, "From what I understand, Mother and Father developed a series of signals to indicate if they needed rescuing. She would tug on her earlobe. He would smooth the tips of his mustache."

"And that worked?"

Narius smiled. "Until Mother got caught at one of these events by a particularly boring Riokan diplomat. The press ran stories for weeks about how they were afraid she had somehow developed an ear infection given how much she tugged on it all night."

Everys snorted, then quickly cast a look around the room. It was good that Narius had saved her from Clarinda, but that just meant that she could maybe go and speak to Ethnarch Rockflow before she changed out of the dress after all.

"Who are you looking for?" Narius asked.

She glanced at him. "Ethnarch Rockflow. I was hoping to speak with him, but—"

"—but you didn't realize your husband spent the first twenty minutes with him."

Her head snapped around, and she gaped at him. "You what?"

"So you don't have to worry about talking to him." Narius nodded toward the edge of the room. "Besides, the way Challix has been watching you suggests it's almost time to change into another outfit, yes?"

She looked to where he was indicating. Sure enough, Challix hovered at the edge of the room, a pained look on her face. Why did she look so worried? By Everys's reckoning, she still had plenty of time.

But better to err on the side of caution. The last thing she'd want is for the power to run out early. She could imagine the scandal if they saw what her dress really looked like once the displays powered down. Maybe she should make the change now.

Everys started to pull away from Narius, but just as she did, music floated through the air. Narius gently tugged on her arm.

"I know you need to change, but would you do me the honor of dancing with me first?"

Everys blinked at him. Dancing? Challix hadn't said anything about that. She started to object, but then she looked into Narius's eyes and her mind froze, even though it felt like fire cascaded through her body.

"Sure," she said.

Narius smiled, and any worry of timing or changing or Challix slipped from her mind. Narius led her toward the center of the room and spun her gently, drawing her into a loose embrace. He positioned their hands: his left and her right on each other's hips, his right and her left held low.

Worry crested inside Everys. "I've never danced this way before," she whispered.

"Don't worry, it's pretty easy," he said. "Just follow my lead."

And then they were off, stepping and turning at the center of the room. For the first few moments, Everys was painfully aware of how all the guests were staring at them, but gradually, others joined them. With each new dancing couple, she felt more and more relaxed.

"Is this protocol? Dancing at a state dinner?" she asked.

"Not usually, but it felt right." Narius chuckled, looking around the room as they spun. "I can honestly say that I've never seen such a relaxed state dinner before, especially with so many different factions here at once. Truly a miracle. One of your making."

Everys blushed. If he only knew. "You're giving me too much credit."

Narius shook his head. "No, I'm sure of it. I've been to enough of these to know how they usually go. People stick to their friends and supporters, everything is very formal. Even if there is music, there's never any dancing. Take a look around."

Everys did so. Close to a dozen couples twirled around them. Those who weren't dancing seemed relaxed as well. People were circulating and chatting amiably, laughing and joking. She spotted Masruq and Oluna chatting up the Plissk Ethnarch. Clarinda had moved on to a new victim, Duke Brencis, who was actually listening to what she had to say with a smile. The only exception was Vizier Paine, who stood in one corner and glowered at everyone else. Everys winced. She hadn't had the chance to make it over to him yet, but she wasn't even sure if he would tolerate her presence.

Narius chuckled, his voice silky. "That dress is quite amazing."

Heat painted across her cheeks, and she wasn't sure what he said. "I... What?"

"Your dress. Reminding us of the Dynasty's beauty. We can get past the ugliness and just focus on the positive. Right? That was your intention."

Everys winced. He was partially correct. That was why she had borrowed the displays, but that was mostly for show. More like a distraction to keep people from guessing what she was really doing. And it had worked, well enough that she even fooled Narius.

He swung her around, almost lifting her from her feet entirely. His smile was dazzling, an expression of joy.

And that was good, right? If he knew what she was really doing, he would be horrified. It was better for her to keep this secret from him along with all the others.

Except...

Except that was what the Dynasty had done with the archives. That was what they were doing with Falling Sword. The weight of all the secrets was too much. Just like the dress, which suddenly felt like it might drag her straight through the floor. She stumbled, almost tripping Narius as well.

"Are you all right?" he asked.

She nodded but pulled herself free. "I-I should probably change. This is..."

It was too much. Too heavy. The dress. The secrets. She had to be free of them. All of them. She could feel the secrets crawling through her mind, wanting to escape. But could she actually do it? Could she really break her promise, the one she had carried with her for so long? Could she really tell him?

She looked into his eyes, the confusion and curiosity warring in them. His golden eyes.

She could.

"Meet me in the gardens in fifteen minutes. Please."

Before he could say anything else, she hurried toward one of the exits. Challix met her there to escort her into an antechamber where Trule and the other girls waited with her other outfit for the night. But as the door closed behind her, Everys turned and looked over her shoulder. Narius watched her, a concerned look on his face. But when their gazes met, his face melted into a smile. He nodded once, then turned toward the glass doors that would lead out to the gardens.

She let out a shuddering breath. She had to tell him. The truth. All of it. He deserved nothing less.

Hopefully it wouldn't destroy everything.

53

Narius fought the urge to rub his hands on his uniform coat. Why was he sweating so badly? He felt like a boy sneaking out to meet some clandestine sweetheart. He snorted at the idea. Ridiculous. These were his gardens, his palace. He was an adult, the leader of the Dynasty. So why was his stomach flipping back and forth?

A couple came out of the state dinner, whispering to each other. It took him a moment to recognize the Dunestrider ethnarch and her husband. Narius couldn't help but stare. He had always seen her as a miserly curmudgeon, but the way they hung on each other, they looked like young lovers. When they spotted him, they sobered, but once he waved to acknowledge their presence, they kept going into the garden. Narius smiled. They would have a nice night for a quiet walk. For once, Bastion's air was crisp and clear, just chilly enough to be comfortable and maybe encourage couples to walk closer to stay warm. And the way the moons' light bathed the gardens... Magical. Romantic. The perfect evening to spend with—

His eyes widened, and he bit off a laugh. What was he thinking? Whatever had infected the dinner was playing with his mind as well, although in his case, it could be stress. Yes, that had to be it. He had been on the run ever since they came back from the Cold Light parley. He knew how tired he was, how his mind had been pulled in a dozen different directions at once. It was understandable his mind was wandering. Maybe he needed to find some time away from Bastion. A smile tickled his lips. He hadn't been to Bluerest, his family's private retreat, in at least two years, maybe longer. His advisers could handle the Dynasty's business for a few days. He could get away, clear his head, maybe spend some time swimming or hiking or—

"Narius?"

The gentle voice turned him around, and his breath caught in his throat.

Everys had changed her outfit, but while she had been amazing in her first dress, now she was breathtaking. The dress itself was a simple sheath, made of a silvery material that shimmered in the moons' light. But unlike her first dress, which competed with Everys for attention, this one simply highlighted her natural beauty. And her girls had changed her hair, sweeping it into a style that accentuated her delicate face and neck. In that moment, her grace and beauty was driven home with the force of a punch to his chest. All thoughts of leaving Bastion retreated. All he wanted was to be near her.

She smiled shyly at him. "Thanks for waiting."

As if he wouldn't. He blinked several times, trying to snap himself out of his daze. "Of c-course. Shall we walk?"

She nodded. Narius tried to keep his breathing even, but he was finding it difficult to even think. And just a few moments ago, he was thinking about how pleasant it was in the garden. So why had it suddenly become so hot? He tried to cut through the silence with some small talk, but he found that he couldn't speak. His dry mouth couldn't form the words.

They wound their way deeper into the gardens until they came across a stone bench, one facing a display of plants transplanted from the island of Maotoa. The scent of sweet flowers drifted across the path, and once again, Narius was struck by how perfect the evening was. A serene garden, the darkening evening, and Everys at his side.

"Why don't we sit here for a moment?" Everys whispered.

He nodded, but as he did, his heart slammed against his chest. He swallowed several times, trying to find his voice. Was she expecting him to say something? He should, right?

"Narius... I need to show you something."

She handed a panel to him, made of thick gray plastic. He frowned. Had she been carrying that the entire time? How had he not noticed?

Then he caught another glimpse of her, and he understood why. He momentarily forgot he was holding anything at all.

He had to force himself to examine the panel. It was three feet square and slightly curved. He hefted it and felt something slosh inside. A liquid? He turned it over and over in his hands. He could see spots where it could be attached to something else. What was this?

He looked up at Everys, a question on his face.

She grimaced. "You said you thought my dress was responsible for the relaxed atmosphere of the dinner?"

He shook his head, holding up a hand. "A figure of speech! I—"

"No, you were right. But not because of the image projectors." She nodded toward the panel. "Because of those. I had six underneath the skirt."

Narius looked at the panel again, frowning. Why? What was the point? Tactical armor? No, it was too flimsy for that...

"You remember the void shields we found in the archives? How there were spaces carved in them in the shape of runes that would be filled with ink?" She took a deep breath. "That's basically what that is."

He almost dropped the panel. "There's toratropic ink in there?"

She nodded. "And pretty powerful stuff too."

"Where'd you get it?"

"I made it out of sap Tall Reach gave me before we left his shade."

His mind locked. Tall Reach gave her what? He started to protest, but she put a hand on his.

"I haven't been completely open with you about who I am. Who my family is." She took a deep breath and nodded. "But I want to be. You need to know the truth."

She took the panel and fiddled with it. The plastic split open along its edges, and she pried it apart, revealing intricately carved channels that resembled twisting vines, with little flares resembling leaves. Amber liquid sloshed through the carvings, glowing in the low light. As he watched, the remaining ink slowly burned away, consumed by the glow. A rune?

"Wh-what does this do?" he asked.

"It's a healing rune, a potent one. The most powerful my people know. Normally it's used for physical healing, but these flourishes—" She pointed at one corner of the rune. "—modifies it to promote 'healing of the heart and mind.' And these right here—" She pointed to another section of the rune. "—cause the effect to radiate, for lack of a better word."

He stared at the rune. "And you had six of these under your dress?"

"I thought maybe the toratropic magic, along with the images of the Dynasty's territories, would promote a sense of peace among the attendees. Break down some walls. Smooth out some rough places."

She shrugged. "I don't know if it'll make a difference or not, but I thought it was worth a try."

That explained so much. It wasn't just relief about the newfound peace with the Cold Light. He had seen the guests relax in Everys's wake as she made the rounds through the dinner. She had been using her magic on the Dynasty's leadership.

"Why?" he asked.

She took the panel from him and sealed it up. "Because I had to try. The Singularity entrusted this particular rune to my family, not to hide it, but to use it. That's why He committed the missing Principalities to us."

His head snapped back. "The missing—?"

Everys nodded. "You have five of the eight Principalities in the archive. Three weren't captured."

He nodded warily. "They were destroyed when Nekek the Bright was sacked."

She winced, looking away. "Actually..."

A cold wave washed over him. "They weren't?"

She shook her head. "No. Before the Ascendancy fell, each Principality had a family assigned to it. It was that family's job to maintain the plinth, to paint the ink on the rune every morning. To protect the Principalities and to listen to the Singularity's will.

"When my ancestors realized the Singularity was preparing to overthrow the Ascendancy, before King Heronus had even left the Xoniel's territory, three families, faithful to the Singularity's will, smuggled their Principalities out of Nekek the Bright and took them into hiding in the surrounding countryside."

Narius couldn't breathe. He wasn't sure he even remembered how. Instead, his mind raced through the history he had learned about the Night of Shards. When his ancestor, Heronus, approached Nekek the Bright with his armies, he had discovered a convoy trying to remove five of the Principalities from the city. He slaughtered the Siporans and captured the Principalities. When the Scriptotum was burned, everyone just assumed that the missing plinths had been destroyed with it.

He finally found his breath. "So the reason why I've never met your family..."

"...is because they're still protecting our Principality."

"Where?"

"I don't know."

"The Demilitarized Zone?"

She shrugged. "Maybe. We're supposed to keep this secret. We're not even supposed to use these runes in case someone figured out where they came from."

"Then why did you use this tonight?"

She flinched again, and he couldn't blame her. His voice was harsh, but he couldn't help it. Too much of his thinking was caught up in trying to untangle this new information, to weave it into his understanding of the world.

"Because I could. Because I had to. We've been hiding these gifts the Singularity gave us. We've created all sorts of excuses as to why we should hide and I realized, maybe the reason why I'm here was to use this rune, to use what He's given me to help make things better. Or at least help people take those first few steps toward—"

"What were you thinking?" The question burst out of his mouth before he could really think about it.

She blinked, her head snapping back as if struck.

"What if you had been caught? What if your girls had figured out what those panels were?"

"Th-they didn't. I told them the panels were to add stability to the imaging system—which they did—and—"

"But what if they *had*?" His fingers curled into fists. "What do you think would have happened if people knew that their queen was performing illegal magic? They'd want you *dead*! They wouldn't care who you are! They wouldn't care what the rune is supposed to do!"

Tears streamed down her cheeks, and she tried to say something, but apparently she couldn't talk either.

"They would demand you be punished, and I wouldn't..." His words caught in his throat. "I wouldn't be able to do anything about it! I wouldn't be able to protect you. Gravedigger's wrath, Everys, if anything ever happened to you, I don't know what I'd... What I'd..."

The full import of what he was saying crashed down on him. If she had been caught, he'd have to turn her over to the mob, to let them do whatever they wanted to her. Exile, execution, no matter what, it would mean losing her and he didn't... He couldn't...

"I-I'm sorry," she whispered. "I..."

He couldn't lose her. Not when he... Not when he...

He reached out, his fingers hovering next to her cheek. Then he gently caressed her skin.

She gasped, her eyes wide as well. He felt a jolt up his arm, as if he had come in contact with lightning. But the connection was there, and he couldn't pull away. Didn't want to.

Instead, that small touch pulled him in. He leaned in, not sure what he was about to do, scared to find out, worried to see how she'd react, hoping she would...

Her eyes closed as she leaned in closer.

"Your Strength!"

The moment shattered. Everys jerked away from his hand, shoving the panel off her lap and into a nearby bush. Narius took several ragged breaths, trying to calm his mind again.

Paine rushed around a corner. Actually rushed! Narius had never seen his friend so worked up before.

"What is it?"

Paine skidded to a halt, his gaze snapping between Narius and Everys, a question forming in his expression.

"Paine! What is it?"

The vizier blinked and pointed back toward the palace. "I'm sorry, Your Strength, to interrupt. But he just showed up. We invited him, of course. How could we not? But he actually showed up!"

Narius rose, holding up his hands in a calming gesture. "Paine, take a breath. Calm yourself. Who showed up?"

"Alezzar. Alezzar has just arrived at the dinner."

Narius frowned. The Dalark ambassador? "So he's a little late to the party?"

Paine shook his head. "No, Your Strength. He says he came to the party on official business. He bears a message from the Emperor himself."

Narius's frown deepened. "Did he say what?"

"The Emperor has finally agreed to a permanent peace treaty." Paine's expression turned grim. "He agrees to all of your terms. *All* of them."

Narius stumbled back a step. No. That meant...

"Alezzar is here to discuss your upcoming marriage to the Princess Innana."

54

Everys followed Narius back into the ballroom, her head spinning. Wedding? To a Dalark princess? How was that possible? What would that mean? For them? For her? And had they just been about to... Had she actually let him... *Would* she have let him?

Alezzar stood in the center of the ballroom, all of the other guests giving him a wide berth. He wore an elaborate series of robes and wraps, all of them brilliant hues and colors, and the imperious way he eyed everyone around him marked him as Dalark.

As Narius entered, Alezzar turned to him and bowed deeply. "Ah, King Narius, blessed by the spirits and potentates, it is but my humble honor to bear tidings from his illustrious presence, Emperor Devroshan the Eighteenth, Bestrider of Worlds."

Alezzar's gaze shifted from Narius to Everys, his expression hardening. Everys felt the distinct urge to step behind Narius, to use him as a human shield. But no, she was the queen of the Dynasty and if Alezzar was hoping a disapproving look would be enough to send her running, he was sorely mistaken. She returned his glare with one of her own, one she hoped conveyed the message: *how dare you interrupt my party?*

Narius, for his part, kept his distance from Alezzar, circling around the ambassador with measured strides. Once he had the grand staircase at his back, he turned sharply to face Alezzar. After he stared at the Dalark ambassador for a full minute, he smiled and looked to the other guests.

"My apologies, friends, but I have business that I must attend to with our friend, the Ambassador of the Dalark Imperium. I would ask that you stay and enjoy my hospitality while I and my advisers listen to the words of Alezzar."

With that, Narius turned on his heel and started up the stairs. Everys tried to follow him, but before she could, Paine stepped into her path and shook his head ever so slightly. She frowned. Why shouldn't she go with him?

As if reading the unspoken question, Paine leaned in and whispered, "While your desire to walk with Narius is commendable, it will not be well received by Alezzar. The Dalark are not nearly as enlightened as the Xoniel when it comes to women. That, and the fact that you are Siporan, would strain what comes next."

Everys bristled and started to object. After all, Duke Brencis, Minister Masruq, and the other members of Narius's council were heading for the stairs.

Paine leaned even closer. "Blessed, I understand your frustration, but this is a delicate moment. We have been issuing invitations to the Dalark to negotiate a permanent peace for the past hundred and fifty years! Please, I beg you, set aside your hurt feelings and let Narius do his job."

She didn't like his tone. She didn't like his condescension. But she couldn't argue. She nodded.

Paine studied her face, his eyes narrowed, then he sighed. "Very well. You may accompany us to the throne room but I insist that you do not interject in the proceedings, no matter what is said. Understood?"

About time he backed down. Paine didn't wait for her to answer. Instead, he quickly fell into step with the other advisers. Everys had to hurry to keep up with them, casting one last smile around the room to the other guests.

By the time she made it up the stairs, most everyone else had hurried toward the throne room. She gathered up her dress and moved as quickly as she could. As she caught up, though, Paine slowed his pace and very clearly stepped into her way, blocking her from moving past him. She ground her teeth. Fine. If that was the way it was going to be.

A few moments later, they arrived at the throne room itself. When Everys slipped through the doors, she saw that Narius had already settled on his throne, Alezzar standing before him. The other advisers took their places throughout the throne room. Where should she stand? She crept along the edge of the room, keeping the massive pillars between herself and the Dalark ambassador. Hopefully that would be acceptable to Paine.

If the vizier noticed what she was doing, he didn't let on. Instead, he stepped to Narius's side and nodded to him.

Narius turned his full attention to Alezzar. "I must admit, I am surprised to see you here. You never responded to our invitation to tonight's dinner."

Alezzar bowed again. "With many formal apologies, Your Strength, I regret my rude behavior. It is not fitting for neighbors to behave as such, yes?"

"Neighbors? Is that what we are?"

"We share such a long border, do we not?"

"Separated by the remnants of the Siporan Ascendancy."

"Do not good neighbors need a fence?" Alezzar laughed. "But his Imperial Majesty, Devroshan, sees it more as a reminder of what Xoniel and Dalark may do when they are united in purpose. He would see what our two peoples might accomplish as one again. Is this not something you desire?"

An uncertain look flickered across Narius's face. "Peace is always a noble pursuit."

"As it should be!"

"But I have made repeated offers of peace since my coronation, and your Emperor has not only ignored me, but from what I have heard, has mocked me for my 'childish dreams.'"

Alezzar actually flinched at the words. Everys wanted to cheer. Clearly Narius scored a hit with that!

"Our great Emperor, inspired by the spirits and potentates, did not wish to enter into such an agreement with someone unseasoned. Even you must admit that you ascended at a very young age. Would you rather not negotiate the terms of such a treaty with both eyes open than with both shut and your hands groping in the dark?"

"Did your king instruct you to question my maturity or is that choice yours?" Narius countered.

Alezzar's mouth clicked shut, and his cheeks turned bright red. He stumbled back a step, mumbling something.

Everys beamed at Narius. He glanced in her direction, and his lips twitched into the faintest of grins.

"M-my apologies, O Great One." Alezzar bowed low. "I am afraid that I speak in the way of the Dalark. We are perhaps too brusque for halls such as yours. The fault and offense are mine and should not be held against my august Emperor or his desire for true and lasting peace. What I meant to say is that the Emperor Devroshan has been most impressed by what you have accomplished in the past few months, especially your forging peace with the intractable Cold Light. He sees you as impressive. If I have given reason for you to think otherwise, I shall submit to whatever discipline you deem fit."

Narius held up a hand. "There is no need to apologize. As we Xoniel well know, sparring sharpens even the keenest of blades. And I have long desired..." His voice trailed off, his expression thoughtful. When he resumed speaking, he seemed to choose his next words more carefully. "A closer relationship with Dalark, this is true. What are the terms of this treaty that your Emperor proposes?"

Alezzar blinked and color crept into his cheeks once again. "Your S-Strength, should not that be a matter left to those more important than I?"

Narius waved away his objection. "The specifics, yes, that will be gone over by many people, debated and refined, as they should be. But that does not mean that you cannot share your master's wishes with me. What would the results of this new peace be?"

"What else could it be? Trade between our mighty realms, free and open instead of clandestine and through hidden channels. Allowing both of our fine militaries to stop posturing and strutting for one another. Bringing to an end centuries of mistrust and conflict. Not a truce, but peace."

Once again, Narius shook his hand as if shooing a pesky insect. "All well and good, yes, but how would this peace be ratified? What is your Emperor's expectation?"

Now Alezzar smiled. "Why, the way that the Dalark have ratified all such agreements in the past: through marriage."

Everys felt everyone look to her, and she ducked her head, hoping to hide the blush that crept across her cheeks.

"Is this not what you yourself have dreamed of for so long? For the Princess Innana to become your wife?" Alezzar asked.

Wait, he had dreamed of what? Suddenly the pieces clicked together in Everys's mind. The woman in the picture next to Narius's bed. That must have been Princess Innana! And he had wanted to marry her? Dreamed of it? From the way he had spoken, fought for it with the Emperor.

And why wouldn't he? She had seen other images of the princess besides the ones Narius had. Innana was lithe and beautiful, the very image of queenly grace. The sort of woman who would inspire love in both her husband and her subjects. Compared to Innana, Everys was... She was nothing.

"Except I already have a wife," Narius said.

Wait, what? Everys's head snapped up. Alezzar looked at her, apparently fully aware that she was in the room after all. She swallowed a groan, wanting nothing more than to shrink down into the floor and disappear from everyone's sight.

"That is, indeed, a truth that the Emperor is aware of," Alezzar said. But he smiled broadly. "But this should not be an impediment to your wishes, yes? You were formerly married to the woman of no repute called Viara, were you not? Is this not a simple matter? Come now, King Narius. Long has the Emperor known of your desire for not only peace, but for Innana as well. While he understands your need for a wife to fulfill your religious obligations to the Perfected Warrior and Water Bearer, would this not be more appealing? Fulfill your personal desire, bring peace to our nations, forge a legacy for yourself beyond the dreams of your ancestors."

Narius shifted on his throne, a pained look on his face. Everys tried to catch his attention, to at least have him acknowledge that she was standing right there. But he didn't. He wouldn't. Instead, a frown creased his brow as Paine leaned over and whispered something to him. A void opened in Everys's heart. He couldn't really be considering this, could he?

Finally, Narius nodded and motioned for Paine to step back. "Is the Emperor expecting a response today?'

"Of course not, King Narius," Alezzar said. "I was merely sent here to make the offer. The Emperor is more than willing to wait for your answer. But he does most respectfully request that you do not deliberate for long. As the spirits and potentates say, 'The world does not wait for the indecisive.'"

Narius nodded sagely. "Of course. We shall discuss your offer and will respond by week's end."

He had to actually think about it? Why? This wasn't just a matter of the heart. He had to consider what was best for the Dynasty, for all of Pedrevor.

"Is there anything else?" Narius asked.

"My message has been delivered as I was instructed."

"Good." Narius rose. "Would you care to join us for the rest of the celebration?"

"Would that I could, Your Strength, but I am afraid I am unable. There are matters of ritual cleanliness to consider, and my Emperor will want a full accounting of what you said. I must return to the embassy with haste." He bowed lowed, but he looked to one side, at Everys. "I do hope you will enjoy yourself with what time remains."

Was he talking to her? Or about her? Either way, she knew she wouldn't. Even though the state dinner was supposed to continue for some time, Everys knew that the celebration was over. So much had ended in the last few moments. All that was left was to go through the motions.

55

Even though Narius, Everys, and the others had returned to the state dinner shortly after Alezzar departed, most of the guests had read the change in their mood and quickly excused themselves. Everys could already imagine what the press would make of that. What was supposed to be a celebration of the newfound peace with the Cold Light had been completely derailed by an offer of peace from the Dalark Imperium. Based on what Challix told her, Alezzar's interruption had overshadowed everything about the party. All of Bastion buzzed with rumors and speculation about what a permanent peace treaty with Dalark would mean. There was no talk of the Cold Light, barely any mention of Everys's dress. The latter shouldn't have irked her as much as it did, but she had worked hard on putting it all together!

Not that she had much time to dwell on her frustration. The day after the party, Narius called for his advisers to join him in his throne room to discuss Dalark's offer. While Everys hadn't been officially invited to the meeting, she knew that she had to be there.

Once again, Narius was seated on his throne, surrounded by his advisers. But unlike the previous night, he hardly looked regal. Yes, he was wearing clothes appropriate for a king, but he looked tired. Haggard. As if he hadn't slept. Everys felt a pang of sympathy. She hadn't either.

If he noticed her entrance, he didn't let on. Instead, he leaned forward in his throne, listening to what Masruq had to say.

"...implications of a peace treaty are staggering, from an economic perspective," Masruq was saying. "Those ramifications alone should make us seriously consider Dalark's offer."

Brencis snorted. "Of course you would look at this as purely about economics."

"How can I not?" Masruq asked. "Consider our present trade situation: An embargo exists between us and them. Yes, we both use intermediary nations to get around those legalities, but those extra steps add unnecessary expense and hassle. With a peace treaty, we could trade directly with Dalark, lowering prices for our citizens and opening up new possibilities.

"And besides, wouldn't an official peace treaty mean that we wouldn't have to patrol the Demilitarized Zone as heavily? We could reallocate our military units and their funding, couldn't we?"

Brencis's expression darkened even more. "There are still plenty of threats out there—"

"Indeed there are," Paine said smoothly. "But wouldn't a peace treaty mean that we could focus on those other threats instead of tying up so many resources along the Demilitarized Zone?"

The duke nodded, but from the expression on his face, it was clear he still wasn't happy about the discussion.

"Have we heard anything from Tormod?" another adviser—Everys thought it was Bokil, the Minister of Internal Security—asked.

"Yes, where is that pesky spymaster these days? It's been a while since I've seen him," Masruq said.

"Tormod has been occupied as of late." Paine's voice was strained. "Personal matters. Why, Minister Bokil? What insight do you think he could provide?"

Bokil shrugged. "I thought perhaps he might have some insight as to why the Dalark made this offer now."

"We all heard what Alezzar said," another minister—Elamek, Minister of Agriculture—said. "They were impressed by the peace with the Cold Light. Simple as that."

"Things are never simple when it comes to the Dalark," Brencis muttered.

Everys chewed on her lip as the ministers descended into bickering about the Dalark's motives. Some seemed ready to take Alezzar at his word. Others were more suspicious. And through it all, Narius watched silently, his face sullen, his features gaunt. He looked like he had aged several years overnight. Everys had to catch herself before she crossed the room to comfort him. Take him in her arms. Hold him close and stroke his hair.

"Enough!" Although soft, Paine's command cut through the arguing instantly. "Friends, regardless of Dalark's motives, I think we all see the benefits. Do we see any reason why the king should decline this offer?"

"Because it's Dalark," Brencis snapped.

"Oh, don't be so short-sighted, Brencis!" Masruq shot back. "Do you have an actual reason, or just your old prejudices? Look at the bigger picture for once in your stunted life and see all the possibilities!"

Brencis grumbled something but fell silent.

The rest of the room did as well, each minister looking down at the floor. The ache in Everys's chest grew sharper.

"What about Queen Everys?" Elamek asked quietly. "The people love her."

"You overstate your case, Elamek," Paine said. "The latest opinion polls—"

"Hang your polls. Fine, *I* love her. She's a far sight better than Viara. And look at the good Queen Everys has done for the Dynasty," Elamek said.

"If you believe the rumors," Minister of Resource Production Filamon said.

"And let's not forget the riots she caused in Bastion the first week of her reign!" Bokil added.

Now it felt like Everys's heart was about to shrivel. She stared at Narius. Why wasn't he saying anything? Why didn't he object or defend her?

Paine held up a hand, once again cutting off the arguing ministers. "My friends, you all know how critical I've been of the queen since Narius chose her."

That was an understatement.

"But even I have to admit that I have been surprised at how well she has taken to her role. Given enough time, I'm sure she would have proven quite the asset to the Dynasty."

Everys blinked at him. Coming from Paine, that was high praise. She leaned forward, a small spark of hope glowing inside her.

"But we cannot overlook this opportunity either. Technically, Dalark and the Dynasty have been in a state of war for two centuries. And now we have the opportunity for peace... Actual peace!" Paine turned to Narius. "Can we really afford to ignore this?"

Narius finally stirred on his throne, shifting ever so slightly away from Paine. He sighed, a heavy sound, one that cut through Everys. He was clearly torn, in pain, so uncertain. And that was only amplifying her pain. But how could he hesitate? She knew how much he longed to make an impact for the Dynasty. Falling Sword, peace with the Cold Light, and now Dalark as well? How could he possibly pass up this opportunity? Unless...

Her eyes widened. Was he really going to let this opportunity pass him by for her?

Hear surged through her and she wanted to laugh with joy. That's what she wanted too. After all, look at how much they had accomplished together. If they stayed together, they could do anything.

But even as her heart thrilled at the thought, reality crashed down on her. How could she be so selfish? Narius had also dreamed of reinventing the Dynasty for years as well. He had been able to take small steps in that direction, but if the Dynasty suddenly knew true peace with the Dalark Imperium, he could take larger ones. Why, with the right queen at his side, he could reshape the world and so easily too!

And he had loved Innana since he was a boy. He had longed for her to be his wife. Maybe he had come to tolerate Everys, maybe even care for her, but he had loved Innana for so long. She couldn't be so selfish to stand in the way of that.

As these thoughts tumbled together, an ache built inside her chest. In that moment of clarity, she understood. And she knew. She knew what had to happen.

She knew what she had to do.

Steeling her spine, she strode forward, brushing past Brencis. The general jerked away as if she were attacking him. Several of the ministers shouted in surprise as she strode to the center of the throne room. As she approached, Narius actually perked up, sitting up taller, a small light flickering in his eyes.

No, she couldn't look him in the eyes. Not if she was going to do what needed to be done. She looked squarely at his chest and nodded to herself. "Narius, I don't know how to do this correctly, so please forgive my ignorance." She took a deep breath and forced out the words. "I hereby vacate our marriage. I release you from your obligation to me." Her words caught in her throat, and she knew if she didn't power through this, she'd break down. "Be free to... to pursue whatever opportunities you wish."

Tears burned her eyes, so she spun away from him and rushed for the doors. The guards barely got them open in time for her. Narius called her name, his shout almost drowned out by the murmurs and whispers of his advisers, but she kept going, hurrying for her quarters.

Someone grabbed her arm and spun her around. Had Narius sicced his guards on her? But no, it was Narius himself.

"What are you doing?" he demanded. "I didn't ask... I don't want..."

She pulled her arm free, took a step back. She didn't dare stand too closely to him. "Don't you see? This is better."

"How is this better?" His voice thundered down the hall. "Everys, how can you do that to me?"

"I'm not doing it to you, I'm doing it for you. This is what we agreed to, isn't it? I would be your queen until a better candidate came along? Yes?"

He blinked, staring at her as if he didn't understand what she was saying.

"And now one has. A real princess. Born to royalty, raised in it. Someone you... you..." She couldn't bring herself to say it, but she forced the word out anyway. "...love. Isn't that what you were hoping for?"

Still he stared, his lips trembling, his eyes raw and hollow.

"I'm doing this for you." Maybe if she repeated it, he would finally understand. "For the Dynasty. For your legacy. Don't you see, Narius? Our partnership worked for a short while, and I'm... I'm glad we had this time together. You deserve nothing but greatness. And now you'll have it."

"But... But..."

No. She couldn't listen to him. Couldn't stand to hear his voice, not if she was going to do what had to be done. Instead, she took another step back. "Contact Alezzar. Accept the offer. Be... Be..." She couldn't bring herself to say *happy*. "Just be."

And with that, she turned and fled down the hall.

"Everys!" he shouted.

No, she wouldn't stop, wouldn't turn back. When she made it back to her quarters, she was relieved that he didn't chase her again.

But that's what she wanted him to do. She wanted him to follow her, to catch her, to take her into his arms and kiss her and tell her that he chose her over Innana, over peace, over the Dynasty. In spite of their differences. In spite of who she was and what she was capable of. In spite of everything that was stacked against them.

That he would tell her that he loved her the same way that she...

The ache in her chest burst into wracking sobs and she collapsed next to the door, wishing that the world would just end so her sorrow could as well.

Packing proved to be the easiest part. She didn't have much that was actually hers. Just the clothes she had worn when she came to the palace. The rest of her clothing had been made for an identity that was no longer hers. Trule insisted that she take some of the outfits she had purchased in the meantime, but those clothes wouldn't fit her life anymore. All told, it only took her an hour or two to scour her quarters and pack it all in a military rucksack, one helpfully supplied by Kevtho.

Once her things had been packed, Everys turned a slow circle, inspecting her quarters. No, not hers. Not anymore. These were the queen's quarters now. Princess Innana would likely redecorate them. A small pang stabbed Everys's heart. When had she started thinking of this room as hers? Why did it bother her so much to think of another person in this space, making changes to it? She shook her head. Best not to dwell. Best not to linger in a room that wasn't hers.

As she turned to leave, she found Trule and the rest of her staff lined up as if for a military inspection. A tremor wormed through her, and her eyes burned. She stepped up to the line and nodded.

"We're going to miss you." Trule's voice quavered. Several of the girls behind her sniffled as well.

"You have all been such a blessing to me," Everys said. "I wouldn't have made it without you."

"Thank you, my queen."

"Trule." Everys's voice caught in her throat. "I'm not your queen. Not anymore."

Tears tumbled down Trule's cheeks. "You will always be my queen, no matter who I might officially serve."

Everys couldn't stand it anymore. She hugged Trule, and the other girls rushed into the embrace as well. Soon all of them were crying and hugging and speaking words of comfort.

After a while, someone cleared their throat. For a moment, Everys thought that it was one of the girls, but then, when the person did it again, she realized the sound was too masculine. She looked up to find Paine standing in the doorway.

"I'm afraid that I must break this up. The guards are waiting."

Everys glared at him. What was the rush? Was Innana on her way right now and needed a place to store her belongings? But given the stern expression on Paine's face, it didn't appear as if he was in any mood to argue. She pulled herself free of her friends and took a step back, nodding at them.

"Serve the next queen as well as you did me, and I'm sure you'll be fine."

Trule looked about ready to start sobbing again, and Everys knew that if that happened, she wouldn't make it out of the palace. So she shouldered her sack and headed for the door, making sure to brush past Paine as she did.

He fell into step next to her. "I've taken the liberty of arranging a stipend for you once you've left the palace. While most nobles would consider it insultingly modest, I'm sure someone of your resourcefulness will be able to make good use of it."

She snorted. "Why are you even offering? To keep me from interfering? Don't worry, I won't. Keep your money."

As she made her way through the halls, she passed by a number of the palace staff. Every one of them paused in their duties long enough to acknowledge her with looks, nods, small gestures, and smiles. Everys acknowledged them all, struggling to keep from crying again. Every time they approached someone, Everys braced herself in case it was Narius. She wasn't sure how she'd respond to him. He hadn't spoken to her since their encounter outside the throne room, and she wasn't sure what that meant, or if she even wanted to see him.

Eventually they reached the palace exit. When Everys stepped outside, she was greeted by two long lines of royal guards, standing at sharp attention. She passed between them, and as she did, they saluted. A military transport waited at the other side, similar to the one she had ridden in all those months earlier. A guard she didn't recognize stepped to the door and opened it for her.

So this was it. Time to go.

Before she climbed into the transport, she turned to Paine. "Happy now? At least you don't have to worry about me wrecking any of your grand plans."

An odd expression flickered across Paine's face. Frustration? Anger? Sadness? Probably not that last one, but for just a moment, his normally stoic exterior cracked. "I realize that we... that *I* did not welcome your presence. But understand, I only ever wanted what was best for Narius."

"And you were so sure that wasn't me?"

Again, that strange hesitation, as if he were weighing her words and his response carefully. "Perhaps. Perhaps not. But if I was mistaken, hopefully history will judge me less harshly than you are now."

With that, he turned and strode back into the palace. Everys watched him go, and then, with a sigh, clambered into the transport, sitting on the uncomfortable bench. The guard outside saluted once more, then closed the door and within moments, the vehicle rumbled to life, and she began her trip home.

Home, it turned out, was an empty hole.

Everys stared at where her building should have stood. She had been in such a rush to leave the palace she hadn't even stopped to consider where she was going. As she stood there, some of the passersby slowed to gawk at her. She shifted on her feet, fighting the urge to run. Maybe it hadn't been the best idea to come back here. What would the neighbors think of their former queen returning? But where else could she have gone? Maybe she should have given this some more thought. But at the time, all she'd wanted was to escape the palace, to get away from it all. To get away from Narius... who hadn't even bothered to say goodbye.

She was attracting too much attention. She had to at least get off the streets. Grabbing the strap of her rucksack, she ducked her head, and did her best to imitate the other residents of Fair Haven as they went about their business. It was like stepping back into a memory, using muscles she hadn't exercised in a while. Her movements were stiff and sloppy at first, but within a block or two, she had taken on the guise of the downtrodden. Hopefully it would last long enough for her to find some shelter.

Away from the hole, down two streets, across the miserable excuse that passed for a public park, and there it was. An apartment building she hadn't ever visited. She went inside and searched the halls until she found the right door. She squared her shoulders, keyed in what she hoped was still the right comm code, and waited.

A few minutes later, the door cracked open and a young woman peeked out at her. "Yes?"

"Does Legarr still live here?"

The young woman sighed. "Look, I don't know what he told you, but I'm his wife and—"

"I know," Everys said. "I'm sorry that we've never met before."

The other woman—Tilash—paused and studied her face. Then her eyes went wide. "It's you. You're her! His sister!"

Everys nodded. "I am."

Tilash looked past her, up and down the hall, perhaps searching for constables. A habit she'd probably picked up from being married to Legarr. "He's not here. Hasn't been for a few days now."

"Oh." Her hopes fell.

Tilash chewed on her lip, then frowned. "I heard you ain't the queen anymore. Is that right?"

"Unfortunately."

"Need a place to stay?"

Everys's mouth popped open. "Y-yes, I do."

"I don't have much. That brother of yours keeps stealing the rent. But we got a roof over our heads for now and you're welcome to share."

"But why? We've never met."

Tilash shrugged. "We're family. Near or far, met or not, that means something, don't it?"

Tears welled up in Everys's eyes yet again. Yes. Yes, it did. And on this day, she would take what she could find.

56

This is what he'd wanted. For so long. He had longed for this turn of events: the envoy, the promise, a new future. It was all finally in his grasp, a dream realized. So why did he feel like he was about to fall off the edge of a cliff?

The Dalark hadn't wasted any time. Once they'd heard Everys had ended the marriage, the Emperor sent word through Alezzar that Princess Innana was on her way. Per Dalark tradition, she would move into the palace with servants, a chaperone, and other attendants. Narius didn't understand the rush, but he didn't object, even though Paine and Zar and a number of others grumbled about how quickly all of this was happening. Additional servant quarters had been requisitioned for Innana's retinue, and Paine was having difficulty controlling the story as it unfolded in the media.

It had only been a week since Alezzar had crashed the state dinner and upended his life, and now Narius stood on the edge of the palace tarmac, dressed in his finest, waiting for the skimmer from Dalark to deliver his newest wife. His third wife that year. He tried to suppress the thought, but it wouldn't go completely silent.

Paine stepped up next to him. The vizier tucked his hands behind his back and looked up at the sky, his face serene. "According to Bastion Control, the princess's skimmer is approximately five minutes out."

Narius frowned. Shouldn't he be able to see it by now? He scanned the western sky.

"Patience, Your Strength," Paine murmured. "She will be here soon enough."

That observation alone set Narius's heart stuttering again. His stomach flipped over and over in time to the beat.

"Am I doing the right thing, Paine?" he whispered.

Paine glanced at him out of the corner of his eye. "What do you mean, my king?"

Narius made a quick gesture toward the empty tarmac, to the spot where Innana's skimmer would soon land. "This. What I've allowed to happen since the dinner. All of it. Am I doing the right thing?"

Once again, Paine glanced at him quickly before turning his attention back to the sky. "Based on current public opinion polls, yes. You are."

"Gravedigger bury public opinion!" Narius snapped. "That doesn't tell us anything! Back in my grandfather's day, the public was completely in favor of everything we did to the Cold Light and look at where that got us."

"In that case, think of how future generations will judge your actions, giving them a more stable Dynasty that—"

Narius snorted. "And bury that too! We don't know how future generations will judge this, and there's no guarantee that they will be correct in their assessment either! Am I doing the *right* thing?"

Paine turned away from the empty tarmac, using one hand to turn Narius away as well. "My king—Narius—I can't tell you that."

"Aren't you my vizier? My chief adviser? Advise me!"

Paine frowned. "That is not something I can do. As you have rightly pointed out, public opinion or the promise of a legacy, none of those things can give you worthy guidance. But I'm not sure why you would think that I would be able to either, not about this. Consider: When you took Tormod's advice and married Everys, I was opposed to your decision. For a very long time, I believed she was a mistake that would bring down your rule. Today, I humbly admit that I was wrong in my assessment. You had the right of it. So the real question is this: what do you think? Do you believe you are doing the right thing?"

Was he? That was the problem: he didn't know. He couldn't. He felt unmoored from any basis for rational judgment. On the one hand, he had his childhood dreams, his desires for peace and stability. He had his longing to craft a worthy legacy for himself and stability for the Dynasty as a whole.

On the other hand, he had... He had... He couldn't bring himself to think of it. To think of *her*.

So how could he know? How could anyone know what to do with any certainty? Public opinion, the future, the past, himself, they were all fallible. How could he *know?*

Paine touched his arm lightly. "This will have to wait, Your Strength. Princess Innana is arriving."

Narius's head snapped around. She was? Sure enough, he spotted the oncoming skimmer soaring over the skyline of Bastion. He frowned. Shouldn't he have heard it coming? Even as it approached, he didn't hear so much as a whisper from its engines.

As it approached, he got a better look at it. Unlike the Dynasty, Dalark apparently prioritized aesthetics in their war machines. For a solitary moment, Narius thought that a large, silver bird of prey soared over his capital. Its wings were flared forward, like a stooping hawk. It came to a halt over the palace, hovering in midair just above the tarmac. And still, even this close, the engines were eerily quiet. Narius thought he heard a high-pitched whine, but he couldn't even be certain of that. Was this a message from the Imperium? A warning about their capabilities? No, he couldn't think like that. As soon as he and Innana were... He shook his head to dislodge the thought. As soon as the peace was ratified, there would be no reason to worry.

The skimmer lowered to the ground and settled with a muffled sigh. Narius straightened, coming to an approximation of attention. No telling who was watching from the skimmer. And the media would undoubtedly have drones in the air around the palace to capture this moment.

After a few minutes, a hatch opened on the skimmer's side, and a long, metallic ramp slid to the ground. A squad of Dalark soldiers in ornate uniforms fanned out onto the tarmac. Their gaze roamed over the surroundings before they took up position. Almost immediately, a man in flowing robes descended the ramp. Narius recognized him immediately: Prince Tirigian, the heir to the Imperium's throne. Narius's eyebrows shot up, and he had to catch himself before he looked to Paine. Had the vizier known Tirigian was coming? He hadn't been mentioned in any of the discussions.

Tirigian marched to Narius, then dropped into an elaborate bow, one filled with waves and flourishes. "I bear greetings from he who shall be your father, O great king. I am Jairavi. It is I who will ensure proper protocol and dignity during the days leading to your wedding."

Narius frowned. Jairavi? He could have sworn that this was Tirigian. Did the crown prince have a twin brother?

Jairavi looked at him expectantly.

He'd have to puzzle it out later. "We have anticipated your arrival... I am sorry, I'm unsure of how to address you."

Jairavi straightened to his full height, which wasn't all that impressive. "Jairavi."

"No title?" Narius asked.

"Jairavi is my title. My name is immaterial. Until the day of your marriage to the princess, I am Jairavi and will answer to only that."

"I see." Narius exchanged a look with Paine, who shrugged. So was this Tirigian after all? Maybe. More importantly, how had they not known about any of this?

"I trust that you have seen to our requirements for the princess and her staff?" Jairavi asked.

Narius focused back on the Dalark man. "Indeed we have. I trust that you will find everything in order."

"I have no doubt." Jairavi glanced at one of the guards, who subtly nodded. "Then in that case, I believe you have waited long enough for this moment, yes?"

Jairavi stepped aside with another elaborate, sweeping gesture. Narius turned his attention to the top of the ramp and sucked in a breath. He hadn't seen Innana in years. All of his anticipation, building up to this moment and...

Innana stepped through the door.

Narius frowned. This couldn't really be her, could it? Was she a decoy? Oh, she looked like the Dalark princess. But her skin seemed too pale, and she was too skinny, a frail slip of a girl. When she spotted him, her face lit up with delight. Narius fought to keep from grimacing. For some reason, her expression didn't seem appropriate. It struck him as... childish.

She hurried down the ramp and looked ready to rush across the tarmac to him, but before she could, Jairavi subtly reached out a hand, signaling for her to stop. She did so, almost comically skidding to a halt, her arms pinwheeling. Once again, Narius had to struggle to keep his composure. Was she drunk? She offered him an impish grin, the same one that had set his heart fluttering when they were teenagers. Only this time, he couldn't muster the same giddy enthusiasm.

"It is good to see you again, Narius." Her voice sounded thready and weak, rather than rich and melodic like he remembered.

Jairavi cleared his throat. Innana blushed.

"I mean, I am honored to be brought under your wing and protection, my husband-to-be." Innana dipped into an elaborate curtsy, her arms practically flailing as she wove them through intricate gestures and flourishes.

Jairavi said something, but his words didn't register. Instead, Narius stared at Innana's strange antics. He supposed it was some sort of display of grace and poise, but it wasn't coming across that way. Paine had to nudge him to bring him back to reality.

"I'm sorry, you were saying?" Narius asked.

The chaperone glared at him. "I said, if it would be acceptable to you, we would like to bring the princess to her quarters so she may settle." Jairavi turned to Paine. "You and I must begin discussions of the ceremony itself."

"Will Innana be present?" Narius asked.

Jairavi shook his head. "No, that would violate our customs. You, however, must be there, but all decisions must be negotiated between your man and myself. You are to be present but silent, yes?"

Narius and Paine exchanged a look. A strange custom, but one they could accommodate.

"I would be most pleased to have that discussion with you, Jairavi." Paine bowed.

"Excellent! Then let us see the quarters you have prepared for—"

"Jairavi, may I please?" Innana asked.

Jairavi sighed but motioned toward Narius.

Before Narius could brace himself, Innana rushed forward and hugged him. He almost stumbled backward, she hit him so forcefully.

"I have longed for this day, my beloved," Innana whispered. "And what we can accomplish together!"

Jairavi cleared his throat, and Innana released Narius, darting around him toward the palace. Jairavi bowed to him, then followed Innana. Then a veritable parade of servants, bearing luggage, crates, and other objects, marched out of the transport, following the princess and Jairavi. Narius watched them pass, and with each step they took, he felt more and more certain: he had indeed fallen off the cliff and he had no idea what waited for him at the bottom.

57

After a full day in the public market, Everys trudged back to Tilash's apartment, the weight of her toolkit clunking against her back. She had worked for twelve hours, and she could feel every minute of it as she dragged herself up the stairs. It had been a decent day financially. By her count, she had made close to five hundred blades doing small repairs in an open-air stall—really just a corner near a busy intersection—and after she paid her part of the rent to Tilash, she would deposit the rest in the hopes of saving up enough to rent a new shop with actual walls and a roof. Sadly, her former status as queen didn't seem to help with Fair Havens bankers. Maybe she should have accepted the stipend from Paine after all, but it was probably too late to ask for it now.

For a while she had considered trying to find Redtale. Maybe her change in status would help mend their relationship, but Everys had no idea where Redtale had gone after leaving the guard. And without the resources of the palace at her disposal, she doubted she'd be able to track Redtale down anyway. Then again, what could she have expected Redtale to have done anyway? Be her personal bodyguard? That wouldn't have gone over well in Fair Havens.

Sadly, she hadn't been shielded from the gossip that had wafted through the market, all of it about the new romance blossoming at the palace. Oh, she had seen the pictures of Narius greeting Innana's transport. She had listened as the shoppers gossiped about the preparations. She had tried to tune out the stories, but people either didn't know who she was as they passed her stall or they didn't care if their words hurt. After such a long day, she wanted nothing more than to collapse and get some sleep.

She pulled herself up the last flight of stairs and came to a quick stop. Tilash's front door was ajar. Everys frowned. Had they not pulled it shut when they left in the morning? No, she was sure she had. And Tilash would never make that kind of mistake.

The hair on the back of her neck stood at attention. She quickly slipped off the toolkit and set it down. She considered finding something she could use for ink for combat runes. But no, she wouldn't be protected by Narius this time around. So instead, she picked up a length of pipe that had been sitting in the landing and brandished it like a club.

Thankfully, the door didn't creak as Everys nudged it open and slipped inside. The apartment was sheathed in darkness. Everys crept into the shadows and raised the club, ready to strike at anyone who might be inside.

"Is that the way to greet someone?"

The voice was right behind her. Everys shrieked and whirled around, swinging the pipe in a vicious arc.

But the intruder knocked the attack aside with a wooden staff, then batted Everys's makeshift weapon out of her hand. Everys stumbled away, desperately looking for something—anything—that she could use as a new weapon.

"Calm yourself, child. I know it's been a while since we've spoken, but that's no way to greet your dear auntie, is it?"

Her auntie? Instead of a weapon, Everys reached for the lights and flicked them on. Sure enough, Auntie Kyna stood in the room, her walking stick on one shoulder. The old fraud still wore a blindfold, which clearly didn't slow her down, given how easily she'd disarmed Everys.

Everys blew a stray lock out of her face and collapsed onto the couch. "What are you doing here, Kyna?"

"Is that any way to speak to me? After all, you're the one who didn't think to check in with me after you returned home." Kyna sank down onto a chair as well. "If you had need of a place to stay, you had only to ask."

Everys snorted. "With you?"

"Or with one of the other members of the conclave. Since most of your family is engaged in divine purpose, your community would have gladly taken you in."

"But I am with family."

Kyna smiled. "Of course, dearie. Of course."

"Is that why you came here? To scold me for not staying with someone else?"

"Such a horrible thing to say! All I've ever done is for your benefit, dearie. Well, not just yours, I suppose." Kyna smiled sadly. "But I did not 'break in here' just to spar with you, verbally or otherwise. I wanted to make sure you were okay."

Everys opened her arms and plastered on a fake smile. "Here I am. In one piece and as healthy as anyone can be in Fair Havens."

Kyna made a scolding noise. "You and I both know that injury can lurk beneath an unmarred surface, dearie. Yes, you may be whole physically, but that is not what I was asking about."

Tears stung Everys's eyes, and a wrenching ache opened inside her chest. Every time she heard people mention Narius, every time the media spoke of his upcoming wedding, practically with every breath she took, her heart twisted inside her. But she didn't want to cry in front of Kyna.

"I'm fine."

"Perhaps one day, you will be." Kyna sighed. "I hurt with you, child. I do. I did not know that this was the path your life would take when I suggested your name as a possible queen."

Ice encased Everys's heart. "Y-you did *what*?"

Kyna nodded. "Oh, indeed. The Dynasty would not have escorted you to the palace unless a family elder agreed to your participation in the search. With your father away, that solemn duty fell to me."

Everys gaped at her. "But how did... How could you have contacted anyone in the palace to do that?"

"Because she knows someone on the inside."

Everys jumped at the new voice, oily and low. Another person appeared behind Kyna, an older man, squat and average looking. It took Everys just a moment to recognize him as the man who had been in the ballroom when she was first brought to the palace, the man she had figured out was Tormod, Narius's spymaster.

"You?" Everys asked.

He nodded. "I understand you've been wanting to meet with me. Well, here I am."

"This isn't how I pictured this meeting taking place," Everys said.

"We rarely get what we want, my queen. But I am here now. So ask."

Everys sputtered for a few moments, trying to organize her thoughts. For one thing, she wanted to know how Tormod had remained hidden when she'd turned on the lights. But she quickly shoved such trivial thoughts aside because there was one question that had nagged at her for months, from the moment she had been dragged out of Fair Havens in the first place.

"Why did you tell Narius to pick me to be his queen?"

Tormod nodded thoughtfully, glancing over at Kyna. "A fair question. I suppose it came as quite the shock, didn't it? To stand in a room with nobility and other powerful women and to be chosen. Why would anyone pick you indeed?"

Everys bristled at the mockery in the man's tone.

"Why would anyone pick a woman with such obvious intelligence and drive? A woman of wit and passion who could do great things for the Dynasty if put in the right position? Let alone the historic import of having a Siporan ruler. Oh, yes. Why would anyone suggest you?"

"But you didn't know me!"

"Is that what you believe? Are you such a mystery?" He chuckled. "Very well. I arranged for your inclusion in the process and pushed Narius in your direction because dear Kyna asked me to."

Kyna wore a mysterious smile. Everys looked between them, trying to comprehend how an old fraud like Kyna could have any influence on Tormod.

"Why would you help Kyna?" Everys demanded.

Tormod sat on a chair near Kyna and smiled at the old woman. "Because that's what siblings do for one another, yes?"

Everys looked between the two of them, back and forth. Once the initial shock of Tormod's statement wore off, she cataloged the similar facial features: the shape and color of their eyes, the turned-up noses, the thinner lips. It would be easy to miss on a casual glance, but once it was pointed out, it was unmistakable.

"So you're—" She pointed between them.

Kyna nodded. "Since Tormod was born. The perks of being older."

"And that makes you—" She pointed directly at Tormod.

He smiled serenely. "A Siporan? Quite."

"Does anyone know?"

"Aside from Kyna, our departed parents, and now you?" Tormod shook his head. "I have been very discreet about my heritage, as one must be in the Dynasty. The Drywell Laws may have been rescinded, but there is still plenty of prejudice within Bastion and elsewhere. Although, I must say, I believe you may have eased that."

Everys leaned back on the couch, staring at Tormod. The king's spymaster was a Siporan? This whole time? What would Paine make of that? Or Narius?

The thought of him caused her mind to stutter. She gulped. "How is he?"

Tormod sighed and mopped a hand across his face. "I have not spent any time with the king in the past week. I've only just returned to Bastion. But from what little I've seen and from what my watchers in the palace tell me, he is putting on a brave face. But he mourns."

Everys digested his words, and the ache in her own heart grew sharper. She bit back a sob, and choked out, "I wish you had never sent me there."

"I know, dearie," Kyna said. "But the Singularity often calls us to walk paths that are difficult or uncomfortable. Take me, for example. Do you think I enjoy pretending to be blind and deaf, wearing these rags, being called fraud and fake by... well, by my own people?"

"Then why do you do it?"

"Because the Singularity asks me to. No, not asks. Demands. As He has for so many of His messengers in the past. Think of all the stories we read of the days before Downcasting, how many times the Singularity called to His wayward people. Do you suppose they relished the mockery and threats they received?"

"So you pretend to be a blind beggar because the Singularity told you to?" Everys couldn't keep the skepticism from her voice.

"Yes. I act blind because we, as a people, are blind to the Singularity's desires. I act as a beggar because that is what we have become. I act deaf because we have stopped our ears." Kyna tugged the blindfold off her head and blinked several times. She then looked directly at Everys. "I am a living reminder of what we have become—all of us—so that we might be reminded of what we have fallen from."

Tormod chuckled. "I understand your discomfort, my queen. She can be a bit intense sometimes, yes?"

Everys looked down at the floor. "Is that why you sent me to the palace? Because the Singularity told you to?"

Kyna smiled. "Perhaps. I wish it were so cut and dry as that. I believe that is what He wanted."

"But why?"

She shrugged. "He rarely reveals His reasoning to me. Or to anyone. But I do have to ask. Have you been seeking His guidance in what you do?"

She winced, Kyna's question a slap in the face. She knew she was supposed to. She had heard the admonitions often enough at conclave. But no, she hadn't been asking. It had never even occurred to her. But still, she had done all right for herself.

Hadn't she?

She shook her head to dislodge the thought. She wasn't going to feel guilty. Not about this. "I hope He got what He wanted. Because now I'm back where I started."

"Are you indeed?" Kyna asked. "The same person? Unchanged by the experiences of the past several months? What a strange miracle!"

"That's not what I meant, and you know it."

"What's more, who is to say that any of this is over? There may yet be more to come. The Singularity's plans are never over in an instant. He often works for years in silence and shadow before we even catch a glimpse of His true intentions. While He has not said this to me directly, I suspect that there is more for you to come. Wouldn't you say, Tormod?"

Tormod chuckled again. "Ah, now that would require me to divulge state secrets, wouldn't it? But I will say this..." He reached into a pocket, pulled out a slip of paper, then handed it to Everys. "We all need a drink sometime. You should maybe go and get one yourself. Not tonight, obviously. Too late for that. But if you were to go late next week? Yes. That would do nicely. Who knows? You might even find a friend."

She took the paper and looked at it. It was an advertisement for a bar in... Defector's Wrath? That was a neighboring area of Bastion, one that made Fair Havens seem like the palace. Why would Tormod want her to go there?

"And when you meet this friend, bring this. It will make your relationship mutually beneficial."

He handed her what appeared to be an ordinary scriber, one she might have sold in her shop if it still existed. Why would she need this?

He smiled and rose from his chair. "I'm afraid that I must go, my queen."

"You keep calling me that. I'm not your queen or anyone else's anymore."

"Aren't you? I wonder. Regardless. I have other matters to attend to. Kyna, always a pleasure."

"Take care of yourself, Tormod. And do eat some more. Mother would be appalled at how sickly you've become."

Tormod guffawed and headed for the door. As soon as he left, Kyna rose and put her blindfold back on. "Now, if you'll excuse me, this 'fraud' has work to do. A symbol is worthless if it is unseen."

And with that, she left the apartment, leaving Everys alone with some very jumbled thoughts. She considered the paper, then the scriber. She glanced at the door, then activated the device. As soon as it had warmed up, a prompt appeared on the tiny screen, asking her for a password. She frowned. Shouldn't Tormod have told her what that was?

She looked between the scriber and the paper. Why was Tormod playing this game? Why not give her everything she needed? This whole thing was pointless! There was no way she would—

Ow! She winced as a rebuke rocketed through her head. She frowned. Why would the Singularity rebuke her? She hadn't drawn any runes! Then her gaze fell on the paper and the scriber. A new rebuke built in the back of her skull.

"Okay, okay! I get it. I'll go when Tormod suggested!"

She braced herself for another rebuke, but nothing came. So that would be fine? She sighed. She'd be so happy when all of this was over, but she had a sinking feeling that wouldn't come anytime soon.

58

Maybe it was too early to make this kind of decision, but Narius was pretty sure he already hated his future brother-in-law.

He sat across the table from "Jairavi," who they had finally determined was Crown Prince Tirigian after all. In spite of that, though, the Dalark prince continued to insist on being called by that title. More frustrating, though, was that no one could determine why. After the Dalark arrived, Paine and Narius had spent hours with the Dynasty's so-called "experts" on Dalark culture, and none of them could explain what was going on. None of them had ever heard of this title. One speculated it was a new development in Dalark culture; another countered that it was a secret related to royal marriages. But all they had were guesses.

Narius glanced out of the corner of his eye at Paine. He still didn't know how the vizier was taking everything in stride. Jairavi's sole purpose seemed to be disrupting life in the palace as much as possible. Right after his arrival, Jairavi had insisted that a group of clerics he called "summoners" be allowed to cleanse the entire palace grounds, a process that involved them entering every room to perform a smelly ritual that took an hour each time. All told, these summoners spread through the palace over the course of three days, getting in everyone's way. Then he had insisted on changes to how food was prepared in the palace kitchens to comply with certain divine principles. And from what Narius had heard, Supreme Prelate Istragon was almost apoplectic from his "discussions" with Jairavi on how to best blend Xoniel and Dalark elements in the wedding. Yet through it all, Paine had remained level-headed and calm.

"I can appreciate your concerns, Jairavi, but what you're suggesting simply isn't feasible," Paine said. "We cannot rebuild the main ballroom in the allotted time frame."

Jairavi, seated across the table from Narius and Paine, sniffed. "Then I once again question your king's commitment to this peace, Vizier. If the king and princess wed in the room as it is presently constructed, the spirits and potentates will undoubtedly smite their union with grief and illness. But if we could make the necessary modifications, the divine geometry could be observed."

"Again, while we would never want the 'spirits and potentates' to be angered, this level of renovation isn't possible." Paine's tone remained measured, even though Narius spotted a hint of tension in his friend's jaw. "Are you certain that there aren't any other ways to satisfy the geometry?"

"Well, yes, I suppose we could bring in more summoners," Jairavi mused. "They would have to work through all four watches to achieve the proper spiritual balance. But I suppose it could be done."

Narius wanted to breathe a sigh of relief. They had been talking about this "issue" for close to an hour. It reminded him of the parley with the Cold Light, except the trees weren't nearly so stubborn. And at least he had Everys by his side then.

He winced at the thought. Still too soon.

Jairavi leaned forward. "Our next subject regards the security and safety of Innana's father."

Narius fought the urge to point out that Devroshan was Jairavi's father as well, but if the crown prince insisted on pretending not to be Tirigian, who was he to fight it?

"I can assure you, Jairavi, the royal guard will be on high alert the day of the wedding. And we will take all reasonable steps to ensure the safety of Emperor Devroshan," Paine said.

"It is not just his physical wellbeing for which I am concerned. The accommodations for the sacred geometry is one thing, but there are other forces that threaten his august personage." Jairavi pressed his hands on the table. "I am speaking, of course, of the many non-humans who serve within these walls. Why, since our arrival, I have seen Plissk, Ixactl, and even an Elbrekkian!"

Narius frowned. "So?"

Jairavi shot him a pained look, and Narius closed his eyes, hoping to forestall the headache. Right. He was to be there but be silent. Trickster's own schemes, these Dalark customs!

"The lesser races are not considered clean by the spirits and potentates. Their very presence has made the summoners' work so very difficult. And, if they are permitted anywhere near the Emperor, their taint will corrupt him. This cannot be allowed."

Narius fought the urge to gape at Jairavi. This was a joke, right? He sat up straighter and raised a hand, ready to make an emphatic point.

But Paine touched his arm and subtly shook his head. The vizier cleared his throat. "I am confused, Jairavi. Are you not concerned about their presence 'tainting' you and the princess?"

Jairavi waved away his question. "The princess, she will live here in their presence after the wedding, yes? The damage will be done, but she is strong and she will adjust. As for me, I am of little importance, hence why I am Jairavi."

Was that bitterness that Narius detected in the prince's voice? Was it genuine or just a performance?

"But the august Emperor, he is the focal point of the spirit and potentate's energies. Should he be corrupted, it will disrupt the Imperium in ways you cannot imagine. And our people would know who is to blame." Jairavi spread his hands. "If this is not rectified, it could threaten the very peace we are trying to create, yes?"

Paine hesitated. "That would be unfortunate, yes. We would hate to jeopardize the relationship between our two kingdoms. What, precisely, do you suggest?"

Jairavi smiled, clearly pleased. "On the day of the wedding, only human servants would be permitted within the palace walls. Surely this is not so great an imposition?"

Narius frowned. Yes, it actually was. It would easily disrupt the staff's duties, during an important celebration no less. That was reason enough to balk. Yet from the expression on Paine's face, he knew that the vizier would want him to agree. So he nodded curtly.

"As for the guards, well, that may prove trickier. We all understand how physical exertion opens one up to the energies of those around them, yes? That means that the guards of your palace have absorbed more of the taint than the regular serving staff. For that reason, we must insist that they all be replaced as soon as possible."

Now Narius gaped at Jairavi. Replace all the guards? "That's ridiculous!"

Jairavi gave him a withering glance. "But I am afraid I must insist. The emperor's spiritual advisers have been most distressed over this subject and have filled my ears to brimming with their concerns. Why, they have even raised the question of whether the wedding should be permitted at all at this point."

Paine frowned. "Because of the guards?"

Jairavi once again waved away the question. "They worry about the corruption that has undoubtedly slithered into the king himself. His former wife was, after all, a Siporan. Who knows what sort of foul pollution now flows through the palace because of her?"

Heat flashed through Narius, erupting through his chest and up into his face. For a split second, he pictured himself vaulting the table and wrapping his hands around the smug prince's neck, squeezing and squeezing.

Once again, Paine dropped a hand on his wrist. The vizier shook his head, then focused his attention on Jairavi. "Let's drop the pretenses, shall we, Prince Tirigian?"

Jairavi's head snapped back as if struck. "I have told you, I am not Tirigian, I am—"

"Enough!" Paine snapped. "It is enough. We have tolerated much from you in the past few days, but your insults and condescension does little to facilitate the peace between our people. You want specific types of food banned from the kitchens? We can accommodate you. You need an army of 'summoners' to do whatever they're doing until the wedding? We can work around them. Do we need to shuffle personnel around to meet your whims? We can do that as well. But I will not tolerate any more insinuations about King Narius's fitness. Do I make myself clear?"

Jairavi glared at Paine, then turned to Narius. "My apologies, King Narius. I was perhaps too... indelicate in my phrasing."

Narius nodded gravely.

Paine cleared his throat. "I will contact Duke Brencis and see what we can do about bringing in human soldiers to guard the palace. Will that be acceptable?"

"Yes." Jairavi took a deep breath, then turned his attention to Narius again. "I believe it might do for us to take a recess at this point, yes? To regather our thoughts and come back with renewed purpose. But before we go, I bear a message from your bride. She wishes to have dinner with you tonight, if you are available. I understand she is doing her best to make a number of your favorite dishes: garic-spiced venison, puff-cloud pastries, and mugs of corat."

Narius's stomach turned at the thought of that meal. Yes, he had liked those foods when he was younger, enough that he may have claimed them as his favorites, but his tastes had changed considerably since then. But he also suspected that if he let on that these weren't his favorites anymore, Innana would take it personally. And who knew what kind of obscure Dalark rituals he'd have to endure during the meal. Given how the past few days had gone, Jairavi would be there, not-so-silently judging him for everything he was doing.

But he had to spend time with her eventually, even if it was with minders and chaperones in tow. He took a deep breath, trying to summon up enough enthusiasm to accept.

Instead, Paine cleared his throat. "I am afraid that the king will have to decline." He turned to Narius. "Remember, Your Strength, you have that briefing with Tormod tonight? Regarding the bark beetles?"

Narius frowned. What was Paine talking about? As far as he knew, Tormod was still out of town on one of his enigmatic missions. But Paine's expression didn't falter. In fact, Narius picked up on a subtle prompt in the vizier's eyes.

"Oh... Yes, I momentarily forgot." He turned back to Jairavi. "Please do share my regrets with the Princess."

Jairavi nodded. "Of course. King Narius, Vizier Paine. Until later."

With that, Jairavi left the room in a swirl of robes.

Narius let out a long sigh, then turned to Paine. "Thank you."

"Of course." Paine started, to rise, but then faced Narius fully. "Your Strength, I have to ask. Is this worth it?"

"Excuse me?"

"This." Paine waved at the chair where Jairavi had been seated. "I know, better than anyone, how long you've wanted this to happen. And peace with Dalark? It's more than any king could imagine. But are you sure it's worth all of this?"

Narius considered it. In some ways, it wasn't. Ever since the skimmer touched down and deposited Innana into his life, he had been chased by a stifling dread. And each day that drew him closer to his wedding felt like another step closer to a bottomless pit.

But was it worth it? He knew that answer all too well. Yes. Yes, it was. His father had explained this to him so many years ago: A king sacrificed. A king served his people. He knew better than anyone what peace with the Imperium would mean for the Dynasty.

Yes, things would be awkward with Innana at first. But he knew he would come to love her again eventually. After all, he had with—

His breath caught in his throat. He clenched his jaw, shoving the errant thought aside. Best not to dwell on the past.

Narius nodded. "It is. It will be. Besides, imagine the diplomatic fallout if we were to back out. The last thing any of us wants is to foment an international incident."

Paine frowned. "I suppose that's so. This is difficult for me. I not only want what's best for the Dynasty. I want what's best for you as well."

Those words, spoken so softly and earnestly, caused Narius's head to snap back in surprise. Paine looked at him, and for the first time in as long as he could remember, Narius saw sadness in his friend's eyes. True compassion. And he understood. He had always known that Paine was his most ardent supporter. Now he knew it on the deepest level he could.

"Thank you, old friend," Narius whispered.

Paine nodded. "If you'll excuse me, Your Strength. I will contact Duke Brencis immediately. Hopefully all of this nonsense will be over soon."

Narius hoped for the same thing. But deep in his heart, he knew that although some of the "nonsense" would end with the wedding, he'd have to deal with the consequences for years. Maybe even longer. He just hoped it would be worth it.

59

Everys took a deep breath and looked up at the Bloodied Blade. This was where Tormod wanted her to get a drink? Bad enough that this... establishment was situated in the heart of Defector's Wrath. But now that she stood in front of it, she definitely didn't want to enter. The bar looked like it had been shelled to the point of collapse. Graffiti covered the front so thoroughly she couldn't be sure what the bricks' original color had been. And from the people she had seen stumbling through the neighborhood on the way here, she fully expected to find nothing but drunks and fighters inside. She reached into her coat and touched the pens she had brought with her. Hopefully three would be enough. It would be a whole lot better if she didn't need them at all, but better safe than sorry.

Taking a deep breath, Everys pulled the door open and stepped inside. She immediately regretted it.

As bad as the exterior was, the interior was worse. A rank odor wafted through the room, enough that her stomach clenched in response. A haze hung in the air, making it difficult to see the bar's patrons. What she could see sent a chill marching across her skin. At least four or five of the patrons were hulking Ixactl, and the others appeared to be just as tough. And unfortunately, they were all looking at her.

Everys froze in the doorway. Their gazes slithered over her body, evaluating her. Dissecting her.

She stood up taller, tried to project an aura of danger. The way Redtale would. Or Kevtho. Or Narius...

After a few tense moments, the patrons turned back to their drinks. Well, almost all of them. An Ixactl brute in one corner flashed her what he probably thought was a charming smile.

"Hey, pebble. Why don't you come over here and sit on my lap?" He patted one knee.

Everys took a step back, toward the door. The Ixactl's friends guffawed.

"Don't be so scary, Stoophawk," one of them said. "She looks ready to bolt."

"Nah, she's just captivated by my charms, ain't ya?" Stoophawk waggled his fingers at her, as if trying to entice her. "C'mere, pebble. I promise, you'll like it."

Everys swallowed hard and considered rushing out the door again. This was silly. She shouldn't be here. Why'd she even come? All because Kyna filled her head with talk of destiny and purpose? All because Tormod had called her his queen? But she was no queen. She was no—

Wait. She may not have the titles anymore. But she didn't have to take any of this.

She rose up to her full height and glared at Stoophawk and his cronies. She summoned up every drop of authority she had once wielded as the Dynasty's queen.

"I doubt that. I'm not here for any of you." At least, she hoped she wasn't. Tormod hadn't said who she was supposed to meet, but she couldn't imagine it was any of them.

Apparently the acid in her tone worked. Some of Stoophawk's friends stopped laughing and exchanged uncertain looks.

Stoophawk shoved his chair away from the table and stood. Much to Everys's surprise, he wasn't much taller than her. From the look on his face, he wasn't impressed with her attitude.

"I think you are." His voice was a growl. "And I think you're going to come over and join us right now. Or else."

A tremor wormed up her spine, but she set her feet and clenched her fists. "Or else what?"

He cracked his knuckles, and it sounded like thunder. "Or I'm going to rearrange that pretty face of yours."

She swallowed the bile that crawled up her throat and forced herself to meet his gaze. "You wouldn't dare touch me. Because if you do, I'll rip off your horns and hang them on my wall as a trophy."

Stoophawk stared at her, his eyes wide, and for a brief moment, doubt flickered across his face. But then he laughed.

"I'd like to see you try." He took another step toward her.

"I wouldn't do that if I were you," someone said from across the room.

Everys froze. She recognized that voice!

"Speaking from experience, this woman has a way of messing up your life."

Everys forced herself to turn away from Stoophawk and toward the speaker. It couldn't be. *It couldn't be.*

Quartus glared at her from his seat on the other side of the room.

Stoophawk looked between Quartus and Everys, fear painted across his face. "Oh, hey, Qulinus. She with you?"

He sneered. "Sure. Why not? I love a family reunion, don't you, *dear sister?*"

She met his glare with one of her own.

Stoophawk, for his part, shuffled his feet and nodded to Everys. "So sorry to bother you. If I woulda known you were here to see Qulinus, I would've left you alone. Made sure everyone else did too."

"It's fine." She forced the words through her clenched teeth.

"Why don't you join me back here and we can catch up?" It wasn't a question, especially given the grim expression on Quartus's face.

"Love to."

She walked over to his table, her body stiff and her mind protesting. This was the monster who got Matron Halis killed. He had manipulated her and humiliated her and tried to assassinate her! She shouldn't be joining him at a bar table. She shouldn't be anywhere near him! Yet Tormod said she should come here. Quartus had to be the one the spymaster wanted her to meet. But why? Shouldn't he know what a bad idea this was?

Everys took the chair opposite Quartus. She eyed the door, just in case she had to run.

"So. Everys."

"So. Qulinus, is it?"

His face darkened. "Given that my dear brother declared me outlaw, it seems wise not to use my real name. You do remember that night, don't you?"

"Hard to forget the assassination you arranged!" she shot back.

His eyes flared and he leaned forward. "I. Did. Not. Do. That."

"Redtale says you did."

"I don't know what 'evidence' Redtale found, but I was framed. Why would I conspire with Viscount Orsin to kill Narius or you?"

"Why would you lie to Matron Halis and have her travel to Olekk?" Everys countered.

His head snapped back. Then he let out a long breath. "All right. I did do that. I shouldn't have. And I've been carrying the guilt over what happened to Halis ever since. But I swear to you, on the Perfected Warrior's entire arsenal, that I am not responsible for the attack on you and Narius. Why would I? If the attack had succeeded, I would have been crowned king. That's the last thing I want."

Everys started to dismiss his words, but she caught herself. He sounded sincere. Completely and totally sincere. As much as she despised him, she believed him.

"Why do you think I'm here?" he continued. "I've been working the past few weeks trying to turn up evidence to clear my name, trying to track down the real perpetrators."

"In Defector's Wrath?" She couldn't keep the skepticism out of her voice.

He nodded. "I've made quiet inquiries to what few friends I have left in the military. One of them has heard rumors about some kind of secret project that operates out of this neighborhood. I have no idea if they're behind the attack on the palace, but I figured it was worth looking into."

She frowned. Some of what he said made a certain amount of sense. Defector's Wrath was mostly abandoned buildings, and it was an open secret that the local constables did nothing to combat the organized crime that operated in this neighborhood. If someone wanted to hide in Bastion, this was the best place to do it.

"But why are you here?" Quartus demanded. "Decided to find a new neighborhood to rescue?"

Everys bristled at the sarcastic question. But she quickly shoved her anger aside. "I'm here because someone told me that I'd find a friend here."

"Really? And who is this individual who clearly doesn't understand our history?"

"Tormod."

Quartus's face went blank. Then he cursed under his breath and looked around the room. "I should have known! That spider was never going to let me out of his web. What, specifically, did he say to you?"

Everys thought back to the previous night. "That I should come here for a drink. That I'd meet a friend here."

He snorted.

Oh! She had almost forgotten. Everys pulled the scriber out of her pocket and set it on the table. "And he said that I should bring you this, that it would be 'mutually beneficial.'"

Quartus frowned at the device, then picked it up. He turned it on, then froze. "It's encrypted."

"I noticed," Everys said.

"You don't know the password?"

"I thought you would."

He studied her face, then poked at the small keyboard. A second later, the device warbled, and Quartus bit off another curse.

"It was my clearance code," he muttered. "Figures."

"You had a clearance code?" Everys asked.

Quartus smirked at her. "What's the matter? Jealous?"

Heat painted Everys's cheeks as she realized yes, she was, a little.

Quartus turned his attention back to the scriber, scrolling through whatever was on it. Then his eyes widened, and he tossed the device back onto the table. "By the breastplate, I should have known!"

"What?"

"I have a lead about an abandoned factory here in Defector's Wrath. I believe the people working on this secret project are using it as a headquarters of some sort," he said. "I've scouted the location, both during the day and at night. But when I tried to hack into the security system—"

Everys snorted. "*You* can hack a security system?"

Quartus glared at her. "The royal family always has to spend some time in the military. My brother chose the infantry. I served in cyber-ops. I was pretty decent at it too."

Huh. Everys would have never expected that. Her estimation of Quartus went up a little.

"Besides, it meant I could stay in Bastion, which meant I got to go out in my military uniform. Women loved that."

And her estimation cratered. Figured.

"The point is, there's no way I could ever crack their security unless I had access to some high-powered intrusion software." He tapped the scriber. "Which this just happens to contain."

Everys's eyes widened. "You mean..."

Quartus nodded. "Don't you find it convenient that, when I hit a wall, Tormod sends you with exactly what I need?"

"Why would he do that?"

"Plausible deniability. Tormod knows there's a conspiracy behind the assassination attempt, but he doesn't know who's behind it. He doesn't want to be outmaneuvered. So he lets me do the digging for him." Quartus's face took on a distant expression. "Now that I think of it, there's probably been half a dozen times he's nudged me in the right direction without me even realizing it. Now he has you deliver these security cracking programs? He wants us to investigate that factory, because he knows that if we're caught, he can pretend that we were acting on our own and see how people react. Or we can discover who's responsible, and he can swoop in when he needs to. The old spider's clever, I'll give him that."

An uncomfortable silence fell on the table. Both of them stared at the scriber. What should she do now? She had delivered the device. As far as she was concerned, she could get up and leave the bar and forget that she had spent any time with Quartus. But the thought of retreating didn't sit well with her.

They both reached for the scriber at the same time, their fingers brushing.

He looked up at her and frowned. "What do you think you're doing?"

"I'm going to go see what's in that factory."

Quartus laughed. "You don't even know where it is."

"Then you can show me."

"Forget it. I'm not putting you in harm's way. I saw the pictures from the state dinner, the way you and Narius were looking at each other while you were dancing. What do you think he'd do to me if something happened to you now?"

Everys's cheeks burned at the thought of the dance, the walk in the garden, the almost kiss. But she shoved those awkward yet pleasant memories aside. "You seem to forget, whoever is behind this tried to have me killed. I have a stake in this too. And I'm coming with you whether you like it or not."

He studied her face before groaning. "I'm going to regret this. Fine. Let's get going." He pushed away from the table. "Stoophawk, you and the boys get the truck ready. We're going to hit that factory tonight."

Stoophawk and his friends let out a quiet whoop and started for the door. But the Ixactl hesitated and nodded toward Everys. "The pebble too? That a good idea, Qulinus?"

Quartus favored her with a wry smile. "You wanna try talking her out of it? Trust me, we'll just be wasting time. She goes."

Stoophawk shrugged and headed for the door. Everys started to follow, but Quartus snared her by the arm and pulled her close.

"Don't make me regret this decision," he whispered.

She hoped she wouldn't regret it either.

60

S toophawk's gang had a transport, one that was used to deliver produce, waiting in the alley behind the Bloodied Blade. Once they had all clambered into the back, one of Stoophawk's friends drove them out onto the empty streets and headed for the warehouse.

The drive didn't last long, which was good. The back of the transport lacked any safety harnesses or seats. More than once, Everys was thrown onto Stoophawk or Quartus or one of the others. All of them brushed aside her apologies, but it happened so often that Everys started to wonder if the driver was doing it intentionally. But then the vehicle slowed to a stop, and the driver pounded on the cab's back wall.

Quartus turned to Stoophawk. "You and the boys go check it out. I'll stay here with her."

Stoophawk nodded and his gang slipped out the back, disappearing into the night.

"How did you wind up with these... gentlemen?" Everys wasn't sure what else to call them.

"They used to work for a petty crime lord named Plion based out of Beyond-the-Wall. He ran the... establishment that Redtale found me in." He cleared his throat. "Turns out, he's the one who had me drugged, then planted the evidence that linked me to Viscount Orsin and the assassins."

She gaped at him. "How did you figure that out?"

"Please. I may have been drinking, but not so much that I'd pass out. I suspected from the beginning someone drugged me. I went back to find out who. The girl I had been with told me about Plion. When I confronted him, he tried to have Stoophawk and his crew 'dissuade' me from asking questions." He shrugged. "I made them a better offer."

"With what?" Everys asked. "Didn't Narius confiscate your wealth?"

Quartus glowered at her. "Thanks for the reminder. No, I bested Plion in a duel."

"You *what?*"

He shrugged. "I proved that I was the better warrior in personal combat. Once I won, Stoophawk and his crew swore their loyalty to me. And they helped me persuade Plion to tell me what he knew."

"Which was what?"

"That someone paid him a lot of blades to come to this factory, get some drugs to slip into my drink, and get a data card that he was to leave in my pocket. According to him, the money was too good to pass up."

"Why didn't you bring this back to the palace? Tell Narius what happened?"

"Outlaw, remember? Just showing up at the palace would have been a death sentence. Besides, it was a story told to me by a criminal, and I didn't have any corroborating evidence." He nodded toward the back of the transport. "Why do you think I want to get into this factory?"

That made sense. Given how angry Narius had been—how angry she had been—there was no way that anyone would have believed this story. But maybe, if there was actual evidence of his innocence, the right thing to do would be to find it and clear his name.

Something hit the side of the transport, and Stoophawk's face appeared in the opening. "All clear, Qulinus."

Quartus gestured for her to go first. She did, and she was surprised when Stoophawk offered her a hand to help her down. The Ixactl led them out of the alley, motioning for them to stay low as they scurried to where the rest of the gang was hiding behind a parked transport.

Everys risked a peek around the vehicle to study the factory. Unlike TelleGlin's facility in Dropport, this was what she expected a factory in Bastion should look like: A towering, dingy building with smokestacks that stabbed at the night sky. Most of the windows were boarded over, and the walls were covered in grime and graffiti in equal measures.

"Any guards?" Quartus whispered.

"None that we saw. What's the plan?"

Quartus mopped a hand across his chin, then turned to his friends. "Everys and I will slip around to the back of the factory and go in through the loading dock we scouted last time we were here. You boys up for a little distraction to cover us?"

Some of Stoophawk's men nodded, but the Ixactl looked worried. "Didn't you say that there could be heavily armed folks in there, Qulinus? What if we make a ruckus and they come out shootin'?"

Apparently Quartus hadn't thought of that, given the way he hemmed and hawed. Everys sighed. Might as well make herself useful.

She slipped out of the hiding place and started across the street.

"What are you doing?" Quartus whispered.

"I'll be right back. Get ready to move."

Everys jogged across the street and quickly spotted the surveillance cams along the factory's second story. She moved parallel to the building, hoping that it looked like she wasn't up to anything. Then she angled for six large storage tanks standing on metallic legs on the edge of the factory's lot. Perfect. As near as she could tell, they would block the view of the cams on the building. That would have to do.

Once she was confident she was out of sight, she ducked between two of the tanks and fished out one of her pens. She hated using the ink for something like this, but it was better than Stoophawk and his men risking their lives. Snapping the pen in half, she winced as the acrid odor overwhelmed her. Then she daubed some ink onto her finger and set to work, tracing a rune on the legs holding up one of the tanks. She frowned as she worked. It had been a while since she had used this rune, but she was pretty sure she got the details right. As soon as she had painted all four legs, she moved on to the next tank. Then the next, drawing the same set of runes on all six tanks.

As soon as she finished, Everys hustled back across the street, ducked behind another transport, and waited. From down the block, Quartus and his men waved for her to get back over to them, but she signaled for them to wait. Any moment now...

The runes didn't activate all at once, which was disappointing, but she had apparently remembered the design correctly. With a shriek of metal, the legs underneath the tanks dissolved. The tanks wobbled, and then toppled, smashing into each other before crashing to the pavement with a thunderous roar.

But Everys didn't watch the destruction. She sprinted back to Quartus's hiding place, figuring that anyone watching the surveillance footage would be paying more attention to the wreckage than a lone woman running down the street.

"What did you do?" Quartus asked softly, staring at the broken tanks with wide eyes.

She smiled and hid her hands behind her back. Hopefully he wouldn't smell the ink. "Caused a distraction. Let's go."

Stoophawk laughed and led the way, his men creating a screen around Everys and Quartus. The former prince seemed too distracted by what had happened. He stared at the smashed tanks before shaking his head and following the rest of the group.

They skirted around the factory with Stoophawk leading the way. Once they were on the other side, the Ixactl led them to a ramp that led to a basement loading dock. Quartus signaled for the group to stop.

"New plan: you stay up here and keep an eye on things. Everys and I will go inside and see what's going on. If there's any sign of trouble, get out of here."

Stoophawk bristled. "We ain't gonna leave you on your own."

Quartus placed a hand on Stoophawk's shoulders. "If we're caught, I doubt there's much you could do about it. So save yourself."

From his expression, Stoophawk didn't like the idea. But he didn't argue. Instead, he nodded once, then motioned for the rest of his companions to spread out around the back of the factory.

Quartus turned to her and made a sweeping gesture down the ramp. "After you."

The two of them hurried down the ramp. At the bottom, there was a large rolling door at chest height, perfect for loading a transport. But there was also a regular door at the top of a set of concrete stairs with a small metal box next to it. As soon as they reached the top of the stairs, Quartus pulled out the scriber and handed it to her, then worked on opening the box.

"What are you doing?" she whispered.

"When we scouted this place, I discovered that I could access the factory's mainframe from this juncture," he said. "But like I said, I couldn't penetrate the system's firewall. I'm hoping Tormod's bag of tricks will help."

He yanked the cover off the box, exposing a mess of wires and data ports. He held out his hand for the scriber and, once she had handed it to him, set to work deftly splicing it into the system. As much as she didn't want to admit it, Everys was impressed. He obviously knew his way around this system. After a few minutes of work, Quartus powered on the scriber.

"Let's hope this works." He clicked a few buttons, then fell silent.

Everys reached into her pocket and wrapped her fingers around her two remaining pens. Hopefully she wouldn't need them.

Quartus let out a soft laugh. "I'm in. Checking the security system..." He frowned. "Look at this."

He angled the scriber so she could see the screen. The image was tiny yet crisp as he cycled through what appeared to be different views from security cameras. Most of those views were very similar: large, empty spaces, although a few rooms had the remains of decaying machines. Then there were brief flashes of empty offices and hallways before the cycle started over again.

"What's the matter?" she whispered.

"I don't see any evidence that this is being used as the headquarters of some conspiracy, do you?"

She frowned as well. Now that he mentioned it, no. She didn't even spot anyone guarding the factory. "Do you think there's a secret entrance somewhere inside?"

He grimaced. "That's entirely likely, but that could take hours of searching to locate. Maybe even days." He hesitated. "Unless..."

Quartus pulled the scriber back to him and set to work. Sweat beaded across his forehead, and he winced a few times, but then he turned to his left, toward the bare wall of the factory's foundation and...

There was an audible click, followed by a hiss, then stone scraped against stone. Part of the wall slipped backwards, then rose, revealing a metal door. Everys braced herself, waiting for the door to open. But nothing happened. She and Quartus stood in the quiet, the only sound the clicking of keys on the scriber as Quartus worked.

"Are you going to open the door?" Everys asked.

"I'm trying. I was able to open the outer shell, but the encryption on this door is proving trickier..."

Another click, another sigh, and the metal doors started to slide open. Everys offered Quartus a congratulatory grin, but his eyes had gone wide.

"I didn't do that," he whispered.

The door revealed a burly man in tan fatigues. He held a hand to his ear. "—checking on what tripped the outer perimeter right—"

His eyes widened, and his gaze ricocheted from Everys to Quartus and back again. He shouted something inarticulate and reached for his weapon.

Everys moved swiftly. She yanked a pen from her pocket and snapped it in half. But there was no way she could paint a rune fast enough. "Quartus! Move!"

Her shout snapped him out of his shock. He dropped the scriber and charged forward, slamming his shoulder into the man's stomach. The two fell back through the door in a tangle of limbs.

"Hold him still!" Everys daubed some ink onto her finger and hurried through the door.

Quartus and the guard struggled on the floor of a small elevator, their limbs tangled. The man flipped Quartus on his back and wrapped his hands around the former prince's neck.

Everys leapt onto the guards back and started drawing. It was going to be sloppy, but she didn't have much choice. He thrashed against her, but she held on with her left arm while she drew with her right hand. Just a few strokes, then the silent command to activate and...

The man's strength drained out of him, and he collapsed onto Quartus, unconscious. Everys breathed out a sigh of relief. Thankfully the sleeping rune was a simple one, otherwise she wouldn't have been able to draw it so quickly and—

"Can you please get off me?" Quartus's words were little more than a groan.

She gasped and rolled off the man's body, then helped Quartus free himself. He dusted himself off and frowned at the guard, then at Everys. "What did you do?"

Then his gaze fell on the broken halves of the pen on the elevator floor. His eyes widened, and they shot to Everys's hand. She looked down as well, seeing the stain of ink on her fingers.

"You're... You're a... a..." he whispered.

She braced herself. Would he attack her? Or shout for his men?

Instead, he swallowed hard. "Does Narius know?"

Everys nodded. "For a few weeks now."

He frowned. "Well, thank you. I'm sure it pained you to save me, but I appreciate it all the same."

She had to force herself to keep from smiling. "That almost sounded authentic."

"It almost was." He looked down at the guard. "How long will he be out?"

She winced. That was a good question. "I don't think it'll last long. I had to work quickly."

He nodded absently, then knelt next to the man. He disarmed him, tucking the gun into the waistband of his pants, then rifled through his pockets. Quartus pulled out an ID, which he handed to Everys. Then he stepped out of the elevator. "Stoophawk! I need some help down here."

Everys startled and quickly snatched up the broken halves of the pen, stashing them in her pocket. Hopefully the ink wouldn't stain her clothes too badly.

Stoophawk lumbered down the ramp and let out a low whistle when he saw the unconscious guard. "You okay, boss?"

Quartus nodded. "Thanks to the lady, yes. But I need you to keep this one under wraps for a while. Okay?"

The Ixactl offered Everys an appraising look, then shrugged and hefted the sleeping man over his shoulder. Without comment, he went back up the ramp.

Once he was gone, Quartus turned back to her. "Are you ready?"

"As I'll ever be."

He motioned for them to enter the elevator. There were no controls, just a small black box set at waist height. Everys waved the guard's ID over the box. With a soft ding, the doors closed and the elevator descended.

Everys blew out a shaky breath, then she realized: she hadn't been rebuked. Not even a twinge. Did that mean the Singularity was okay with what she had done? With what she was doing and might do? Only one way to find out.

61

They rode in the elevator much longer than Everys had expected. It felt like they had dropped ten floors, maybe more, before the elevator came to a gentle halt and the doors opened. Quartus held up a hand and peeked through the doors. He bit off a curse and yanked the guard's gun out of his waistband.

"Surrender now!" He hurried out of the car.

Everys risked a peek herself. Apparently Quartus had surprised another guard. The woman had her hands out in surrender, glaring swords at him.

"Can you knock her out too?" Quartus asked.

Everys nodded and stepped forward. She pulled out half of the broken pen and smeared more ink on her finger. The woman flinched away from her, but at a grunt from Quartus, the guard went still. Everys was able to apply the ink more carefully, tracing out a rune that would render the guard unconscious for eight hours. As soon as it was done and activated, the woman slumped to the floor.

The immediate threat taken care of, she took a moment to examine her surroundings. They stood in a cramped room, just a box with the elevator behind them and what appeared to be thick metal doors in front of them. There was a large mirror to their right and three metal cabinets in the wall to their left.

Quartus eyed their surroundings, then looked at the mirror. He nodded once, then opened fire on it. The flechettes embedded themselves in the glass, but it didn't shatter.

"Thought so. That's where they monitor the folks who come in here. If I had to guess, those are remote guns in the boxes." He jerked a thumb toward the cabinets.

"So you decided to test your theory by shooting at the glass?"

He shrugged. "If I could break through, it'd be a shortcut. Unless you have a way of cutting through the doors?"

She scowled, but she understood his reasoning. "Let me try something."

Quartus stepped out of the way, and she walked over to the mirror. If she squinted, she could catch the barest glimpse of a room beyond it. As near as she could tell, no one was in there. Best not test their luck. She daubed more ink onto her fingers and traced a rune on the glass. She activated it and stepped back.

With a loud crack, the glass shattered, pieces dropping to the floor. Quartus flinched, then gaped at the hole. "Handy power."

"It can be." She gingerly knocked away some of the remaining glass and slid through.

Everys dropped into a room no bigger than a closet. There was a small desk with monitors shoved up against the wall with the broken windows. The monitors showed what looked like a lab, some offices, and... Were those prison cells? And an operating room? What kind of a place had they found?

Quartus slid through and checked the monitors as well. His scowl deepened. "We'd better keep moving."

They went through the only door and found themselves in a long hallway dotted with more doors. They crept down the hall, poking their heads in each door as they passed. One was an armory, with guns and weapons stored on racks. Another led to a barracks with neat rows of cots. Another door brought them into a lounge area with a vidscreen, several metal tables, and a small kitchenette.

But then they found a pristine laboratory, something similar to what she had seen on her tour of TelleGlin. Gleaming white tables stretched out before them in orderly rows, the room's walls obscured by computer banks, cabinets, shelves, and diagramming boards. Each table was covered in scribers, devices in various states of assembly, and on one, what appeared to be large glass bottles containing foggy liquids in different colors. Everys took a cautious step forward and winced, waiting for alarms or guards or something to indicate that people knew they were there. Nothing happened. She took another step. Then another. Still no reaction.

"Well, let's see what this is all about, shall we?" Quartus asked.

They took a different row. Everys glanced at each table as she walked past. She picked up one scriber and scrolled through its contents, but she couldn't decipher the notes, chemical symbols, or equations. She did stop at one table with a partially disassembled machine of some kind and gave it a closer look. In spite of her experience with repairing broken technology, though, she couldn't fathom what the device was used for.

"What do you suppose this is?" Quartus asked.

Everys went over to where he examined a machine. It looked like some sort of robotic arm poised over a flat surface. She frowned. It looked familiar. She knew she had seen something like it before. It was...

"A biofabricator," she whispered.

Yes, that's what it had to be, similar to the units she had seen when she had toured TelleGlin with Clarinda Gaines. But these were so much smaller, compact, streamlined. Everys suspected that if Gaines saw one of these, she'd either be jealous or furious. Maybe both.

There were several of the units in a row against a back wall of the lab. She walked quickly from machine to machine, looking them over, trying to find some clue, some hint of what they had been making. Nothing. So she searched one of the fabricators until she found the power and switched it on. The machine hummed and clicked for what felt like years before a small screen lit up on the fabricator's side, only to display a rotating icon that Everys didn't recognize.

"What are you doing?" Quartus asked.

"These machines can create organs out of donated tissue. I want to find out what they were fabricating."

After a few tense, silent moments, the tumbling icon on the screen vanished, only to be replaced with a menu. It took some experimentation, poking at different buttons and selecting random settings, before Everys was able to call up a list of potential "constructs" the fabricator could make. Unfortunately, the listings didn't tell her much. Each one was labeled as a graft, followed by a series of indecipherable letters and numbers. She scrolled through the list but couldn't make sense of what she was seeing, so she selected one at random and opened the design. The display panel above the fabricator lit up. The image almost looked like a tree or plant, with a thin stalk splitting into multiple branches that whirled and twisted around each other, forming loops and swirls.

"What is that?" Quartus asked.

Everys glanced down at the screen. "According to this, it's a vein graft along with a microvalve right..." She studied the larger display and pointed to a small bulge where the delicate branches forked off the stem. "...there."

He frowned. "What about the other designs?"

Everys fiddled with the controls, calling up a different design. A new image formed on the display. According to the information, it was another vein graft, complete with microvalve, but the overall pattern was different. Everys frowned and called up another design, yet another vein graft, but this one was simpler, smaller, fewer branches and much more linear.

"Are those supposed to connect to an organ of some kind?" Quartus asked.

Everys shook her head. "I don't think so. It looks like the smaller veins and capillaries just dead-end and aren't intended to go anywhere."

She pulled up the first design again, studying the way the different branches twisted and turned. There was something vaguely familiar about all of this, but she couldn't quite place what it was.

"Let's keep looking," Quartus suggested quietly.

Everys nodded absently.

They moved on, checking over the lab tables. With each passing moment, Everys's anxiety grew. Where was everyone? Were there really only two guards? That didn't seem smart, but maybe it made sense. If they had finished whatever it was they were doing here, maybe they would only leave two people behind to guard the facility. Maybe. Or they could run into more. Her hand snaked into her pocket, and her fingers wrapped around her remaining pen. She'd hate to use it, but she had better be ready just in case.

They didn't find anything else of interest in the lab. At least, nothing they could understand. So they started looking in the other doors. There were three identical offices, with the same desk and two chairs plus computer terminal. The only difference was a painting that hung in one that looked vaguely familiar to Everys. But a quick check of the desks revealed that they were empty.

The next room they checked had a long table along one wall which was covered with beakers and vials and bottles. But when Everys checked the labels, she couldn't figure out what any of the chemicals were or what they might be used for.

"Everys?" Quartus called.

She stepped over to the table and froze. Various scalpels, syringes, and bottles were scattered across the table. But that wasn't what caught her attention. Instead, there were eight large, brown lumps. They had been shaped like teardrops at one point, but someone had torn them open, exposing the fibrous interior.

"What are these things?" Quartus poked at one of them gingerly.

The answer caught in her throat. She knew what they were all too well. Cold Light seed pods. They had been opened and harvested of their sap. What did they do with it?

"Let's keep looking," she whispered.

Quartus shot her a suspicious look, but thankfully, he didn't press the question. They moved on, although Everys shot an uneasy look back at the empty pods. What was going on here?

Then they checked the last room, another office of sorts. Two desks with deactivated computer terminals faced each other. But the walls caught Everys's attention. They were covered with individual sheets of paper, each one with different patterns printed on them, jumbled lines that looped and swirled and...

Everys's eyes widened as she realized what she was looking at. Toratropic runes. Dozens of them, all printed out and on display.

"Are those... Are those runes?" Quartus asked.

She nodded absently, stepping into the room to take a closer look. While she knew what they were, she didn't recognize any of them. No, that wasn't entirely true. She could identify some of the smaller components: sworls and dashes that denoted timing, duration, sequence. She used those same patterns in her own runes. But she couldn't decipher what any of them might possibly do.

Then her gaze hitched on one of the designs. Jagged lines criss-crossed each other, doubling back and running parallel, creating a pattern that almost looked like a broken hexagon. And while she didn't know what that rune would do if drawn, she knew she had seen it before, just moments earlier. She quickly tore down the drawing and rushed back to the room with the biofabricators. Thankfully, she had left the one unit on, so it didn't take her long to call up the second graft they had looked at. Once the graft design was on the larger screen, she held up the paper with the rune. Sure enough, they were almost identical. As near as Everys could tell, the only differences were due to actually crafting the rune out of veins. But why would someone want to—?

The answer hit her so strongly, she thought she had been rebuked. She stumbled, catching herself on the table.

"Everys?" Quartus rushed to her side. "What is it?"

"Blood," Everys whispered. Then she quoted one of the first lessons she had learned: "'Blood is the strongest of the inks, but it is forbidden for your people to use. It is an abomination to the Singularity who has given you the runes as a gift.'"

"What are you talking about?" Quartus asked.

The pieces were all falling into place. "They're fabricating runes out of blood vessels and then...implanting them into people. The valve opens, the vessels fill with blood, then when the rune is triggered it does... something."

"'Something?'" Quartus snorted. "Shouldn't you know what that pattern does?"

Everys wanted to glare at him, but her head was spinning. "The mage-kings used many forbidden runes that my people thought were forgotten." She looked down at the paper in her hand and dropped it. "That could easily be one of them."

"So what could those runes do?" Quartus demanded.

"I-I don't know, not for sure," Everys said. "According to the old stories, the mage-kings could make people stronger or impervious to pain or injury. They could cause them to go into a berserk rage or shoot fire or lightning from their..."

Her voice trailed off, and she quickly pulled up the last design they had looked at. Sure enough, the simpler graft design resembled a combat rune, similar to the ones she had used when defending Narius.

Her stomach twisted. What kind of monster would do something like this?

"C'mon," Quartus whispered. "Let's keep looking."

They quickly moved through the remaining rooms. Sure enough, they found an operating room. While it was clean, she thought she spotted evidence of it having been used recently. Across from that were a row of cells. Everys barely spared them a glance. They were probably as empty as the rest of the facility. She turned to keep going, but then she heard it: a muffled groan, coming from the last cell in the row. She froze in the doorway. Had she really heard that? Better check to make sure.

She hustled down the row, peeking in each cell as she went. All of them were indeed empty until she came to the last one. Someone was stretched out on a cot, tubes running into both arms, his chest heavily bandaged. His skin was pale and covered with bruises and thick, black lines, as if someone had traced every one of his arteries and veins from the inside with dark ink. The man groaned and shifted on the cot, trying to lift up his head. As he struggled, Everys got a good look at his face. With a start, she recognized him.

"Legarr?"

It couldn't be. It couldn't be her brother. But he froze at the sound of her voice.

"Ev-Everys?" His voice, while weak and raspy, was unmistakable.

"Quartus!" She searched the cell door for some way to open it.

Quartus rushed to her side. Thankfully, he figured out what she was trying to do. He gently moved her aside and set to work on the lock. Everys popped up onto her toes to look into the cell. Legarr tried to sit up, but he collapsed onto his back with a watery moan.

Then the door rattled open. She slipped through as quickly as she could, rushing to Legarr's side. She pressed a hand to his forehead, then snatched it away. He was burning up.

"Who is this?" Quartus asked from the doorway.

"My brother," she whispered. "Legarr, what happened? Who did this to you?"

"D-don't... know. Doctors all wore... masks. Didn't know... any of the guards." He struggled to sit up again, but it was clear that he was too weak. He flopped down with a groan. "Don't know... what they were trying... either. But apparently... didn't work... with me. The lines... been getting darker... since the surgery."

"They didn't say what was happening to you?"

"Not directly..." He smiled, a faint echo of his usual lazy grin. "Not big... on communication."

She studied him, trying to determine what she could. True, her family were stewards of the healing rune, but that didn't impart any special medical knowledge or wisdom. "You didn't overhear anything?"

He shook his head, a bare twitch.

Everys turned to the tubes and medical devices. "Then we're going to get you out of here. Maybe we can find someone who—"

"No!" Legarr swatted at her hands. "No... time. Don't know... what they did to me. But I do know... why."

She frowned. "What do you mean?"

"They're planning... an attack. A big one."

Her eyes widened. "Where?"

He licked his lips and coughed weakly. "The... The palace. They're gonna... attack the palace."

A chill swept through her. "When?"

"D-during the... the wedding. Narius's wedding. They... They're going to kill him."

She stared at him, stunned. For a split second, her mind couldn't process what he had just said. Then the full meaning crashed down on her.

"What? How? Who?"

Legarr struggled to speak, his hands twitching like he was groping for answers. Small hissing words slipped out of his mouth. Everys leaned in close, hoping that he would whisper some vital clue, some detail that would...

No, he wasn't whispering. He was choking!

She sat back, staring in horror as her brother convulsed on the cot. The darkness in his veins spread through the rest of his skin, consuming his flesh rapidly. His eyes widened and he gasped. His back arched and his arms stiffened. Then, with a muted gurgle, he went limp, his head lolling to one side.

Everys pressed her fingers against his neck. No pulse. No! This couldn't be happening. This couldn't—

"Legarr!" She shook him by his shoulders. "Legarr! No!"

Quartus touched her shoulder, and she shrugged off his hand. Tears streamed down her face, blurring her vision. This couldn't be happening. She had promised Papa. She had *promised!* How would she tell him? How would she tell Tilash?

"Everys, we need to go. If what he says is true, we can't stay here." Quartus's hand settled on her shoulder, squeezing it gently. "Come on. We have to do something."

She couldn't leave him. Not like this. Not with so many unanswered questions. She had to... She had to...

Narius. In danger. That thought cut through the panic. Quartus was right. They had to do something.

If only she knew what.

62

I t should have been the best day of his life. Narius had been dreaming of this day ever since he first met Innana. He should have been ecstatic.

Instead, he felt as though he was getting ready for an execution. His.

He lay in bed, staring at the ceiling. He had never noticed how cracked and chipped the plaster was before. This had been the bedchamber for dozens of kings, each one lying under the same ceiling, each one pursuing greatness the way the Perfected Warrior would expect. Each one striving and, in some cases, dying so that the Dynasty could remain strong. Each one believing that their legacy would withstand the test of time. Ignoring the cracks. Ignoring the slow decay. Ignoring how the weight of everything they had built would eventually collapse in on itself.

Narius chuckled mirthlessly. Happiest day of his life indeed.

He rolled out of bed and plodded over to the armoire which held the clothes that had been carefully selected for this day. Istragon and Jairavi had painstakingly worked out the details. Narius sighed and rested a hand against the armoire's cold wood. At this point, he was little better than a puppet. He'd wear his costume, go through the motions, spout his lines, and in the end, he'd have a new wife. And the Dynasty would be on a path to stability with the Imperium that might last for generations.

He carefully went through his morning routine, washing and shaving and preparing himself. The eyes of the world would be on him. It wouldn't do to have a single hair out of place. Then he opened the armoire and carefully dressed in his wedding outfit, modeled after formal Dynasty military uniforms. But where formal uniforms were stark and functional, this one was decidedly not. At the Dalark's insistence, there were numerous artistic embellishments added to the uniform: patches and medals that symbolized his role as the Xoniel king, as the leader of their military, of the new peace between their realms. All of the additions made it look like a rainbow had vomited on his clothing. He wouldn't look regal in that outfit. He would look like a joke. How Viara would have mocked him if he ever wore something like this in her presence!

His head snapped back at the thought of his first wife. In some ways, this day was going to be an echo of what had happened with Viara. His first marriage had been one of political convenience. He had never really expected to genuinely love her. They never really got past tolerating each other. He still had no idea what had gone wrong, but given how their relationship had started, maybe he shouldn't have been surprised.

But then Everys... Well, she'd complicated things. Yes, their marriage had simply been a way to keep the prelate mollified. And many in the Dynasty would applaud the way things turned out. Everys had turned out to be a worthy partner, helping him achieve his goals. She even enabled him to make this union with the Dalark as well. With laying the foundation for Falling Sword, pacifying the Cold Light, and brokering peace with the Imperium, he could possibly be remembered as one of the Dynasty's greatest kings. And he was still young! There was no telling how much more he might accomplish. So many in the nobility were already praising him for his shrewd marital alliances, each one taking him to new heights.

So why, as he pulled on his wedding outfit, did he feel so defeated?

Thankfully, the colorful uniform wasn't all that complicated to put on. He examined himself in the mirror, making sure that everything was straight and—

"Narius?"

He winced at the high-pitched voice. What was Innana doing here? According to Jairavi, they weren't supposed to see each other until the ceremony itself started. Innana was supposed to be in a time of secluded meditation to "align her thoughts with the relevant spirits," whatever that meant. He turned to look at her and realized she wasn't alone. A Dalark servant stood near the door, a disapproving look etched on her round face. Clearly the servant wasn't happy about this impromptu visit either.

His gaze swept over her. Her outfit, like his, was a strange pastiche of styles and colors. He recognized some hints of the classic Xoniel wedding attire, and he suspected the gauzy blue material wrapped around her waist was supposed to be an homage to the Water Bearer. But he couldn't identify what the other pieces represented. The press would probably dissect her outfit for days, maybe weeks, afterward, calling the design "bold," "innovative," and "unifying." But to him, it looked like a child had been given permission to dress herself for the first time. He winced as the thought crossed his mind. Not helpful, not now.

Thankfully, Innana didn't seem to notice his reaction. She spun. "You like it?"

"It is... just as unique as you." He fought back another wince. What was wrong with him?

Her smile broadened, and she darted forward, skidding to a halt a mere second before colliding with him. She smiled at him, her eyes alight with impish joy, and she reached out to snare his hands. "Are you ready for today? I've been waiting for this for so long."

He grimaced but managed to force it into what he hoped would pass for a genuine smile. "So have I."

And he really had. So why was he struggling so much with this?

Then he realized that she had pressed something into his right hand. He freed himself and looked down. It was a dried wildflower, its petals and leaves delicately preserved. He stared at it, unsure of what this meant. Was it a part of a Dalark tradition he wasn't aware of? Was he supposed to have brought her some small memento as well?

Tears pooled in her eyes. "You don't remember?"

Narius's jaw worked as he tried to form words, anything, that might defuse the situation.

"It's the first flower you gave me," she said. "Remember?"

He desperately wracked his memory. When would he have done this? When they met as children? Or during the summit meeting when he had kissed her the first time?

But then he remembered! It had been on the trip when they first met. During one of the negotiating sessions, his mother had taken Quartus and him to tour a park near the Dalark embassy in the Beach-head. He had snuck away and, ignoring the signs that forbade him from doing it, plucked a single bloom from some flowering bush. He had intended on giving it to his mother, but when they made it back to the embassy, he had run into Innana instead. He had given it to her, even tried to perform the correct courtly bow.

"Of course. I do," he said. "After we first met, right before my family returned to the Dynasty."

Her face lit up, and she lunged forward, kissing him on the cheek. She squeezed his hands, then stepped back. She started to say something, but her gaze slid toward the watching servant by the door. A moment of frustration flitted across her face, but it was chased away by the same childish giddiness. Innana giggled, then scurried for the door. He watched her go, followed by the servant woman. His sense of relief was chased away by overwhelming shame. Shouldn't he have remembered the flower faster? The story? Any of it? He hadn't really noticed before, but for some reason, it had become increasingly difficult to remember the details of their strange, long-distance relationship. Now, whenever he tried to remember what had attracted him to her, he struggled.

Should he really be doing this?

The question caught him by surprise. Obviously he had to. It was a matter of duty. Of honor. Of strengthening the Dynasty so it could continue in its grand march through history. No matter how his feelings may have changed, he really didn't have a choice. It was what needed to be done.

No matter how empty that thought left him.

63

War raged inside Everys's mind. Part of her shrieked that they shouldn't have left Legarr in the lab. But what choice did they have? Plus, there was the information he had shared. An attack on the palace, targeting Narius, by unknown forces? Exhaustion dragged on her. She had been up for so long, she wasn't even sure what day it was or what she had done the day before.

But out of the chaotic, tumbling thoughts, one kept rising to the forefront: Narius was in danger. They had to do something.

But what?

Her first reaction had been to try to contact Tormod. The spymaster had set them on this course, after all. But he hadn't left any way to contact him. A flash of irritation temporarily chased away the exhaustion. Why would he have sent them into that underground lab, knowing that something was going on, and not have a way for her to report back?

But obsessing about it now wouldn't do anything to save Narius from whatever was about to attack him.

She looked across the table at Quartus. After retreating from the hidden lab, they had found a small restaurant to hide in, get something to eat, and plan their next steps. Quartus's goons had taken the two guards to some undisclosed location to make sure they couldn't contact their superiors, so the two of them were alone. Quartus looked as rattled as she felt.

"What do we do now?" Everys asked.

Quartus shrugged, his gaze vague and unfocused. "No idea."

"But we are going to do something, right?" Everys leaned forward, trying to press home the point.

That seemed to snap him out of his reverie. "I suppose we have to, don't we?"

Everys gaped at him. "Yes! We do!"

He scowled. "Look, the irony of this situation isn't lost on me. The brother Narius banished and his second wife, uncovering a threat against him. You're asking what do we do, but the better question is what *can* we do? Call the constabulary? Storm the palace gates? There's a reason why Narius has some of the best soldiers in the Dynasty guarding him. He'll be fine. You'll see."

But he wouldn't. Everys knew that clearly. The more she thought about what she had seen in that lab, the more certain she was. Someone had been crafting new runes that did Singularity-knew-what, then implanting them in people. She shuddered at the thought. While the ancient texts didn't say anything specifically about this, she knew how the scriveners would react if they ever learned of it. Abominations. Desecrating a precious gift. And using blood as ink? Whatever those runes would do, it would be difficult to counter, especially by soldiers who didn't know what they were dealing with.

She shook her head. "No. We need to do something. We have to at least warn him."

Quartus sighed and nodded. "I suppose that is true. Let me try to contact some of my former guards. Perhaps they can get a message to Zar or even Narius."

He slid out of his chair and stepped over to a public comm terminal.

Everys closed her eyes and massaged her temples, trying to unwind the knot that was twisting behind her eyes. She wanted to collapse, but she shook her head, trying to focus. Narius. She had to save him. She had to. Because if something happened to him, if he were injured or even... No! She couldn't accept that. Wouldn't. They'd find a way. They had to.

Quartus came back to the table, a strange look on his face. He sat down, staring at an undefined spot on the table's surface. Then he blinked and looked up, his features changing into a frown. "I wasn't able to get in contact with any of my former guards."

"That's not that much of a surprise," Everys said. "You were banished, after all."

He shook his head. "No, that's not it. I didn't try to contact them directly. I called someone who could pass a message along. And she said my entire team had been temporarily reassigned. Not only that, your guards got reassigned as well. And so were Narius's."

Ice sluiced through Everys's veins. "You mean..."

Quartus nodded. "That's awfully convenient for whoever is going to attack the palace, don't you think?"

Everys burst out of her chair and headed for the door. Before she could make it, though, Quartus grabbed her arm and spun her around.

"What are you going to do?" he asked.

"I-I don't know. Something! I'll stand at the front gate and demand to be let in. I'll see if I can't contact one of the guests and see if they can help. I'll... I'll..." A sob shuddered through her chest, and she swallowed, trying to keep it together.

Quartus pulled her into a tight hug. She jerked, surprised at the sudden move. Part of her recognized what he was trying to do. But no, she didn't want this. Not from him. Not given their past. She shoved him away.

"There has to be something we can do," she muttered. "Some way that we can get in without being noticed. How did you slip away for your... trysts?"

He arched a brow. "Trysts, eh? Well, I usually had to bribe a few of my guards to get them to look the other way while I slipped out the main gate. I don't think that will work for us this time."

No, it wouldn't. "There aren't any secret ways in? Hidden passages? Tunnels?"

He shrugged. "Believe me, if there was a back door, I'd know about it."

Her eyes widened. Actually, no, he wouldn't. There was a way into the palace that not even the guards would know about. Only Narius. And her.

"Do you have the contact information for the royal archivist?"

"That fool? Why would you—"

"Just call him!"

Quartus went back to the public comm and tapped in a code. He waited a few moments, then raised it to his mouth. "Archivist Turron? This is Prince Quartus. I'm here with former Queen Everys and—"

Everys snatched the comm out of his hand. "Turron, is it? I need to know where the secret entrances to the royal archives are in Bastion and how to open them. It's an emergency."

Someone spluttered on the other end of the signal before he could speak again. When he did, his voice sounded hollow and thin. "That's ridiculous! I don't have to tell you. You shouldn't even know about that!"

"But I do. And I also know what's down there."

"So does the entire Dynasty, thanks to you!" he shot back.

"True, but I don't think anyone has mentioned the Principalities yet, have they? Or the *ur-keleshen*? As far as everyone in the Dynasty still knows, all of those dangerous Siporan artifacts were destroyed four hundred years ago. Do you think they'd be so understanding if they learned the truth?"

Turron went silent on the other end. "You wouldn't dare."

"Oh, but I would. And if you don't tell me what I want to know right now, I'm going to make sure that everyone knows who you are too."

He spluttered on the other end, then sighed. "Fine. Where are you right now?"

"In a restaurant in Defector's Wrath," she said. Smudges, why didn't she pay attention to the name?

"There's an entrance to the archives in Defector's Wrath. Do you know the old armory in the Hollows?"

She had no idea, but she could find it. She *would* find it. "Go on."

"If you go into the prelate's chamber, there's a rack with the ceremonial weapons. Switch the Spear with the Sword, and it'll open a door to a tunnel. There's a cart you can ride to the Archive itself."

"Thank you." She handed the comm back to Quartus.

He stared at her, then chuckled. "You are an amazing woman."

She brushed aside the compliment. "No time for that now. Let's get going."

She just hoped they weren't too late.

64

Unfortunately, the costume proved worse than Narius had anticipated.

It wasn't that the outfit was uncomfortable. No, the palace tailors would never stand for that. The clothing was soft and supple enough that he could have fallen asleep in them if he wanted. But he suspected he'd still see the riot of colors through his closed eyes.

He paced a tight circle in an antechamber down the hall from the main ballroom. The ceremony should have already begun. His isolation was, again, a compromise between the prelate and Jairavi. In a Dalark ceremony, the bride and groom weren't supposed to even participate. Their proxies would negotiate the terms of the marriage, nailing down all the details regarding family loyalties and obligations, financial considerations, and the rest. The couple wouldn't actually appear until the post-wedding feast, when the guests were supposed to act like they had been married all along. In the end, they had decided that Paine and Jairavi would conduct abbreviated negotiations to satisfy Dalark expectations. Once those were completed, Innana and Narius would be summoned to complete a shortened Xoniel ritual. Jairavi had grudgingly agreed, but he'd insisted that during the negotiations, Innana and Narius remained separate and isolated.

Narius glared at the walls, the furniture, his impatience rising. How long could these negotiations take? By his estimation, he had been trapped inside this room for at least two hours. He was half-tempted to storm out of the room, down to the ballroom, and take over for Paine. But he knew he couldn't; if he did, the Dalark would likely condemn his behavior as a bad omen for the marriage and call an end to it all. Then again, maybe that wouldn't be such a bad thing.

There was a quiet knock at the door. Narius turned to face the door, and Duke Brencis slipped inside.

"Your Strength, are you ready?" he asked.

Narius nodded. Brencis stepped out of the way with a sweeping motion, indicating for him to take the lead. Narius stepped out of the room, then stopped. Twenty Dynasty soldiers stood in two straight lines along either wall. He looked up and down the wall and realized he didn't recognize any of them. It still rankled that Jairavi had insisted on the removal of Zar and the rest of the guards. It would have been nice to have some familiar faces walking with him.

Narius marched to the doors of the ballroom and waited. The timing had to be perfect. Two of the soldiers jogged up to the doors, getting ready to open them when the time came.

A low gong crashed inside the ballroom. This was it. The signal. The soldiers hauled the doors open. Narius squared his shoulders and stepped through.

The guests were seated in wedge-shaped sections, all facing a center ring. As Narius stepped into the room, Innana entered on the other side. Narius blew out a shaky breath and started toward the center, trying to match his gait to his future wife's. Again, the timing had to be exact, with both of them reaching the prelate at the exact same time.

As he walked down the aisle, he studied the people he passed. All of them were from Dalark. Innana would walk through the Dynasty guests. Some sort of symbolism, probably. He caught sight of Emperor Devroshan to his left. The Dalark Emperor had arrived the day before, but due to his bizarre insistence on ritual purity, he had refused to meet with Narius before the wedding. He took a moment to size up his soon-to-be father-in-law. The last time he had seen the Dalark Emperor, Narius had been a young boy. Devroshan had towered over him and seemed like a god. Now, though, Narius could clearly see the man. Older. Worn out. Fragile. The years had not been kind.

Standing next to Devroshan was Jairavi. Or could he call him Tirigian finally? However he identified himself, the Dalark crown prince looked bored, almost half-asleep. When Narius caught his gaze, Tirigian had the audacity to roll his eyes and flick his hand toward him, as if shooing him. Narius ground his teeth. The least he could do was pretend to be interested.

Supreme Prelate Istragon stood in the center of the ballroom, dressed in his finest robes, his face split by a cheesy grin. Across the way, in the front row, stood his council of advisers. Masruq and his wife were practically beaming. There was an empty space where Brencis likely sat before going to get him. Painc sat at the end of the row, his expression dour. At least one person seemed to mirror how he felt.

And then he stood face-to-face with Innana. Somehow, her outfit had become even more ludicrous since she'd snuck into his room earlier. But she beamed with such excitement, such energy, such enthusiasm, that he couldn't help but return the smile with a nervous chuckle.

"For the good of the Dynasty," he whispered to himself, and he hoped that he actually meant it.

This had taken too long already.

Oh, things had been going smoothly enough. The archivist hadn't lied to them. They'd found the entrance in the abandoned armory, a motorized cart waiting to take them to the archives. But even as they zipped through the darkened tunnel to the palace, Everys couldn't shake the feeling that they were too late. The wedding had to have started already. For all she knew, Narius and Innana were already dead.

"Can't this thing go any faster?" she muttered.

Quartus, who sat at the cart's simple controls, shook his head. "Sorry, but no. I've opened the throttle all the way. There's nothing more that we can do other than ride."

Everys curled her fingers into fists, wanting to hit something, someone, anything. Her fingernails dug into her palms, the pain a welcome relief. Visions of Narius, sprawled on the ballroom floor, his wedding attire stained with blood, kept assaulting her mind. She didn't know what...

The cart tipped as it rounded a corner, and light spilled over them, faint at first but growing brighter. Everys sat up straighter, leaned forward to get a better look.

And then the cart rolled through an archway and slowed to a halt in a small stone room, one with no decoration or indication of where they were. Aside from the tunnel they had just come out of, the only exit was a thick wooden door on the far wall. Quartus shut down the cart as Everys clambered out. She jogged over to the door and gave it an experimental tug. It took a little bit of effort, but thankfully, it wasn't locked or latched. Without waiting for Quartus, Everys dashed through.

Yes! Shelves and displays stretched out in front of them. They had made it. She raced past the rows of artifacts and stolen treasures.

Then she emerged into the center of the room where the five Principalities stood their quiet sentinel. Even though she knew they were here, seeing them again sent a quiet jolt through her. She was about to rush into combat with people who had created some sort of new toratropic runes, and she barely knew anything about combat runes or how to counter them. Maybe she should even the odds.

She stepped over to the rack of *ur-keleshens*, thankful that they were still here. According to the old stories, those blades, even in unskilled hands, were almost unstoppable thanks to the runes carved into their sides. Armed with one of those swords, she would be able to face any threat, protect Narius, save him. She reached out, her fingers hovering over the hilt. All she had to do was take it.

But no. Even as she considered the possibility, she knew she couldn't do it. These swords had been the beginning of her people's downfall. Even if toratropic runes were being misused, fighting that evil with older evil wasn't the right way to proceed. She turned back to look at the Principalities. Even here, tucked away and forgotten in an ancient basement, there was still a presence here, lingering in the air, drawing her in and closer. She stepped into the middle of the pillars, turning a slow circle to look at each of them in turn. Unlike the runes that they had found in the lab, these radiated peace. Calm. Certainty. She took a deep breath, drawing the presence that seemed to hover over the pillars into herself. She didn't know what was going to happen. She couldn't. But she knew that she wasn't going into this battle alone.

Once Quartus caught up with her, Everys led the way through the displays, past where the Cold Light's Hearth once rested, and to the steps the led up to the garden entrance. With a ponderous groan, the hidden mechanisms wrenched the door open, allowing bright sunlight to pour down the stairs. As soon as the opening was wide enough, Everys squeezed through and charged for the palace. Hopefully she wasn't too late.

65

Would this ceremony ever end?

By Narius's estimation, the prelate had been droning on for at least fifteen minutes, extolling the virtues of the Perfected Warrior and the Water Bearer, encouraging the new royal couple to be "exemplars of that divine ideal," whatever that meant. Once again, Narius wondered if the prelate actually believed the words he was spewing. He knew the Dynasty's subjects held to their own beliefs and traditions, and the Dynasty's citizens, well... most of them held on to the Perfected Warrior and his Armory so they could use the different weapons and armors as ways to curse. Everything about this day was so pointless, from the enforced isolation to the prattling about divine weapons exemplifying sought attributes, it was all worthless.

Well, maybe not all of it. Narius's mind drifted to Everys, to what she had been able to do through her toratropic runes. That had been real, and Everys had said that the power for the runes came from the Singularity. Was it real? The runes certainly indicated that it was. He had seen Everys do incredible things with them. But if the Singularity was real, then why did it... he allow the Dynasty to overthrow the Ascendancy the way it did? The prelate would have said that it was because the Warrior was stronger than the Singularity, but that couldn't possibly be true. Narius pursed his lips. He wished Everys was still around. Maybe she could have answered some of his questions. Maybe she could have...

The prelate cleared his throat.

Narius snapped his attention back to what was happening. The prelate looked at him expectantly. Innana blushed a bright red next to him.

"Wh-what?" he asked.

Soft chuckling rippled through the assembled crowd. Paine's eyes narrowed at him, and he mouthed something, but Narius couldn't make out what.

"I said, 'Will Your Strength pledge to embody the ideals of the Warrior, not only for the good of the Dynasty you rule, but for the wife, your Blessed, that you now protect?'" The prelate's tone was strained, clearly annoyed.

A pit opened in Narius's heart. He should have known they had reached this part, the traditional vow that would join them together as husband and wife. This was the moment. This was the time. This was what historians would talk about in years to come, the moment when Xoniel and Dalark's long-standing feud came to an end. And he hadn't been paying attention.

He swallowed, then coughed, trying to get his voice to cooperate. He knew what he had to say. It wasn't supposed to be scripted, but a genuine pledge of loyalty, of love, of fidelity. This had been Innana's request, that when he offered these words, they would invoke his deepest values and beliefs. He had been mulling over these words for the last few days, trying to craft just the right sentiment with the correct emotional heft. But now that he was there, in the moment, he couldn't speak them. He couldn't say anything. Because he realized that whatever he said to Innana would be a lie. Whatever he said would be meaningless because the wrong woman stood next to him.

The prelate cleared his throat again and nodded. Narius could read the prompting in the older man's eyes. He sighed. What could he do? He could either lie by saying something hollow and meaningless, or he could try to live up to his honor and be the man he wanted to be by speaking the truth, no matter how hurtful it was going to be. His people, his advisers, history all demanded he respond one way. His heart screamed for him to respond the other. And in the midst of that war, Narius knew. He knew what he had to say. He knew what he had to do.

He turned to Innana and took her hands into his. Her smile brightened, relief flickering across her face.

"Innana," he said. "I—"

"Stop!"

The shout was punctuated by a slamming door and chased by anxious whispers. Someone had burst through the garden doors. Narius whirled around to see who it was, but the crowd jumped to their feet, pushing and shoving each other to get a better view themselves. Brencis shouted some sort of command for the soldiers, but apparently they weren't moving fast enough because the intruder made it through the crowd.

His eyes widened. "Everys?"

She looked like she hadn't slept since the state dinner. Her hair was unkempt and wild, her face was covered with grime and sweat, and her eyes had a haunted look to them.

She had never looked so radiant.

But then he spotted someone following in her wake, and his stomach curdled. "Quartus?"

His brother skidded to a halt behind Everys and grimaced.

Everys didn't seem to care. She strode forward, reaching into her pocket.

"What is the meaning of this?" the prelate thundered.

"We don't have time for this." Everys crossed the distance. "Narius, we have to get you out of here. You're in danger." Her gaze flicked toward Innana. "You both are."

"Is this..." Innana's voice was thready, breathless. "Is this her? Is this Viara?"

Everys glared at her. "Introductions will have to wait. We have—"

Someone in the back of the room screamed, and the crowd parted. One of the soldiers who had escorted Narius into the throne room stumbled forward, clutching at his stomach. Dark liquid exploded from his mouth, and he groaned.

"Inkstains!" Everys whipped something out of her pocket and snapped it in half.

A pungent, familiar aroma filled the room. Everys dropped to her knees, her hand tracing patterns on the stone floor. Narius immediately knew what she was doing. The fact that she was willing to do so in front of the prelate, the advisers, and everyone else told him the threat was real. He quickly stepped forward, interposing himself between Innana, Everys, and the convulsing soldier.

The man's head snapped back and his mouth ripped open. Green light flashed across his temples, then snaked down his neck to beneath his shirt, which smoldered, then disintegrated, revealing jagged patterns glowing just underneath his skin. Toratropic runes. The man's body swelled, his chest and arms thickening while jagged claws erupted from his fingers. Within just a few seconds, the man sagged forward, but then his head snapped up and murder shone in his bloodshot eyes.

The crowd screamed and scattered, revealing that other soldiers had undergone similar transformations. They snarled and growled, baring their teeth and behaving like little more than animals.

Then Brencis appeared at his side, snaring his arm. "Your Strength, come with me immediately! We have to get you to safety."

Narius shook his head, looking around for a weapon, anything he could use to protect himself and Innana. "Get the guests out of here first! Everys?"

"Almost got it..."

"Your Strength, now!"

The first soldier bellowed and charged at them. Innana shrieked, but the soldier slammed into an invisible wall and ricocheted off. Narius looked down at Everys, who had an open hand pressed into the middle of a glowing rune. She looked up at him. While she may have looked tired and maybe a little frightened, Narius recognized the determination burning in her eyes.

"I'll be fine. Go," she said.

Brencis tugged on his arm and pulled him and Innana back toward one of the exits. Narius allowed himself to be pulled away, but he kept his gaze locked on Everys, who drew more runes on the ground around her. Much to Narius's surprise, Quartus rushed to her side, brandishing a weapon—where did he even get that?—and opened fire on the charging monster. The assembled guests screamed and hurried around the room, but apparently they couldn't find a way out. Thankfully, though, two soldiers who hadn't been transformed stood near an open door, which Brencis steered them toward.

"You know what to do," Brencis shouted as they passed.

The soldiers nodded, and as soon as Brencis had pulled them through the door, they slammed it shut. Narius twisted around as they did so he could catch one last glimpse of Everys. She didn't look up as she continued drawing on the floor, and he hoped that wouldn't be the last time he saw her.

Another transformed soldier slammed into the barrier. The rune next to Everys flared brighter, and she could see the ink burning away rapidly. If she wanted the rune to keep protecting them, she'd have to touch it up soon, but she only had so much ink. And a barrier was defensive. Right now, they needed offense.

"Not to criticize, but can you scribble any faster?" Quartus opened fire on the nearest monster, but the flechettes couldn't penetrate the creature's skin. The monster roared in anger and looked ready to charge them again.

Everys groaned and looked at the half-completed runes around her. Every time she started sketching out an idea on how to stop the attack, she realized it wouldn't work. She had no idea what to do. People screamed around them, their shrieks mixing with roars and growls. The other creatures must have been attacking the guests. Thankfully, only two or three seemed focused on them, but that would have to change.

She looked up at one of the transformed soldiers. She could see the rune-veins burning brightly beneath his skin. And it wasn't just one. From what she had seen, there were at least three or four in each soldier, each one pulsing and burning at a different rhythm. It made a certain amount of sense. From what she had learned from her teachers, creating an abomination like this was entirely possible using toratropic magic, but the problem was that the transformation could only last as long as the ink did. Once the ink burned away, the victim should revert to their usual form. But because these runes were made out of veins, they could constantly refill with the victims' own blood, prolonging their attack. Granted, they'd run out of blood eventually, but apparently that wasn't going to happen anytime soon.

"Everys! Today!" Quartus thundered.

Everys winced. Right. There'd be plenty of time to figure out how this all worked if they survived. So how could she make that happen?

Another soldier slammed into her protective rune, but instead of bouncing off, he pressed up against it, clawing and slathering. The rune next to her flared even brighter. It would give out any second, and it wasn't doing anything to protect the other people trapped in the ballroom with her. If only there was some way to help all of them all at once, some way to...

Her eyes widened. She couldn't. But she knew someone who could. And she knew just the right runes for the job.

She dabbed the rest of her ink onto her finger, and rather than draw on the floor, she drew the runes on her arm. She knew them well enough; they were the same runes that every Siporan was supposed to trace on their doorframes—the ones used during Downcasting, the same runes that the scriveners had drawn on their arms in that picture she saw in the book she found in Tall Reach's shade. The runes that invited the presence of the Singularity.

Then, as quickly as she could, she sketched out the runes for healing. For sleep. For peace of mind. All of these in a row up her left arm, stitched together by a single bold line she hoped would mesh them all together. Then, taking a deep breath, she activated the rune of invitation.

At first, nothing happened, and she was sure she had wasted the last of her ink. But then, after a heartbeat, all of the runes on her arm lit up with the brilliance of the sun. Heat coursed up her arm into her chest, where it built in intensity but strangely, not in pain. Quartus shouted in surprise, but his voice was soon drowned out by the sound of rushing winds, surging waters, the roar of the ground being split open beneath her feet.

And under it all, a gentle whisper that caused her heart to soar.

A wave of pure light burst from her chest, slicing through the people in the room. The soldier trying to get through the barrier was knocked backward. The other monsters crumpled. The panicking people stilled, the injured stopped crying out, and soon, calm settled on the ballroom. Another wave flowed out of her, rippling across the gathered people. More of them collapsed as they drifted off into a peaceful slumber.

And then a third wave crested, blowing across the room. Quartus gasped, but Everys couldn't see why. Her head had fallen backward, staring up at the ceiling. But instead of seeing the room, she saw the light pouring through it, light that couldn't be contained or kept out, light that burned away shadows and sickness, light that was both intolerably bright and soothing as a gentle kiss. And it all funneled into her, flowing out in those brilliant, overwhelming waves that threatened to carry her away.

But then the sensation faded. The light dimmed. And Everys felt all of her strength drain out of her. She fell to her knees with a shuddering gasp.

"Everys... What did you do?" Quartus whispered.

She opened her eyes and looked around. The room had gone still, everyone lying on the floor, sleeping. She got up and stepped gingerly through the fallen. Many of them wore torn clothing, obviously ripped during struggles with the transformed soldiers, but it didn't look like any of them were injured any longer. And the soldiers? They were unconscious as well. While they still bore the marks of their transformation, those were starting to fade as they reverted to their original form.

She breathed out a sigh of relief. It was over. It was—

"Open fire!"

The shout jerked her around. Soldiers had appeared in the balconies overlooking the ballroom, each one armed with a large rifle. Everys gaped at them, but Quartus snared her arm and dragged her out of the line of fire. Flechettes sliced through the sleeping guests, the fallen soldiers, everyone. Everys screamed and covered her head as Quartus dragged her through the room and underneath the balcony. The sleeping people's bodies jerked, blood spreading across their chests, their arms, their legs. One of them caught her attention, an older man dressed in robes that marked him as Dalark. Was that the Emperor?

"Now what?" Quartus shouted.

Everys checked her pen. Still a little bit of ink left in it. Just enough, hopefully. With a shaking finger, she sketched out a smoke rune on the floor and activated it. A column of smoke erupted from the floor, quickly rolling through the room and obscuring the fallen guests. The soldiers shouted in surprise as they continued to shoot, but soon, the smoke billowed up toward the ceiling. Then she drew a shattering rune on a wall and activated the spell. The wall crumbled, creating a hole into the servant's kitchen. Quartus didn't waste any time, pushing her through before following.

"This doesn't make any sense!" Everys said. "Why would they start shooting now? Unless..."

Quartus nodded. "They're part of the plot."

Everys's eyes widened. The last she had seen Narius, he was being pulled out of the room by Duke Brencis. Was he even safe?

She picked herself off the floor and checked her ink. Nothing left. And she didn't have any pens either. But that didn't matter. Narius needed her. Ink or no ink, runes or no runes, she was going to help him. No matter what.

66

N arius stumbled as he rushed into the throne room. Innana almost slammed into him from behind. Brencis hurried inside and pushed the door shut.

"Are you okay?" Narius asked Innana.

She gulped several times, looking as though she might start bawling at any moment. Narius couldn't blame her. In the distance, he heard the chatter of weapon fire. Reinforcements? Other attackers? He had no way of knowing.

Brencis paced next to the doors, his hands pressed against his temples. He looked sick, stricken. Narius couldn't really blame him. While he wasn't personally tasked with palace security, technically the royal guard fell under his purview. But nobody would have expected him to predict or prevent this attack. It wasn't his fault that Prince Tirigian had objected to the royal guards. But the duke appeared to be on the verge of collapse.

"Duke! Status!" Narius tried to inject some steel into his words, hoping that the order would snap Brencis out of it.

Instead, the duke shot a glare at him and kept pacing.

Narius frowned. What was going on? "Duke Brencis, report!"

"I heard you the first time, Narius," Brencis snapped. "And you can stop posturing. No one is impressed."

Narius gaped at him. "Excuse me?"

"Oh, you're so good at playing soldier, aren't you, boy? You say all the right words, make all the pretty speeches, look so handsome even in that ridiculous get-up. But you and I both know the real truth: you are not a true Xoniel king."

Heat flashed across Narius's face. He took a step forward, but he realized that Brencis had a gun pointed at his chest.

"Here you've claimed that you're going to bring the Dynasty into a glorious future, but you forget what made us great in the first place. You're supposed to exemplify the Perfected Warrior's traits, but what do you do instead? Divert military funding into secret projects. Seek peace with rebels you should have burned to the ground! And to top it all off, first you married the scribbler, and now, you marry this idiot?"

Innana sobbed. Or maybe it was an indignant gasp. Narius couldn't be sure. Instead, he focused on the weapon. He was too far away from Brencis to try to disarm him—the duke would shoot before he could close the distance. Calling for help wasn't an option either. Not only was it unlikely that anyone would hear them, but there was no guarantee that if someone did, they would be willing to help. And Brencis would still shoot him and possibly Innana as well. Best to keep him talking.

"So this is what? A coup?" he asked.

Brencis smiled thinly. "Don't make it sound so implausible. The newly married king and his insipid bride—oh, shut up, Innana!—are killed in a terrorist attack. In the resulting chaos, the Dynasty needs a firm leader to take the crown, someone with the experience necessary to keep things secure and level."

"You?" Narius couldn't quite keep the sarcasm from his voice.

"And why not? My family is pure Hinaen, descended from the ancient kings, just like yours. Unlike you, I do more than just pay lip-service to the Warrior. I live out his ideals. Oh, there will be chaos. There will be blame thrown around. But when the dust settles and the smoke clears, the people will be grateful to finally have a true king on the throne once again." He clenched his jaw. "But you were supposed to die in the ballroom, a victim of the chaos, not back here. If it wasn't for the interference of your scribbler witch and your brother, the plan would have been completely successful."

Narius's heart skipped a beat. Everys! Was she still all right? For a moment, he sucked in a breath and hoped that her deity would somehow protect her, even if he died in this room.

"But then, this is more fitting, isn't it? The Xoniel way. 'When you face your enemies, let them know it was you that wielded the knife that delivered the killing blow and do not flinch from the honor.'" Brencis sneered. "That's a quote from the Warrior's Counsel, in case you forgot."

Narius stiffened at the verbal jab. He had recognized the quote.

"Goodbye, Narius. I promise that when I'm done, the Dynasty will be free of your pathetic—"

The door burst open, and someone rushed inside. Brencis whirled around and fired. Someone grunted and tumbled to the ground. Narius froze, surprised at how quickly it all happened, but then leapt forward for the gun. Maybe he could...

Brencis whipped back around and fired. Pain sliced through Narius's shoulder, his chest, and he stumbled to the ground. Innana screamed as Brencis kept firing, diving for cover behind one of the pillars. And then someone was at his side. He tried to speak, to urge them to get to cover, but he couldn't talk. The words wouldn't come out. Whoever it was rolled him over onto his back, sending burning knives slicing through his heart. He could feel the strength leaking out of him as he landed hard, facing the ceiling, staring at...

Everys.

No, no, no! Not like this! Not like this!

Everys's hands hovered over Narius's wounded chest. Dark circles spread across his shirt, and already his skin was pale and cold. He mouthed something at her, but no sound came out. Tears stung her eyes as she tried desperately to think of what she could do in this situation. No ink! She didn't have anything to draw the rune except... except...

Her gaze landed on the pool of blood that slowly spread across the floor. Blood was the most powerful ink. And it wouldn't be wrong to use it to save Narius's life, would it?

Before she could come to a decision, though, Brencis came around the corner, muttering curses. But when he saw Everys, his scowl twisted into a feral grin.

"Lost one, but I found the one I really wanted to kill." He leveled the gun on Everys. "When we were putting together this operation, I was disappointed that we wouldn't be able to eliminate you as well. I'm so glad you graced the king's wedding with your presence. Goodbye, Everys."

Everys braced herself for the shot, but it never came. Instead, Brencis's face twisted into a rictus of agony as a rune blazed into existence on his right temple. His mouth tore open in a silent scream, and he dropped the gun, clawing at the rune.

"But why? Don't stop me now, we have the opportunity to—" He doubled over, almost falling to his knees. "Very well."

The light at his temple faded, and Brencis glared at her. "You're lucky. He wants to spare you. And..." He winced as the rune flared to life again. "...yes, yes. Enjoy your reprieve, Everys. It won't last long."

Brencis scooped up the weapon and darted out of the throne room.

Everys whirled to Narius. His features had gone slack, his skin ashen. She frantically checked his wrist, his neck, for a pulse. It was there, but barely.

"Help! Someone help!" Her throat was raw, and probably nobody could hear her.

Then someone stumbled around one of the pillars. Quartus clutched at his shoulder, but when he saw Narius, his eyes widened, and he rushed to his brother's side, falling to the floor. "Narius! Broken Sword, don't you dare die on us!"

Everys got out of the way as Quartus set to work, ripping open Narius's shirt and tearing the fabric into makeshift bandages. Then Innana hurried up to the scene. She gasped, then rushed for the doors, shouting for help.

"If you have any tricks up your sleeve, now would be the time," Quartus whispered. "It looks like Brencis hit an artery. He's not going to last much longer."

Everys sobbed and looked down at the pooled blood. Yes, she knew she could use it to save his life, but she had never violated that prohibition before. But when she looked at Narius, saw how close he hovered over death, what else could she do? She knew she would be rebuked for using blood as ink, but in that moment, watching Narius's life spill away, she knew it would be worth it. How else could he survive? And he needed to survive. The Dynasty needed him. It needed him a whole lot more than it needed her.

"Get Innana to safety," Everys said. "I'll do what I can."

Quartus studied her face, then nodded grimly. He moved quickly, snaring Innana's hand. The Dalark princess screamed and cried as Quartus dragged her out of the room. As soon as they were gone, Everys knelt next to Narius. She dipped a shaking finger in the blood and set to work. While she wanted to hurry, she knew she couldn't. She had to keep her lines and patterns precise. If the rebuke for doing this was going to be as bad as she suspected, she wanted to get it right the first time. It felt like the time it took her to draw the rune stretched into an eternity, but then it was ready. She took a shuddering breath and activated the magic.

The lines blazed with red light, and Narius gasped, his back arching. Color spread through his body, and the wounds in his chest knit themselves together again. Narius groaned and pushed himself up to sitting. He looked around the room, at the blood on the floor, before his gaze landed on Everys.

"Everys?" His voice was hoarse. "What did... What did you..."

Fire blossomed inside her chest, searing through her and burning into her arms and legs. She convulsed, and a scream tore out of her throat. She had never been rebuked this strong before. The pain mounted, wracking her body. Gray nibbled at the corner of her vision, and the last thing she heard was Narius shouting her name as she collapsed into darkness.

67

V oices buzzed around her.

"There are troops massing in the Beachhead..."

Who was that? Who was talking? Why was his voice so muffled?

"And an uptick in graffiti in the outlying cities and rumors of unrest in Maotoa..."

She didn't know that voice either.

"Thank you, gentlemen."

Her heart thudded heavily. She knew that voice. Narius!

Her eyes snapped open, and she sat up in bed. It only took her an instant to realize that she was in the queen's quarters in the palace. But the room was sadly empty, devoid of any personal touches, almost like a hotel room rather than a person's bedroom. No, wait, there was some medical equipment standing next to her bed like silent guards. Then her gaze landed on Trule, who stood near the bedroom door. Everys smiled, although the effort seemed to tire her out immensely.

Trule gasped and threw open the door. "She's awake! Get the doctor!"

Then Trule rushed to the bedside and threw her arms around Everys, hugging her tight. "We were so worried about you, Blessed. We thought you would never wake up!"

Never wake up? What had happened? Why was she here? And who was "we?"

Two women in medical uniforms jogged into the bedroom. They smiled when they saw her.

"Ma'am, how are you feeling?"

That was a good question. As far as she could tell, she felt fine. Tired, but fine. But she also knew that she shouldn't be feeling that way, but she couldn't quite remember why. Was that because of... The rebuke? Yes! She had been rebuked for... Her last clear memory was trying to save Narius in the throne room, his blood pooling on the floor beneath him, soaking into her clothing and...

"Narius?" She tried to get out of bed. "Narius?"

The doctor put a hand on her shoulder and gently pushed her back into the bed. "He's here, and he can see you soon enough. But I want to check you over first, all right? You gave us quite the scare. How are you feeling?"

Everys shrugged. "How long was I asleep?"

The doctor snared her wrist. "Five days. We couldn't determine a medical reason for your condition. We wanted to move you to a hospital for further tests and observation, but the king wouldn't allow it."

Oh? She looked toward the door, and the doctor chuckled.

"All in due time, ma'am. All right?"

Everys sighed and sat back on the bed. The doctor and her assistant set to work, taking her vitals, barraging her with questions. Everys answered them as honestly as she could, but as they talked, more of her memories filtered back. Narius injured. Drawing the rune. The rebuke. That had to be why she had been unconscious for so long. So she answered as vaguely as she could. The doctor appeared frustrated by her answers, but after a few minutes of poking and prodding her, she finally nodded.

"Well, I'm going to prescribe a little more bedrest before you try getting back on your feet. We want to make sure you're fully recovered from whatever trauma caused your condition. But I suppose it wouldn't hurt for you to have a visitor or two right now."

Everys looked over to the bedroom door and there he was. Narius looked like he hadn't slept for days, and stubble lined his jaw. But when he smiled at her, warmth spread through her chest, and suddenly, she felt a whole lot better.

The doctor and her assistant stepped out of the room, followed by Trule. Narius crossed over to the bed so slowly that Everys wanted to scream. She wanted him to be there, by her side, his arms around her. She wanted to jump out of the bed and meet him halfway.

"Are you okay?" she asked.

"Thanks to you, yes. Just some minor internal injuries and some bruising," he said. "And they don't suspect anything. Quartus can be a very convincing liar. It came in handy in this case."

She laughed, frustrated at how weak her voice sounded.

"The more important question is, are you okay?" he asked.

Everys nodded. "I think so. But what's happened?"

Narius sighed and sat down on the edge of the bed. So close to her, but not close enough. "Quite a bit. We're still trying to piece together the sequence of events."

"Duke Brencis?"

His face turned stony. "Escaped in the confusion. He has much to answer for. Quartus told me what you did to protect the guests, but Brencis's troops shot and killed many of them anyway. And that includes Emperor Devroshan."

That's right. She remembered seeing him in the ballroom. "Innan a..."

"No, she's fine. Very grateful to you."

Everys's stomach soured. "Is she still here?"

Narius blew out a long breath. "No. She and the rest of the Dalark left almost immediately. Prince Tirigian managed to escape the carnage, and as near as we can tell, he'll be the next Emperor. Unfortunately, he seems uninterested in pursuing any sort of peace, temporary or otherwise. His troops are massing in the Beachhead."

Her heart fell. "I'm sorry."

"I am too. Tirigian is claiming that the wedding was an ambush to decapitate their leadership using special Siporan commandos."

"That's ridiculous. They tried to kill you too!"

"That's not what he's telling the Dalark. War very well may be inevitable."

"What else has been happening?"

He sighed and ran a hand through his hair. "Now's not the time to—"

"You can't go in there!"

Trule's shout caused Everys to jump, but the doors to the room banged open, and Supreme Prelate Istragon stormed in, flanked by two of his guards. Trule rushed in after him, with Paine bringing up the rear. Unlike Narius, the vizier looked calm and collected, as always. And was that a sneer tugging at his lips when he saw Everys? Looked like he hadn't changed much.

The prelate stabbed a finger at her. "There! The Siporan witch! Guards, arrest her!"

The guards came around the prelate and advanced on her bed. Narius rose and stepped between her and them.

"Stand down. Now." Narius crossed his arms. "Prelate, you have no authority to do this."

"Don't I? There were multiple witnesses who saw what the former queen did. We all know what she is now. The people will demand her arrest and execution!"

Narius looked back at Everys, his face turning a brilliant crimson. She could see the conflict written across his face. She sighed. There really wasn't another solution. The prelate had seen everything. So many people had. And the last thing Narius needed, what with war on the horizon and more unrest in the Dynasty's holdings, was trouble with the prelate.

"Very well, I—"

"Everys, lie down. You are in no condition to move."

Much to Everys's surprise, it was Paine who spoke. He glided across the room to stand at Narius's side. He glared at her once, then turned his gaze onto the prelate, who visibly flinched.

"I was in the ballroom as well, and yes, there was what appeared to be toratropic magic at use," Paine said. "But by the attackers, not by the former queen."

Wait, what?

"There was a great deal of confusion in the ballroom during the attack." Paine smoothed his robes, his face impassive. "I consider myself most fortunate that the Warrior's Shield protected me from the attacking foes. But the queen didn't do anything to save us. Just look at her. Does that look like a dangerous mage?"

Everys bristled at the snide tone in Paine's voice, but she caught herself before she reacted. Instead, she did her best to look weak.

The prelate sputtered, turning to the guards. They looked even more uncomfortable than when the king opposed them.

"But I know what I saw! Everys drew something on the ground and then those creatures weren't able to attack us!" The prelate actually stomped his foot. "She is a witch and I demand she face justice."

Paine crossed his arms and arched a brow. "Interesting. So what you're saying is that *if* Everys is a toratropic mage—and I'm not conceding that she is—she used her unnatural and evil power to protect the life of the Xoniel king and his new bride? Is that really the story you're going to tell the people of the Dynasty? Do you not think that perhaps they will be grateful for her intervention, no matter what form it supposedly took? You seem to forget how popular she was, Prelate. Do you really want to risk the public's wrath over something that only you saw?"

"But you must have seen it, Vizier. You were right there!"

"I saw nothing."

The prelate sputtered, looking from Paine to Narius to Everys, then back to the vizier. Then he growled something under his breath, spun on his heel, and stormed out of the room. The guards hesitated a moment before hurrying after him.

Narius turned to Paine. "Thank you, old friend."

But Paine wasn't looking at Narius. Instead, he stared at Everys. "Your Strength, if I might have a word with her. Alone?"

Narius shot her a questioning look, but she nodded. Paine had just defended her. She doubted he would be a problem now. At least, she hoped he wouldn't.

Once Narius had left the room, Paine turned to her and let out a long breath. "Of course, I saw everything. I saw the runes. And given the amount of blood in the throne room, I suspect you used more of your abilities at some point before we found you."

"So why didn't you turn me into the prelate?" Everys wished she could inject more venom into her voice.

Paine's face turned stony, more so than usual. He crossed over and sat down on the bed next to her, staring down at his fingers as they twined and twisted together.

"It's no secret that I have never believed you worthy of Narius," he whispered. "But then I didn't believe that Innana was worthy either. Nor was Viara. There is no one worthy of Narius. No one. But..." He sighed heavily. "...you have proven that you, at least, have his best interests at heart. You risked your life to protect him. The least I can do is repay you in kind by protecting you from small-minded fools."

He rose from the bed and adjusted his robes. "But make no mistake. If a time comes where I believe that you are more of a liability than an asset, I will suddenly remember the truth of what happened and let the prelate know. Are we understood?"

Everys glared at him, but she nodded.

"Very well." He went back to the door and opened it. "Thank you, Your Strength. I will move the other advisers from the living space to the Amber Office. I will keep them occupied until you can join us."

Narius walked back into the room, watching Paine as he departed. Once the vizier had left, he turned back to Everys. "What did he want?"

She hesitated. Should she tell him? No. Narius had enough to worry about as it was. Better to focus on what really mattered. So she shrugged. "Just wanted to say thank you."

Narius studied her face with such intensity that she blushed. She couldn't stand it.

She cleared her throat. "What happened to... Is Quartus...?" How could she phrase this?

Narius smiled. "He's fine. He's still in the palace, being debriefed by Tormod's people."

Everys sat up in bed. "The lab. Did they tell you about—?"

Narius nodded. "They did, but it appears the conspirators cleaned out the lab during the attack. We were able to recover some scribers, but I suspect it will take them a while to decipher whatever it was that Brencis and his co-conspirators were doing there."

"What about Legarr?"

His face fell. "I'm sorry, Everys, but they didn't find his body."

Oh. She looked down at her hands. She knew she should have felt sad. Or angry. But suddenly she was very aware of Narius, his calm demeanor, his physical presence, his... everything.

"So now what?" she whispered.

He looked down at the floor. "I'm not sure. We don't know if the Dalark will actually invade or if this is mere posturing. We don't know if the uptick in unrest is due to Brencis's schemes or—"

"Narius. That's not what I meant."

"I know."

He stood still for a few heartbeats, then lunged for the bed. She jumped, unsure of what he was actually doing until she realized he was kneeling next to her.

"I do know. Everys, I was miserable after you left. You were... You were a good partner for me. Everything that the Emperor thought I accomplished was because of you. I need you by my side so I can continue to move the Dynasty in the right direction."

Oh. She tried to hide her disappointment.

He looked down at the bed. "When we first brought you here, we didn't give you a choice. We didn't... *I* didn't ask what you thought or seek your permission. I treated you like someone I could just order around. And that's not what I want anymore. I want to do this right, starting now. Everys... May I kiss you?"

She stared at him, his words not registering. Could he... May he...

Then she grabbed the front of his shirt and pulled him into a kiss, snaking her hand behind his neck to hold him there so she could enjoy the feel of his lips against hers. He gathered her into his arms and held her tight.

When they finally let go, he whispered in her ear, "I never should have let you go."

"I never should have gone in the first place," she whispered back.

"Everys, I want you to be my queen again. More than that, I want you to be my wife. Will you please marry me again?"

"No rival candidates?" Everys asked. "We could see what Clarinda Gaines is doing."

"Not a chance," Narius said. "It will be you or no one else."

She smiled. She leaned forward and kissed him again, savoring his taste.

"I will. On one condition."

68

The scrivener looked absolutely terrified, and Everys couldn't really blame him. It wasn't every day that a simple Siporan cleric was invited into the royal palace. It had taken some persuasion from Everys (and some overt threats from Auntie Kyna) to convince him to travel from Fair Havens to the palace itself. But once he realized that this wasn't a trap, but was, instead, an actual wedding, he relaxed. At least, enough to do his part.

His hands still trembled as he mixed the ceremonial ink. Everys watched him work, stirring in the different ingredients, but she stole glances at Narius from time to time. Narius seemed completely enraptured with the process, studying the scrivener's gestures and movements as the elderly man added the various dyes and ingredients to create a sticky but sweet-smelling paste.

"When the Singularity painted the world into existence, He began with the deepest seas and the highest heavens," the scrivener said as he worked. "With His finger, He drew the sacred runes into the ground, the water, the sky, drawing forth the land, the air, the animals, the plants. And finally, the people. But because the Singularity was complete in Himself, He wanted the pinnacle of His creation to be complete in community as well. And so, He gave them marriage as a way to help and strengthen one another."

The scrivener threw in another handful of pigment, sending up a bright blue cloud. Narius flinched, and Everys stifled a chuckle.

She glanced around the ballroom, so large and cavernous with so few people there. The official wedding, performed by a very reluctant Supreme Prelate Istragon, would take place the next day. But Everys didn't want the Xoniel ritual to be the only one. After all, she hadn't saved Narius and so many of the wedding guests. It had been the

Singularity. It had been the gift He had given His people that had made the difference. This time, she wanted Him to be a part of their marriage too.

Narius hadn't objected. Neither had Paine—at least, not that Everys had heard. The vizier had probably given Narius an earful at some point, but he hadn't made any more trouble. Everys suspected that it hurt Narius that Paine had refused to attend the private ceremony, but that wasn't a hill worth dying on.

Her gaze landed on Quartus. Siporan custom dictated that there should be at least two people present during a wedding to serve as witnesses. Unfortunately, there were very few people she would have trusted to be a part of this moment. She never thought Quartus would be one of them. But she did now.

"Everys, Narius, please extend your hands," the scrivener said.

They did so, Everys's hand on top, Narius's on the bottom. The scrivener took a brush and dipped it into the ceremonial ink. He set to work, his brush dancing across the back of Everys's hand. The rune itself wasn't complex, a simple circle with crescent shapes along the inside, creating a pattern that looked like a stylized flower. Once it was complete, the scrivener gently turned their hands over so he could paint a similar pattern on the back of Narius's hand. Once he was done, the scrivener set aside the brush and clasped his hands over theirs.

There was no toratropic magic involved. No flash of light. No miraculous effect. But all the same, Everys felt a shiver worm down her spine. When the scrivener withdrew his hands, the deed was done. The ceremony was over. She and Narius were married once again.

Before the scrivener could speak, she pulled Narius into a passionate kiss, one that she had kept pent up inside of her for far too long. He kissed her back with the same intensity. Eventually Quartus cleared his throat.

Everys broke away and beamed at Narius. He looked a little dazed.

"Your majesties," the scrivener said. "It has been a pleasure I won't soon forget."

"Thank you, scrivener," Narius said. "Please, allow me to escort you back to your transport."

As he left, Quartus stepped forward. He looked ready to hug her, but he hung back, uncertainty on his face. She didn't blame him. A lot had happened between them, a lot of very hurtful things. And while she had pushed past it during the crisis, the hurt lingered. She didn't know if she would ever get past it. And maybe he understood that.

"Thank you for including me," he said, his voice stiff.

She nodded. "Did Narius reinstate you?"

Quartus cleared his throat, then shook his head. "No. No, he didn't."

That surprised her. Granted, she didn't know Xoniel custom all that well still, but she would have thought that Narius would have rewarded his brother to thank him for his help.

"Why not?" she asked.

"Because I asked him not to."

Everys jumped and whirled. Tormod smiled broadly. Had he been there the whole time? Shouldn't she have noticed him at some point?

Tormod strolled forward. "Quartus impressed me. He showed resourcefulness that I need. I've asked him and his... team to keep digging into Brencis's schemes."

"But why them?"

"Because he was able to uncover a plot that my best people overlooked." Tormod's face darkened. "That either means that Brencis and his co-conspirators are extremely skilled, my teams have been too lackadaisical, or..."

Everys's eyes widened. "Or they've been compromised."

Tormod nodded. "Precisely. I need unconventional operatives if we're to navigate these uncertain waters. Once Quartus leaves the palace, he will work for me. And only four of us will know that truth. To the rest of the world, he will still be an outlaw."

"Isn't that asking an awful lot?" Everys asked.

"In ordinary circumstances, yes. But these are far from ordinary. The open use of toratropic magic certainly indicates that, wouldn't you say?" Tormod's face darkened. "These are dangerous times for our people, my queen. Dangerous indeed. If we are not able to figure out who Brencis worked with to create those abominations, we may play directly into their hands. I would prefer for that not to happen."

"So what can I do?"

Tormod blinked, then smiled. "Right now? Enjoy the night, my dear. The days ahead will be hard enough. We should all find enjoyment while we can. For me, that means a fine vintage in front of the fire. For you..." His smile broadened. "Well..."

She blushed furiously as Quartus guffawed.

"With that thought, I will bid you farewell too, dear sister. Please, be gentle with Narius, especially his heart," Quartus said.

She glared at him, which only made him laugh harder. When she turned back to Tormod, the spymaster had disappeared. She turned a quick circle. Where had he gone?

A few moments later, Narius returned. He exchanged a stiff hug with Quartus, then he turned to Everys. "Are you ready, wife?"

She took a shaky breath and nodded. For whatever the Singularity wrote into their future.

Ackowledgments

This was maybe one of the strangest writing journeys I've ever taken. And a lot of people assisted me along the way.

First of all, thank you to the participants of the 2017 One Year Adventure Novel Summer Workshop. They were the ones who witnessed this idea taking hold of me. And you were my earliest cheerleaders, encouraging me to actually write the story back when it was only known as #gottabebae. This book would not exist if it wasn't for you.

To my (former) long-suffering agent, Amanda Luedeke, who looked at my earliest ideas for this story and nudged me in the right direction. I appreciate everything you've done for me and I definitely miss the disapproving looks.

A special thanks goes to Michael Charron, Lizzy Hite, Katelyn Coker, and Chawna Schroeder for serving as alpha readers. You helped me see that there was a viable story in here and that I should keep on working.

A special thank you to Megan Gerig of MG Literary Services for the editing and proofreading. I am so glad for our partnership!

My beta readers were helpful as well. Thank you to Lisa Godfrees, Lee Hillshire, Stephanie Tuman, Tom Evans, Chris Gordon, Lisa Sauter, Logan Martin, Bill Merrill, JR Forasteros, and especially Katie Vincent for your insights and feedback.

I also want to thank the people who went above and beyond in backing my Kickstarter project. So big thank you to Timothy Bicknase, Meghan Clark, Tatianne Dobbin, Lisa Godfrees, Chris Gordon, Rosie and Lydia H., Christine Krenz, Rod and Miriam Lindemann, the Montgomery Family, Chawna Schroeder, Jimmy Schroeder, Jill Williamson, and Jason Worley.

And most of all, thank you to my God, Father, Son, and Holy Spirit, who lifts me from the ashes and draws me ever closer to Him. Soli Deo Gloria.

About the Author

John is a PK, a pastor's kid. He grew up in Columbia Heights, a suburb of Minneapolis, with his parents and younger sister and brother. They were the terror of their local library because, every few weeks, they would come and check out crates full of books, increasing the workload of the poor librarians. In high school, though, John worked at the same library, so it balanced out.

After high school, John attended Concordia University in St. Paul, Minnesota, where he majored in theatre. Upon his graduation in 1996, he moved on to Concordia Seminary in St. Louis, Missouri. He graduated with his Masters of Divinity in 2000. He served as a Lutheran minister in Blue Earth, Minnesota, and South Saint Paul, Minnesota. He currently serves as an associate pastor in Blue Springs, Missouri, where he lives with his wife and kids.

John is a lifelong writer. He started with badly drawn comic books in the fifth grade. When he realized that he was a lousy artist, he moved on to badly written novels in middle school. He's tried his hand at screenplays (don't ask), stage plays (a little better), fanfic, teen mysteries, and religious fiction. But his first love has always been speculative fiction.

His debut novel, *Failstate*, was published by Marcher Lord Press in April of 2012, and was a finalist for the Christy Awards in 2013. He has gone on to publish four more novels with Marcher Lord Press/Enclave Publishing, two of which, *Numb* and *Failstate: Nemesis*, were finalists for the Christy Awards in 2014 and 2015. John looks forward to telling even more strange tales that point people back to God and His incredible grace.

Everys's Adventure Continues...

What will happen now that Everys and Narius are reunited? Find out...

Learn more about Vizier Paine

Haven't gotten enough of Vizier Paine? Find out more about his rise to power in the ebook exclusive novella, *The Storm's Eye*. It's available wherever you buy ebooks!

Get a free short story!

D id you enjoy this book? How'd you like to get a free short story set in the Dynasty?

Head over to John's website and sign up for the Geeky Grace Newsletter. When you do, you'll receive the short story *Cage and the Outpost of Monolith* absolutely free!

johnwotte.com/subscribe

Also By...

The Failstate Series

Failstate
Gauntlet Goes to Prom (ebook exclusive)
Failstate: Legends
Kynetic: On Target (ebook exclusive)
Failstate: Nemesis

The Ministrix Duology

Numb
The Hive

Anthologies

Into the Bewilderness
Just Dumb Enough (Contributor)
The Memory Eater (Contributor)
Spirited: 13 Haunting Tales (Contributor)

Kickstarter Backers

This book wouldn't have come into being without the help of the
following people:

Mike A., Gillian Bronte Adams, Megan Archer, David Bauer, David
Beagley, Jake Bellinghausen, Bobbi Boyd, Branson Boykin, Joshua
C. Chadd, Edward Cloutier II, B. Cluppert, Sam "Duke" Downs,
JR and Amanda Forasteros, Kate Force, Dawn Ford, Lindsay A.
Franklin, Morgan Freeman, Noah G., Rachel Garner, Megan Gerig,
Tiffany Goldman, Leah E. Good, Josh H., Michele Israel Harper, E.
A. Hendryx, Lee Hillshire, Lizzy Hite, Luke Italiano, Robin 'echo'
Johnson, Andy and Stephanie Jones, Jason C. Joyner, Joel Kovach,
Ryan Kuecker, Tom Langemo, Scott Lemmermann, Grace Licht-
enberg, Bob and Sandy Logan, Mary and Kevin Low, Mark Lund-
gren, Brian McCauley, Jill McConnell, Justin McRoberts, Alex Mellen,
Bill Merrell, Matt Mikalatos, CJ Milacci, Celeste S. Mora, Meagan
Myhren-Bennett, Marie Norris, Josh Olds, the Olson Family, Bill and
Dea Otte, Mark Otte, Gabby Penaflor-Barnett, Jaina Peveto, Aaron
Plattner, Dominik Plejić, Tracy Popey, Rachel Reinke, Bob Riggs,
Gena Roberts, Janna Ryan, Lisa Sauter, Rachel S Stohlmann, Daniel
Schwabauer, Rachelle Y. Sperling, Lena Karynn Tesla, Ida Thomason,
Katie Vincent, Justin Walker, Kathy Wildschuetz, Tracy Jo Workman,
Eron Wyngarde, Peter William Younghusband, Bryce, DarthCollectus,
Devin and Christabel, Elizabeth, Jenelle, Joel, Josh, and Kevin